THE
PERFECT
SOLDIER

Books by Ralph Peters

Bravo Romeo
Red Army
The War in 2020
Flames of Heaven
The Perfect Soldier

THE
PERFECT
SOLDIER

—

RALPH
PETERS

POCKET BOOKS

New York   London   Toronto   Sydney   Tokyo   Singapore

This book is a work of fiction. Names, characters, places, and incidents are either the product of the author's imagination or are used fictitiously. Any resemblance to actual events or locales or persons, living or dead, is entirely coincidental. The views expressed in this book are those of the author and do not reflect the official policy or position of the Department of the Army, the Department of Defense, or the U.S. government.

 POCKET BOOKS, a division of Simon & Schuster Inc.
1230 Avenue of the Americas, New York, NY 10020

Library of Congress Cataloging-in-Publication Data

Peters, Ralph, 1952–
    The perfect soldier / Ralph Peters.
      p. cm.
    ISBN: 0-671-86583-8
      1. Korean War, 1950-1953—Prisoners and prisons, Soviet—Fiction. 2. Soldiers—
United States—Fiction. I. Title.
    PS3566.E7559P47 1995
    813'.54—dc20   94-45908
                                                                                     CIP

First Pocket Books hardcover printing September 1995

10 9 8 7 6 5 4 3 2 1

POCKET and colophon are registered trademarks of
Simon & Schuster Inc.

Printed in the U.S.A.

This book is dedicated to those U.S. POWs from Korea who were transported to the Soviet Union, imprisoned, and eventually, murdered by the Soviet security services. It is also dedicated, with the deepest humility and respect, to the family members who loved those men, and who never forgot them as the world and the business of government moved on.

He was the perfect soldier:
he went where you sent him,
stayed where you put him,
and had no ideas of his own
to keep him from doing exactly
what you told him.

—Dashiell Hammett
The Dain Curse

THE
PERFECT
SOLDIER

PRELUDE

HIS ABILITY TO HOPE AMAZED HIM. EVEN NOW, WAITING TO DIE, WAIT-
ing for the bullet in the skull that would resolve his suspended
life, he hoped against all logic that he would be spared. He was
intelligent enough, and still sane enough, to realize his folly.
He was going to die. And all his inextinguishable dreams of
rescue were going to end, here and now, on this gray morning.
The last shot before the one that would kill him had already
echoed itself to death in the maze of scrubby ravines. The bastards were taking their time about it, killing them one at a time,
as the morning matured into a chill, briny day, with the wind
coming in from the Pacific to the east, skimming over the waste-
lands the way his aircraft had skimmed its fallen belly over the
Korean marshes so many years ago.

He had considered himself a very good pilot, buoyant with
young-American pride, until that other morning when the antiaircraft rounds had knocked the flight out of his F-86 and he
had done what he could to steer it in, too low to eject, too late,
maybe too afraid. He woke up to blows from shouting men with
furious faces, pummeling his broken arm until the skyrockets of
pain made him shriek. Then he went half-stumbling, driven
like a bad animal, through the ankle-deep wet and up onto a
diked road. His Korean captors had been vicious, his Chinese

interrogators worse. It had been a relief at first to come into the custody of the Russians, who were comparatively humane. They had taken him by vehicle across an unseen border, to a town where the residents spoke a different, if equally unintelligible, language. They questioned him for days, holding him in a separate cell. Yet, he had known that other Americans were present. He had sensed them in the way you could never explain.

Then the Russians shuttled him along, bundling him into a train car during the night, under guard. The windows were covered over, yet the senses told so much. He could feel the vastness all around him, the forlornness of the pauses on rural sidings, then the arrival in a city, with its different noises, smells, texture. This time they put him in a cell with three other Americans, two pilots and a navigator, men whom he would get to know painfully well in the course of their mutual captivity, and one of whom, grown to be his brother, would die in his arms of a simple untreated fever.

None of them had imagined that the Russians would keep them. They had all assumed that, when the war ended, they would be repatriated. But the war had been over for months before they heard news of the armistice. They were seventy by then, almost all Air Force officers, held in the first of a series of primitive, isolated camps. The shock of the news that their war was already a part of history while they remained prisoners was such a blow that one man committed suicide by running straight for the wire, perfectly anticipating the sweep of the guard's machine gun.

Even then, they had believed it was only a matter of time. Their government would never forget them, never abandon them. They were *Americans*. They were special, blessed. America took care of her own.

Years passed. Only the camps changed. For a time, they worked in a gold mine, where they had limited contact with Soviet prisoners. Three men died in a cave-in. Then, one night, the remainder of them were trucked to yet another wilderness railroad siding and they rode a boxcar to a river, then traveled by barge to a trackless place, where typhus lurked in the moss. Eleven of them died there. They served endless months in

mountain camps and torrid desert prisons. Intermittently, one
of their number would be taken away, never to return. The
optimists insisted that those who disappeared had been repatriated. But no one really believed that.

The Russians never tortured. Not the way you thought of
torture. They simply held you in purgatory, with poor food and
ill-managed work. And you dreamed away your life.

He dreamed, as he aged prematurely, of the infinite softness
of the wife he had left behind, recalling the private folds of her
body until he thought he would die of emotion. He thought of
the daughter whom he had never seen except in a baby photograph. Despite all evidence to the contrary, he never fully gave
up the belief that he would see them again.

Even now, on this last morning, a part of him refused to
believe that he would never rejoin his wife and daughter. He
realized that his wife, with her loveliness and her needs, must
have long since remarried, that she would have gray hair now,
that she would have become a different person. And his daughter would be an adult woman, with a husband and children of
her own. Yet, his heart could not accept it. Ronnie would always be his smiling girl, her hair all sunlight, while his daughter waited patiently, reaching out tiny hands to welcome her
father home.

He had learned so much about the human heart in the camps.
It seemed a terrible shame to die now, like this, for nothing,
when he had never been able to put his knowledge to use. He
believed he had discovered in himself a nearly infinite capacity
to love.

He had hated God. Cursing Him for stealing everything that
mattered, for giving him life only to sentence him to a living
death. But he had only been journeying toward God on a particularly troubled road. And in the end, God sustained him. He
recalled a sampler hung on his grandmother's wall in Abilene:
"Bidden or unbidden, God is always present."

He understood God's love now. The camps and his fellow
prisoners had taught him that, too. Nothing was more important
than the ability to love.

Still, it was hard to face death. His body shook as he sat on
the cold earth between the guards. The killings took place in a

ravine just behind a low crest. The guards had taken the prisoners one by one, some struggling to the last, some resigned, others smiling gently and wishing their friends a last good-bye. They marched up the slope and disappeared down the other side, and after an immeasurable stretch of time, a single shot ended each life.

They were all dead now. Except him.

Why now? Why, after letting them live so long, after feeding them just enough to let them survive, why kill them now? What had changed? This last camp had been so small and remote, the new regional commandant so vicious, that they had learned nothing of the outside world in the past few years. Had something happened out in the world beyond the wire? Something terrible?

It didn't matter.

All that mattered was that the years of waiting had come to this. A bullet in the head in the morning.

He struggled against bitterness, against the sin of despair. God would welcome him soon. And perhaps . . . maybe the United States government had never known about them, had believed they were all dead. . . .

He found a flashing reason to hope: they had saved him until last. Perhaps there was some significance in that. Perhaps they were going to spare him. Perhaps there was some hidden logic he could not intuit. . . .

He closed his eyes and saw his wife, whose love he knew he had never lost. Even if she had married again, she still loved him. He knew she still loved him. And his daughter loved him, too. She would throw her arms around him and cry until her tears soaked through his shirt. And he would hold them both in his arms. It was impossible to imagine that he would never see them again, impossible to think like that.

Even now.

The two guards who had been responsible for fetching each prisoner to his death bobbed up over the crest of the ravine and came down the slope toward him, soft figures in the flannel light. The wind rose slightly and he imagined he could smell the distant sea.

He prayed, sentences becoming fragments. He was afraid

now, despite himself. He asked God to give him one minute, just one single minute with his wife and daughter again. To let him breathe the air of home and feel the Texas sun just until the quick hand on the watch went around once.

The features of the guards grew crisper. He knew them both and they averted their eyes. They were not such bad men. He sensed that they did not want any part of this. But in their shame, they grew brute. They jerked him to his feet, and although he walked forward peacefully, relieved to find that his legs still half-obeyed him, the guards prodded him nervously with their rifle barrels, hurrying him up the slope.

Please, God. One minute.

The dry grass broke against his calves. A pair of small birds jinked about in curiosity.

Behold the work of Man.

Help me be strong, Lord.

He trod up over the crest and saw three men standing at the end of a line of corpses. The position of each death was slightly different, but the overall impression was of good order. The three living men watched him descend this steeper slope.

His legs felt as though the bones were gone. How can I be doing this? he wondered. Why does a man walk willingly toward his death? When he felt no willingness in his heart?

He had seen one of the three executioners before. The man was a subcommandant, responsible for the local chain of camps. He had sharp, southern features and eyes full of death. He looked like the perfect executioner. The other two men were ethnic Russians, one markedly older and smaller than the other. Each of the three men wore the uniform of a general officer in the security services. The southerner and the younger Russian each had a single star on their epaulets, while the older man, who looked like a clean-shaven Santa Claus, all red cheeks and bright eyes, had three stars on his shoulders. Santa Claus wore a thin-lipped smile that might not have been a smile at all, while his Russian protégé held, of all things, a camera. Only the southerner was armed. At the moment, he was snapping a fresh clip into his pistol.

The decision to kill the prisoners must have been taken at a very high level, he realized. If the executioners were general officers . . .

The guards pushed him over the corpse of his best friend, who lay twisted and open-eyed. He had to jump to avoid tramping on the body, and he couldn't help kicking it slightly. His friend looked up at him in astonishment.

A small realization jarred him. He had always believed that the bullet came at the nape of the neck. But each man, as far as he could see, had been shot in the forehead, just above the nose.

These executioners were not afraid to look their victims in the eyes.

He began to recite the Twenty-third Psalm, trying to speak it out, broken-voiced. He had become an infinitely fragile creature.

The guards knocked him to his knees, manipulating his posture with blows from the stocks of their automatic rifles.

The younger Russian general came in close with the camera and snapped a picture, then stood by, ready to take another.

Afterward.

In the end, there was only the Trinity of God, his wife, and his daughter. Nothing else remained of reality, of this world. After all the waiting, after years and decades of waiting, the end came quickly. The general who looked like a sweet grandfather stepped back slightly to avoid having his uniform mussed with waste. The southerner stepped in with his pistol. Even though the barrel didn't actually touch the skin, you could feel its heat.

The prisoner turned his eyes up to the gray sky.

ONE

In the days when the sky was falling, two friends stood in a desert town. They wore identical uniforms, each with the insignia of a major, but they were different in most other ways. The one who smiled—the one who was forever smiling—was named Ben, and he was shiningly American. He stood under medium height, but no one noticed that at first, because he was so full of life. He had a big, genuine smile, with marble teeth, and eyes of the sort women who remained forever girls found irresistible. He was the high-school hero grown into robust, responsible adulthood, serving his country in far, sorry places with courage he wore as easily as an old pair of khakis. Ripening into his thirties, he still had a boy's face and manner. His wife of several years was a bit younger—a wonderful girl—and very far away now, expecting their first child amid the shopping malls that gave focus to lives strewn throughout the suburbs of Washington, D.C. She joked that she didn't know how she would manage with *two* children on her hands.

The two friends stood at the tailgate of a truck in a place luminous with heat and poverty, passing food parcels across a makeshift table. They wished the recipients well in Russian, since neither man spoke the arthritic local dialect of Persian. The women understood the simple phrases, and their sunburned hands—quick, tiny animals—shot out from heavy, bell-like sleeves. As Ben released a package, a woman's shoulders condensed under the weight and she scuttled off, protecting her gift with a lunatic incantation.

These women never raised their eyes when they came in close—unlike their brazen sisters back in the capital city, who had been allowed the piecemeal liberation of literacy and legal status as long as the republic was still officially Communist. But those days were gone now, and here, in the desert hills, the old order had never really been disrupted, anyway. Rulers came and went, and stray power lines adorned the Middle Ages.

Antiquity was creeping toward the capital again, reversing history with a vengeance, flowing into the vacuum left by the collapse of successive governments. These fetid country women, clothed by male rules, were again coming into their own, while the women of the drab, polluted capital, with its veneer of human rights and dog-eared fashion magazines, lived in fear. Many of the city women had taken to covering their hair voluntarily, hoping to keep worse things at bay.

These village women were afraid, too, of course. But their fears had not changed for thousands of years and so were less dynamic and more comfortable. There were laws that had to be observed under threat of physical violence, even death. But at least the laws were known, and these women had learned how to crowd up to the threshold of custom without crossing it.

They did not lack curiosity, these women who had never even traveled to the next valley. Although they grew frightfully modest standing before the two Americans, so long as they remained safely blurred in the waiting line, a smear of color and dark eyes, they inspected the foreign intruders with simmering interest. They looked at Ben Williams, who was not much taller than their own men and who smiled as though God had deprived him of at least a tenth of his reason, and they giggled, whispering to one another behind callused palms. The women obviously enjoyed admiring such a man, unexpectedly saucy in their downtrodden sisterhood. But their reaction was very different in regard to Ben's friend, who lacked the shorter man's contagious warmth. The women looked at the second man only in short glances, the way people throughout the failed parts of the world steal a look at a police station as they hurry past.

Ben's friend was taller and more angular, with a transient, unhelpful smile that he clearly considered part of his duty. If Ben Williams was a summer full of ball games, Christopher Ritter was a northern winter. Ritter was a man who, born earlier, might have been one of those theologians who lived like clenched fists, defying the Mother Church over minor points of Scripture. He was the sort of man who could not bear to do a thing badly, and his intensity was often mistaken for ambition. The women who loved him never quite got over him, shocked to life, even a bit crippled, by the experience of meeting a man who paid attention. He had married a Mexican-American woman whom he loved boundlessly, only to see her devoured by cancer, and he nursed his grief like a drink he could not bear to finish, struggling to be the perfect soldier in penance.

These two friends stood in this desert town, dispensing their nation's bounty, and the sky fell all around them, but they were accustomed to that. They had come a long way since they had trained together to serve as the U.S. Army's experts on an empire's corpse. Ben had gone quietly to Croatia and Bosnia, without his uniform, charged to sort out relative guilt by policymakers who had already made up their minds. Maj. Christopher Ritter had nearly been killed in the bloody splendor of the Caucasus, stupidly reckless in mourning the loss of his wife. Veterans of other people's wars, the two friends were more at home in this timeless village than on the gunnery ranges in Texas or in the quick mock wars in the Mojave where their contemporaries dreamed away their careers, fantasizing about another war as delicious as Desert Storm.

Anyway, the sky still had a long way to fall. Its succulent blue poured down over the ice-cream peaks to the east, barring the way to China with beauty, and the two friends felt only the sun pressing on the shoulders of their uniforms. Ritter bent to inspect a woman's identification card, made a tick in his notebook, and straightened his back again, feeling his sweat thick as butter. Ben, a grinning advertisement for America, thrust out another cardboard box. The line caterpillared forward, rustling up a bad scent.

Except for the bullet-chipped and burn-scarred municipal building before which they stood, all of the structures in the village were single story and of the same color as the earth. The fallen Communist government had tried to convince the population of the utility of the two-story home, which was cooler in the summer and whose upper floor was easier to purge of vermin, but reason counted for nothing against tradition. Adherence to tradition provided a man's primary claim to worth. The crumbling hammer-and-sickle ornament above the entrance to the municipal building, good for target practice, had been too inconsequential to scrape away fully. Here, in a valley so parched and poor that only the shabbiest of conquerors had fussed with it, the old religion still defined the terms of life—even though the people had forgotten its theological intricacies. The men, privileged and proud, sulked in the garden of a pitiful teahouse while their wives lined up for charity under the eyes of a few elders. On routine days, the women hacked at the ruined soil and carried home parasite cocktails from the communal well, while the men played dominoes in the shade and philosophized about the harshness of fate. Intermittently, they conducted a civil war against their brethren to the north, sponsored by other kinsmen across the Afghan border to the south.

Wherever the two friends went in this time-skipped land, local military escorts accompanied them to provide protection against the bandits, rebels, and government representatives who might wish to help themselves out of turn to America's largesse. Depending on the size of the delivery and the route to be traveled, the escorts varied in size from a lonesome squad in a light truck to a full company mounted in armored personnel carriers. Today's mission merited a reinforced platoon of idiot-eyed conscripts with armored vehicles, commanded by a captain who looked impossibly young and uncomfortable in the relic of his Soviet uniform. The captain was very nervous about the bandits—about one in particular, who was virtually a government unto himself—and like his peers with whom the two Americans had worked, he seemed unclear as to the authority to which he ultimately answered. At times he spoke as though he had committed body and soul to the fledgling army under the control of the regional capital. But then he would revert to the old phrases learned from the Russian officers who had trained him and who still broadcast orders from Moscow for anyone who might be persuaded to pay attention.

The captain emerged from the gutted municipal building where he had been avoiding the sun and marched toward the Americans with the haste of a man who has struggled to keep his patience but failed. His eyes snapped from side to side as though he expected to be attacked at any moment. A few of his dozing soldiers perked up and renewed their grips on battered rifles.

The captain took up a position equidistant from the two foreigners so that the three men together made a triangle. The shadows of their shoulders and heads lay across the dust like the silhouette of a mountain range. The air was hot and thick as mashed potatoes, and at the appearance of the officer, the women still waiting in line began to mutter and nudge forward, sensing bad news.

"My most esteemed friends," the captain began in accented Russian, "this cannot go on." He was markedly smaller than either of the two Americans, just a local boy suckered into serving a failing system. He looked up at them, switching his eyes from one to the other and back again. "We must go now. It is too dangerous. We must cross the Gobur Pass before the darkness. Rakhman's people will come."

The Americans looked at him mercilessly, two Calvinists in Sodom, then Ritter spoke:

"We're not finished. These people have been waiting in the sun for hours."

"We will leave the packages on the ground," the captain said. "It will be all right." He seemed as distraught as a peasant worried about vampires.

"You want a riot?"

"No, no. They will distribute the food themselves. It will be fair. I know these people."

The captain was a poor liar. Ritter leaned over him, ready to dress him down, but Ben wedged between the two men. Smiling with all the generosity of his homeland, he said:

"Ali, my friend. Just a little longer, all right? We'll hurry."

The captain looked at his military watch and shivered in the heat. "It is not necessary. Truly. These people have enough to eat. You see the fields all around."

"Those are cotton fields," Ritter said.

"It's all the same. They have very good crops here."

"Those are cotton fields," Ritter went on coldly, "because some asshole ordered them to plant cotton with his ministry's dying breath. And now they've got nothing to eat, and nobody gives a damn."

"There is civil war. It is very hard."

Ben edged in again. "Half an hour, Ali. I promise. We're wasting time talking."

The captain sulked, realizing the impossibility of talking sense to these Americans, who would soon fly back to their immeasurably rich country. "These packages," he said bitterly, "they will make no difference. These people will go hungry anyway. You only give them false hope."

Neither Ben nor Ritter said anything for a moment. They had been discussing the same issue for months and knew that, on this point at least, the captain was right. The food distribution was a gesture. To make important, well-fed men and women back home feel committed to humanity. Like tossing a quarter to the homeless.

But it was the mission they had been given. And they were dutiful officers.

"Half an hour," Ben said with finality.

The captain looked down at the earth in disgust. Then he gathered his last dignity and squared his shoulders, trying to rise to the Americans' height, to impose some slight authority.

"We *must* cross over the Gobur Pass before the darkness. Rakhman—"

"Piece of cake," Ben said. But the expression did not translate well and the effect was lost.

The little officer strutted off to curse his subordinates, and the conscripts made a halfhearted effort to greet him with a display of military bearing. But the heat had penetrated their bodies like worms, and their actions had only the slight life of a sleeper's kiss.

Ben looked at Ritter thoughtfully. "Maybe we ought to speed things up."

There was never enough time to do the job right. And they had been going even faster than usual, aware of the danger here. Now they caught a light case of the captain's fear, a re-awakened sense of their ultimate helplessness. According to the rules laid down by their own country, they were not allowed to carry weapons on these forays, and they depended entirely on the local military for their physical safety.

"Roger," Ritter said, and he turned back to their work with a muscular generosity foolish in such a climate. But his eyes were elsewhere.

The women in line had grown very unruly, concerned that the Americans would leave before each of them had received her package. Only a few really looked malnourished—and that was likely an illusion created by disease. They would be hungry when the winter came, but it wasn't like Africa, like Somalia or the southern Sudan, where you only had to step off the ramp of a back-country relief flight to be forever scarred by what you saw.

Ben shook his head and, shifting a stack of boxes, looked up at his friend with a smile that had taken on a harsh edge.

"What in the name of Christ are we doing here?"

Ritter gave his friend one of his fleeting smiles in return. "Making the world safe for democracy." He handed off a parcel to a woman who grasped it fiercely to her belly and scurried off like a tent on two legs.

The captain came back, unable to stop picking at his sore.

"My friends, I am so worried."

"Right."

"We know."

Ritter waved the next woman forward and Ben doled out the goodies.

"I think," the captain went on, "that we have made a great mistake."

"We make great mistakes every day," Ben said with a laugh that sought to cancel any intimation of danger. "It's part of our job."

The captain was undeterred. "This Rakhman . . . he is not like the others. They say he may even be the new president. We should have given him a gift."

"Ali," Ritter said, "if we gave a 'gift' to every chickenshit warlord in this country, we'd have nothing left."

"But Rakhman is different. He is a big man. Perhaps he is not even afraid of my guns. Perhaps he is not even afraid of America."

Ben offered up his dependable smile. "Ali, our government says we don't pay bribes. And *your* government says we don't pay bribes. So we don't pay bribes."

The captain took offense. "But we do not speak of bribes. Only of a gift that is customary."

Ritter turned on the little man whose uniform bore the old sweat stains of a desert homeland, of an impoverished country that had very recently been found to possess some of the world's richest oil and natural-gas reserves under its sand and dust. The American wielded a voice of jagged ice:

"Rakhman is a thug and a murderer surrounded by thugs and murderers. He's an enemy of your government. And the United States Army is not about to kiss his ass."

To a stranger, such as the captain, Ritter's voice sounded firm and strong. But to Ben, who knew his friend with the intimacy of shared dangers, there was more than a little worry behind the forcefulness. To Ben's ear, what Ritter was really telling the captain was:

"Here we are in the middle of Buttfuck, Nowhere, with the hills full of cutthroats who have lost all fear of punishment. We aren't even allowed to carry our own sidearms, and we have to rely on Our Gang with rusty rifles to keep our asses alive. *Of course,* we know that the smart thing to do would have been to buy Rakhman off—especially since your government is going to be lucky to last another couple of months and that pig Rakhman really is a contender for the Sheepshit Throne. But we have been expressly forbidden to do the sensible thing. And, *of course,* we know that the ride back to your plumber's nightmare of a capital city is going to be riskier than a date with a feminist lawyer who's had a bad day. But we've got a job to do. We didn't choose it. We didn't even get to offer advice. We were just ordered to go out and do great and glorious things by self-righteous State Department sopranos and politicians who don't know Dushanbe from Disneyland. And we're giving it our best shot. So why don't you stop whining, pal, and try to act just a little tiny bit like a soldier, okay?"

"But this is Rakhman's territory," the captain pleaded, hearing nothing but stubborn folly in the American voices. "It is the custom to give a gift to the big man when you come to his home. Even if you do not agree with him. It is a courtesy, a tradition from the days of the caravans and the Silk Road."

"Ali," Ben began, forever the peacemaker, "we have our orders. You have your orders. Right now all we're doing is wasting time."

The captain shook his head in sorrow, mourning the future. "We must go very soon," he said in a voice gone hopeless. And he walked away. This time he did not even pause to chastise his shaven-headed soldiers.

In wordless accord, the two friends shoved the aid parcels into the women's waiting arms as swiftly as they could without allowing all order to break down. Rakhman, they knew, was a special case, indeed. He had ordered one government representative skinned alive for the crime of attempting to negotiate with him, and he had seen to it that the man's hide was delivered to his superior in the capital city. Rakhman had massacred entire villages whose dominant clan was loyal to the government of the moment. During the years of Communist rule, he had been an honored state figure, rising to a general's rank in the security services. Now he presented himself as a freedom fighter, and some sources claimed he had experienced a revelation that caused him to return to Islam. He was also reported to love action videos, especially those featuring Arnold Schwarzenegger, and he led his warrior bandits across the desert from the backseat of a red Mercedes that was said to be the gift of an Italian oil company with an eye on the future. He was financed, depending on which furtive voice you distrusted least, by the Russian security services or by the Iranians or the Saudis, by the Pakistanis or even the Chinese. Several multinational oil and gas companies were rumored to be courting him even as their representatives tried to cut deals with the legal authorities back in the capital. It was an environment in which anything could happen, the chaos one minute before the end of the world. The only things the embassy resident officer had been able to tell Ritter and Ben with any certainty about Rakhman were that he was deep in the drug trade with the Afghans and that he kept a blond Ukrainian mistress. According to the ambassador, who had met Rakhman in the days before the socialist heaven had collapsed, Rakhman also believed that all foreign aid was filth intended to corrupt the souls of his countrymen.

"Screw Charlee Whyte," Ben said suddenly.

Ritter cast off another parcel in silence, too preoccupied even to offer a perfunctory greeting to the recipient.

"I met her once," Ben went on. "Back when she was still working on the Hill. Before Cromwell dumped her on the Pentagon and got himself a younger main squeeze—I mean, talk about new levels of palimony. Anyway, she called us all in for a 'briefing.' Which consisted of a lecture from Ms. Whyte on how the military can't do anything right. She didn't hear a single word we said. Mind made up in advance. Typical, you know? *Hates* the military. And what do they do? Cromwell leverages her into her own starring role in Defense. The Honorable Charlene Whyte, Assistant Secretary of Defense for Humanitarian Assistance. Since when do we need an assistant secdef for humanitarian assistance?"

"Since we became humanitarian assistants," Ritter said calmly. He paused to slug down a drink from a brown, unlabeled bottle of mineral water. Taste of salt and history.

"To hell with that, too. If it weren't for Charlee Whyte's pigheadedness, we wouldn't be in this shithole."

"Well," Ritter said in a voice drier than the desert, "it'll be a great story to tell your grandchildren. One of those experiences that's a lot more fun in the remembering than it is while you're going through it. Anyway, you can't just blame Charlee Whyte. It's the president's policy. 'New missions for the new military.' "

"Crap. Anyway, old Charlee's the detail person. She's the one who wrote the goddamned rules. No sidearms. Full matériel accounting. Nonpartisan distribution—I mean, what the hell is that, really? Every breath you take in this neck of the woods is partisan."

"She's a D.C. person. They undergo a lot of sensory deprivation. Especially regarding any sense of what the world's really like." Ritter heaved a parcel and sighed, scrubbing the sweat from his face with an equally sweated forearm. "In any case, I suspect she means well. She just doesn't realize the implications of what she does. Good intentions gone wrong."

Ben put down the parcels he was shifting off the back of the truck and looked at Ritter in what appeared to be genuine astonishment. Usually, when Ben brought up the subject of Charlee Whyte, Ritter simply remained silent. Now, in this place, of all places, on this day, of all days, he appeared to be sticking up for perhaps the most hated woman in Washington and certainly the official most despised by the military.

Ben, who was forever smiling, who would be forever smiling in Ritter's memory, gave his friend an unusually sullen look.

"Yeah. Well, one of these days her 'good intentions' are going to get somebody killed."

The big-wheeled armored personnel carriers scuttled over the desert hills like cockroaches bred on amphetamines. The lone delivery truck snorted along in the center of the swarm, emptied of everything but a lonely boy driver in mustard-colored fatigues. Ritter stood up, torso thrust through the open hatch of a carrier, savoring the rush of air as they raced for the pass. Ill-tended engines sharpened the air with diesel fumes, and Ritter could feel his face griming. But the cooling effect was more important to him than a clean snout.

When he looked down, he could see the top of Ben's head in the cramped interior of the war machine. Ben gesturing and laughing. The squad of conscripts assigned to the vehicle crowded against one another with the happy male familiarity that marked the region, greasing their mouths with their rations while the exhaust system filled the hold with poison. They were curious about the Americans, alternately shy and bold. At the moment, Ben was half-yelling to be heard over the engine noise, shooting the bull with a sergeant who, it had quickly emerged, had a black marketeer's soul.

Ben had a finger stuck in a book. He had been trying to read in the bouncing, jarring carrier, captivated by his cause of the moment. Ben always had a cause, and this time it was the POWs who supposedly didn't come home from the last half century of America's wars. It was a subject Ritter regarded with a lot of skepticism and little interest. As far as Ritter was concerned, the POW/MIA groupies who trudged around the Wall on the Mall in their desecrated uniforms came from the same loony bin as the UFO crowd and the trailer-court residents who saw Elvis at the convenience store. The conspiracy junkies. Oliver Stone bottom-feeder stuff. Ritter had been surprised when Ben developed an interest in the subject, and after a bit of notably unsuccessful proselytizing, Ben had agreed to keep his latest crusade to himself. They were the kind of friends who could handle differences like that. Ben, for instance, hated the desert, while Ritter felt powerfully drawn to it.

Ritter knew that no desert was a congenial place for man. He did not underestimate the desert's harshness or dangers. Yet reason perished in the flood of memory as soon as he found himself in the dry vastnesses of the earth. Because the deserts were always Lena. Beautiful and endless, transcendent without ornament. He rode the battered troop carrier through a bleak landscape made poorer still by human folly, and his soul sailed away, leaving behind the cage of tended muscles and the armor of his uniform, to drive down another decade's roads, the two-lane blacktops of southern Arizona, with the desert twilight coming to life and his irresistibly vain, explosively intelligent, too generous, too beautiful love beside him in the sports car without which no new lieutenant could exist.

Magdalena Navarro, destined to become Lena Ritter and squander herself loving him. The grandee's fabulous daughter, picked up in a Tucson art-film house, amused at his temerity. The graduate student telling him about her thesis on San Juan de la Cruz, drinking beer from a long-necked bottle in the sweet night and lecturing a sexually ballistic young Army officer on sublimation and transcendence in the poetry of Sister Juana. His Lena, too proud to sleep casually with fools, who made an exception in his case. His desert rose, whose pure-blooded Spanish family fled the Mexican revolution and wound up owning half of Tucson. The Navarros were a bouquet of glass-mannered old men, hypnotic young gallants, and madonnas in Anne Klein dresses. The family's paternalistic racism toward the more typical Mexican-American's Indian blood first shocked him, then made him laugh with its antique extravagance.

Lena perched above his naked chest, leaning forward with her palms on his shoulders, moving and moving, her dark eyes closed and lips parted as her hair fell around his face like a personal midnight. Her sudden cry, as though she had been bitten. All deserts were Lena, and his life was a desert without her.

Once, on a mountain-hiking vacation in Italy, she had laughed and quoted Eliot, telling him he was "the still point of the turning world," and he had been miffed because he thought of himself as a man of action, muscles ever in motion. It had taken him a long time to understand that she was talking about *her* world, and by then it was too late and she was miserably, impossibly dead.

He looked eastward, with the late sun doting on his back. The far mountains that had served as a barrier first between civilizations, then between religions, then ideologies, shone pink where the high snows lay, blue in the lower gloaming. Between Ritter and the mountains lay a broken land.

The light quit too fast. They would not make it across the pass before dark. Perhaps they had been foolish. But it was all foolery, anyway. He didn't quite think of Rakhman, but the warlord hovered just beyond the realm of active thought. Another ghost.

A choke of black fumes from the carrier just ahead rumpled the evening, and a hawk or falcon brushed the sky. In that moment, which no watch could tame or measure, Ritter's dead wife was more real to him than his mundane surroundings. He remembered the deep touch of her lips in crippling detail, heard her voice. It was more than a year since he had lost her, yet he still could not understand how she could not be alive.

"Hey, dude," Ben said, popping up beside him. The friends crowded together in the narrow hatch, casually savoring the universe.

Ritter smiled automatically to feel his friend beside him, and they scanned the landscape together. Ritter had recently been threatened—again—with a Pentagon desk job, and he feared it would take him away from this sumptuous comradeship and these barren places where he belonged.

Ben made his voice big against the chugging of the carrier:

"What a raggedy-ass place. They can give it back to the Indians."

"The Indians already took it back."

Ben set his elbows on the worn rubber seal of the hatch and nodded, weighing the thickening darkness.

"So what's up?" he asked Ritter. "You watching out for bad guys, or just playing tourist?"

"Both, I guess."

Their voices meandered languidly, drained by the day. Nothing-talk between friends.

"Well," Ben said, "thanks to the United States Army, I can say I've seen many a place that few, if any, of my countrymen have seen. Of course, most of them are places nobody *wants* to see . . ." Ben giggled. He was one of the few grown men Ritter had ever encountered who actually giggled. In Ben, it managed to be an attractive quality. Ben Williams, who wore his uniform as though it were a letter sweater.

"I've been powwowing with Sergeant Sabayev," Ben went on. "He offered to take me home to meet his sister. I think he wants to go to America."

"Everybody wants to go to America."

"I told him I'm married. Not that it fazed him much. I think these boys are looking forward with some enthusiasm to the return of the system of multiple wives. Anyhow, I told him you were available." Ben smiled, an eternal boy. "Besides, you go for those serious, dark-eyed types."

Ritter let it pass. Then he said, "So how's Karin? You didn't update me on the last letter. Don't future godfathers have a right to know?"

Ben snorted. "Says she's big as a house. Christ, I hope she loses the weight afterward."

"You are a genuinely charitable and understanding man."

"I try." Ben waved it off. "You know Karin. She's a trooper.

She can handle anything. She just wants me home in time for the gory event."

The banter could not fully absorb a new undertone rising between the two friends. Rakhman was no longer on the periphery. They were entering the heart of his territory, and the night had come tumbling down with that suddenness peculiar to the desert. A shared sense of danger tightened around them like leather straps. They were just short of the near side of the Gobur Pass, and you could sense the rock walls up ahead, breaking the desert's skin. Ritter wondered where the boundary lay between a sense of duty and folly. Well, wherever that boundary lay, they had crossed it. Dumb shits, Ritter thought.

"Think old Rakhman's up for messing with Americans?" Ben asked, roping in their mutual thoughts.

Ritter explored the notion a bit further, then said, "I'm not sure how much of a conception he has of America. America's far away."

"Yeah. No shit. You still want to join the Charlee Whyte Fan Club?"

No. Ritter did not want to join the Charlee Whyte Fan Club. But that was another matter.

"I'd feel better," Ben went on, "if I at least had my own bullet-launcher."

Ritter shook his head. "If Rakhman wants our asses, he'll get them."

"Ah, the fatalist. *La vida es sueño*, right?"

"That's me."

The vehicle had been climbing gently for a long time. Now its nose lifted as if it had suddenly sniffed danger. They were entering the approach to the Gobur Pass.

"Fun, travel, and adventure," Ben said with mock zest.

The vehicle choked, then caught its breath in a lower gear. The climb steepened again. Ritter was glad of the dark on one count: it would be impossible to see the sheer drop-offs that lay ahead.

Ben leaned lightly against Ritter's shoulder. "Thinking about Lena again?"

Ritter shifted his weight, moving a little bit away. "I always think of her. It's a fact of life. I breathe and I think of her."

"Sooner or later . . . you've got to let it go, dude."

"Maybe later. Not sooner."

"You need to get back in the fight."

But there had been no fight with Lena. Only his growing selfishness and her unreasonable, inexplicable tolerance. She had taught him how to love. And he had been such a poor pupil.

"I'm not ready yet." Ritter had twice spent an evening in another woman's company during the past few months. But neither of the women had been able to reach him. They seemed so trivial and unaware, so undeveloped, and he was certain that neither of them would be able to love him the way he had grown accustomed to being loved. He drank wine with them, found no common ground, and ultimately annoyed them with his inability to long disguise his lack of interest. They tried, he didn't, and the nights went nowhere.

As the vehicles climbed, the temperature dropped. After the oven-dry day, the mountain night raised the hair on your forearms. Ritter tugged at his rolled-up sleeves until they flapped about his wrists. He felt overcome by affection for Ben, who tried so hard but did not understand. Ritter wanted to speak truly to his friend, to offer him something of value. His throat felt raw from carrying on their conversation above the noise of the military vehicles and from drinking dust, but that was a minor thing. In the Army, you learned to have the most intimate conversations in that harsh, strained voice you took on above the rumble of the tracks or the thumping of the big guns or the gargling of a helicopter in flight. What held Ritter back was the inadequacy of words to express anything important and true.

Abruptly, he took Ben by the upper arm, feeling the outsized muscle beneath cloth stiffened with dried sweat. "Listen to me, asshole. I want you to do something for me. For you. For Karin." He looked at Ben in the memory of light. Ben the eternal boy, eyes shining. "Grow up. Get out of the Army and just love your wife and the kid that's coming and don't ever leave them. Don't wait until it's too late. You can always find another job. Anyway, you could both live on what Karin makes with her computer business." Ritter tightened his grip. "Get out before something dumb happens to you or to them. You don't need the Army. And you said yourself you don't believe in the bullshit they've got us doing now."

Ben laughed like a delighted child, voice musical above the grunting war machine. "And when are *you* getting out?"

"I'm different."

"Bullshit."

"Ben, I'm serious. You want to leave Karin and your ankle-biter with a fistful of photos and your serviceman's insurance? For this?"

Ben laughed, a medium-size furred animal howling at the moon. "I can't believe it. My best friend's turning into my wife's twin." He looked at Ritter with eyes that gleamed with wonder, lighting the darkness. "You and Karin have been talking, right?"

The night opened up like a knife wound. Bleeding fire. Up at the head of the column, a new mountain appeared—white, yellow, orange, red—hurling lights off into the valley on the left side of the road. Burning trails stretched downward into infinity. Then the mountain of light faded and all that remained was the glow of cooking metal. Tiny chips of light chased one another through the darkness and the huge noise arrived.

Rakhman's people had blown the road, catching the lead vehicle.

An instant later, another blast tore away the roadbed behind them.

Their carrier groaned to a stop on the edge of a precipice, its tires bitten by old brakes. Small-arms fire pelted the metal.

"Shit," Ben said.

They couldn't stay in the carrier. That was a guaranteed death. They both knew it, yet they hunched down in the machine's belly for several seconds. With the soldiers crowding together like frightened animals. Ritter looked at Ben in the eerie interior light, with the sky artificially vibrant overhead. Ben nodded:

Let's move.

Ritter grabbed the nearest soldier by his load-bearing harness. "Come on," he shouted in Russian, hoping the local boy understood at least a minimum of the supposedly universal tongue. "Get out of here, let's go."

The soldier looked at him in horror, then began to swing his automatic weapon in the cramped space. Trying to point it at Ritter.

Ben kicked the weapon out of the boy's hands, then scooped it up for his own use. The rules didn't apply anymore.

The other soldiers in the hold cowered together even more closely, watching as though they expected the Americans to slaughter them.

"You've got to get out," Ritter screamed at them in Russian. "You'll be killed in here."

The uniformed children looked at him in wonder.

Ben hit Ritter on the back with an open hand. "Fuck 'em, if they can't take advice. Go. I'll cover you."

Ritter followed Ben's example and tore a weapon from a boy's shaking hands. With a vaguely directed prayer, he launched himself up through the hatch, rolling down over the vehicle's side with his legs and arms tucked so he wouldn't snag on the clutter of fittings and ports. He struck the earth with his boots together and rolled toward the cut between the side of the road and the upward slope of the mountain. All the while, Ben fired above him in short, sharp bursts.

Ritter rose to his knees and squeezed off a burst in the direction of the thickest cluster of muzzle flashes.

Different sound. A deep thump. The trailing carrier lit up from within as though it were a lampshade. Part of a second later, the vehicle's hatches exploded, volcanoes shooting fire and gear and human remains heavenward. Ritter felt the heat, as though he had stumbled too close to a bonfire.

Rocket-propelled charge into a fuel tank: the reason you did not remain inside an ambushed armored vehicle.

Ben flopped down beside him, striking the earth so hard the air went out of his lungs with a sigh audible over the sounds of battle.

"All right?" Ritter asked.

"Fucking bastards."

"You all right?"

"Yeah. Yeah. Okay."

Unexpectedly, the fire slackened. A moment of terrible silence followed. Then a voice called out in some local dialect.

No answer.

After a few seconds, the firing picked up again, contagious. The mountainside streamed with light. As nearly as Ritter could tell, all of the rounds were incoming. None of the surviving escort troops bothered to fire back.

"I'm going forward," Ritter half-shouted toward his friend. "See if I can find Ali."

"I'm right behind you," Ben told him.

Ritter arched like a sprinter in the starting blocks, then launched himself up alongside the column, keeping close to the lip of earth on the side of the road. There was too much light, thanks to the burning carriers and the headlights of the truck—which seemed to have been abandoned. None of the vehicle crew members who were still alive had the presence of mind to switch off their running lights, let alone man the heavy machine guns in their turrets. They simply hid in their steel coffins, waiting to die. Children playing dress-up in army uniforms had met the real thing.

A trail of bullets followed Ritter as though someone were stringing Christmas lights at his heels. Just in time, he flattened himself against the bank of earth along the roadside and let the gunner run his aim ahead of him. He resumed his dash only to trip over a corpse and nearly shoot himself with the automatic rifle in his hands. The spit of bullets chipped the roadside just in front of his face as he fell.

Ritter lay on the earth in a high-noon sweat. Not hurt, he thought, I'm not hurt. He wondered how many rounds, if any, he had left in the Kalashnikov. He switched the selector down to single shot.

Ben bellied in beside him, splashing gravel.

"Chris? You hit? You hit, buddy?"

Ritter tried to speak and found he was out of breath. He bullied himself toward normalcy. But his nerves were burning.

"Fell over my own fucking feet."

The sky sizzled. Another carrier clanged and whomped, burning its human cargo alive.

"What I admire most about these bastards," Ben said, "is their sense of gratitude."

Behind them, one neatly contained blast followed another.

Grenades.

The ambush party was skimming the little bombs down the slope, trying to get at the dead space at the side of the road. Where the Americans lay.

Ritter half-crawled, half-ran forward, seeking the captain, who was nominally in charge. In the fading hope of organizing some resistance. And he found the man. The captain crouched behind a boulder, weeping and praying.

The little man looked so far gone that Ritter did not try to rouse him at first.

The firing dissipated again, then ceased. Just ahead, a carrier burned magnificently, crackling and flaring as though it were a separate little war all its own. The hulk sent off the smell of fuel and molten rubber, of cordite and flesh.

The same voice that had called out earlier sounded again. The opaque syllables reminded Ritter of a Muslim call to prayer.

Ritter felt a cold rush of fear that the battle noise had been unable to trigger. Suddenly desperate, he squatted and shook the captain by the shoulder.

"What's he saying? What do they want?"

Ben crowded in. Three men behind a shrinking rock. "Ali, come on, man. You don't want to die here, do you?"

The voice from the mountainside spaced single words now. Speaking as if to children whose understanding remained incomplete.

He's counting, Ritter realized. It was a countdown.

"Ali, would you—"

The captain surprised them both. He stood up boldly. As he did, he brought up his automatic rifle, pointing the compact barrel at America. Neither Ritter nor Ben had time to react.

The captain shouted something in a fractured voice. Then he called out again, and the voice from the mountainside answered.

The captain switched to breathless, awkward Russian:

"You must put down your guns. Place them down. *Place them down.*"

The weapons clattered onto the earth, their metal alive in the firelight.

The captain straightened his back as if on parade. But he was still a little man. With a gun. He screamed in the local tongue, a fey opera spoof, frightened at some sudden possibility.

Ritter realized that it wouldn't take much to get the captain to pull the trigger.

The mountain's voice responded, its tone commanding. For Ritter, the world, the night, took on an authenticity that seemed to expose a reality behind common experience. He slipped into a feeling of calmness, of *oneness,* an uncharacteristic passivity. Yet his heartbeat was so powerful it felt as though someone were thumping him rhythmically on the spine. He listened to the snapping sound of the blazing machinery and to the scuffle of dozens of pairs of feet coming down the mountainside toward them.

The captain looked terribly frightened, even though he was the one with the rifle in his hands. The fear in his firelit eyes struck Ritter as unruly and sad, and he realized that there was nothing left that he personally feared with the extravagance of the little officer's fear. Ritter's body was afraid. A silver cold pierced his bowels and bones. But that didn't really matter. The body wanted to live. But the body's fear had no power over the utter stillness in his soul.

Yes, he thought, yes. The still point of the turning world. Yes, Lena. Yes.

The mountain's voice had come closer now and it called out a sharp order.

"Stand up straight," the captain translated. *"Straight."*

Ritter half-expected the man to shoot them both in anticipation of the ambushers' desires. He marveled that he felt so little fear. It almost made him smile.

Maybe, he thought, I'll be half as brave as she was.

"Chris," Ben said quickly, "tell Karin—tell her I love her, if—"

"Only Russian," the captain screamed. *"No English."* The little man had stepped into the cast of the truck's headlights, and his shadow flowed off into the night, enormous.

A little avalanche of stones preceded the ambush party.

One day, near the end, Ritter had surprised his wife in prayer. The lapsed Catholic who cherished religious poetry. The Catholic forms, the rites, had such strength, even emptied of belief. But where could a fallen Lutheran hide?

His body wept with sweat. Yet Ritter still did not believe that he was afraid. He felt exhilarated and sick in the stomach at the same time.

Countless hands fastened onto the Americans.

With the artful suddenness you encountered in a well-made horror film, an unforgettable face appeared in the firelight. The face stood out from all of the dark-haired, dark-eyed, tawny-skinned locals as completely as could any face on earth. The man was an albino, with patchy white hair. He looked too young for the alert deference the other bandits paid him, yet it was finally hard to read his age. Neither did his features offer a clear reference to the man's ethnicity. The shape of the eyes, the nose, looked at least partly European. But that could have been a trick of the flames—which gave his skin its only color. The albino wore an arctic expression perfectly suited to his coloration, and Ritter instantly pegged him as one of the lost men, often Afghan vets, who wandered over the corpse of the Soviet Union hiring out their phenomenal capacity for violence. One day a street thug, a paramilitary chief the next, their lives were adorned with cruelty. They migrated from trouble spot to trouble spot like the mercenaries of Renaissance Europe, living off death and dying young, usually murdered by one of their own kind.

This man—white, walking death—approached the Americans. His subordinates yanked the captives out of his path, beating Ritter and his friend on the neck and shoulders until they bent into a posture of respect. Ritter took the blows as though he were merely watching it all on film. He noticed that the captain had lowered his automatic rifle only to find himself taken prisoner as well.

The albino wasn't Rakhman. Just a semitrusted subordinate, a hireling. Ritter got the message. He and Ben and the aid convoy were not of sufficient importance to merit Rakhman's presence.

The albino wasted no time on the captain. He showed his gratitude for the man's betrayal by casually lifting a pistol and firing into the captain's skull from a foot away. The little officer's head snapped back and lolled, while the nearby bandits flinched as the pollution of blood and brains spattered them.

The shot echoed down ancient valleys. The albino turned to more important things.

He laid the hot barrel of the pistol against Ritter's cheek, savoring the automatic recoil of the flesh. The albino used the barrel as a steel finger, roughly turning the foreign face from side to side. Ritter saw eyes bred to keep secrets.

Abruptly, the albino moved on to Ben, inspecting him just as he had gone over Ritter. Buying horses at a mountain bazaar.

With a beautifully flowing gesture, the albino thrust the pistol up into the night, then brought it back down, smashing the butt into the side of Ben's cheek. It made the sound of a branch snapping in two. His friend's blood swept across Ritter's face like a gust of rain.

"Who do these Americans think they are?" the albino asked the heavens in peculiar Russian. "Who are these great and powerful Americans who come to our homes and behave without respect? Who are these sons of whores?"

Ritter could not fix the man's accent. Local, with some speech impediment? The albino had mastered the regional turns of phrase, to a degree. The theater. But he did not speak with the halts and slurs Ritter had come to expect east of the Caspian. The albino's Russian was as mongrelized as were his facial features.

The camps, Ritter realized with the force of revelation, *he's one of the kids who grew up in the prison system.* Ritter could never have explained why he knew this, but he was convinced of it. He would have bet anything on it, if he had had anything left to bet.

The albino fixed his attention on Ritter. He stepped back so that he would not have to tilt his head to look the taller American in the eyes. Ritter felt as though he understood this man. And there was only death at the end of such understanding.

Something displeased the albino and he spit a command. Ritter found himself smashed down to his knees.

I will die for nothing, Ritter thought. But it was little more than a casual observation.

The albino came intimately close. Crotch inches from Ritter's face. He rested the pistol's muzzle on the bridge of Ritter's nose.

Ritter calmly closed his eyes and waited. He thought of Lena, her lips just opened.

So much to regret.

But reality would not quit. He smelled the stink of gunpowder off the metal, the dirty body of the man who stood over him.

Ritter opened his eyes again, reawakening to life. It seemed to him that he was living a very long time. And the night air was beautifully cool. He raised his face until he and the albino were staring into each other's souls.

"You're just a fucking bozo," Ritter said in a perfectly normal voice, in English. And he waited for the bullet.

The albino broke the stare and gave another command. A great smear of hands lifted Ritter back to his feet. They stood him at Ben's side. The hands kept him firmly in their grip and Ritter was glad of it now. His legs felt as though all of the muscles had been stripped from them. His body was so afraid. And he did not want to give this man, these men, the satisfaction of seeing him collapse.

Ben's jaw hung at a cartoon angle, broken.

"Tell me, my American friend," the albino said to Ben, "do you think I am afraid of America?"

Ben could not, or would not, answer.

For God's sake, Ben, Ritter thought. *Try* to give him what he wants.

Ben's breath whispered over a slime of blood.

"But why don't you answer me? My name is Zhan. You can call me by my name because we are friends. And you can tell me why General Rakhman should be afraid of America." Zhan smiled. He had the standard deplorable teeth of the old Soviet underclass. A mouth like a burned-out building. "Talk to your friend Zhan. Tell him why you have come to piss on his country." He jabbed the pistol into the wreckage of Ben's face and Ben jerked backward in pain.

The albino shook his head. He understood the necessity for drama. If he wasn't a local native, he had a brilliant gift for mimicry. And now he was playing to the locals:

"We do not want to talk to our friend Zhan. Zhan is not worthy of America's respect." He stepped in close, nudging between the two Americans. Their captors twisted them to accommodate the albino.

"I have a problem," Zhan confided. "If I kill both of you, I will have no messenger to send to the president of the United States. To tell him what happens when he shows no respect and tries to buy the loyalty of Rakhman's people with a handful of rice." He looked from Ben to Ritter and back to Ben, infinitely amused.

Ritter tried to catch Ben's eye. But their captors held them too rigidly, and Ritter could only half-see and half-sense the silhouette of Ben's body.

"I would like to kill you both," Zhan said mildly and pleasantly. "But, you see, my hands are tied. Rakhman wants you to deliver a message. So I am forced to kill only one. But how shall I choose between twin dogs?"

Ritter did not think. He spoke automatically:

"Kill me," he said in Russian. "Kill me, you little sugar-coated faggot."

Zhan stabbed his pistol up into Ritter's cheek so hard that Ritter felt bones ache in his neck. Head forced back at a miserable angle, he waited for the end that had been delayed. His eyes consumed a sky fantastic with stars.

He felt nothing but the pain in his neck and an intimation of unknowable vastness.

Lena.

The pistol pulled away and Ritter's head rolled forward, neck all hurt. When the pistol fired, it was so close to his ear that the report struck him like a physical blow. The sound was as big as the sky. As dark as the reaches of space between the constellations.

Ben lay at his feet, scumming the earth with his blood. His boy's eyes were open and fixed in endless surprise.

"No," Ritter shouted.

Everyone around him laughed. This was splendid entertainment. The shot dwindled into eternity, swallowed by the mountains.

Ben's blood flowed downhill, making an island of Ritter's right boot. His carcass lay like a sack of waste.

Ritter wanted to vomit.

"And *you,*" the albino said, closing on Ritter again, kicking Ben's arm out of the way, "you can go back to your nation of whore wives and whore mothers and tell them of Rakhman. Go back and tell them of Rakhman's justice."

Lena was gone now, a culture and a corpse away. Ritter thought of another woman, of Karin, Ben's wife. With Ben's ghost swelling in her.

There should have been a better end than this, Ritter thought.

Ben stared into the settling fires, his child's wonder frozen forever. He would go unavenged, Ritter knew. This was a sideshow of a sideshow, and the president was not going to send in the Marines. Maj. Benjamin Thomas Williams, killed in the line of duty. Karin would get the flag that covered the casket. If they recovered the body.

Zhan, the pale death vendor, smiled. As if he could read Ritter's thoughts.

"Go back to your country. Tell them what you have seen."

He pointed his pistol at Ritter's right leg and shot him just above the knee. The binding hands fell away and Ritter collapsed in instant agony. No more transcendence or bravado. Just pain.

Ritter rocked over the ground like a madman, clutching the hurt.

"Go back to your country," the albino repeated. "But *crawl* back."

TWO

RITTER LIMPED ALONG THE PENTAGON HALLWAY. JAPANESE TOURISTS in their quaint native dress of designer windbreakers and camera necklaces listened as a Navy yeoman assured them she would not forget to stop by the bust of MacArthur. Workmen nibbled lazily at a water-damaged wall, and a disabled black man in an electric cart beeped past on his way to deliver boxes of photocopy paper. Junior officers hurried, colonels prowled, and an occasional flag officer paraded by. The younger secretaries tacked along on the tile-over-concrete floors, provocatively alone, enriching the universe, while their older sisters plodded in pairs, reporting to one another on settled lives. The innermost ring drew the Men-in-Suits, forever seeking shortcuts to an office with a view out on the E-ring. The Men-in-Suits came in three essential varieties: the intermittently important, the buffoonishly self-important, and the nervous young apprentices who wished they could be just a little more important. No one noticed Ritter.

Bright antitobacco posters and blaring videos threatened smokers in their flight toward the outdoor landings where they could light up and grow whole again. A fine glass display case celebrated Native Americans in the military, while another exhibit flirted shamelessly with women in uniform. A glorious fat cartoon of a bureaucrat hippoed down the hall with a fistful of glazed doughnuts and a styrofoam cup of coffee steaming scent. Absorbed in his dream of calories, he almost collided with Ritter, who had to twist sharply on his bad leg to save himself.

"Jesus Christ," Ritter said. He could not stop the words, but he had the self-control to restrain their volume. The doughnut king surged by, oblivious, with the incomparable assuredness of the tenured government worker—to whom all those in uniform were as identical as they were inconsequential and transitory.

Ritter stood still for a moment, then reached out and braced a hand against the wall. He closed his eyes. He hated the pain in his leg for the weakness it revealed. He tried to clear his mind. Breathing deeply. Then he snapped to and forced himself to move on, unwilling to make a spectacle of himself. He despised his limp and struggled to hide it, making the pain worse. With each step, hot little bullets of hurt shot up his thigh, skipped his torso, and impacted high in his skull. The reconstructed mess atop and behind his kneecap made him hate the hard flooring and the infernal distances in the building. The Pentagon Circus. He just didn't want to be one of the clowns.

He would be able to run again. Eventually. Maybe. If he took his therapy seriously. And he would walk normally. He had made the doctors and therapists promise him that much. In the meantime, he refused to use the cane for which he had been forced to sign a receipt.

He knew officers who preened over the damage their careers inflicted on their bodies, cherishing their marks of manliness. But Ritter just wanted to be able to travel between two points with inconspicuous dignity. He *marched* through the Pentagon in the hard old Army sense of the word, facial features bullied into inscrutability. Until the bone gravel crunched in his knee and it became all he could do to stop himself from sitting down in the middle of the hallway and slamming his eyes shut.

He passed a series of large black-and-white photos, taken during the Korean War, of GIs. Winter suffering. Suddenly, he felt unspeakably ashamed at the tininess, the near luxury, of his discomfort compared to the miseries endured by the men who had fought their way to the Yalu only to find themselves overwhelmed by the stunning manpower of Red China.

"You pussy," he told himself.

A lieutenant colonel, swollen in his black polyester sweater, pondered the choices offered by a candy machine. Ritter could tell at a glance that the man would not survive the next round of personnel cuts.

Ritter did not look forward to the impending interview. Col. Jeb Bates had called him—the first official call since Ritter's release from Walter Reed—and asked him to drop in. Ritter understood that this meant a job offer. He had known Bates for years, the casual way you got to know good officers for whom you never really worked but who shared bits of the same over-arching mission. Bates was a walking slice of history, a man with a reckless past that made him a superb officer but that would likely keep him from a general's stars. He was the kind of officer about whom his peers told admiring stories—from Vietnam, from edgy Berlin before the Russians went home, from the career-killing swamp of Central America. Under other circumstances, Ritter would have looked forward to seeing Bates again and would have been more than ready to work for him. But he had heard that Bates was working the POW/MIA issue with the Russians at the moment. Yesterday's news and maybe a decayed corpse or two.

Ritter had overdosed on death and the past. He wanted a real Army job doing real Army things. Away from the Russians for a couple of years. Away from other people's miseries. A job where the concerns were straightforward, the hours long, and the press of the training schedule kept you from thinking too much. Where the duty language was American English. Where he could lick his wounds and heal up just a little. No matter how good a man Jeb Bates was, Ritter was not about to go chasing ghosts for him.

He turned down a corridor piled with furniture removed from offices undergoing renovation. A computer-generated sign, taped to a chair, alerted passersby that the furnishings were not excess property. The building was a living thing, its microorganisms forever erupting, metamorphosing, disbanding, then reincarnating under a new acronym. Missions and responsibilities migrated about the vast structure like nomadic tribes. The Pentagon was a world unto itself, waiting for an anthropologist to make his or her reputation by explaining its folkways.

Polite to a degree still fashionable only in the military, Ritter stepped out of the way of a rushing woman who looked as though she had not thought of anyone but herself in ten years. She left a wake of asexual perfume behind her. She had not seen him. But he had seen her. Her face was the Washington face of oblivion.

He marched. Almost there. He turned into the D-ring and counted down the numbers until he found the little blue sign that said U.S.-RUSSIAN POW/MIA WORKING GROUP.

Ritter paused to straighten his uniform, his back, his soul, then opened the door.

The office was in chaos. The space had been stingily allotted, and too many people were trying to do too many things with too many phones and too much paper. Keyboards ticked. The blank blue screen of a computer, unattended, looked promiscuous and neglected amid the confusion. Another computer lay in shiny pieces on the floor at Ritter's feet.

Bates stood in the middle of the room, colonel's eagles on his shoulders, Kabuki-mask face, and a telephone pressed to his ear, its cord tortured across the room. He didn't see Ritter at once. Simultaneously with his telephone conversation, Bates paged through a clipboard thick with message traffic and gestured to a subordinate who looked desperately in need of a good leave. Bates nodded, but it was impossible to tell whether he was nodding at something he was hearing or at what he was reading. He looked older than Ritter remembered him, the oval mask forehead driven farther back into the hairline, the skin under the jaw noticeably less elastic. Bates had been a bird colonel for a long time.

He spotted Ritter. Delayed reaction. Then he smiled as though he were genuinely glad. Old counterintelligence hand, Ritter reminded himself. The bugger knew how to glad-hand you. Watch out.

Bates flipped the message sheets back down onto the clipboard and held up one finger in Ritter's direction:

Wait.

"Listen, Danny boy, let me call you back, okay? I've got an important visitor. . . . Right. Sure, you bet. Out here."

A moment later, Ritter felt the clasp of the colonel's big, warm hand.

Bates. Skin splintering at the corners of his brown eyes. Northern European brown eyes, not the night windows of Lena's kind. Up close, the colonel's breath smelled faintly of medicine. One of the many ailments that came with age and hard service.

In Vietnam, the story went, Bates had lived out in the villages. Alone. With a pistol and an ear for languages. In Germany, Bates had been involved in cracking the worst spy ring in the history of the U.S. Army. And in El Sal, both sides had wanted him dead—the rebels because Bates was so damned effective, and the government troops because he refused to keep his mouth shut about human-rights abuses.

"Can't talk in this madhouse," Bates said. "Come on. We'll use the general's office. He's out running."

Bates led Ritter next door, past an enlisted woman functioning as a secretary, and into a smallish office that had a distinctly provisional look. There were none of the usual Leavenworth or Carlisle class prints or diplomas, none of the cherished, ugly unit plaques and allied military paraphernalia that gave the average senior officer's inner sanctum a jumbled, flea-market feel. Only two forlorn plants and a nearly empty bookcase topped with a few family photographs. It was the office of a man who expected to move on in short order.

Bates sighed as though breaking down to a walk at the end of a hard run. "Chris, you look good. Sit down, sit down. Heard about the dustup you got into—sorry about Ben Williams, by the way. Didn't really know him, but I heard he was a good man."

"A very good man." Ritter smoothed his rump into one of the "serious-meeting" leather armchairs.

Bates nodded and held up empty hands: What can you do? "Leg doing okay? It was your leg, wasn't it?"

"Coming along fine."

Bates took on a knowing look. "Yeah. Well, don't be a hero.

Give it time to heal. Do what the doctors tell you." He snorted, laughed. Ether-breathed. "And always take your malaria pills. I can tell you that, personally."

Bates veered off for a moment, mind chasing some private devil. The silence was the sort everyone usually rushes to break. But Ritter wasn't saying anything. He had come to listen. Then to decline and go.

Bates looked up, capturing Ritter's eyes. "Chris, I want you to give me a snap answer. No hesitation. What do you think of when I say 'POW/MIA'?"

"Lunatic fringe. Nonissue. Fat guys with beards and beat-up field jackets who can't get on with their lives."

Bates rolled his head back as if an invisible blow had made him dizzy. Then he leaned in toward Ritter, the father, the coach. "I can see I've got my work cut out for me." The friendly smile dissolved into seriousness with the magic of a computer image. "Listen, Chris. I've got a problem. And you're going to be in a position to help me. Just listen to what I've got to say for a few minutes."

"When colonels talk, I listen."

"No. I mean *really* listen. One no-bullshit officer to another."

"Sir, I came to listen."

Ritter could read Bates well enough at the moment. The colonel had worked as an agent, an interrogator, an agent handler. He knew more about human nature than any thirteen psychologists. Bates was looking for "the angle," the point of entry. Ritter let him search.

"Chris," Bates began again, "how much do you actually know about the POW/MIA issue? As it relates to our little Russian brothers?"

"I know the Russians are their own worst enemies."

Bates raised his eyebrows. It was not the sort of reply the ex-interrogator expected. Then he nodded. "Granted. But I'm talking about the nuts and bolts. What-they-did and when-they-did-it stuff."

Ritter shrugged. "It's never been a topic that interested me. I scan the newspaper articles. But it just strikes me as all so much history. Trying to raise the dead. I mean, I *don't* believe there are tens of thousands of Americans hidden in some secret

camp in Siberia longing to return to their loved ones." Ritter
looked hard into the older man's eyes. "Am I wrong?"

Bates sat back against the brown leather, the pale green of
his shirt framed by brass upholstery tacks. He appeared frankly
disappointed at Ritter's bluntness, at his evident unwillingness
to play the game.

"No," the colonel said slowly, "you're not wrong. There
aren't tens of thousands of POWs hidden away in some last
bastion of the GULag. There may be a few shadowy cases where
the Soviets turned a guy and let him live out a dull life somewhere in the boonies, I can't say for sure. But—"

"But the Soviets weren't, and the Russians aren't, stupid
enough to let a pack of POWs live to tell the tale. *If* the Soviets
ever took any of our guys in the first place."

Bates looked at him thoughtfully. This time, Ritter could not
read the man.

"Oh, they took them, all right," Bates said softly. "They
took them."

Despite himself, Ritter quickened, straightening his spine. It
occurred to him that Bates had a great voice for telling ghost
stories. But Ritter's cynicism had weakened markedly over a
few words. After all of the sensationalism in the press, here
was a sober, honest—if clever—man stating, "It happened."

Ritter shuddered on time-delay.

He noticed how the colonel's eyelids had begun to fill and
sag with the years, how the remaining hair was losing its color
in its long retreat. The skin, not only around the man's eyes,
showed the depreciation of years spent in the tropics, outside
of the protective vaults of civilization.

"Chris, let me give you the exec summary of what happened.
The Sovs played World War Two relatively cleanly with us.
They cheated here and there on the repatriation issue, but only
on gray-area cases—dual citizenship and that sort of thing.
They've let us into their archives on that one, and they've
owned up to what they did. Case closed for me." Bates shifted,
relieving some old injury. "At the other historical end, Vietnam, it looks like they were smart. They let the North Vietnamese do the dirty work. Besides, the North Vietnamese realized
the value of U.S. POWs early on, and they weren't about to make

the Sovs a gift of one of their most valuable assets. So, if the Sovs took any of our POWs back to the Motherland from Indochina, it was only a matter of a very few people with highly specialized knowledge. And they just might be clean on that one."

The colonel leaned forward again, slipping back into his ghost-story voice to continue. "On the Cold War . . . well, that was such a mess we may never sort it out completely. Everybody in the universe was running secret ops. I personally believe they may have recovered one or two of our downed aircrews, or at least a couple of survivors. And maybe they killed them after a while, maybe they died from the harsh conditions. Maybe some guy rolled over and got to survive for a while. Now, I say we may never sort it all out, because it's such a goddamned mess. But we're actually making surprising progress on the Cold War shootdowns, both working with the Russians and in our own archives. We've gotten some breaks." Bates smiled sadly. "You know, it's funny how bureaucracies work. Back in the fifties, we démarched the Sovs right and left, trying to get back flight crews we thought they were holding. The Sovs just stonewalled us. And as people changed jobs over in Foggy Bottom or here, as administrations and priorities changed, we just sort of lost track of the whole business. There was no conspiracy, no overarching cover-up. Just bureaucrats shuffling papers. Human lives reduced to card-file entries, then shipped off to the archives. We never had much evidence. And you know how it is. There's always some issue of the moment making you jump through your ass."

Abruptly, Bates dropped his musing tone and sharpened his expression. "Listen. What I really want to talk to you about is Korea. The Korean War POW/MIA issue. *That's* where our little Russian brothers have blood on their hands."

Ritter's curiosity was up. He couldn't help himself. But he tried to maintain a controlled exterior, sitting back in his chair. A still point. He told himself that he did not want to be drawn into this. No matter what the Soviets had done forty years before, it was history. And nothing more.

"Sir . . . whatever may have happened in Korea . . . it's over. The world has moved on."

Bates nodded. But the gesture had no agreement attached to

it. "Chris, you're resisting me. Why don't you just listen? With an open mind? Have you got some sort of thing about this?"

"Sir, I'm serious. I don't understand the importance people attach to this issue. Oh, it's interesting enough to hear you talk about it. But I can't let myself get sucked into all this."

The colonel's face rumpled. Into another mask. The Great Mask of Hurt and Misunderstanding. Almost a woman's face. "And what's that supposed to mean?"

Ritter half-smiled. "It's just . . . Christ . . . we're talking about the dead. And I honor those who died for my country. But they're *dead.* I find this entire POW/MIA cult morbid and unhealthy. And . . . I guess it's tied into my personal affairs, my personal life. Too much of a downer. The whole business just makes me want to run for the trees."

Death, Ritter thought. Stinking up this sterile Pentagon office. Death and more death. He didn't want to smell it anymore. Not the hospital variety, and not the middle-of-nowhere midnight kind, either. In Tallinn, a paramilitary officer from the new, independent government had given him a tour of the basement of the old KGB building, bullying him into the windowless cells where a man could only stand up, couldn't even turn. Then they went into the subterranean chamber hacked down into the bedrock, hidden deep under the building, muffled so that no one in the crowded neighborhood would hear. It was the execution room, where the muzzles brushed the hair at the nape of the neck. There were no lights, you moved over the broken floor guided by a cigarette lighter. And death kissed you, caressed you, ran its fingers down your belly and up into the crack of your ass. There was so much cold death in that little black room that you had to swim through the air, with your soul struggling against the currents of eternity. There were thousands of such rooms on the earth.

Ritter just wanted to breathe clean air.

Maybe I've used it up, Ritter thought. Maybe I've lost the vocation. After all, soldiering isn't about much else, in the end. *Death.*

Bates was a very good interrogator. He bore down. "Chris, I understand you've been through a lot. I do my homework. I know it's not just Ben. I know where you've been and what you've done. And I know about your wife."

Ritter flinched. As though Bates had just hammered a nail into his bad knee.

"I understand better than you think," Bates went on. "But I *need* your help. And all I'm asking you to do at the moment is to listen to me. Let me tell you about the Korean War POWs. About our fellow soldiers. We've been building this case. Painstakingly. Agonizingly, if you will. From scraps and shreds of information. As near as we can reckon the scenario, the Soviets culled the POW population in Korea and took the cream of the crop. Pilots. Navigators. Engineers. Officers with technical or organizational knowledge. Men with something to offer. They took them back to the Soviet Union—"

"How many?" Ritter interrupted coldly. "What kind of numbers are we talking about?"

"Not sure. A Soviet veteran confided to us that he believed the numbers were in the dozens to the low hundreds. But he only had access to part of the picture. Maybe his numbers are right, or maybe it was several hundred. But we can follow the shadow they cast in the GULag. A report from a released prisoner who served in this camp or that, someone who saw Americans at a transit point or shared a holding cell with a pilot for a few days. You have to work with hundreds of tiny pieces, some of them absolutely false or damned doubtful. But, when you assemble the mosaic, it makes a powerful case. The Soviets took our POWs. And they didn't give them back. And I will go to my grave believing that."

"They killed them?"

Bates shrugged. "It looks that way. But it's frustrating. We don't know who, when, or where. Oh, we've got some ideas on prisoner identities. But Korea was an absolute mess. Personally, I read it this way: they held on to these POWs for several years, until they realized the poor bastards were nothing but a liability. Then, say sometime in the late fifties, or when the Berlin Wall went up or during the Cuban missile crisis, the poor bastards each got a bullet in the back of the head. When some bureaucrat was having a bad day."

Ritter felt another chill, hating the extent to which the colonel's speech moved him. Bates was a persuasive man, and the effect was compounded because Ritter knew Bates was a sincere and decent man, as well. The colonel's commitment to caring for his subordinates was legendary, and he could always be counted on to do the right thing. Now he was trying to care for the dead. And Ritter felt himself being drawn toward an utterly unwanted fate.

Ritter caught himself, and he flushed away the excitement of making new mental connections. "Fine. So we get to the shocking revelation that our newly beloved Russian counterparts haven't always been democratic saints. So what's new? Even the press catches an occasional glimpse of the obvious. But all this POW business . . . it's still nothing but history. If they're dead, they're dead. I mean, I understand wanting to bring them back to Dover with a flag over each and every casket. But this is a job for Mortuary Affairs."

Bates smiled gently, evidently not displeased with the progress he was making. Ritter sat back and waited to hear the next installment, refortified against the colonel's psychological siege operations.

"Chris . . . maybe it's my personal Vietnam hangover. You're a little too young, you didn't go through that. But, when your buddy goes down, you want to bring him back, you know?"

Ritter knew. Ben's body had never been recovered. Karin still got a flag. Forced on her. They delivered it to her after she got out of the hospital. Premature labor and a dead, underweight infant. And a survivor-assistance officer trying to do the right thing, aching to be elsewhere. Karin would not attend any ceremonies. She did not even want to see Ritter. So he knew a little bit about wanting to bring the bodies back.

"Anyway," Bates went on, "the victims aren't all dead. Because the POWs weren't the only victims. They weren't even the most numerous. Chris, the tragedy now, the living tragedy, concerns the families. The survivors. The ones who waited. For years. Hoping. The ones who are still hoping after forty years." He grimaced. A horrid smile. One of the innermost masks. "Dealing with the POW family members has been one of the most difficult things I've had to do in my military career." Bates dropped his eyes. "I'm not talking about the obnoxious sons of bitches who use Vietnam as an excuse for their own fuckups, or who never miss a chance to cry in front of a camera. Those are the bastards who are turning you and the average citizen off. And you know the goddamned thing about it? If you pin down a lot of those grungy maggots parading around in uniform shreds and more badges than a Latin American dictator, you'll find out that, not only aren't they real vets, but that they have no personal connection to any POWs. They're just misery freaks. A lot of those clowns never served a single day in the military. But they've found an issue that's the psychological equivalent of a banana split. If they hadn't stumbled onto the POW/MIA thing, they would've joined some whacko religious cult or picketed abortion clinics where they could terrorize teenaged girls. They do a disservice to everybody. Like the journalists who'll print any lie for a headline, who get the POW/MIA families excited, then blame every disappointment on a government conspiracy.''

Bates sat back and let out a long breath. Then he leaned back into the fight. "Human misery *always* attracts parasites. And, as far as the POW/MIA issue goes, there's plenty of misery out there. It makes you just want to club the shit out of those jokers. Because they hurt the wives and sons and daughters of the men who didn't come home, and because they alienate people like you, people who should care, who could make a difference. But . . . Chris, the *majority* of the people involved, the family members, aren't like that. These are good people, good Americans. The people you and I are proud to defend. They just want to know what became of their husbands or brothers or fathers. Sure, they wish we could bring them back alive. Wouldn't you? I mean, I've got to tell you honestly, Chris. The U.S. government has not always handled this issue well. And not everybody in this town is committed to handling it well today. If men in uniform don't fix it, it won't get fixed. There are just too many vested interests. We've got to take care of our own, because, frankly, except for a couple of good men on the Hill, nobody gives a shit. They just wish the problem would go away. POW corpses are bad for business. And they're apt to upset State's beloved diplomatic status quo—brought to you by the careerists who gave the world Yugoslavia and Somalia, thank you."

Bates extended his hands in front of him as though he were cradling a globe. His eyes, scorched by old tropical diseases, had emerged from behind the last mask. Ritter understood that the colonel was trying from his heart to reach him.

"Chris, there never was any kind of conspiracy. No cover-up. Nothing like that. But, by God, there was plenty of incompetence. And, sometimes, a gross and fundamental lack of simple decency on the part of Washington officials. We usually knew more than we told the families. We held back information on national-security grounds that ... hell, it makes me sick to think about it."

The colonel's hands had closed into fists. Ritter, shut inside the castle of self, was surprised at the level of emotion Bates was willing to betray.

"It all leads back to Korea," Bates said. "We were convinced they took our boys way back when it was all going down. But the whole damned thing just looked too hot to handle. Everybody just wanted to close the book on the war. And we didn't have a smoking gun, just a lot of circumstantial evidence that the Russians took our POWs. What were we going to do about it? Declare thermonuclear war?"

Bates smirked, almost spit. "So we told the young wife of First Lt. John Smith and her three-year-old daughter that her husband was classified as killed in action, body not recovered. Or some other caveat. Case closed. But that case was never closed for Mrs. Smith. And the daughter grew up remembering. Chris, I don't wear my heart on my sleeve. But it just tears you up to talk to these people, to hear what they went through at the hands of their own government. The stupid official lies and half-truths. The bureaucrats too busy to return calls. The lost files. And the lost years." The colonel's eyes were slightly wet. "Chris, this city's full of monuments. Every one of the homeless has his own Civil War general. But there are two monuments missing. One is to the POWs who didn't come home, who gave more than *anyone* else, whether in Korea, Manchuria, or Siberia, from the Cold War or Indochina. And the other missing monument is the one to the families they left behind, to the wives and parents and children who never lost faith."

Bates smiled at himself, realizing how far he had gone, and

he relaxed a little. "Oh, hell. Sorry. But it just goddamned humbles you to deal with these people. It makes you hope and pray that, if you ever go missing, your wife and kids will think that much of you."

Yes, Ritter agreed. Certainly that. "But . . . what you're telling me . . . is that you're being straight with them now?"

"We're damned well trying. Not everybody's happy about it. You've got sons of bitches who are still afraid to declassify forty-year-old dinner menus. But we're making progress. And the military, the Army, is absolutely determined to get it right this time. Chris, I've seen so many good men put their careers on the line over this issue that it just makes me proud. The Army is committed to telling the truth. But, as soon as you leave the company of the uniformed brethren, the Potomac starts to stink." Bates paused. "I'm not being fair. There are good people in every agency. Trying to do the right thing. But it's a thankless job. And, in the end, only the military has the moral clout to get this job done. You can't let it become part of a political agenda."

The colonel waved a hand at the great capital city beyond the walls. "We're not going to make a lot of people happy. Some of the family members have been treated so badly for so long that they'll never believe what we tell them. And there are others who've just become obsessed with the issue. Even if you could give them proof they could hold in their hands as to the fate of their loved ones, they'd have to reject it. Without this issue, they'd be rudderless, as if they'd lost their religion. So they'll keep on believing in the Big Lie conspiracy theory, because they have to. It's all they've got to fill up their lives. And other family members, the ones who still quietly hope that dad's going to walk in out of the taiga—they're likely in for a hell of a disappointment. But we're going to tell them the truth. Or at least as much of it as we can uncover with our little Russian brothers."

Bates sat back, spiritually winded. He hooked an arm over the chairback. "This may be the most miserable job I've ever had. But I've never felt so committed to anything. Not even in Vietnam. I'd warn you, but I guess you've already figured it out. I've been on the road to Damascus. It's *my* cause now. And it always will be, God help me. So be careful. Or it'll become your cause, too."

I don't need this, Ritter told himself firmly. I won't be suckered into it. Bates is one slick old bastard.

The colonel looked weary, a man near the end of his speechifying. "Chris, I believe our men are dead. I told you that. But, as a fellow soldier, I want to bring their bodies home. Even if I have to go to Siberia and dig them up myself and walk home with them. They're my brothers. And they're yours, too. Maybe that's too romantic for you to buy into. But scratch an old soldier and you'll find a romantic. Anyway, I think they deserve to rest in their native soil. Honored by those for whom they died. If they're going to be forgotten, let them be forgotten at home. Not in some frozen, godforsaken trench or pit where all they got for their courage was terror and a bullet."

There were unmistakable tears in the old colonel's eyes. The sight startled Ritter, who was struggling to deal with his own emotions, resisting them with all his strength. He hated this, wanted to be anywhere else.

Then he caught himself. *No.* No way. Bates was a master at this. He was not even above this kind of trick to draw somebody into his game. *Yes,* it was tragic. *Yes,* you had to feel for the dead and their survivors. But you didn't have to take a bath in it.

You didn't have to become one of them.

Ritter shifted his leg and winced at a flash of pain. He straightened his back, going formal. Military.

"Sir . . . it sounds like you're doing a great and good thing. But I'm going to be honest with you. I don't want this job. And I'll fight you if you try to drag me into it. I can serve the Army better elsewhere."

Bates looked at the younger man with a bewildered expression that Ritter could not understand. Then the colonel smiled. A moment later, he began to laugh.

"Oh, Jesus. Oh, Christ. I'm sorry." Bates shook his head at some powerful private joke. The laughter faded into intermittent chuckles, but the colonel could not control his grin. "So *that's* why you're being such an asshole—you thought I was pitching you for a job?"

It was Ritter's turn to feel bewildered.

"Good God," Bates said, "I'm too smart an old dog to try to rope in a fast burner like you on something like this—you mean nobody's told you?"

"Told me what?"

"About your assignment? Nobody's said anything?"

Ritter was utterly at a loss. "Sir . . . I've been on medical leave. I've—"

Bates could not stop shaking his head. Slowly. In boundless amusement. "Well, I guess it's not really my place to break the news to you. Oh, Christ." He spurted laughter. "I'm sorry. Chris, I really am. I've made a mess out of this. Haven't I?"

"So what's my assignment?"

"I guess they were going to call you in. Notify you formally . . ."

"Come on, sir. You can't do this to me." But Ritter was smiling, too. He suspected that he had nothing to smile about. But the colonel's glee was infectious.

"Chris, for God's sake. Don't let on I told you, all right?"

"All right. Fine."

"You're going to be the military aide to Charlee Whyte. To the Honorable Charlene Whyte, Assistant Secretary of Defense for Humanitarian Assistance. She picked you by name—what's the matter? You look snakebit."

Ritter wished it had been a job interview after all. And that he had been in a position to accept.

"It won't be so bad," Bates went on. "I mean, she *selected* you. She must have her reasons. And you'll survive it. And you just might be able to do a lot of good for the military. Talk some sense into her."

Ritter could not speak. Out of all the things he had expected in life, this certainly had not been one of them. She's crazy, he thought. Fucking nuts.

"Chris, that's why I called you in. I need your help. There's something going on—are you listening to me?"

"Yes, sir."

"Charlee Whyte's got her finger in something. Something to do with Korean War–era POWs. I've got a source. I'm not going to tell you who. You know the rules. But I've been tipped that she's trying to run some kind of independent operation. And I don't trust her, Chris. I can't for the life of me see why she'd want to get mixed up in POW/MIA affairs."

"Well . . . it *is* a humanitarian matter."

Bates shook his head. "Not her kind. If it doesn't have to do with a certified liberal cause that involves at least a percentage of foreign radicals who hate everything this country stands for, Charlee Whyte's not interested. I don't believe she has the least interest in POW/MIA matters on their own merits. There's something going on."

"Like what?" Ritter was trying to listen and think at the same time. And there was plenty to think about.

"Don't know. I just don't know. But my source tells me that there are some kind of documents for sale right here in this country . . . smuggled in from Russia . . . proof that just might explode the whole Korean War POW business. Now I can't swear it's true, my source is an F-6 if ever there was one. But Charlee Whyte seems to believe it. And she's a loose cannon, Chris."

"Where's her office? I've got to talk to her. This can't happen."

"What can't happen?"

"I can't work for her."

"Oh, yes, you can. And I suspect you will. Charlee Whyte tends to get her way."

"I *can't* work for her."

Bates shook his head. Mirth in the pink-brown eyes surrounded by ruined skin. "Oh, you can, indeed. From what I hear, she's dead set on you. It was all we could do to keep her from dragging you out of the hospital before the doctors were ready to let you go."

This cannot happen, Ritter thought. She's off the fucking deep end. I will not permit this to happen.

"Where's her office?" Ritter demanded. "E-ring? Where? Which floor?"

Bates shrugged happily. "Of course, she's on the E-ring. She's an E-ring kind of girl. Our visionary assistant secretary has to have a good view, doesn't she?" The colonel dropped his smile. "But she's not there at the moment, so hold your horses and keep up your physical therapy. Ms. Whyte's off in the Balkans, doing good. I'm sure we'll all see her on CNN." He leaned over and touched Ritter on the forearm. "It'll be okay. And you'll be in a position to find out what the hell she's hiding on the POWs. I need you to find out what's going on. Before we screw things up again." He firmed up his grip on Ritter's flesh. "I know you'll do the right thing, Chris."

Ritter lowered his head in frustrated anger. And in genuine sorrow at this folly.

"This is going to end badly," he said.

THREE

THE OUTCAST SAT ON THE COLD EARTH, APART FROM THE ROWS OF squatting prisoners. He wore scrap trousers torn open to the lower thigh and a cardigan sweater dyed in the hard chemical colors that were one of the legacies of Balkan socialism. Exposed skin showed pink as perfectly cooked beef, with indigo spots and large maroon stains where he had scratched himself leprous. Pus welled through his sores the way yellow cream runs from an overstuffed éclair, and the older ulcers on his calves looked like fountains of disease. The eyes of the other prisoners—still eyes set in hundreds of swarthy faces—transmitted fear of the moment and of the hours ahead when the inspecting delegation would leave and the guards would come into their own again. But the outcast's eyes registered only the annoyance you encountered in the unimportantly mad. The Honorable Charlene Whyte cataloged each nuance.

With her friends, with her few remaining friends, with her ever-fewer friends—those who had been able to keep pace, who had not given up, who had not learned to disguise their surrender with words and phrases such as *compromise* or *the art of the possible*—with the handful of people who remained almost her friends, Charlee Whyte would joke that she had become a connoisseur of misery. Except that she never joked. Not really.

She saw that the ragged man sitting apart was unbalanced and that he had an aggravated case of scabies. Along with a medical encyclopedia full of other ailments. His hands had been bound behind his back with strips of cloth, probably by well-meaning fellow prisoners. But the restraints only robbed him of his single source of pleasure—the fleeting, luxurious relief that came from scratching at the parasites wandering under his flesh. He sat in the high-autumn cold, gurgling and lolling his head off to the side in a rhythm only he received. The wind shaved his skull.

"That one is sick," Charlee's government escort said in careful English. He was a revoltingly handsome young man in a trim uniform, inflated with sexual self-confidence.

"I can see that," Charlee said.

Her escort tapped two fingers against his temple. "Sick this way, too."

"I can see that."

Charlee turned away for a moment, wanting to breathe cleaner air. She looked back down the line of prisoners. Far fewer than there were supposed to be. Where had they taken the rest? Men with beards or heavy stubble. Dark eyes that did not hope. Those who had been in the camp the longest had been starved until they had taken on an ethereal, tubercular look. She had tried to speak to them, to explain that she had come to investigate their condition as a representative of the United States government. But the guards—adolescents with machine guns and their bulge-bellied superiors—had coached the prisoners well. Not one prisoner dared speak. The guards fingered their weapons or pistol belts, stinking of plum brandy. The prisoners squatted as though they had been broken down to a primitive ape-essence. Their smell was of their own spoiling humanity.

Charlee glanced at her preening escort, then at the camp commandant standing behind him, arms folded. The commandant wore bandoliers, holstered pistols, and an oversize knife. And a thin little rapist's smile. She had seen him before, many times. Along with his henchmen in their camouflage-pattern jackets. She had seen the same weapons in the same hands throughout all of the "developing," the "underdeveloped," and the never-to-develop countries to which she had dedicated her life.

But this was Europe.

Europe, or at least its fringe. Where old, brutal empires had kissed along river lines. A land that had passed itself off as European, demanding the respect due a high civilization. This country had exercised leadership abroad, giving counsel to the wretched of the earth. It had offered itself as an example of a sane middle way between the devils of East and West. Until history opened the lock to the cell door. *How had this happened?* Massacre, atrocity, a formal program of rape along ethnic lines that slammed thousands of women down onto the camp bed, the concrete floor, the earth. How had this happened in a place where, just a few seasons earlier, it had been politically correct to vacation and lie topless on the beach?

Charlee had mastered the art of the official mask over the years. Now she wore an expression that was technically impartial but that managed to convey an arctic displeasure. No one jostled her or tried too anxiously to hurry her along. The worried attaché, a U.S. Air Force colonel who had accompanied her from the embassy, followed at a watchful distance. Behind him came the staffers, the journalists and cameramen. They were all waiting for something they could not articulate.

They were all waiting for her.

Even the once-admired novelist and poet who had shocked the educated world by heading the ethnic-cleansing campaign in this subregion of a substate could not steel himself to violate the invisible border Charlee had constructed around her outrage.

Suddenly, the ragged madman noticed her. He woke from a dreaming swoon and saw a woman from another planet before him. She was too healthy for this ripped place. Too well fed and far too clean. Day-tripping into irremediable horror in a Gore-Tex parka, her blond hair shampooed the night before in a luxury hotel open only to foreigners, black marketeers, and those corrupt officials who held hard currency. The wind came cold and teased a veil of her hair across her lower face. Her golden hair that had made her attractive to men who never really saw her at all.

The madman's expression changed wonderfully, hideously. He opened his mouth and showed the world the insides of an oily, broken machine. Charlee could almost feel the sores on the man's face cracking open as his muscles shifted. His eyes filled with the delight of an infant confronted with bright motion.

It stopped her. For a moment, she lost control of her expression as she realized that this pathetic, diseased human being was laughing at *her.* With laughter as rich and beautiful as his physical parts were revolting. He laughed the way tenors laughed in the opera, confident of impending delights. He laughed and bobbed his head and shoulders, transcendently happy to see her.

The madman said something to her in his own language, repeated it, then lost his verbal equilibrium and toppled back into laughter. Sitting there in the midst of so much fear, ripe with sweat and shit, he took more delight in her than had any man in a long time.

Yes, she thought, I'm a joke.

The madman coughed out a few more words, in a changed voice.

With the swiftness characteristic of thugs and bullies everywhere, a guard brought the butt of his rifle down against the side of the man's face. The madman's jaw crunched like an ice-cream cone and distended—a character from a sick cartoon. Blood and bits of fleshy mass splattered over the man's rags, the earth, Charlee's boots. Then the madman crumpled to the ground.

The government bullies everywhere went for the mouth first, robbing their victim of the power of speech. Then they broke the fingers.

The madman's hands struggled against the rag binding them, desperate to touch his ruined face. But he could not free himself. He lay on his side, crushed jaw down dead on the earth, not fully connected to the rest of his face. His eyes were radiant with astonishment as he whimpered through the pulp of his mouth, crying as best he could.

Charlee felt the hundreds of prisoners tensing behind her, afraid that something terrible had been set in motion.

She stepped forward, cloaking the madman in her shadow. But his eyes still caught the bright, cold day. He quivered the way she had once seen trussed lambs shake outside a Greek country restaurant as they waited to have their throats cut.

Charlee knelt down, reaching out with a gentleness she had to force. The madman recoiled, anticipating another blow, more pain. He dragged his smashed jaw over the earth, away from her.

"It's all right," she said, wishing, as she had so many times in so many places, that she spoke the victim's language. "It's all right."

In close, the man was vastly more repulsive than he had been from a distance. Diseased inside and out, he seemed a clinical example of how low the human animal could descend. She smelled the rot-sweet flesh, as though he were already dead, and she wanted to vomit, tasting poison at the back of her mouth.

But this was the test. You had to love this man, too. Not just the picturesque children and the sexless old.

"It's all right," she said again. She forced her hand down over the man's temple, stroking his filthy hair. His scalp broke open under her palm as if it were made of saltine crackers.

"Get a doctor," she commanded.

No one stirred. The madman shivered under her touch like a dying animal. She looked up at her handsome, tailored escort.

"Get a doctor for this man."

The officer stared down at her contemptuously. "He is very sick. You will become sick, too."

"If he's sick, he should see a doctor. And the guard who hit him committed a criminal act."

Her escort officer smiled down at her. The camp commandant smiled, too. And the guard showed her his gold front teeth.

"He said a thing that was not nice about you," the escort officer said. "These people must learn the good manners."

Charlee met the handsome officer's eyes. *This was the enemy.* His kind was always the enemy. And the commandant. And the guard. All of the guards. And the officials who gave them their orders.

Charlee forced her head back down, making herself look at

the living being before her. She continued to skim her hand gently over the man's scalp and he calmed a little. But it was terribly hard not to just quit, not to run away. Her palm had slimed with the man's blood, with the grit of his dying flesh. She did not know what she was going to do. Off to the side, she could see the media people flocking together like wary animals, not nearly so brave now as they had been at the press conference in the capital.

The attaché came forward and knelt beside her. He was typical of the American officers she despised: annoyingly well-trained, full of conditioned responses, confident that he possessed the right answers—and bursting with practical considerations and reasons why a thing could not be done.

"Ms. Whyte," he whispered, "confrontations don't work with these people. Let me talk to their head honcho off-line. Maybe I can get him to let us evacuate this guy."

Charlee looked at him through a glacier.

"You tell that bastard I want a doctor brought *here. Now.* These sons of bitches just want us out."

"Ms. Whyte . . . we can't stay here forever."

But you could. A part of you did. And the ghosts of these places boarded the plane home with you, leaching the life out of you.

"I'm not leaving until this man is treated and until we find out what's been going on in this camp. I wasn't born yesterday, Colonel."

"Keep your voice down," the attaché said. Then he realized his tone had been too peremptory, too military. "Please."

"Colonel, why don't you just do what I tell you? Put your tax-dollar language skills to work. Help a sick man."

"Ms. Whyte, this man is highly infectious, he has—"

Charlee turned on her countryman. "I damned well know what he has. I've had it, too."

One of the penalties of commitment. That had been Haiti. But you went home and good doctors fixed you.

The madman began to weep again, terrified by the hard tone of the foreign voices arguing above him.

The colonel stood up and marched off, leaving Charlee alone

in a world that made her insides feel the way the man under her hand looked on the outside.

No one spoke or moved for a long time. The madman whimpered and shivered under the cold blue sky.

Charlee rose partway and took off her parka. With great care, she laid it over the human wreckage.

She saw a glint of metal off to her flank. A journalist had found the courage to raise his camera. Charlee hated the theatricality of it all. But you had to use the press. So often, the silly, self-important bastards were the only weapon you had.

A prisoner rose, tentatively, to his feet. Then another stood up beside him. The two men stepped forward, silently asking permission with each slow step. The guards shifted, but made no move to stop them.

After walking through a tunnel of invisible fire, the two half-starved inmates knelt down beside Charlee.

"Please, madame," the older of the two began in a professor's English, "this ill gentleman is our brother. We shall care for him. But you must go away."

The man who spoke had a gentle, wonderful, sadly intelligent voice that could be trusted instantly. Charlee stalled on her knees a moment longer, wondering what was best.

The man smiled, showing a broken denture. "You must go. It is for the best. We will care for this gentleman."

As she moved to rise, he leaned closer, as if aiding her with Old World politeness, and whispered:

"Look behind those trees beside the camp. *Go there.* That is where they kill us."

Then he let her go and turned back to the hopelessness and contagion for which he had taken responsibility.

It would have been easier to understand the cruelty had the sky not been so blue. It was an imperfect sky, with a few clouds flying southwest, disregarding borders. But the clouds only made the blue richer by contrast. It was the kind of autumn sky you saw in the landscape painting of Holland's golden age, work you had loved before you found you had no time for such indulgences, and it was the sort of day that might have made you want to speak poetry aloud, except that poetry, too, no longer had a place in your serious life. The sky was extraordinarily blue, and the surrounding hills tumbled their brilliant decay into the valley. Had the cold air not been steeped in death, had there been no fear or rabid hatred, it would have been a glorious day to be alive. But mankind, the ruining species, had soiled it beyond redemption.

Charlee climbed into the second seat of the van, leaving behind the cold and the camp that had been sanitized for her visit. A young staffer dropped into the seat beside her, yanked the sliding door shut to get rid of the world, and drew a pound bag of M&M's from the pocket of his parka. He offered some of the candy to Charlee, but she could tell from the tentative way he held out the bag that he feared some infection from the hands that had touched the sick prisoner. She declined, disgusted anyway that the young man, for whom she had once had high hopes, could be so astonishingly immune to all he had just seen.

The attaché got into the front seat beside the local-national driver. The colonel had tried to give Charlee his own jacket after she left her parka draped over the madman. But she wasn't having any of that nonsense. She was accustomed to living with the consequences of her actions. So the colonel had followed her around the camp, sheepish, with his jacket held stupidly under his arm, another fool in uniform.

The media people climbed into their pool van, clicking off the last useless shots as they mounted. They, too, were repugnant to her: the way they judged all things solely in terms of their ability to make headlines, their humanity reduced to ambition. She could not stomach their cynicism or their off-camera cowardice. But she needed them. The way she needed so many others who did not believe. She needed the journalists and photographers to spread the gospel of the world's suffering, just as she needed the soulless diplomats to open doors. She even needed the military to deliver food or to separate warring sides. She hated the way the structure of the world forced her to consort with the enemy in order to accomplish anything worthwhile, and she struggled with the iced passion of a Robespierre to avoid contamination.

Better the diseases of the slums than the diseases of the heart that blinded her own kind to the needs of this world. You had to be willing to risk all, to struggle without cease, to *give*. The alternative was to murder your conscience with comfort and consumption. Charlee would have preferred to lie in the dirt beside the lunatic prisoner.

It was only that you grew so tired. She was always tired these days. She closed her eyes as the driver warmed the engine. Gathering her strength for the ordeal still to come.

Behind her eyelids, the starved, beaten-down faces of the prisoners merged into a single face. Dark eyes huge with malnourishment and sickness, the off-tone skin stretched over the cheekbones. The beard that would continue to grow after the living prisoner had become a corpse. Fear, fear, fear. The face could have been Croat, Serb, or Bosnian, Armenian or Azeri, Turk or Kurd, Arab or Persian, or culled from a hundred barely surviving tribes and clans, Osireks or Ossetians, Abkhazians or some religious minority. There was no end to the potential victims. By modulating the skin tone just a bit, you attained a universality of suffering. In the end, the faces were the same, the miseries identical, as humanity slaughtered itself over slights a thousand years old.

Once, she had believed in the ultimate triumph of love and reason. She had believed that the horror could actually be stopped, that a shimmering future awaited mankind. All that Age of Aquarius shit, she thought bitterly, wistfully. She had long since given up her hope of a perfect world in her lifetime. But she would not, could not, give up the fight. Now the struggle was simply to lessen the agony. And perhaps a little more. To resist for the moral sake of resistance. Because, when good, capable men and women gave up the habit of resistance, the little warlords bulked into great dictators, and the horrid atrocities metastasized across borders as contagiously as a pop hit or dance craze. No, you could not give up. You had to continue to fight for what you knew to be right, just, and true. Even if you were no more effective than a child beating at a locked door. You could not surrender and hide behind the castle walls of citizenship and station. Even if your effect was statistically negligible, you had to *try*.

I'm just so damned tired of being tired, she thought.

The van pulled out in the wake of an escort jeep.

She had watched them load the madman into a military ambulance. That was the best she could manage. For all she knew, they would just drive him around the next curve, throw him out by the roadside, and shoot him. She had taken his name. And the camp commandant's name. And the name of the guard. But it was all a bluff, and everyone knew it. There would be no war-crimes trials here. There weren't enough jails or judges. There weren't enough lawyers in the world. Everyone everywhere was smeared with blood.

She opened her eyes, ready again. She did not look back at the camp. She looked ahead. Watching for the end of the grove of trees beyond the barbed-wire fencing.

"Colonel," she said to the attaché, "would you ask the driver to pull off onto that farm trail just ahead? At the end of the trees?"

The attaché turned in his seat and looked at her questioningly.

"Please be a gentleman," Charlee said. "Don't make me be explicit."

"Shouldn't we go a little farther from the camp?"

"Colonel, please."

The attaché gave in. "Well, I guess we could all use a quick stop. It's a long way back to town." He switched into the local language and gave the driver instructions.

The driver flashed his lights to alert the escort vehicle up ahead that something was up. Charlee had tried to get the timing just right, and now she waited anxiously. She knew the colonel would be furious that she had not told him what she was up to. But there had been no time. Anyway, he didn't matter. He wasn't a player.

The van turned off onto a track that had seen recent use. The fringe of trees shook down golden leaves in welcome, and the vehicle's undercarriage jounced.

"Tell him to go a little farther," Charlee told the attaché.

The colonel had just begun to speak when the first shots sounded.

The driver hit the brakes.

"Tell him to keep going," Charlee commanded, casting off the armor of pretense and politeness.

Another burst of fire.

But these were only warning shots. She had the pageantry down pat. There was no real danger yet.

"Get down on the floor," the colonel yelled. "I'll sort—"

But Charlee was already climbing over the bewildered staffer, opening the van's door.

"Ms. Whyte—"

Charlee jumped out onto a lip of dried grass by the edge of a thicket. Men came running from the escort vehicles, waving their rifles.

Excited children. Every male between the Danube and the Great Wall of China was a case of arrested emotional development. Maybe every man everywhere.

Charlee turned her back on them all and began walking.

She could smell the death.

She had smelled it the instant she shoved back the door of the van. That piercing, unmistakable smell of human remains ill-buried. She knew that scent far better than she knew any of the latest generation of perfumes in the shopping-mall department stores back home.

Home.

This is my home, she thought.

The wind picked up and shot through her clothing. The trees lining the field reached out to rain leaves down on her hair, the grabby knit of her sweater, the rutted trail. The fine far fields up the valley looked like a photograph taken to illustrate the beauty of Thanksgiving. Charlee wondered, just for an instant, if she might die here. But she swallowed the thought like a pill. And kept on marching.

A man in a dark olive uniform ran just past her, then turned, blocking her progress with his body and a rifle held diagonally from hip to shoulder.

He barked at her in his own language.

She stepped around him.

He sidestepped. Then there were more soldiers.

"Ms. Whyte, what are you *doing?*" The voice of the attaché.

An officer from one of the endless splinter militia groups jogged up, puffing. He was one of the midlevel thugs who lived too well to be quick on his feet. But he was self-assured. Since he was dealing with only a woman, after all. Charlee noted that he had not even bothered to draw his pistol.

"Ms. Whyte," the thug-officer began, still gasping, "you cannot go here. You have not permission."

"Bullshit. Your government gave me permission to go wherever I wanted."

"Yes. But that was only for the camp."

She looked at the man. No taller than she. The sort who reveled with whores and neglected his wife. Hiding his double chin with a beard.

Charlee shoved her way between the officer and one of his criminals in uniform. The action was so unexpected that it worked.

The officer came after her, grabbing her by the arm.

Charlee turned on him with a look so hard that he let her go at once, staring down at his hand as though it had been scalded.

Charlee noticed that the media types had come up as close as the guards would let them. Scenting blood.

Charlee put on her speech-giving voice:

"You think I'm a fool? There were supposed to be two thousand men in that camp. I didn't see more than six or seven hundred."

"They have been moved," the officer said quickly. He spoke the last word in two syllables, "mov-ed."

"You killed them. And buried them right down there. I can smell it."

"You smell the unfortunate sanitation of the camp."

Charlee looked at the man with inexpressible disdain. He was the sort of coward who would not fight, but who loved to kill. The archetype. From Somalia, Mozambique, Sudan. Whom you found in the Kurdistan that did not exist. In El Salvador. He ran so many countries that you came to suspect that wanton cruelty was the common denominator of the human race.

No. You did not believe that. You never let yourself believe that.

"Kill me, if you want," Charlee said in a quieter voice. "If you think you can explain it to the government of the United States. But, if you don't kill me, I'm going to keep walking down this trail."

And she began to walk.

The world took on a silence as big as the sky. She could hear her footsteps on the grass between the ruts, on the autumn-hardened earth. On the leaves that died so gorgeously, at their appointed time.

She heard the action slap back and come forward again on a rifle. But she didn't look back.

I should have taken more time to look at the world, she thought. It's so beautiful, really.

The smell of human death was so strong it brought her insides to a boil. Her stomach yearned to empty itself. Any way it could.

It was an indescribable smell. Yet, once you had smelled it, you could never forget it.

Will I smell that way? she wondered.

Of course.

She thought of the conscienceless boy, so well-educated in the formal sense, gobbling his M&M's in the van. His was the true lost generation.

A voice spoke behind her back. But not to her. Local language, but with an accent. The voice of the attaché. Poor bastard, Charlee thought. All that skill and no vision. The military always had an excuse why they couldn't do what really needed to be done.

Footsteps jogged up behind her.

The attaché. Of course. She didn't have to look. She kept her eyes on the golden blue horizon beyond the end of the trees and the rolling fields.

The colonel would try to stop her. For her own good. But he would not dare touch her. And the words he would use would be as paltry as his narrow sense of duty.

"Ms. Whyte, for God's sake. These people are *serious*."

He settled his pace to hers. She could feel his exasperation, sensing that he wanted nothing so much as to pick her up and drag her back to the van.

She marched on in silence.

"Ms. Whyte, you're destroying every agreement we've reached with these people. You're only making things worse."

She didn't look at him. She could not bear to look at him.

"Don't talk to me about your fucking agreements."

"Ms. Whyte—"

"Your agreements are a joke. They promise, you believe them, and the killing goes on. But you've got a piece of paper to ease your conscience."

"Ms. Whyte, these are dangerous men."

She laughed in genuine wonder. As if she didn't know that.

"They're killers," he said in a hushed voice.

"If you're afraid, go back to the van."

He'd like to slap me for that, Charlee thought. But he deserved it. They all deserved it. They were all cowards.

She caught herself. That was unfair. The colonel wasn't really a bad man. Just weak. Shortsighted. The perfect soldier, doing what he was trained to do. Carrying on all the glorious traditions that had brought them to this.

She was too hard, she knew. She was always too hard on the ones who wanted to help but could not see the way.

Death was so thick in the air it had begun to grease her skin.

A covey of dark birds lifted off just ahead. Another rip of shots made her flinch. But she forced herself to go on.

They wouldn't dare shoot her. They were all bluster. Empty threats.

She had won. She was sure of it.

Ahead of her, just where the trees broke, a blackened forearm reached up out of the earth.

It had rained heavily a few days before as the embassy sedan skidded through the streets of the capital city on the way in from the airport. The rain was supposed to make things clean. But out here in the history-drenched countryside, in a big horseshoe-shaped field cut back into the trees, the rain had uncovered a local holocaust.

They killed the last ones in a hurry, Charlee thought. The bulldozer or whatever tool the men with the guns had used to bury their victims had pushed only a few inches of dirt over the corpses. The rain had uncovered arms and legs, exploded skulls, naked buttocks and bellies chewed by small animals from the woods.

"My God," the colonel said.

Charlee had seen a lot of horror. But this was an example

that deserved to be recorded. It wanted a Goya or Callot to capture its perverted glory.

Booted feet trod the earth behind her. But she was not afraid now. She was only angry, with the scorching, holy anger that had shaped her life. She looked down at the smashed remains of a human face, wondering if they had killed some of the more unpredictable prisoners on her account, if her visit had hastened the extermination process.

No. You could not allow yourself to think that way.

"I have supped full with horrors," she recited to herself. It was a line a wonderful boy had left her as a joke, a boy who loved Shakespeare and whom she had loved until he betrayed everything in which they had both believed and left her with a broken heart and a handful of useful quotations.

In her cold, disdainful, customary fury, Charlee turned on all those who had followed her: the uneasy militiamen like children caught in an act they knew to be terribly wrong, the fat, self-adoring officers, and the media reps, who were so careful to stay out of the line of fire.

A male photographer, new and too pretty to be really good, recoiled at his first encounter with stale, mass death. He bent and vomited into the dry grass.

Charlee waited until the silent men came on line with her, letting them appreciate their handiwork through her eyes. The press group, heroes of the mahogany trench back in the hotel bar, inched forward. Charlee briefly considered them, the icons with the Nikons, hating the extent to which she depended on them to inform a world that didn't really want to know.

She found the eyes of the young photographer who had lost control of his insides.

"Take your fucking photographs," she told him.

It was a long ride back to the capital. They had a U.N. escort part of the way, grunting white troop carriers drawn from the unit that had been dispatched to safeguard the burial field and its contents. After the shock had worn off, the bureaucratic wrangling had begun, the arguments over jurisdiction and the pompous, bluffing threats. Charlee didn't stay for all that. The press had their photographs, she had her proof.

The heater had gone out in their van—the local driver's small revenge—and her staff aide had run out of candy. He complained about being cold and hungry until the attaché gave him the remnants of a brown plastic packet of military rations. The vehicles in their little convoy had to clear countless roadblocks. All of the checkpoints were utterly male and self-important. Sometimes the men with the searchlights and machine guns were drunk. But they were a danger only to their own former countrymen.

Charlee felt nastily tired. Weary. Old beyond her age. Blowsy. The cold would not let her rest, and she imagined itches, thinking of the diseased madman she had tried so ineptly to comfort.

It was all just one more thing to get through. And she knew she would get through it, reminding herself how trivial bothers loomed unreasonably large when you were exhausted and out of patience with the world.

Tomorrow, they were scheduled to cross the Danube into a neutral country, from which they would fly to the capital city of one of the other sides in a civil war as complex as it was irrational. The participants looked the same, ate the same mediocre food, spoke essentially the same language, dressed the same, and behaved with the same desocialized manners. But they had discovered differences worth butchering one another over: ancient land claims, nuances in the religions none of them really practiced, ethnic virtues and shames dredged up from the deepest pages of fantastically imagined history books. They shed their neighbor's blood with an intensity and abandon that sometimes struck Charlee as uncomfortably sexual. Not that she had anything against sex in theory. It was just that the reality was so often so damned disappointing. Like visiting a third-world country whose leader you had long admired from afar.

After the stopover in the other capital and the chance to look at the buffet of atrocities from the other side, she would fly back to Washington. The prospect was especially attractive to her this time. She needed the same warm, clean bed every night for a while. And she promised herself dinner at Red Sage, then wondered whom she might invite to accompany her. She quickly deferred that problem and began mentally composing the cable she would type out in the morning in the embassy's secure bubble before hurrying to the airport. And the attaché was bound to go bitching to the ambassador about her behavior, so she would have to waste half an hour soothing a vulgar old businessman's ego. The man wasn't fit to be ambassador to Las Vegas, let alone to a country in the middle of a no-holds-barred civil war.

The attaché tried to start a conversation with her, to admit that he had been wrong and she had been right. But Charlee cut him off. He was a big boy and he'd placed his bet. Fuck him.

The hotel, reached in the early-morning hours, was a sliver of heaven. With the swing of a door, she was back in a clean, safe world with hot water. Her bathroom had both a tub and a separate shower cubicle, and she ran a hot bath as she showered, then soaked in the bath-oil beads she always carried in her luggage in a halfhearted effort to hold a bit of youth in her skin. She thought again of the madman, of his scalp under her palm, and she scrubbed herself savagely, beginning with her hands, then moving on to every part of her body, scrubbing with merciless roughness, as though she might scrape away all the filth of the world. When she was done, she sat on the edge of the tub and cried for her failed life.

After he had washed, dried, and put away his dishes, Ritter looked over the day's newspapers for the third time. The Honorable Charlene Whyte, Assistant Secretary of Defense for Humanitarian Assistance, had made the front pages of both the *Times* and the *Post*. The photo run by the *Post* showed her comforting a wretched-looking Slav, while the *Times* captioned their shot with a reference to still more newly discovered killing fields in the Balkans. Charlene Whyte looked marvelously honorable in both snaps, a WASP Joan of Arc, outfitted by L.L. Bean. The photos and the inevitable op-ed pieces had drawn merciless comments from his comrades in the Pentagon when he dropped by ODCSINT between therapy sessions. But Ritter had carefully stowed the front sections of each paper in his briefcase. Now he examined them patiently in the lamplight, sitting in his old leather chair by the sliding door to his apartment balcony, letting in a dose of cold, fresh air and smiling despite himself. Finally, he shook his head, dropped the last paper, and put on a John Coltrane compact disc.

He kept the volume low—too low for his tastes—because the fine-looking building in which his apartment lay hidden had been constructed to standards better suited to the third world than to northern Virginia, and his neighbor beyond the living-room wall did not like music of any kind. She was a typically gray young woman of the sort who flocked to gray Washington jobs with sterile futures, careful never to date anyone whose job might be less important than her own, careful in all things. She had complained to the management one Saturday morning when Ritter put on Schubert's *Death and the Maiden*. When he went next door to try to make peace, she met him with a gray, unprepared face and dead eyes. At his attempted apology and explanation, she simply clutched the documents on which she had been working more severely to her chest, threw back a strand of colorless hair with a sharp, impatient gesture, and dismissed him with the observation that she didn't have time for small talk. She looked to be in her late twenties, and Ritter saw her future with such clarity that he felt sorry for her for long minutes after she shut the door and snapped over the bolt. Since then, he had kept his music very low out of consideration not for her work but for the desert of her life. He never heard her with a lover or a friend. Other than an occasional clack from her kitchen, the only signs of life that came through the wall were the hypnotic lullabies of CNN or C-SPAN on her television.

It was hard on Ritter to feel that he dare not play his music loud enough to get its spiritual texture, and that he should not play certain types of music at all. Music and books were his prime remaining comforts, and the chance to drown briefly in the artsy rock he and Lena had been able to agree upon, or to slink into one of the operas she had so perfectly loved, was medicine for his soul.

Coltrane's sax line soared and dipped through the room like a tiny, hopped-up seagull, and Ritter sat on the carpet, putting his leg through another bout of the miserable therapy that might let him walk properly and run again. He preferred the self-therapy sessions to those he got at the clinic, because here, in his book-lined cell, he could make faces and curse. He could even cry, when it really got him down, which was something he could not bear to do in front of the captain-nurse or the earnest young enlisted woman who put him through his drills in a room full of other defective pieces of humanity.

After he finished his leg exercises, Ritter ground coffee and prepared the tools for the next morning's breakfast. He repacked his gym bag for the next day's lunchtime session in the weight room at the Pentagon Athletic Club. Then he turned off the music and went into the bedroom where the light was best for reading. Three books lay on his nightstand, as always: one in Russian, one in German, and one in English. But he did not take up a book immediately. He paused for a long moment in front of the picture frame on his chest of drawers. Lena. Smiling. With her dark hair down. A Spanish-American woman in a German autumn. The princess who condescended to marry an officer. Then clutched the darkness in her arms, dying before he was done loving her. He had brought her the poetry of words, stolen from Shakespeare, Donne, or Auden, and she had responded with the brilliant poetry of her flesh. His incomparable love. Who went too soon into that dark night.

Ritter had always been confident of his strength. He had believed he could bear any pain. But, more than a year after his wife's death, he returned each day to rooms as lonely and empty as the day he had returned from her funeral, fleeing the theatrical dignity of her family's sorrow and his own inability to open his mouth and speak any sense at all. She had filled his life more fully than the black cancer had filled her body. And then she had left him with intolerable speed.

In the impossible days after her death, when he had been waiting for an assignment that would take him far away and fill his days and nights with so many things to do that no man could accomplish them all, in those unbearable days when he had volunteered for everything that made other men pause, the chest of drawers had been an altar laden with photographic icons of Lena, as crowded as the side altars in one of those Mexican cathedrals known for miraculous cures. Under the pretense of discipline, he had forced himself to remove the photos one at a time. But the truth was that he could not bear their weight. Now he had reduced her to a single photograph: a dark, laughing young woman, her reserves of love inexhaustible. He had never tired of her sexually or intellectually. He had enjoyed each day with her, even as he had neglected her because duty always came first, because he took his uniform and flag with an old-fashioned seriousness that cost her dearly. She had borne his folly with remarkable patience, sacrificing her talents, her education, her earlier dreams. In her willingness to suffer for him, she had been astonishingly Catholic, and his fears that she would not be able to endure the mundane garrison life of a peacetime officer, the inanity of the wives' clubs and the petty jealousies, had proven groundless. She had shouldered all of it, casting off her plans to go on for her doctorate and all of the other ambitions she had worn as beautifully as other women wore good jewelry. She had loved him relentlessly, inexplicably, as he plodded through the routines of field exercises and annual gunnery, the grinding business of being a lieutenant in a line unit, then the staff-officer frenetics of a captain scooped up by a general's hand, the official travel that left her behind with her books and the beastly women who wore their husband's rank and slighted the childlessness he enforced because he feared the time he would lose to a child, time he needed to spend soldiering.

She had begged him to have a child. But she had possessed too much dignity to lie about the time of the month or birth-control measures. She was cursed with a dignity and honesty that were ill-matched to the times. And he had taken her qualities for granted. Pushing on to this achievement or that, studying languages, attending staff college ahead of his peers: all of it not out of the common hunger for high rank—which seemed so cosmically trivial—but out of the need to accomplish things, to *do,* drugging himself with the narcotic of higher ideals.

He had not served Lena half so well as he served the Army. And at Fort Leavenworth, as he fought to keep his eyes open while memorizing badly written doctrinal texts, she had sickened. She did not tell him about it at first, unwilling to trouble him. And he had been too self-consumed to notice. Oh, he loved her. But there would always be another day to show her how much. His evenings were devoted to the methodology for calculating airlift capacity and troop-list priorities. He first alerted to her sickness as her sexuality began to fail in little ways. And he discovered that this magnificently educated, fiercely intelligent woman had been ill for months but had not gone to see a doctor. He made her go. Sentencing her to the knowledge of her death, the terrible word:

Cancer.

Her body brought to the disease the same passion it had brought to sex. No drug or savage treatment could slow its progress. And she refused any treatment that might make her lose her hair, knowing how he loved it, insisting that, if she had to die, she intended to die with as much dignity as possible. They opened her with knives, taking first a little bit, then more, until Ritter pictured her as a hollow, beautiful shell through which he might poke a finger. She lost weight until her eyes grew so brown and huge they reminded him of the dreadful paintings tourists bought in Mexican border towns. She grew tiny, girl-like, and her breasts withered. But she had so much inner strength, and he loved her so much, that he never really thought the fight would end. They were going to go on struggling against the disease forever.

Then it was over. With shocking suddenness.

And now his wife was a single photograph in a worked-silver frame they had bought on vacation in Potosí, when their love had been greater, deeper, and richer than the ore-veined mountains.

He turned from the photograph and stretched out on his side of the bed, nursing his leg. For half an hour, he read a German translation of Swedenborg, trolling for belief, then he switched over to a Russian ministerial study of ethnicity in the northern Caucasus. Finally, he rewarded his discipline by allowing himself to read in English. He was rereading a translation of one of Kundera's novels. It was a book both he and Lena had cherished. And, as he read toward sleep, his miraculous Lena was both Teresa and Sabina, the one forever opening her legs, the other opening her heart.

When he had grown tired enough to sleep, he put down the book, stirred himself long enough to brush his teeth and wash his face, then turned out the lights.

He lay in bed dressed only in an old Army T-shirt, willing himself deeper into the timeless darkness. But sleep would not come after all, and he touched himself, trying to imagine it was Lena's hand. She had loved to touch him. She would take him in her hand with a good-girl-gone-bad laugh and bring him against her. And, for a moment, it was almost as if he could recapture her. He could almost feel her, almost smell and taste her.

He clicked on the night-table lamp, stood up in his half-nakedness, forgetting the pain in his leg, and took up his wife's picture. He inspected her beauty in the yellow light. Then he laid the picture on the pillow beside his own and brought the darkness back down over them.

He dreamed of his dead wife. She sat apart, as if in the reaches of space, cradling a child in her arms. The little creature shared its mother's physical harmony, her grace. Mother and child looked toward Ritter with guileless eyes. But he could not be certain whether or not they saw him. Time fractured like the wall of an old house in an earthquake, and Lena and the child became a stylized pietà, painted wood, of the sort you saw deep in the Mexican countryside. The colors had mottled, the surfaces bore scars from the bad times when the Mother of God had been forced to hide, hastily, from anticlericalists or bandits. But there could be no mistake. The image was still Lena and her child.

In this sumptuous dream, Ritter took up an ax and split the statue's skull. He hacked on until only splinters remained, unrecognizable and beyond all possibility of reconstruction.

He slept soundly thereafter. The sweat soaking his T-shirt was not uncomfortable enough to wake him. It was as if his mind, or perhaps his soul, had learned over the past months that this dream never came more than once on a given night.

FOUR

BLACK WING-TIP SHOES. SHINING, TOOLED WITH RARE PRECISION, THEY were by far the most impressive thing about the young staffer who fielded Ritter's arrival in Charlene Whyte's office suite. Ritter wondered if the staffer's father had handed down a tradition of buying from a particular shoemaker, or if the shoes were a gift from an exasperated mother. Whatever the case, Ritter would have bet his next pay that the young man had not chosen them without aid: his suit was dark and safe, but poorly fitted, and the staffer had thoughtlessly chosen his tie from the pattern of an active British regiment. Except for his gorgeous, indecently expensive shoes, the staffer's clothes seemed a perfunctory attempt to hide an inner vacancy. Personally, Ritter would not have worn shoes with such elaborate workmanship. But he could admire them the way he might admire a fine old dagger in a tribal chieftain's belt. While despising the chieftain.

The staffer did not offer a handshake or even the token cup of coffee granted the poorest guest in the poorest Pentagon office. And Charlee Whyte's office was far from poor. The suite was unusually large, even by E-ring standards, freshly carpeted and outfitted with antiqued leather sofas the General Accounting Office did not permit mere bureaucrats-of-the-line. Entering the reception room, the guest immediately sensed power. But, at least in Ritter's case, he did not feel much of a welcome. Even the secretaries ignored him.

The staffer gestured toward one of the sofas and said:

"Ms. Whyte's behind schedule. You can wait over there."

Ritter sat down, more amused than insulted. Thus far, his expectations had been fulfilled. The staffer sat down behind a desk that was much too big for him and stuffed his hand into an oversize bag of M&M's. Ritter leaned back and admired the empire to which he had been sacrificed. The secretaries and assistants, all female except for young Mr. Wing Tips, looked excruciatingly politically correct: little or no makeup and encoded clothing that, while proper, hinted at a dark desire to be ravished by the ghost of Chairman Mao in a rain forest. They were cartoon commissars for whom sex could be only a biological function or a tool of repression, smart, unlucky children who came to Washington so they would never have to grow up. Ritter smiled, imagining the collisions between the military leadership, with its well-intentioned courtliness toward women, and Charlene Whyte's acolytes.

Even the choice of magazines laid out on the coffee table was determinedly out of step with every other Pentagon office Ritter had ever entered. Instead of military and aerospace journals or the latest copies of *Army Times,* Charlee Whyte's guests got a choice of the latest U.N. study on hunger in Africa or a brochure from Amnesty International. But the most telling features of the office hung on the walls.

Where the average office might have had a clumsy print celebrating Desert Storm, the anniversary of fighter aviation, or some instant of glory from the Civil War, this activist space hosted a photo exhibit of suffering. Starving children awaited rescuers. Political prisoners displayed impossible scars. Bodies lay in mounds like dark pasta or waited under shrouds in neat rows. Cheerful working environment, Ritter thought, eyes moving on. Refugees fled in faded tribal costumes, literally carrying the weight of their world on their shoulders. Travelogue Kurds smiled, an emaciated African mother bore her dead child in her arms, and a chubby, grinning Cambodian displayed a regiment of skulls. One photograph caught a Balkan woman in mid-shriek, arms raised to the sky in outrage, while the next showed dead-eyed men behind barbed wire, each of them starved thinner than the most neurotic fashion model. A few of the photos, brilliantly placed, tricked the viewer into looking more closely in his or her effort to figure out exactly what the subject was. Then the viewer saw that the openmouthed boy was showing the stump where his tongue had been cut out, or that the abstract composition beside it was in fact an example of what electric burns do to human flesh. It was a grim, powerful display, a splash of ice water in the face of the gung ho guest, a stroke of brilliance. Ritter would have admired it even more had it not been so thoroughly dishonest.

The display was clever propaganda for Charlee Whyte's view of the world. Not one of the photographs included a U.S. soldier or Marine risking his life or health to lend a helping hand in Shitsville. The chain of expensive operations to protect the weak or alleviate some shred of the world's misery went unacknowledged. In Charlene Whyte's world, nothing had been done, everything remained to be done, and the United States damned well needed to get moving. There was, Ritter noted, no snapshot of Ben Williams dead in the dust.

But that wasn't the worst of it. The exhibit rewrote history as shamelessly as any Leninist scribbler. All of these victims suffered in a guiltless vacuum. No black gunmen had been included in the photos of mass graves in Africa. No homemade knives disemboweled the opposition voter, and no local entrepreneurs starved their own people because it was a good career move. No Sudanese or Ethiopian or Somali politicians or soldiers were responsible for that man-made famine or this enforced migration. None of the photos captured the masked monsters of Sendero Luminoso as they wiped out entire villages of uncomprehending *indios.* Gassed Kurds died under the smothering paws of some European chemical concern, not at an Arab's whim. No Persian executioner fixed a noose around a Bahai's throat, and no black mobs adorned their fellow citizens with necklaces of burning tires. The exhibit was not about truth. It was about guilt fantasies: the Honorable Charlene Whyte's conviction that each American who lived a comfortable life bore personal responsibility for the world's miseries.

At another time, in another office, the photo display might

have angered Ritter immensely. But now it only saddened him. He recalled a line one of his mentors had offered him:

"Liberals . . . are just poor bastards who can't live with themselves—and conservatives are the poor bastards who can't live with anyone else."

It struck him that Charlee Whyte resembled the early Christians in Rome—those first Marxists—who were so fanatical about the virtues of the underclass and intolerant of the values of the average Marcus or Julius that the poor, badgered Romans ultimately had no choice but to bring in the lions just to get some peace and quiet.

He shifted his leg. He had pushed a little too hard during his home therapy session the night before, and his knee was stiff and unwilling. Well, he figured, he and old Charlee had that much in common—they both tried too hard. He wondered if she was trying to make some point by letting him wait so long.

Probably not, he decided. She had the sort of personality that always took on too much, then fell behind schedule by midmorning. He closed his eyes, putting himself in order.

But it didn't work. He could not maintain full control over himself. His pulse had quickened. It was all so damned complicated. Foolish.

Foolish, foolish, foolish.

If I had half a brain, he told himself, I'd walk out of here this minute.

A door opened. An Air Force three-star took off out of the inner office as though piloting the last flight out of a burning city. A moment later, a lieutenant colonel followed. The general looked furious, but his subordinate only wore a look of collapse.

The two officers fled out into the hallway without a word. The token-male staffer tossed a last spray of M&M's into his mouth, then ambled into the inner office, shutting the door behind him. He appeared to have forgotten Ritter entirely.

But the staffer was gone for only a minute. He reappeared, even more sullen than before, and spoke to Ritter without really looking at him:

"Ms. Whyte's not ready for you yet."

*   *   *

Charlee closed her eyes for a moment and tried to calm herself. But her heart was going, and she knew it wasn't just anger at the latest son of a bitch with stars on his shoulders who was trying to sabotage her work.

Maybe it *was* a mistake. Perhaps ... it was a terrible move and she was setting herself up for humiliation. She knew she hadn't thought it through, and that was unlike her. But there had been no time. And she needed help.

Her admin chief poked his uninspired head through the doorway. When Charlee didn't respond, he came in and shut the door behind himself. Chewing. His fucking M&M's. She wondered why he never got acne or gained weight.

"That Army guy's here," the staffer said. "That major you wanted."

"Tell him to come in. No. Wait. I'll buzz when I'm ready." She looked at her watch. "Jonathan, I want you to go down to the metro entrance and personally escort Mr. Morozov up here. He doesn't speak English worth a damn, and I don't want the guards harassing him. I want you to walk him through."

"Yes, ma'am."

"Meet him at the turnstiles and carry his bag for him. He's bringing me something and I don't want the guards or anyone else involved—understand?"

"Yes, ma'am. I'll walk him through."

"He might be early. He's nervous. Try to make him feel comfortable."

"Yes, ma'am."

The boy was the disappointing son of a father who had been instrumental in helping LBJ design the Great Society. She had given him a chance, at Ollie Cromwell's request. But the kid had neither the brains nor the heartfelt commitment that might have compensated for a lack of intelligence. He would marry well and wake up one morning surprised at the extent of his unhappiness. The younger generation were all such self-centered little shits.

The staffer knew when he had been dismissed. Alone, Charlee took a deep breath. She was nervous. She had to admit it to herself. Well, that was natural, wasn't it? After so long?

Perhaps it was an utterly stupid thing to do.

Crazy.

Nuts.

Insane.

Maybe the best thing would be to cancel the whole business. God, why did she have to be so pigheaded? Why on earth had she set this in motion? With so much else going on?

Hastily, furtively, she drew a little makeup case from her desk and examined herself in the tiny mirror.

God.

Was that her face?

She stared at herself as though she had not looked into the mirror for twenty years. Then she stroked back her hair, her last really good feature, and thought, Yeah. Charlee, you ass.

She slapped the makeup case shut, then hid it in her desk again. She was all right. Strong. She took a deep breath and rebuilt her face, then buzzed the outer office on the intercom:

"I'm ready for Major Ritter."

The two ex-lovers did not shake hands. They stood in the disappearing office, stupid-faced, each examining the other through the prism of the self. They had not breathed the same air for more than seventeen years, and the last time they had seen each other one of them had been carrying a box full of books to his battered car while the other wept, certain she was on the edge of madness, pride wrecked. He had been glad to go, although he had tried not to show it too heartlessly, and she had been certain that no man in history had ever been guilty of a greater betrayal. It had been one of those civilized good-byes played out just one ill-chosen word away from savagery.

"Hello, Charlee," the man said at last.

"Hello, Chris."

She wondered what she had ever seen in him, why he was the one who had to be remembered. She had known other lovers with as much power and finesse. He was intelligent, but she had shared dessert forks with men whose brilliance moved the world. Handsomer men had been accessory to her evenings. And nearly all of the men who had fumbled with her adulthood of zippers and clasps had made better use of their lives. Why was it that memory held fast to moments and lovers of so little objective value?

Was it simply the ravishing deceit of nostalgia? The longing, the narcotic human need to believe that *once* had been better than *now,* the aching for the lost golden age? Or was it a perverse reaction to the thoroughness with which he had rejected her, to her failure to save him for her life's crusade?

Well, she knew about failure. It always made her wince to recall the man, a senator, the great Ollie Cromwell, with whom she had shared a decade, only to find herself set aside when he decided to amend his life with a clever, young proposition.

She had known folly. In her save-the-downtrodden-by-sleeping-with-them phase, when her inner-city lover had not only proven a physical disappointment but had stolen her jewelry and given her a venereal disease.

But, in the end, she had gotten the important choices right. She was even right in her failures, and she knew it was her willingness to be proven a fool, her determination to *try,* that allowed her to accomplish whatever worthwhile things she had brought off in her life.

Why did he remain? Of them all? The lover as apostate, heretic, betraying not only the casual flesh but the soul.

Perhaps, she thought, it was that she really had loved him. But that just brought her back full circle to the question of *why* she had loved this one so much. How much of it, she wondered, had been him and how much her earnest half-child's idealization of him as a reflection of her?

No one else, not even Ollie, had ever rejected her so profoundly. Cromwell had, at least, presented her with the job she wanted as a consolation prize. And he still phoned when he was feeling sorry for himself. But this man, this *fool,* had never even sent a Christmas card.

She wondered what she had ever seen in him. Where was the burning, handsome young undergraduate who had set fire to the seminar she, an infinitely wiser graduate assistant, had inherited from a disinterested professor? He stood there shifting his weight uncomfortably, hair laughably short now. His temples showed the first hints of gray, although he was younger than she was by more than three years. He was bigger in the chest and shoulders, but not in the waist. The line of his nose was not quite right—a souvenir of some nonsensical Army horseplay, no doubt. He had strutted in like a windup toy soldier, a caricature, as he struggled with his bad leg. She knew all about that. She knew a great deal about him. Professionally, at least. His file, his reports, his memoranda, had lain open on her desk, defenseless. As he attacked her programs, her designs, her vision of the world.

Why should the sight of him move her even now? She had hoped for a more satisfactory disappointment.

Older, used hard, a trivial major in the Army. He had chosen a life whose biggest reward was a booby prize. Generals came running when she called. In Washington, in life, a major was nothing. Why had *he* chosen this wasted life? When he could have made a difference?

Only his eyes had not changed. But they had always been old and closed to her, mirrors, not windows. He had beautiful eyes, and beauty always fooled you.

Had he been a street person hustling change downtown, she could not have regarded his choice with more scorn. She found the homeless far easier to understand than the heartless. To her, men in uniform—in *any* uniform—would always be the enemy.

How could he, of all men, have chosen that path? When he had been so true to the willed shape of her life, so fine a fit to the books and bed they had shared?

No man had ever embarrassed her so by leaving.

"Long time," he said.

"Seventeen years."

"Almost eighteen."

"You're looking well," Charlee said.

"So are you."

"Oh, shit. The truth is you look like hell."

"You look splendid, Charlee."

"I look like hell, too."

"You're just tired."

"I feel like I've always been tired." Then she added quickly, "But I'm not too tired to do the things that have to be done."

Ritter glanced around the office, seeing it for the first time.

Relics of Charlee's travels, Charlee's causes. An African mask and an explosively colored rug from the Caucasus. Good paintings and a tall water jug of the sort women elsewhere carried on their heads.

"I don't expect you to agree with everything I do," Charlee said.

"I don't. I can't."

"Listen. Sit down, for God's sake. Are we at least going to be able to talk to each other like adults?"

"I don't know."

She looked at him with an expression that had become more guarded. "Are you going to be a bastard, Chris?"

He felt sorry for her. He did not need to step close to see that age had begun to press her unfairly. She looked at least five years older than she did in the newspapers or in the sound bites, one of those rare human beings who suit cameras. The public image was of a woman forever harried who could be a knockout if she would only take the time to put herself together. But the woman who had resumed her seat on the other side of the great desk was plummeting into an early middle age.

He smiled inwardly, remembering how she had always hated any exercise other than sex.

He was beginning to feel far too kindly toward her when he caught himself—she had always had that effect on him. She had almost convinced him it was his duty to graft their lives together. In an instant, he recalled the aspects of her from which he had needed to rescue himself: her ability to make intolerance sound like compassion, the close-mindedness she could mask as commitment, her readiness to give away all that was unimportant so that she would not have to share the truly meaningful . . . and the sexual selfishness. He almost grinned remembering the explosion of outrage he had touched off when he teasingly called her a "sexual fascist." Yet it was true. She wanted it all her way and only her way, often—but loutish, and boyish in the brevity and directness of her desire. Quick to come and then impatient with any art or prolongation. Loud, theatrically passionate, and tender as Mussolini on a bad day. Sex with her had become a duty, then a bore.

So he felt sorry for her, a woman once beautiful with whom he had remained for two years not out of desire but because she had threatened to kill herself. He, a naive child, had believed her. And, to be fair, he had been drawn by her intelligence. Today, summoned to the expensive discipline of her office, he thought that, had she only been a man, they might have been great, enduring friends.

"Chris, I need your help."

"Come on, Charlee. You don't need anybody's help."

"I'm serious. Please. Listen to me. Consider how much of my pride I had to swallow to ask you to come here."

"I was ordered to come."

"You wouldn't have come, otherwise. Isn't that right?"

"Yes."

"This is awkward for me, too."

"It's not awkward. It's crazy. Charlee, you've got more enemies in this town than anyone else I know."

"That's why I need your help."

"Don't you get it, for Christ's sake? If they find out you've recruited an ex-boyfriend—and an Army officer, at that—they'll make you the laughingstock of the year."

"Don't you think I've considered that? Anyway, I'm not going to tell them. Are you?"

"Of course not. But nothing in this town stays a secret. And you've got a high profile, Charlee."

"I'll risk it."

"You could be throwing away everything you've ever worked for."

"Wouldn't that suit you? You're against everything I do. You should jump at this chance."

"Charlee, I'm not against everything you do. I'm just against the things you do wrong. I'd like to see you out of this building. But not that way."

"Ever the soul of honor."

"Maybe I'm just protecting my own career."

"Oh, bullshit. I've seen your file. You've done all the wrong things. But you did them so well you blew everybody away. I *hate* what you do. But I need you. Because you're the one person in this building I can trust to think of something beyond the next promotion or reduction board. You're the *only* one I can trust, Chris."

"Charlee, you *can't* trust me. A friend of mine just died because of one of your programs. Because of the idiotic restrictions you placed on us. How could I possibly be loyal to you?"

"I know about your friend. I'm sorry."

"Tell his wife."

"I'm sorry, Chris. But there will always be losses. You're supposed to know that. And think of how many people that program kept alive."

"Charlee, I was *there.* That program didn't keep anybody alive. It was a feel-good giveaway. A total waste. And, in the end, all it did was get people killed."

"Even if that were true, it doesn't matter in the great scheme of things. Not every program can be a success. You know that. It's the cumulative effect of all the programs, over the years. That's how you change things."

Ritter shook his head in disgust. "That's crap. Every snake-oil salesman in this town likes to talk about the 'great scheme of things.' Waste is waste, wrong is wrong, and dead is dead. A man who was like a brother to me died for nothing. Because of your self-righteousness, Charlee."

"And I need you because you'll always tell me the truth. Everybody's afraid to tell me the truth."

Ritter smiled. "They're afraid to walk down the same corridor as you."

"You could tell me the truth. If I'm wrong about something, convince me. I can listen."

"Charlee, you couldn't hear the voice of God unless he was saying something you scripted."

"Don't be flip. This is about real issues, Chris. Life and death. I need somebody I can trust. Somebody who . . . somebody who understands this men*tal*ity better than I do. They're all against me, Chris. I need someone to build a bridge. And someone to help me on a very special project."

"I'm the wrong man. I don't believe in what you're doing. I'd undo most of it, if I could."

"You only see a small part of what's going on. You don't have access. There are things going on in this town—"

"There are always things going on in this town."

"Not like this," Charlee said quietly.

"What?"

"Not like this. Chris, I'm coming up against something big. Something terribly big. And I don't understand. It's . . . all out of joint."

"What're you talking about?"

"Damn it, Chris, I don't *know* what I'm talking about. That's just it. I've brushed up against something. By accident. I didn't even want to get involved. But you know how things go."

"I know you can't keep your fingers out of other people's rice bowls." Ritter shifted his weight. "So what are you trying to tell me, Charlee? Are you in some kind of danger?"

"No. I mean, I don't know. I don't think so. But I find myself dealing with people . . . with a kind of people I don't understand. And I'm finding locks on doors everywhere I turn."

"You've made a lot of enemies. Eventually, they network."

"It's not that kind of thing."

"Well, what is it, then? You must have some inkling."

Charlee looked at him with slow seriousness, as if she still had not fully made up her mind how much to tell him. Ritter let her work through it on her own, and finally, she spoke:

"It's about prisoners of war. From long ago."

"POWs?" Ritter wondered how his voice sounded. He was, by nature and by training, a direct man. Now he found himself acting, with Jeb Bates feeding him cues. He didn't like the feeling much. "Charlee, that's a political mess. And it's not within your purview. Is it?"

"Technically speaking, no."

"But you've just got to stick your paw in it."

"Somebody came to me. It wasn't my choice."

" 'And some have greatness thrust upon them.' Why don't you refer whoever it is to the proper organizations?"

"This person doesn't trust anybody else. He's afraid."

"Charlee, I don't want to hear any more." And it was true.

He did not want to be put in a position where he might feel obliged to betray her confidences to Jeb Bates. Or to anyone else. He just wanted to stay out of the entire mess. "You're just empire-building, Charlee. POW/MIA affairs fall under Personnel. Not under Humanitarian Assistance."

"But it *is* a humanitarian matter."

"You're rationalizing. I know you, Charlee. Oh, for Christ's sake—haven't you got a full plate?"

Charlee looked at him for a long moment. She appeared genuinely saddened by his intransigence. And she looked very much alone. Ritter wondered how much of it was her near-genius for theater.

"You won't help me?" she said at last.

"I can't."

"So. What are you going to do then?" A slight spice of resentment flavored her voice now. "What's so important that it has to prevent you from helping me?"

"Charlee, I'm a soldier."

She laughed. "You *were* a soldier. You can't just go back to playing Army with that leg."

"My leg's going to be just fine."

"That's not what the reports say."

"My leg's going to be *fine.* And maybe I'll just get out of this town and go back to Germany or down to Hood and do something sane for a couple of years."

"You're throwing your life away."

"It's mine to throw away. Anyway, the worms don't care whether you're a private or a president."

"That's just New Age bullshit. What does your wife think?"

"What?"

"What does your wife think about going to Fort Hood or wherever? How does *she* feel about your throwing your life away? And hers, too?"

"Charlee," Ritter said gently, "my wife died last year."

"She—"

"Cancer."

"Oh, God. I'm sorry. Oh, God, I'm such an ass. I mean—your file. I don't . . . I must have read it wrong."

"You probably got an old ORB. It happens."

"Chris, I'm so sorry. I'm just so stupid sometimes."

Ritter smiled. Tried to smile. "I wish I had that on tape. Anyway, it doesn't matter. Water under the bridge."

"I really am sorry."

"Forget it."

They sat very much apart in the fouled silence. Ritter felt oddly crushed, unable to understand himself. He massaged his knee without thinking about it. Charlee stared down at her desktop for an instant, then turned her eyes toward the window. Sweet autumn day. Where was the promised rain?

"You really won't help me?" she said without looking at him.

"I can't."

She nodded. "I guess that's that."

"I suppose so."

"Just think about it, all right?" she said with sudden impatience.

"I'll think about it," Ritter lied.

"I could order you to work for me. I could make it happen, you know."

"That's your prerogative."

"Chris, *why* do you always have to be such a bastard?"

"I'm doing the right thing, Charlee. I can't believe you don't see that."

She rose. Even more impatient now. A busy woman in a busy world. She looked indescribably tired.

"Call," she said. "We can have lunch."

"Bad idea."

"You don't leave a girl much to hang her hat on."

"Good-bye, Charlee. And thanks for not forcing the issue."

"I'm still considering it."

"Good-bye."

As he left Charlee's office, Ritter came face-to-face with the staffer with the elaborate wing tips and realized from the expression on the boy's face that he had been listening at the door. But that was Charlee's problem. With an internal shrug, Ritter took one last look at the Jacobin secretaries and said:

"Don't get up, ladies. I was just leaving."

Their expressions did not change, and Ritter had no doubt that they could send him to the guillotine without a tremor of spirit.

There was one sign of genuine human life in the office, though. A little old man, Santa Claus with high cheekbones, sat on the sofa where Ritter had waited half an hour before. The man looked as tense as if he were awaiting his own execution. He clutched a big, worn briefcase in his arms, guarding it by pressing it back into his stomach and down onto his thighs. It was a cheap, dreadful, gray vinyl briefcase, and it was clear that the man would sooner die than part with it. His hair had gone a bit wild, tufting out of his ears, and his eyebrows were great cobwebs. Red cheeks reported ill health, not a love of the outdoors. Dressed in a horrid brown checked suit, the old man looked as out of place as he clearly felt. Ritter knew immediately that the man was Russian.

God only knows what the fuck-all she's got her fingers into, Ritter thought. He saw her overtired face again. Heading for a breakdown? It was safe to feel sorry for her now that he was leaving. And he recognized that, underneath all her arrogance and willful stupidity, Charlee wanted with all of her heart to do the right thing. She just had trouble with definitions.

With a last glance back at the Russian, he pushed out into the E-ring. Within seconds, he joined the lunchtime crowd in the axial corridor. An admiral steamed against the current, and a mentally disabled janitor tried to sweep the floor as a fleet of secretaries and staff officers headed for the complex of cafeterias.

Unexpectedly, Ritter heard Charlee's voice. Calling after him. It was uncanny. In that displaced instant, she sounded younger, alive again, calling across a green campus mall to her beloved:

"Chris. Wait a minute."

He turned. And saw a stress-marked woman hurrying awkwardly on high heels, a woman slowly gaining weight and losing the confidence that would let her shed it again. As she closed the distance between them, the smooth, brightly intelligent face he had summoned from memory aged painfully. Only the golden hair remained.

She caught up with him.

"Chris, I really *do* need your help. Just for fifteen minutes, okay? You just have to agree to forget everything you hear." She was out of breath from her short run. "I've got this Russian in my office—doesn't speak much more than survival English. A friend was supposed to send me an interpreter, but he hasn't shown up. Could you just translate for me? It's important."

He looked at the woman he had once known so thoroughly, whom he had admired, if not loved.

"Sure."

The force of the explosion threw her against him. He caught her briefly in his arms, then they tumbled to the floor. The shock wave passed, but the noise left a souvenir of temporary deafness in its wake. Ritter grasped immediately that the blast had occurred back in the E-ring. He and Charlee had been just far enough down the right-angled corridor to be protected from serious danger.

As his ears came back, the first thing he heard was a woman's voice screaming.

A great deal of blood was visible under the smoke. But Ritter discounted it. The people he saw were stunned, but not badly injured. The kind of flesh wounds caused by flying bits of debris looked vastly worse than they in fact were.

Ritter centered in on the density of smoke and the pattern of destruction: the explosion had taken place either inside of or very near Charlee's office.

"My God," Charlee said, struggling up to her feet. A moment later, she was running toward the blast site in her high heels.

"Charlee," Ritter called. But he knew she would never listen to him. He got up and hobbled after her, dodging the other survivors.

He caught up with her just where the corridor ended and the E-ring opened up. The smoke in the hallway was too thick and black to enter. All Ritter could see were a few ghostly hints of flame down where the door to Charlee's office had been.

A bell shrilled hugely, followed by a siren.

Ritter stepped back from the smoke. He coughed. And looked down.

At his feet lay the remains of a finely made black wing-tip shoe.

FIVE

COL. JEB BATES SAT OVER HIS MISERABLE RATION OF SALAD WITH A dab of dressing and a diet Coke, absently watching the lunchtime pageant. The vast Pentagon cafeteria had already filled with officers in haste and unimportant visitors, with secretaries whose calorie allowance was even less generous than his own, and with slumped, swollen males whose diets were as poor as their polyester suits. The perfume of frying food teased through the air, and an Ethiopian immigrant pushed a rack of dirty dishes toward the scullery. Bates had worked counterintelligence for so many years he could tell at a glance who was having an affair with whom and which of the customers merely led a rich fantasy life. But that wasn't a game for today. He had spent his morning on the phone with POW/MIA family members who were still convinced their husbands or fathers were going to come strolling in from Siberia. Their combination of misery with beautiful, relentless faith made Bates think back to Vietnam.

He had learned to love the Vietnamese people. Not the confused throngs of Saigon or Da Nang, but the villagers among whom he had lived so long and so luckily. His love had been slow and earned, not the condescending sort professed by those who passed through in order to fashion a book and make their academic careers. His love was born of awe. He had come to the Vietnamese countryside as a soldier, to fight, teach, and control. But the fighting had been an oddly ephemeral thing, an occasional dream, not particularly good or bad. He had learned far more than he had ever taught. And in the end, he had controlled nothing.

He had been astonished by the ability of men and women who possessed little and lost that to endure with good hearts, even with grace. What a journalist or bureaucrat might have described as "simple," Bates had come to understand as ineffably clear and rich. Amid the squalor of a particularly horrible war, he had found resources of human goodness that nothing in his education could explain. And when his own kind finally called him off, when the sweep of history carried him along like so much dust, he left behind only unintentional lies and hard fates for all who had trusted him. Speaking for his government, he had told them all, "We will never abandon you." And he had meant well, it was true. He had not imagined that his government could go back on its word. He had believed in his mission with a white faith he knew he would never attain again. He had been so rich with belief it seemed unfathomable now.

He did not need to close his eyes to see their faces. The old men and perfect young girls. Boy-men with helmets and rifles too big for them. The old women with lacquered smiles that revolted you at first. And children whose Saturday-morning cartoons were the clouds in the sky.

He had loved Vietnam, with a love he doubted anyone else would ever understand. He had even married the country.

Funny, his wife had never really wanted to leave. For her sake, he had stayed as long as he could, ending up in an embassy compound surrounded by terrified Vietnamese who had bet their lives and the fates of their families on Uncle Sam. And with his own wife and child safely on a carrier out in the South China Sea, he had stood behind the grille of the gate, wielding his best Vietnamese, swearing to everyone shut out that they would be evacuated, if only they would be patient. After all he had seen, he had still believed that. Then the station chief jogged down from the ops center where the last documents were dying, shouting to him over the huge throb of blades as another chopper settled onto the roof:

"The ambassador wants you on the fucking helicopter, Bates. *Now.*"

Bates just stared at the man, at his white, sweating exasperation, until the station chief lost it and bellowed in his ear:

"It's the last fucking one, man. We're unassing this place."

Good-bye.

His wife had cried to leave her country. She had nurtured no downtown visions of the Land of the Big PX. She had been as simple as she was beautiful, and he had loved her for both qualities. He had bullied her into coming with him. And now, two decades later, she was frightened and sick in a cold country she had never mastered. She did not fit a single one of the prevailing clichés about Orientals. She was simply the woman he had possessed the scorching vanity to love. His souvenir. Of a lost war whose veterans were passing from the ranks. And of his naive, lost, lost, lost conviction that love could overcome any obstacle.

Bates lingered uncharacteristically over his tray and paper plate, reluctant to go back to his office and take on any more of the pain of strangers. Ritter had good instincts, not wanting to get involved. No job since Vietnam had troubled Bates so much. He looked down at the oily jewels left behind by his salad, at a wisp of lettuce too small to merit forking. At first he had wondered why the Army leadership had selected him to work the POW/MIA issue with the Russians. His language was Vietnamese, his understanding was Vietnamese. He had learned to love working in quiet. And the Russians were all loud, brazen, and terribly foreign to all he valued. But, over the months, the point of the assignment had become clear: the organization had enough Russian speakers and Russia experts. What they needed to tie it all together was a good counterintelligence man, whatever his background. A counterintelligence man—and a man who understood human misery. He had been the right man for the job, after all.

And it was like Vietnam in at least one respect: the enemy was everywhere. Chasing the ghosts of missing servicemen from half-forgotten wars, he had encountered nearly as much resistance from bureaucrats in Washington as from the unrepentant murderers in Moscow. He thought for a moment, thirsty and sucking on the remainder of an ice cube. Well, it was like Vietnam in another way, too. It was programmed to fail.

Unless the hand of God descended. Unless they got a lucky break. Official Russia was stonewalling. They needed a touch of magic.

And his instincts told him that he needed to know whatever it was that Charlee Whyte knew. He hoped Ritter would come through. The Brooks Brothers saints over at Justice had turned down another request for a wiretap. Everybody was afraid. Even when the legal justification was there. It was a town terrified of doing anything. And a good part of the town was scared of Charlee Whyte, too.

Bates wasn't afraid of her. He knew, quietly, that he wasn't afraid of very much. Only of more broken promises.

He was gathering himself to rise and return to his office when he heard the bomb.

His veteran's ears told him immediately that it was a bomb. Exploding far away, in the distant rings of the great building. The sound was muffled, the thump of a great drum, and the follow-on shock wave was enough to raise eyebrows but not to ignite panic. Everyone around him was so unscarred and innocent. They just didn't know. Bates caught a look of renewed alertness, of concern, on the face of one civilian employee who was of the right age and had the right look to have served as an NCO in Indochina. But everyone else soon tucked back into their burgers and fries.

Bates wondered whom the bomb had touched, where exactly it had gone off, and who had placed it. But he did not rise immediately. He knew he was in no danger. And he could offer no help. It was an art, knowing when you could help and when you couldn't. When you had to turn your back. He waited for the sirens that would inevitably rise to clear the building.

A bell rang first, piercing. Then a siren rose, the voice of a waking dragon. Now the first nervousness arrived. The women and the younger officers rose first, looking around, as though they might see through the walls. Without instruction, people began to move for the doors. The pace of the crowd quickened as its individual members collected one another's fears. Voices sounded like night traffic on a highway in the middle distance.

Perhaps, Bates thought, the bomb had been set by a group representing groundhog rights on military reservations. Or by Arabs determined to blame America for their failed culture. Or by a single madman who could not otherwise articulate his rage. The Pentagon made a show of security, but the truth was that the building was wide open. It was amazing to Bates as a counterintelligence man that nothing like this had happened before.

Well, he hoped no one had been injured. Maybe there had been a warning.

No. They would've cleared the building.

He wondered, with professional curiosity, what it was all about. Then, as he stepped out into the broad ramp corridor, Bates saw a thing that filled him with mirth and delight. It was as if he had come upon a cluster of angels playing poker. Charlene Whyte ran madly through the crowd, pushing mere mortals out of the way, red-faced and a bit pathetic in heels. It was clear from the locked expression on her face that her mind was racing far ahead of her body's ability to keep up.

But the spectacle of Charlee Whyte parting the crowds was, for Bates, the lesser half of the show. What really made him smile was the sight of Chris Ritter fighting to keep up with her, pumping along on his bad leg, shame-faced and pain-faced because a woman could outrun a warrior.

Poor Ritter. He was a hard case. So proud and honest he'd crack apart like frozen iron someday. The thing with his wife had nearly destroyed him.

Ritter would come through. Or die trying. He wouldn't know when to stop.

Bates had the warm feeling that the gods had taken charge. He understood immediately that Charlee's chase had to be related to the bombing. A junior CI guy on his first case would've figured that out. Bates watched the pathetic couple hurry down the ramp toward the concourse. Ritter came so close to him at one point that Bates could see that the younger man was almost in tears from the pain in his leg.

That's my boy, Chris. Go get 'em.

Ritter didn't see him. But Ritter was that kind. The upright dreamer who saw only what he chose to see. Ritter would think of himself as hardened, cynical. But he didn't know the first thing about cynicism. He was an innocent.

Amazing that Ritter had survived so long, Bates thought. A very lucky man, in his way. His type tended to end up in a body bag early on. But then, there truly were some lucky ones. God's chosen. The buggers who could make every mistake in the book and still come through wearing a grin and carrying the enemy's nuts in their fist. Luck. The Vietnamese had understood all about that, too.

Luck. And fate.

Maybe Ritter really would turn out to be one of the lucky ones. Hard to believe, though, given the bleak business with his wife.

But you never knew. You never knew what tribulation would turn out to be a blessing.

Bates read his horoscope every day in the *Washington Post.*

He stood by a pillar and watched Charlee and Ritter disappear down on the concourse. Two sorry cases. Bates knew that the two of them had been lovers back in their college days. You didn't survive a quarter of a century in counterintelligence by being an idiot. Even if you were lucky.

He would have liked to tell Ritter a little more about the case. But he didn't know that much more himself. And Ritter was the type who worked best starting with a blank slate. He had to discover things for himself. To gain belief. Besides, there was always the chance that he'd wind up back in bed with Charlee Whyte and blab everything.

Bates moved placidly with the crowd. He knew where Charlee was going, where she was leading Ritter. He had the externals pretty much figured out. But he had not been able to break inside to the meaning. Really, it was a crying shame they wouldn't issue a wiretap order on her. He decided to try again. Sooner or later he'd get a judge with a pair of rocks. Probably a female, he figured.

He wondered if the Russians had placed the bomb. One of the several Russian factions that might reasonably have taken an interest in the case. But he dismissed the possibility. The Russians knew the rules, the limits. No bombs in the Pentagon.

No, the bombing had to be the act of a maverick. And mavericks were always dangerous.

What if it was a Russian maverick? He rethought his position and decided he had been too hasty. It was too early to rule out the Russians. They had a genius for doing things that were breathtakingly stupid. It was their only redeeming quality.

Ritter sat adjacent to Charlee at the front of a metro car, marveling at the expression on her face. A woman of stone. Her office had just blown up, her staff members were either dead or terribly injured, and she had narrowly escaped death. Yet her face revealed neither fear nor sorrow, not compassion, not even a case of jumped-up nerves. Her eyes stared ahead as though possessing the power to strike men down into the dust, and her mouth was fixed with a cold will that would have done credit to the sort of man who saw a revolution through to its conclusion—or carried out the bloody reaction against it. She had been strong when he had known her. But now there was a determination about her that struck him as almost inhuman. And she was certainly decisive. Her formal duty would have been to remain at the scene of the bombing, to answer the questions from the security boys. But she had immediately chosen to follow a different priority. Ritter believed that, had she been a general, she would have won battles by brute strength, taking horrendous casualties in the process.

"All right, Charlee," he said, leaning toward her, "what's going on?"

Her breath was still heavy with exertion, the makeup on her forehead broken with sweat. Golden hair clung to her temples. She looked at him with the eyes of a bloody queen and said nothing.

Behind her, a young man wearing an X baseball cap bobbed his head to the rhythms from his Walkman, while a woman in a business suit studied an investment magazine. Across the aisle, a naval officer sailed off into a daydream, while two mall dolls with Gap and Benetton bags spoke poetry:

"And he goes, 'Like don't tell Angela,' you know? And I go,

'Like no way am I doing that.' I mean, it's like crazy, how he gets. Like I should care."

"Like we all should care. So how's your dissertation going?"

The train burst up into the sunlight and pulsed across the Potomac. Just across the river, a wall of gray clouds moved in over the city, eating the day's early brightness. Ritter could smell Charlee's sweat. It made her instantly familiar to him. After so many years. Her smell. For which he had not much cared.

His leg hurt badly and it made him sour toward her, toward the world. He wondered how many weeks of therapy he had undone. Following her like a fool. Just because she had looked at him with something approaching honesty, a woman who had just done an end run on death, saying:

"Chris. I *need* you."

He had overtaken her only at the entrance to the metro, where she had waited, purseless, for him to buy her a ticket. To a part of town where few went by choice.

Ritter stretched out his aching leg and tried again:

"Charlee, you've got to tell me what's going on. If you expect me to help you."

"Not here." A shade too peremptory. A woman who had become used to having her own way.

Ritter glanced over their fellow passengers again. No one cared. Each passenger wore his or her own suit of armor.

"Here and now," Ritter said quietly but firmly. "Or I'm getting off at the next station."

On cue, the train began to brake. Weak light lit a sterile platform.

"We're both getting off," Charlee said. "We need to change lines."

The train stopped with a final jerk. In seconds, the doors opened. Charlee got off, confident that he would follow. And he did.

They stood apart, alone, between the crowded hours. Waiting for another train.

"Talk to me, Charlee. Where are we going? What's going on?"

Charlee looked at him dismissively, as though her office exploded once or twice a week and all of this were no big deal. "We're going to see a woman."

"And?"

"A Russian woman."

"And?"

"Her father was just in my office. He was supposed to bring me a package. We were going to make a trade."

Ritter looked at her. "And he brought a bomb instead?"

A lightning-fast tic of her eyes told him she was terribly confused after all, just holding herself together by strength of will. He glimpsed one tired, shocked woman behind the mask.

"I don't know," she said in a quieter voice. "I don't—maybe the bomb was already planted. Maybe—"

"What do you *think?*"

She looked at him. With considerably less haughtiness. Almost civilly. "I think he brought the bomb in with him. But . . . I just can't figure it. It doesn't make sense."

"Tell me about it."

"I can't now."

"Try."

"I can't. Later. I have to think."

"Let's think together. Two brains are better than one."

"I didn't figure him for the suicide-bomber type."

"Me, either. I saw him in your waiting room. Father Christmas. Looked nervous as hell, though. Clutching his briefcase for dear life."

Charlee looked at him. "Chris, could the kind of bomb— could you fit a bomb that powerful into a briefcase?"

"Sure. You could fit in two or three. Seven or eight, if you're a chemistry whiz."

Charlee looked down at the tile floor. "It just doesn't make sense."

"Why?"

Charlee looked up. He could tell she was considering how far to go with her answer.

"Well, I had money for him."

"For what? What was supposed to be in the package?"

"I can't tell you."

Ritter grimaced. "Oh, screw that, Charlee. If you want me to play, you have to share the toys."

"I'll tell you later. I promise."

They stood in silence for a moment. Ritter considered turning his back on the whole business. But he couldn't make his feet go. It was Bates. The bastard. He'd sucked him in. For the duration. He couldn't walk away now. He swallowed and spoke:

"All right. So who was this guy with the briefcase? Saint Nick of the Nihilists?"

"A general. A retired Russian general. A KGB general."

Ritter felt his face betray him. Yes. *That* was a surprise. "So you invite retired KGB generals into your office?"

Charlee looked at him, the coldness returning to her eyes. "If they have something I need."

"Charlee, let's stop playing games. What was supposed to be in the package? Does this have something to do with the POW business you were talking about?"

He caught the look on her face in the moment before she masked herself again. Yes. POWs. Sweet Jesus.

"I can't tell you."

"Why, for God's sake?"

Charlee looked at him with her high-tribunal expression. "Because . . . I'm not sure yet that I can trust you."

Ritter shook his head. "In your office you said you wanted me because you needed somebody you could trust. You can't have it both ways."

"I *do* trust you. I just don't trust anybody more than I have to."

"Well, thanks. And trust goes both ways, sweetheart."

They fell into another silence. As if the world were a size too small for them, holding them in tightly, holding them apart.

"Can you at least tell me about this KGB general?"

Charlee nodded.

"Defector?" Ritter guessed.

"No. Just a poor old retired bugger nobody wanted anymore. Changed world. His daughter brought him out. She got into the country on the arm of a Jewish husband, then dumped the poor sap. Immigration isn't thrilled. Case pending. But she sure as hell wants to stay."

"Sounds charming."

Charlee smirked. The lamps beside the track began to blink, announcing a train.

"Oh, you'll like her," Charlee said.

"And what makes you think that?"

The train's headlamp shone down the tunnel, rushing toward them.

"She's the kind of woman all men like," Charlee said.

They emerged from the metro station into an unkempt D.C. street. Liquor stores with brilliant discount signs highlighted the rows of derelict storefronts and ethnic groceries. The sky had gone the gray of dirty cement, and when the wind blew, the neighborhood smelled like ashes left in a fireplace. It was cold. Neither Ritter nor Charlee had coats, but Charlee didn't show any discomfort, and Ritter didn't feel much beyond the gravel-shift in his knee. It annoyed him, though, that he didn't have his cap. Soldiers never went outside without their head-gear, it was ingrained to the point of absurdity, and Ritter could not shake the feeling that some all-seeing sergeant major was about to pop out of a doorway and demand an explanation.

Old rag of a day. Late fall or early winter, you could call it either way. A disheveled man in a knit cap lurched toward the intruders. Wise, he quickly corrected his course to avoid Charlee. He asked Ritter:

"Spare a quarter, general? I gots nothing to eat."

Knowing better, Ritter released a shower of change into the man's palm.

"Bless you, sir. God bless you."

Ritter hastened after Charlee. Thinking: Well, I can probably use all the blessings I can get.

It wasn't the worst sort of neighborhood. When you read closely, the street's text revealed a message of hope as well as of despair. A variety of immigrants had chosen the area as a starting place, while the indigenous minorities alternately strutted and slumped toward the irredeemable neighborhoods a few blocks away. Still, it was not a place Ritter would have visited after dark without a definite purpose.

Charlee never looked back. Simply assuming he was behind

her. Her blond hair took the wind and flew in the gray light. Ritter had to admire her will to action, her decisiveness. A woman who had come within half a minute of dying. She had reserves of strength, or at least of nervous energy, that few soldiers possessed. Ritter was not sure now whether he still had the capacity to summon such power from within.

He recalled, in crisp-cut images, the summer when they had volunteered to teach English to the Vietnamese refugees at Fort Indiantown Gap: 1975. Charlee had gone back to their off-campus apartment early, unable to make the politics of the whole business come straight, while he had remained, awed by the fate of his students as they struggled with survival grammar. He had learned shame. Recognizing his comfortable cowardice in hugging the university as worlds came to an end. Then one evening, after a late class, he had stopped by the orderly room to mooch a cup of coffee and an officer he had come to admire suddenly turned on him, all black circles and rage, crying, *"You.* You're to blame for all this—you know that? Smart-asses like you. Too good to wear a uniform and serve your fucking country. Just too fucking smart."

The next day Ritter spent a great deal of class time assuring a Vietnamese father who spoke daunting French that it was all right to drive on U.S. highways at night, that there were no bandits waiting to kill him and kidnap his daughters. That weekend, Ritter drove up north and moved his things out of the apartment he had shared with Charlee, who wept and hated the weeping. A few months later Ritter joined the Army as a private.

Such a long time ago: 1975. He smelled the summer nights again, the lush scent off the pastures and the late coolness settling from the hills. Ruby and emerald lights jeweled the little fort's helipad, and the occasional churn of blades made the combat veterans and the refugees start until they remembered where they were. Before she bolted, Charlee and he had made love on an old iron cot, on a mattress seared with disinfectant, until they were luminous with sweat, and she had refused to discuss the refugees, whom she taught with a rigorous, effective aloofness Ritter could not master. Then she left, telling him she couldn't allow herself to be part of a program that was nothing more than a sop to Nazi consciences. Upon her departure, the same chronically exhausted officer who later shamed him commented, "That girlfriend of yours. She loves the *idea* of humanity. But she doesn't really like people very much. Does she?"

And now. Here. D.C. street life in the red-and-white-and-blue third world. Another ruined man, drunk or mad or both, meandered down the sidewalk. Charlee registered on him only when they almost collided. The man stopped, absentmindedly pawing at his crotch.

"Oh, baby," he said. "I love to jump you all day and all night. How I would love that."

Charlee hurtled past the invisible man.

Ritter met the man's eyes and said, "No. You wouldn't."

The names posted in the battered lobby ranged from Latino to East African to the unidentifiable. Amid the cultural confetti, a faded piece of tape read MOROZOV.

They did not need to buzz to enter the building. The inner door was broken. They climbed the stairs through ghosts of dinners past and pending. The graffiti was mostly in Spanish, although someone had taped up a bilingual flyer announcing a rally in support of an independent Kashmir. Washington, D.C.—capital of the world. Ritter figured the slums of Rome had probably been just like this in the days of the high Caesars. The streets of Rome, too, had been dangerous at night, and the whores had whispered in accents as exotic as their trade was mundane.

Ritter paused on a landing, unable to make his leg go on. The pain came bright red now.

Charlee turned on him from above, looking down in exasperation. "Come on. It's right up here."

He straightened his back and pulled his leg up the stairs behind the rest of his body.

Charlee waited for him at the door to the Morozov apartment. Rock music blasted from inside, a nameless song from a faceless group. The music had been cranked up to a level where the speakers distorted. It was instantly familiar to Ritter, very Russian. As if they feared being shortchanged by anything less than the fullest possible experience, craving sensation of any kind. You could never talk in a Russian club.

"This is it," Charlee said.

"I can tell."

Charlee looked at him without comprehension but without really caring. She rapped on the wood, then rapped again.

No response.

The music was very loud. As Ritter's eyes found Charlee's, he sensed that they had both had the same thought at the same moment:

Something's wrong.

But they were mistaken. The music dampened abruptly and a woman of unnerving beauty opened the door.

She held her hand to her forehead as if fending off a blow. Then the hand ranged on in a gesture as flawless as if it had been learned for the stage. Wiping away the sweat of exercise, the hand—shaped like a white flame—slipped aside as though drawing a veil. To reveal a flushed, delicate face and eyes that jarred the man who truly dared to see them. Her eyes were the tone of the darkest amber, flecked with gold, but they held none of the warmth or the illusion of warmth that usually lit brown eyes. Her eyes said that they had seen a great deal, much of it unpleasant, but that experience had not so much scarred her as left her immovable. She had the alert, ducal eyes that haunted old portraits in the Uffizi and a matching strength in her beauty. Although she posed an extreme example, Ritter had encountered the phenomenon before, in Moscow. It was as if the painters of the Italian Renaissance had drawn their models from Russia. She raised her hand again, smearing salty wet across her brow.

She had drawn back her hair, but a single dark blond strand had fallen free, trailing down over an ear. She wore an overlarge T-shirt advertising Baltimore's Inner Harbor and Lycra spandex tights with an oval tear just inside a thigh. Slender, she might have been a girl masquerading as a page or one of those ravishing androgynous boys who shattered the vocation of priests. Perhaps thirty, her beauty pretended to fragility and reserve. But what Ritter caught from her was the scent of a sexuality almost unmanageable, as if she had greeted him by running her hand between her legs, then across the lower half of his face.

Even Charlee, whom Ritter assumed had met the Russian woman before, seemed momentarily stunned by the sight of her. Beside the Russian, Charlee appeared too large and almost shapeless, her bright blond hair pale and obvious. Ritter sensed Charlee appraising the Russian woman as a man might have done. As he himself was doing.

In the unexpected fragment of silence, the Russian woman's facial expression shifted from mild curiosity to incipient alarm. But her eyes never changed. They revealed no concern whatsoever. An open window behind her back let a flood of cold air wash through the apartment and into the hallway. The draft carried with it the scent of a woman's perspiration and a little more.

With a start that might even have been visible, Ritter realized that the Russian woman had focused on him, ignoring Charlee. She considered his uniform, black sweater with gold leaves on its epaulets, and the dark green trousers. She looked at his shoes, too, a habit bred into the Russian genes. Then she brought her smart, cold eyes back up to meet his.

"May we come in?" Charlee asked with a slight break in her voice. "It's important."

The Russian woman turned her head slightly, regarding Charlee with unmistakable disdain.

"I remember you," she said in a voice that sounded as though it had been whispering and smoking cigarettes all night. "You have visited with my father."

"Yes. May we come in?"

The Russian woman stepped aside and invited them in with a gesture that was little more than a hint.

Untidy, the apartment was furnished with the uneven poverty typical of recent émigrés. A sleek television coupled with a VCR, but the sofa, chairs, and odd tables looked as though they had been gathered in, not bought. There were plenty of books shelved and littered about, and a disorder of prints brightened the walls—everything from a copy of a dreadful Glazunov painting to a travel poster for the Virgin Islands. Although it did not show quite the clutter Ritter had come to expect even of educated Russians, the apartment reveled in the standard Slav disregard of color combinations, the hunger after vividness at any cost.

The woman slipped through her possessions with a grace that always left the eye one frame behind. First, she shut off the stereo completely, then, just before the observer caught up with her, she closed the window, blocking out the world. She moved quickly, but without haste. Ritter might have guessed her for a dancer except that her legs were too fine. He wondered what she had been in her earlier life.

Charlee stood heavily in the center of the room. "Miss Morozov," she began, oddly unsure of herself, "I'm afraid I have to tell you something. It's something important. . . ."

The Russian woman paused by the window, backlit and perfectly articulated by the gray light. The scent of her haunted the room.

Abruptly, Charlee turned to Ritter. Her makeup had failed her and her skin looked mannish and mottled.

"Tell her in Russian," Charlee said. "So she understands."

"Tell me what?" the woman said in English, faintly impatient. Ritter noted that she was taller than she had appeared at first. Her appearance of delicacy had made her seem small. So much about her seemed to be an illusion. "I understand when you are talking," she went on.

Something in the atmosphere made Ritter want to turn on his bad leg and leave. His instincts shot off one warning flare after another. But Charlee stood there unable. Unfairly weak at an unfair time. And the Russian woman looked at him in wary expectation, her small chest lifting and falling under her T-shirt.

She's a tough one, Ritter told himself. He felt something akin to anger. Meeting her stare, he decided to find out just how tough she really was.

"Miss Morozova, your father's dead."

The woman's facial features changed in slow motion, and a hand rose to her mouth. But her eyes were the same, the same, the same.

"I'm sorry," Ritter continued, "but I have to be frank. You may be in danger."

"Tell her she has to come with us," Charlee said.

The Russian woman touched her lip. Even dressed for exercise, she wore lipstick. On a small, full mouth. She drew her finger down to the seam of her lips once, then again, then a third time, each time a bit rougher with herself, brushing away invisible crumbs. Her eyes never left Ritter's. Until she suddenly reached out a hand for a support that was not there and fell onto her knees. She hit the floor hard, uncontrolled. Her head lifted briefly to look at Ritter, as though she were making sure of something, then she rolled forward and clutched her body together, almost as if she were continuing her aerobics program.

"Get her up," Charlee commanded. "We've got to get her out of here."

Ritter ignored his old lover. The Russian woman had made herself tiny, with the renegade strand of hair feathering over the back of her neck. Her T-shirt had climbed to show a sliver of flesh at the small of her back, and her buttocks had spread from the stress of her posture. Ritter shocked himself with the bluntness of his feelings. After slapping a stranger with news of her father's death, he found himself sexually alert, drawn to a woman with a bluntness he had not known for a very long time.

It struck him that this was the kind of woman men died for.

"Get her up," Charlee ordered. "Get her dressed or something. I'll throw some of her clothes in a bag." She stalked off into the bedroom.

Ritter waited for the Russian woman to cry. Or to shriek. To move. But the news he had delivered had gripped her like an irresistible bully, and she held still in her posture of defeat and submission. Only the advance and retreat of her breathing promised that she was still alive. He stared at her, ashamed of the selfishness of his feelings, memorizing the lines of her back and the push of her hips. He was afraid to touch her.

"Miss Morozova," he said finally, "I'm sorry."

No movement. No sound. Just a woman's perfect form on a

carpet rummaged from someone else's trash. In the background, Charlee hunted noisily through a series of drawers.

Suddenly, the Russian woman began to uncoil. She rose heavily, each movement testing the air to see if she could struggle through its weight and force herself back to her feet. She looked at him again, and her eyes changed at last. The impenetrable surety was gone now, replaced by tentativeness. He had hit her so badly with the news that she seemed as though she had been physically beaten. As if he had smashed her to the floor with his fist. She rose as though expecting another blow.

She was unspeakably beautiful.

She came toward him, learning to walk all over again. Conditioned to economies of space, she came closer to him than any American woman would have come to a stranger. A single drop of blood swelled at the corner of her mouth, then broke away and trailed down her white throat. Another drop replaced the first. She had bitten herself or chewed open the inside of her lips.

Ritter was convinced he had struck her. With an invisible hand.

The top of her head came just up to his mouth. Her hair smelled of cheap, fruity shampoo. She seemed oddly surprised to find him in front of her, her expression that of a blind man who had walked into a wall. She trembled at the edge of touching him.

Charlee slammed a closet door.

The Russian woman grasped the breast of Ritter's sweater in her small, strong hand, pulling the knit away from his heart, forming a ball of material in her fist. She bent down slightly and wiped the blood from the corner of her mouth, smearing it onto his sweater and over her chin. He could not see her eyes.

"My father's dead?" she asked in Russian.

"I'm sorry."

She released his sweater, dropped her hand away. Then she lowered her forehead so that it touched his chest, and she began to cry and laugh at the same time. Time jumped, and Ritter found himself holding her in his arms without knowing how such a thing had come about. He could feel the print of her bones.

"My father's dead," the woman said. For a moment, laughter dominated her tears. Then the tide shifted. "My father's dead." The words had a singsong quality, Ophelia near the end.

She put her arms around the lower reaches of Ritter's back and clutched him with the desperation of a lost child.

"I told him this would happen," she said.

Timidly, Ritter soothed his hand over her hair. He had a sense of far planets changing their orbits. Slowly, lethargically, he realized the implication of what the woman had just said:

She knew something. At least enough to get hurt by the kind of people who had the ruthlessness to risk bombing the Pentagon.

He pressed her head to his chest and lowered his lips toward her ear. "Be quiet now," he whispered in Russian. "Don't say anything. You can tell me all about it later."

Charlee marched out of the bedroom, lugging a vinyl weekend bag. Two steps into the living room, she halted as if responding to a barked command. At first, she looked generally at Ritter and the woman in his arms. Then she looked straight into Ritter's eyes. Her mouth opened, but it took a few seconds before she found her voice. Even then, her first words had no consequence.

"Now where to?" Ritter asked. "Back to the Pentagon?"

Between them, Charlee and Ritter had wrapped the Russian woman in a long winter coat, guiding her to the metro station, since no cabs cruised this particular street. It struck Ritter as comical, preposterous. Not at all the way movies or thrillers conditioned you to imagine things. There were supposed to be car chases and cleverness. Instead, the three of them stood on a metro station platform, waiting in the slow, midday dreariness for public transportation.

"Don't be ridiculous," Charlee said. "We can't take her to the Pentagon."

"She'd be safe. And she'll have to be questioned. She said—"

"Chris, are you absolutely crazy? She's not involved in the bombing. This is separate."

"Charlee," Ritter said coldly, "you don't know that. Or if you do, explain it to me. This isn't a joke. People are dead. And the investigation—"

Charlee rolled her eyes. "Oh, screw the investigation. This is more important."

The Russian woman stood slackly beside Ritter, visibly preferring him to Charlee. Her face looked pale and ill.

Ritter tried to force Charlee to meet his eyes. But she avoided him. He insisted, "We need to turn all of this over to the professionals."

"Bullshit."

"Charlee, this is a *crim*inal case now."

"We can take her to your apartment. Then I'll go back to the Pentagon."

Ritter shook his head, marveling at Charlee's obstinacy. "That is one of the lousy ideas of all time."

"Scared?"

"Oh, fuck you, Charlee. Yes. I'm afraid. Of doing something colossally stupid. We live in a country with laws . . ."

Charlee looked at him impatiently. "You won't have to put her up for long. Just until I can talk to some people, sort things out. And, if they're looking for her, we'll take her right in. I promise."

"And why my place, for God's sake? Why not your place?"

Charlee looked at him briefly, then looked away again. "My house would be the first place they'd look for her."

"Who's 'they'?"

"Whoever. Whoever sent the bomb."

"Charlee, you're not being straight with me."

"Trust me, Chris."

"Why?"

The lights embedded in the floor by the edge of the track began to blink. The rattle and rush of a train haunted the distance. The Russian woman's eyes had a gone, drug-addict look.

"Because," Charlee said, "in the end, you and I believe in the same things. We want the same things. We just differ on the means. It's us against them, Chris."

"Nonsense."

"It's true. And you know it. No matter how much we may hate each other's choices, it's us against them all in the end."

The train sleeked into the station. Shaking his head, Ritter led the Russian woman into the carriage. She had stopped crying, stopped bleeding. Outside, in the gray light, her skin had seemed translucent. Here, in a moving compartment under the earth, she looked like a beautiful corpse.

"Charlee," Ritter said, "you're a two-legged catalog of bad ideas. And you and I do not believe in the same things." He sat beside the Russian woman, close enough to sense her powerfully. Charlee sat just in front of them.

Charlee put on her business face. In the hard light, it struck Ritter again how harshly she was aging. "Just take her to your place for now. I'll try to think of something else. I need time to think."

"I know you're using me, Charlee. I understand what you're doing."

Charlee snorted. "Everybody uses everybody. Where've you been?"

"I guess I've been away."

"Well, welcome home. Listen. I'll make you a deal. Take her to your place. For a day. Maybe two. And, if I can't sort this out, I'll resign."

She was bluffing. Ritter was positive she was bluffing.

"Word of honor, Chris. Just give me two days. And, if I can't get this sorted out, I'll resign. And all of your buddies can pop open bottles of whatever cheap champagne substitute military officers drink."

Ritter grinned. "Great try. But I don't believe you for an instant."

Charlee didn't smile in response. She looked old and sober. "Chris, this whole business is more important than you know. To me. Personally."

"You're a bad liar."

"No, I'm a good liar. If I were lying, I'd have you convinced already. Anyway"—Charlee paused, unfolding a fan of fingers in the direction of the Russian woman—"you don't really want to see her killed, do you?"

An unkempt young man left a bookshop in Brighton Beach, thinking about lunch and Pushkin. He wore a suit, neither brown nor gray, that could only have come along in a suitcase from Russia, and his prematurely thinning hair clotted together as though he had forgotten to wash it for a week. He wore glasses. He was the sort of man born to wear glasses and to love books too much. His bad suit covered very little physical substance, and any Russian could have told you at a glance that he would skip a meal to buy a book. As he thought about lunch, he was sorry that he had not made himself a butter sandwich with the stale bread in his apartment, since it would have saved him a few more dollars toward the turn-of-the-century edition of Pushkin recently acquired by the owner of the bookshop where he worked. He chastised himself for being far too self-indulgent, too ready by far to squander his salary on knishes or *pelmeni*.

A foul smell came in off the sea, enlivening the traffic fumes. Clarinet music sounded from a storefront. An old woman from Minsk looked at the young man pityingly, knowingly, relieved that her granddaughter was about to marry a dentist and not such a one as this. The ones who loved books too much, who walked the streets in such simpleminded blindness, never amounted to anything. A man who read too many books wasn't really a man at all.

The old woman watched as a stranger approached the young man. The old woman knew everyone on the street, by sight if not by name, and she had never seen this interloper before. She would have remembered. The stranger was not very old, yet his patchy hair was winter white. His skin, too, was unnaturally white, his eyes and lips pink in a way that made her think of a fat albino rabbit she had kept as a pet during her childhood. One day her father had come for the rabbit, and that night the family had eaten the pet. But this time it was the bookish young man who was about to be eaten. The old woman had seen enough of life to know when a terrible thing was about to happen, and she saw it now in the convict gait and brutal features of the stranger.

She was not certain that she had ever seen a man who looked so cruel. And the stranger's actions soon proved her right. After exchanging a word or two with the young man from the bookstore, a recent émigré who had been of no interest to any of the mothers or grandmothers of eligible young women, the white stranger simply picked him up and threw him into the backseat of a big American car. The sight chilled her and made her turn away for a fateful moment as she recalled the way the Germans had thrown the bodies into the pits during the war.

When the old woman opened her eyes again, when she had mastered her feelings sufficiently to look back toward the stranger's car, it had already pulled away. The distance was too great for her to read the license plate. She sighed, having lived long enough to know that neither she nor anyone else on the street was likely to see the sad young man from the bookstore alive again.

"Drive," Zhan said. "Let's go."

The big, fine car bullied its way out into the American traffic. Zhan kicked his prisoner down flat with his heel, forcing him deeper into the space between the seats. The prisoner shook like a frightened animal and fought like a girl, pawing at his captor with half-fists held wrong, scratching, annoying. At a red light, Zhan put a stop to that by opening a door and slamming it first on one of the prisoner's hands, then on the other.

The prisoner moaned. Irritated, Zhan picked up the young man's glasses where they had fallen and tossed them out of the window. Then he planted a shoe on the prisoner's temple.

"You're making me angry. I don't like men who cry."

The prisoner wept helplessly, unable to find a bearable posture for his crushed hands.

"I'm not a cruel man, but I find people like you unreasonable." Zhan tapped the prisoner's head with his shoe, seeking his attention. "A man has to take responsibility for his actions. Can't you see that?"

The prisoner wept.

"Did you shit yourself?" Zhan asked, catching a rising odor. He lifted his foot off his prisoner's skull as if he might become contaminated. "What a filthy creature you are."

"He stinks," the big man behind the wheel said. His military-cut hair revealed a gashed, chipped skull. "They all fucking stink, the Jews." Like Zhan, he spoke in the criminal accent of the camps.

Zhan rested his foot on his prisoner's shoulder. "It's very important," he told the prisoner, "not to make Mitya angry. He has prejudices that interfere with his judgment."

Mitya shook his scarred head and passed a taxi as though he had been driving in New York all his life. "I just hate it when a guy shits himself," he said. "It embarrasses me."

Zhan increased the pressure of his foot slightly, pushing down his prisoner's shoulder. The young man felt so frail that he reminded Zhan of a woman.

"You're embarrassing my colleague," Zhan said. "And you're offending me. This isn't a good thing."

For the first time since he had been hurled into the car, the young man found his voice:

"What do you want from me?" His voice sounded like that of a woman being raped by the third or fourth man in line. Both Zhan and Mitya recognized the tone.

Zhan rested his foot more lightly again, watching America go by. He had never been to the United States before, and although he tried to conceal it from Mitya, who had already been on one wet-work project here, Zhan was intimidated. At home, in the world he knew, he felt an enormous confidence, the self-satisfaction of a minor mortal god. But he sensed that this was a more challenging reality. He pulled rank and made Mitya drive the rental car their contact had provided. But the truth was that he was afraid to drive, unexpectedly afraid of America. He had never felt afraid in his adult life, and the feeling made him mean.

"That's an interesting question," Zhan told his prisoner. "I mean, I was convinced you'd ask that. Everybody does. Even though they know exactly what's wanted from them. I think the psychology of our relationship is very interesting, don't you? You know what I want. Yet you feel that you have to ask me, anyway. Even though you know that you know. Human behavior fascinates me."

"The bastard really did shit himself," Mitya said from the front seat. "People are disgusting."

Zhan ignored his associate. "It's like the theater, isn't it? I mean, I've never been to the theater myself. But I imagine it's like this. Everybody plays a role, even though they know they're really somebody else."

"Don't hurt me anymore," the young man pleaded.

Zhan smiled gently. "That's up to you," he lied. Then he bent down over his prisoner. "Listen. Let's just be honest with one another. I'll ask you a few questions, you answer them, and it's all over. All right? First question: Where are the photographs?"

"What photographs?" the prisoner asked.

Zhan erupted into motion. He picked up his foot and smashed it down on the young man's closer broken hand. Over and over again. Wherever the hand went, Zhan's foot followed. The young man screamed and Zhan slammed his heel into his mouth and nose, careful not to catch the jaw and knock him unconscious or kill him. When he lifted his foot away, the prisoner's face had changed dramatically.

"Where are the photographs?" Zhan repeated, bending low.

"I got to open the goddamned windows," Mitya said. "The little turd."

"Where are the photographs?"

"I don't know." It was amazing that such a bloodied face could still speak clearly. But the words were the wrong words. Zhan burst into violent life again. This time his feet came down on the side of the prisoner's ribs, cracking the young man's chest like a dried biscuit. The young man screamed, then screamed again at the sudden pain of screaming.

"You're scared of the wrong people," Zhan told him.

SIX

"STAY HERE," RITTER SAID. "YOU'LL BE SAFE HERE."

It was time to go to meet Charlee. He had spent the afternoon imprisoned in his apartment, with the woman curled up on his bed, staring off through walls and across oceans, crying occasionally, while he mostly sat in the living room by the sliding door to the balcony, trying to read and waiting for the phone to ring.

The woman looked up at him as though struggling to remember his identity. Her amber eyes were gold and pink with weeping.

"Just stay here until I come back. It might be a while. But I'll bring you back some dinner. In the meantime, you can help yourself to whatever's here."

She looked at him with an expression shifting between numbness and great sorrow.

"And don't worry," he said, wanting somehow to reach her, to earn a response. "You'll be perfectly safe."

He did not know for certain whether or not that was true. He did not know who, if anyone, might have an interest in hurting her. And he felt foolish and used. Yet, he instinctively felt that this particular woman in this particular state was far better off crying herself to sleep in his apartment than wandering off into the wonderful world of the Washington evening. And, ashamed of himself, he had to admit that he did not want her to go.

Now and then the magnitude of events struck him. God only knew how many people had been killed or injured in the Pentagon bombing. As soon as he and the Russian woman entered his apartment, he had clicked on CNN: *Bombing in the Pentagon,* with shots of smoky, blocked-off corridors, of thousands of officers and employees milling around the vast parking lots, and of paramedics hustling gurneys up and down ramps. But the details were slow in coming, and the last time he had turned on the television to snare the headlines, Charlee's name still had not come up.

Not yet.

She had gone back to the building. To do her part, she said. But he realized she was capable of lying to anyone, at any time. So long as she believed the cause was just.

Ritter sensed that he was making one mistake after another. But, at the same time, the conviction had been growing in him that this was his mission, after all. He knew that, at the very least, his actions could end his career. But careers were so unimportant in the end. Events had begun to rhyme fatefully, bringing him to an odd, restless wakefulness. He began to sense that he had been asleep since Lena's death.

The beautiful zombie on his bed reached up and touched him with an exploratory hand.

"Don't go away."

He looked down at her, thinking that a man would be a fool to leave any bed on which she lay.

"It's all right. You'll be safe."

"Don't go."

"I have to."

"I'm afraid."

"It's all right."

"I don't like her."

"Who? Charlee?"

"Yes. That woman."

"She wants to protect you."

"I don't trust her. She came to see my father. I didn't like her then. And I don't like her now."

"She's a very important woman."

"I don't care. I don't trust her. I only trust you."

That might be a mistake, Ritter thought. "But you don't know me."

"I can tell about people."

If you could, Ritter thought, you would run away.

"I know you're a good man."

"Debatable. But it doesn't matter. The important thing is that you stay put. Until I get back. Not a vegetarian or anything, are you?"

"No."

"Chinese okay?"

"What?"

"Do you like Chinese food?"

"I will have a hamburger please. Or perhaps quiche. But I will eat a pizza, too."

Ritter smiled. It was a warm smile of a sort to which he had grown unaccustomed. "I'll manage something. Listen, help yourself to anything. There are towels in the closet in the hallway."

"I will stay here."

"Good. Now, I've got to go."

"Don't go."

"I have to. It's important. It's about you."

"You're going to see that woman."

"Yes. She's figuring out how to take care of you."

"You will take care of me. And I will stay here."

"This . . . is a provisional arrangement."

"It is best that I stay here. You will protect me. But I don't trust this woman."

"She could do a lot more to protect you than I can."

"She's jealous."

"What?"

"She loves you."

Ritter shifted to a higher alert level. "That's silly. And wrong. I'm just useful to her at the moment."

The Russian woman looked at him with her drained amber

eyes. "But she *does* love you. It's obvious. But she hates you, too."

"Listen. When I come back, I want you to tell me everything you can think of about who might have wanted to hurt your father. I know it'll be hard on you—"

"I will tell you now."

"I have to go." To meet the woman who loves and hates me. "But when I come back—"

"They're from the mafia. The Russian mafia. I know it. They're terrible people. I warned my father. 'Don't get involved with them,' I said."

Ritter decided that Charlee could wait a little while.

"He wouldn't listen. I don't really think he had a choice. They knew something about him. Everyone in Russia has something in their past. They held it over him. Or perhaps he thought he was doing it for me."

"Doing what?"

She looked at him as though surprised that he didn't know. "The business with the photographs."

"What photographs?"

"I don't know. I only know there were photographs."

Ritter sat down on the edge of the bed, careful not to come too close to her. For her sake and his own.

"What was he going to do with these photographs?"

She looked at him with a kindled wariness. He had not worried about her demanding to be taken to the police because he understood the deep distrust all Russians harbored of officialdom. Now he caught himself sounding far too officious. He decided to shut up and let her talk.

The suspicion passed from her face.

"What does any Russian do when he gets his hands on something valuable?" she asked with sudden cynicism. "He was trying to sell them, I think. To whoever would pay the most. I think they were worth a lot of money."

And Charlee always knew where to get a lot of money, Ritter thought.

"Miss Morozova—"

"Nadya."

Nadya. From Nadyeshda. The Russian word for "hope."

"Nadya, when my friend came to see your father—is that what they talked about?"

"I don't know. He made me leave the apartment. He didn't want me to become involved. But he couldn't hide everything. I found out little things. And that woman is not your friend. Just because someone loves you, it doesn't mean they're your friend."

"All right."

"He had one of the photographs in the apartment. He hid it. But I found it. I think he used it as a sample. I asked him about it. And he became angry with me. He told me I must forget it, that I must never mention it again."

Ritter did not want to spook her into silence. But he had to ask: "What was the photo of? What did it show? Do you have it?"

"He hid it again. I don't know where. But it showed a man. There was an information block that gave his name as Char-less Tarner. It said that he was an American pilot."

Ritter did not feel surprised. He felt fear. And he could not say why.

He knew how Russians transliterated. How they spoke. "Char-less Tarner" would be Charles Turner. Bates's people could run a records check on the name to see if a Charles Turner had gone missing in action in Korea. Or in Vietnam, for that matter.

Ritter looked at the hurt, splendid woman on his bed. Smart eyes in the face of one of Lippi's angels.

"Is that it? Was there anything else?"

She shook her head slowly. "No. It was just a black-and-white photograph. Of this American. He was just lying there with a Russian officer standing over him." She looked away. "I almost cried when I saw it. He looked so sad. With his hands tied behind his back like that. But I suppose people always look sad when they've just been shot."

"Tell me about the photographs, Charlee."

He had her. He saw it in her eyes, her frozen mouth, in the way she held her forkload of vegetable chop suey in midair. But she was a veteran and she recovered with amazing speed.

She glanced around the food court: oblivious after-work crowd, with the riches of Imperial America on sale in the tiers above them. The mall had been positioned brilliantly in a no-man's-land between the Pentagon, an array of offices, and the dormitory apartment buildings where Ritter and his peers slept and washed. He and Charlee sat on neutral ground, amid numbing opulence.

"You pick the damnedest places to ask questions," Charlee said.

"You suggested meeting here."

"I wasn't thinking."

"Charlee, you're always thinking."

Charlee chewed and considered, then moved to the flank. "So how's our little femme fatale? Doing gymnastics in your living room while she regales you with helpful information?"

"What about the photographs?"

Charlee put on her annoyed face. "I was going to tell you about them."

Ritter smiled and shook his head. He cut a piece of orange chicken in two with his plastic knife and fork.

"Morozov was supposed to bring them to me today. We had a deal. I had one million dollars in cash in my office."

Ritter worked at keeping his face impassive. "Tell me about the photographs themselves."

Charlee sighed. "I never saw any of them. We only talked about them. For some reason, Morozov was reluctant to show them in advance."

Ritter leaned in over his food. "Maybe it was a bluff. Maybe there were no photos." He wanted to hear her response now, after what Nadya had told him about the single photo she had seen.

Charlee shook her head. "No, I'm sure the photos exist. Unless he had them with him and they went up in the explosion. I mean, he was *supposed* to have them with him."

"But he wasn't supposed to have the bomb."

"No." Charlee tried to fork a sliver of broccoli. But the plastic utensil had too much flex. She settled for a mushroom cap.

"Charlee, I still don't see Morozov—a retired KGB general— as a suicide bomber."

"No." She tensed her dark eyebrows under her golden hair. "Well, maybe someone else planted the bomb?"

"The timing would be awfully coincidental."

Charlee nodded. "Nobody wants to die. But, I suppose—"

"Men are willing to die for what they love."

"What?"

"Nothing. Charlee, please be honest with me. Is there anything else you know about the photos?" He was sure she had seen at least the sample photo of which Nadya had spoken. None of it made sense otherwise. And why lie about that?

"Well, I know they're from the KGB archives. They're stolen, Chris."

"And old Morozov stole them?"

Charlee chewed and swallowed. "I think there may have been others involved. But he had some special role. Honestly, Chris. I have as many questions as you do."

"I doubt it. Charlee, listen. Nadya says—"

" 'Nadya'?"

"That's her name. It's short for Nadyeshda. She says her father kept one sample photograph in their apartment. She believes he showed it to you."

If Charlee was acting, she was playing her finest role. The look of denial on her face seemed utterly genuine.

"Chris, I swear. I didn't see it. I asked him to give me some proof, but he was reluctant."

"Didn't that make you suspicious?"

"Yes. Of course. But we—I had another source of information."

Ritter put down his drink. "Good enough to make a million-dollar deal go."

Charlee nodded. "The money wasn't the problem. A million dollars is nothing in this town. And if the photos turned out to be genuine—well, an asking price of one million was nothing. Morozov and his friends were thinking small."

Two fully veiled Middle Eastern women, refugees from the adjoining luxury hotel, sat down at the next table. From the bounty of possibilities offered by the food court, one had chosen a Philly cheese steak and fries, while the other had selected a Mexican combination plate and an ice cream sundae. She treated the ice cream as an appetizer.

"Well, that tracks," Ritter said. "The Russians do think small. They're still learning. They either have lunatic delusions of grandeur or they sell cheap. They can't find the middle ground. Anyway, a million U.S. dollars would sound pretty impressive to a retired KGB general. Or to most of the thugs running around the garbage dump that was the Soviet Union. Hell, it sounds pretty impressive to me. So tell me about your other source."

Charlee set her elbows on the table, one hand up in the air as if holding an invisible cigarette. She looked off to the side.

"Come on, Charlee. We have to be straight with each other. Who's been feeding you information?"

Charlee looked back into his eyes, then looked slightly away again.

"Ollie Cromwell," she said in a lowered voice.

Ritter got it. Sen. Oliver Cromwell. Select Committee on Intelligence.

"So Cromwell's behind all this? That's why you're interested?"

"Yes. I mean, he asked me to help him. But I'm interested in it for other reasons."

"Which I don't suppose you're going to share with me?"

She surprised him. She reached across the table and closed her hand over the back of his.

"Chris . . . please give me time on the motivation business." She looked impossibly earnest. "I told you I have a personal interest in this. And I'm not sure it's good for you to know. And it doesn't matter. All that matters are the results."

Ritter withdrew his hand. Gently. "Charlee, I'm sorry. I just don't get it. I can't understand why you're interested in the POW/MIA issue in the least. I mean, be honest. You *hate* anybody who wears a uniform." He smiled sourly. "Christ, you act as though a soldier took away all your Christmas toys when you were a kid."

Charlee paled. But Ritter barely noticed. His thoughts had already moved on. "Anyway," he said, "Ollie Cromwell's the biggest glory hound on the Hill. And he's got staff. Why throw you a bone this juicy, when he could suck free publicity off a POW/MIA breakthrough for years? Christ, I can hear the sound bites: 'Sen. Oliver Cromwell, working independently, uncovers POW fates.' It's too good to be true."

Charlee shrugged. "Chris, don't you think I've wondered that myself? I mean, give me some credit. I *know* there's more going on than Ollie's telling me. And I'll tell you something else—I'm starting to get the feeling that there's more going on than Ollie knows." Suddenly, she smiled. "You know me, Chris. Charlee Whyte, control freak." The smile disappeared. "And I just don't feel in control of this one."

"Charlee . . . you're scaring me. I'm almost starting to believe you're capable of a measure of honesty."

"You always knew how to flatter a girl."

"Tell me what Morozov told you. About the photographs. What were they going to reveal, exactly?"

Charlee rested her fork in a pool of soy sauce.

"He said the photos would show the executions of individual U.S. POWs at Russian hands. And that there was a name associated with each photograph."

Ritter looked down at the tablecloth. Thinking. Wishing still that he had no part in this.

"And Cromwell's information confirms Morozov's claims?"

Charlee rested her jaw on her hand. She hesitated before answering, and Ritter could feel the resilient suspicion in her. She really had no friends.

"Yes," she said finally. "Yes. Ollie has a source. The photographs definitely exist. And they really were stolen from the KGB archives. But . . . that's about all Ollie knows. He's manic about getting his hands on the photos, though. I've never seen him like this."

"It's a coup."

Charlee shook her head. "Chris . . . none of it feels right to me. I have to say that."

"Charlee, if all this about the photos is true . . . I can think of a dozen interest groups that would kill to get their hands on them—or to get them back under control. Let's just start with the obvious. On paper, the KGB doesn't exist. Now we've got the Russian Foreign Intelligence Service and a domestic division and some ash and trash. All freedom-loving democrats, of course. Except that they're exactly the same people. The road to Damascus has been pretty crowded lately. Anyway, if Morozov stole something that provocative from his own people, they wouldn't take it lightly."

"So you think the KGB, or whatever they're called now, bombed my office?"

"No. No, I really doubt that. They know the rules. And they're scaredy-cats when it comes to the tit-for-tat department. So I don't think the *organization* was involved. I mean, they might've gone after Morozov. But not you. That would be totally out of character. Only . . . if some faction, some renegade bunch with a vested interest . . . I mean, it's too early to rule anything out. But my gut feeling—against all human logic—is that Morozov carried that bomb into your office and knew he was doing it. God knows why. It's a contradiction only a Russian could swallow."

"Maybe he was being blackmailed?"

"It would take a pretty heavy threat."

"Maybe they threatened to harm his daughter?"

Ritter had already decided that was as good a bet as any. He decided to think more about it later.

"You're the expert, Chris. Tell me about the Russian security services. Hundred words or less. What are they really like now? I mean, if they *are* out to kill me, I'd at least like to know where they're coming from."

Ritter shook his head. "Charlee, I honest to God don't believe they're out to get you. At most, you'd be collateral damage. Unless there's something you're not telling me." He looked at her intently. "First of all, they don't want that kind of a fuss. Secondly, the really sharp ones are too busy getting rich. The old warhorses like Morozov, most of them are living out impoverished retirements. But the ones who hit general-officer rank just at the right time, they're wearing Hugo Boss suits, driving Mercedes, and looting the corpse of the old Soviet empire." Ritter drained the last of his drink. "You see, they're the only ones who really knew what was going on. They know where the bodies are buried. Figuratively and literally. They know how to work the system. How to move money, how to launder it. Out in the provinces, they're feudal lords. And half of them are mixed in with the high end of the Russian mafia, even while their underlings fight it out."

"Chris . . . if you were a sharp Russian security man today . . . where would you look to make your fortune? In the archives? Dredging up secrets? Like these photographs?"

Ritter considered the question. He'd never approached the problem in exactly those terms. But it wasn't hard to answer.

"If I were clever, I'd stay a million miles away from the archives. It's too dangerous. Too many people have too many secrets. Blackmail doesn't pay enough. And you end up dead. Selling stuff to the press is even more small-time. That's for the unimaginative." He turned his plastic knife over the last little hills of fried rice, a landscape as brown as Central Asia. "If I were in their position, there's no doubt about what I'd do. I'd work raw-materials deals. Export contracts. I'd facilitate things, use my knowledge of the system to 'help' the international business community do business. Charlee, the art of the deal is everything in Russia. And only the security boys know how to make a deal stick. They're still the only ones who can dependably deliver the goods, whether we're talking about rare metals, gold, diamonds, or oil and gas—and *that*'s where the really big bucks are. In oil and natural gas. They've got so much they can't even measure it. Charlee, are you all right?"

"What?"

"You look sick. Are you okay?"

"Yes. Yes, I'm fine." She tried to smile. "The day's just catching up with me."

Ritter smiled sympathetically, unaware of how far he had fallen into trusting her. "Well, it's not every day somebody tries to blow you up. Or at least blows up your office. How was it back in the Building? Bad?"

"Horrible." But Charlee's voice was vacant, her eyes elsewhere. As if waking, she glanced abruptly at her watch. "I've got a press conference. I really have to run."

"Charlee, you really don't look well. Are you sure you're all right?"

She shut her eyes for a moment, then took a deep breath and freshened her smile.

"I'm fine. Just tired. After the press conference, I'm going to go home, take a hot bath, and go to bed. Tomorrow's going to be a mess. And then there'll be the funerals." Her smile faltered. "God, it just never ends. Sometimes I feel so tired."

"Is somebody providing you with protection, surveillance on your home?"

"No. They wanted to. I refused it."

"Charlee, your office was just bombed."

She looked at him wearily. "You said yourself that the KGB or whatever they're called now wouldn't come after me."

Yes. He had said that. And now he was sorry. So much was unclear.

"Charlee, it's not just the Russian security services I'm worried about. Maybe there are some lone guns out there, special interests . . ."

"Oh, to hell with them all. I'm not afraid. And I will not sacrifice my privacy to watchdogs in polyester slacks and penny loafers."

Ritter smiled. "You can take the girl out of the country club, but you can't take the country club out of the girl. How's your family, by the way?"

Charlee smiled as if relieved at the chance to talk at last about something simple and undemanding. "Oh, Mom's great. As always. Obsessing on her golf game. And my stepfather just keeps getting richer. He's becoming a positive embarrassment."

"Life's tough."

"Yeah. Well, I really do have to run, Chris. Can't keep the press waiting. Thanks for dinner."

He held out his hands in a gesture of playful generosity. "We Army officers live in style. Next time I'll call out for pizza."

Suddenly, she looked at him with terrible sadness in her eyes, with a frankness that was painful to see, and it struck him how alone she must feel. For a moment, he was afraid she was going to say something she would later regret, and he helped her by turning the conversation back to business.

"One last thing, Charlee. When all is said and done, I *still* don't get it. This is all supposed to be about prisoners from the Korean War, right? That's forty years ago. It's history. Now, I understand that the Russian government isn't eager for further embarrassment. But they could make nice with us by coming clean and laying it all off on Stalin and the boys the way they always do. Maybe I'm thick, but I just don't understand why everybody's *so* excited about this particular issue."

Charlee stood up to go, looking down at him with eyes that seemed to have aged decades.

"I think I do," she said.

After Charlee had gone, Ritter sat for a bit, watching a young Hispanic man clean tabletops. He was very conscientious. As soon as customers departed, carrying their trays to the trash barrels, the young man hurried in with his rag, scrubbing away the ketchup and the crumbs, fueled by his vision of America.

Ritter asked himself what the smart thing to do would be, what the moral thing would be, and what the dutiful action would be. The smart thing, he knew, would be to bail out. But he wasn't going to do that. The moral aspect was tougher. It boiled down to whether it was better to trust Charlee or Jeb Bates. As far as duty went, his mission was clear: work with Bates. Drinking the water his cola's ice had left behind, he decided to continue working with both Charlee and Bates as honestly as he could, occupying the strategic center. He needed more information in order to make a good decision. In the meantime, he didn't see that he was doing any harm.

He rid himself of his tray and bought a few slices of pizza and a plastic container of salad to take back to the Russian woman. Then he went to a pay phone. With the rich, contented noise of the mall behind him, he dialed Bates's work number, confident the colonel would still be shifting papers around his desk.

Bates answered his own phone. The kind of guy who shooed off his subordinates so that they could have lives, while he stayed behind and did what needed to be done. An officer's officer.

"Sir, this is Chris Ritter."

"*Chris,* how's it going? Sounds like you're calling from an airport."

"Shopping mall. I come for the women. Listen, sir. Can you do me a favor? Check out a name, 'Charles Turner.' Or any likely variant thereof. Check the unaccounted-for list from Korea. If he's not on that, you might want to try Cold War shootdowns or Vietnam."

Bates's voice had sounded as tired as Charlee's when he answered the phone. Now his tone picked up as though he'd had a shot of caffeine straight into an artery.

"Sounds like you're coming on board with us, after all. That's my boy."

"Sir, I've got to tell you honestly. I hate this stuff. And I don't feel any kind of commitment to it."

Bates laughed. "Chris, you were born committed. You're an idealist. Anything short of a grand passion's just jerking off for you."

Ritter grinned despite himself, holding the warm, fragrant carton of pizza in his hand.

"Sir, you're a lousy judge of character. The guy you're describing is on the other end of the phone."

Bates laughed. There was no sound, but Chris could tell.

"All right, Ritter," Bates said happily. "Just send me the occasional postcard from the crusades."

Charlee stood behind the thicket of microphones, wearing a sober, determined mask. The lights were too high, too warm, and she had disregarded the need to freshen her makeup, deciding that it might not be a bad tactic to look like hell this time. The faces she could see between the pools of glare were anxious, greedy, amazingly untutored. The media. That great, dangerous tool. Silent, waiting.

"As you can imagine," she began, speaking with funereal slowness, "this has been a terrible day for me. A shocking day. So I have only a brief, informal statement." She noted a camera lens zooming in from the side of the room, hunting for imperfections. She took a deep, calculated breath, raised her eyes briefly to the ceiling as if searching for the god of soundproof panels and insulation, then focused on a point just above the heads of the gathered journalists. Speaking to deep space, to America, the world.

"In this tragic incident, I have lost not only valued colleagues, but cherished friends. Words cannot express my feelings of personal devastation. My sympathy—no, my full heart—goes out to the loved ones my coworkers left behind." She paused, counting beats. "We do not yet know who perpetrated this senseless deed. But let me assure the murderers that they will not stop us. Our work, our service in the cause of humanity, our struggle to lessen the suffering on this small, wounded planet, will go forward. Clearly, there are forces that feel threatened by our work. Some of those forces are becoming desperate. It doesn't mean we're losing the battle. On the contrary, it means we're *winning*. The forces of evil, of prejudice and inhumanity, of greed and willfully inflicted misery—those forces can feel the tide turning against them. Our struggle is a slow, agonizing process, and we could easily become discouraged. But *we* will not give up. *Nothing* will stop us—not hatred, not corruption, not bureaucracy, and not even bombs. My coworkers—my friends—have not died in vain. I promise them that. And I promise it to all of you." Charlee waited, feeling the pace of the crowd, then said, "I'm ready for your questions."

A network man who had built a career on disrespect for everyone jumped to his feet and began to speak without waiting to be recognized.

"Ms. Whyte, our sources tell us that you disappeared for a few hours after the bombing. The emergency teams even feared that you were among the victims. Can you tell us where you went and why?"

Charlee smiled graciously, displaying her vulnerability for all to see. "Sam, I know you think I'm superhuman, but I've got to let you in on a little secret—I'm not. When the bombing occurred, I just happened to be around the corner from my office. So I was very fortunate. Blessedly fortunate. But I saw what happened. I experienced it close-up. One moment I was hurrying down a corridor, and the next thing I knew I was picking myself up from the floor. I ran to see what had happened. And when I realized my office had been hit so badly, I just lost it. For a couple of hours I hardly knew who I was. I'm sure the doctors have a fancy name for it. But I'd just say I needed a little time to gather myself together. After the sheer physical shock compounded by the sense of emotional loss." She smiled again. "I lost it. 'Nough said?"

Beaten, the network man sat down. Charlee took control again. "I'm really a bit out of it tonight. As I'm sure you all understand. So I'm only going to take one more question—Dolores?"

The correspondent from National Public Radio stood up as the other bidding hands fell away.

"Ms. Whyte, you referred to 'forces of evil.' Now we might normally think of such forces as foreign, as speaking a strange language. But it's been said that you have many enemies right here in this building. I certainly don't want to put words in your mouth, but do you think there's even a remote chance that some element within the uniformed services might have been behind this bombing, perhaps some reactionary cabal?"

Charlee looked at the tall, plain woman, her familiar features blurred by the dazzle and halos of the television camera lights. She mimicked the correspondent's zealous expression.

"At this time," Charlee said, "I don't think we can rule out anything."

Ritter leaned against the rear of the elevator, resting his leg. He had gotten beyond the pain for a little while, as if the nerves had short-circuited, but his body's awareness of what he had done to it was beginning to return now. He told himself it would be all right to swallow a couple of the painkillers that sat, determinedly avoided, in his medicine cabinet.

The green numbers above the door marked progress, and the diffusing warmth of the pizza comforted his hand. He felt weary. But when the elevator doors opened at his floor, he alerted, sensing that something had gone off the rails. He felt people, heard rock music thumping in the background. Somebody having a party. Then he turned the corner toward his apartment and saw two Arlington cops and the night manager standing in front of his door, with various neighbors strewn down along the hallway.

"There he is," the night manager cried.

The cops, exasperated twins, looked in Ritter's direction.

Ritter closed the distance. In the immediate background, he saw his careerist neighbor, the young woman with the sensitive hearing.

"Buddy, you want to open this door and turn down your stereo?" one of the cops asked. He had a been-there-and-seen-it look.

Ritter nodded, fumbling for the key, almost dropping the pizza box and the perched salad.

"We can't have this sort of thing," the night manager said. "You've been told about this before."

Ritter glanced at him. "Sorry. I've got a guest. She's a foreigner and she doesn't know the rules. Sorry."

He opened the door. The stereo tuner lashed them with heavy-metal guitar whips, beating them with drums. Ritter dropped the takeout on the breakfast bar and hurried across the room to kill the music. Midway, he realized that the apartment was empty.

"Nadya?" he called in the big, fresh silence.

"Hey, buddy," the been-there cop said, "I got something for you to sign."

"Nadya?" Ritter stalked through the abbreviated hallway. The vinyl overnight bag lay at the foot of the bed where he had dropped it hours before. Nadya's exercise togs lay scattered over the unmade bed, found art.

He looked in the bathroom. He sensed recent damp and towels were on the floor.

"Mr. Ritter," the night manager called from the living room, "I hope this is going to be the *last,* truly the *last,* incident of this nature."

The seen-it cop met Ritter in the hallway. "Buddy, would you sign this so we can get out of here?"

"She's not here," Ritter said, speaking to himself out loud.

"And don't put us through this again, okay? I mean, look at you. A grown man and a military officer. You're supposed to be a responsible individual."

"She's gone," Ritter said, trying to think through this new development.

"Just sign the paper. Then you can sit down and cry."

Ritter looked around again. No signs of violence. On the

breakfast bar, a half-eaten microwave dinner sat cooling, while a carton of skim milk warmed and a bag of chocolate-chip cookies waited their turn.

The cop put on a disgusted face. "So what is it, buddy? You want to make out a missing-persons report or something? If not, we got work out there."

"Where do you want me to sign?"

"Here. And initial down there. It says you've been counseled by your friendly neighborhood patrolman. And that you will never give any of your neighbors an excuse to call nine one one ever again."

"It doesn't say that."

"Just sign it, okay? I'm giving you a break."

Ritter signed the form. The cop gave him a pink undercopy, looked up and down Ritter's uniform one last time, then turned to his partner:

"Doesn't look like the MTV generation to me. Does he to you, Jack-o?"

The quiet cop shrugged. "Takes all kinds."

"Don't I know it. So do us a favor, buddy. If your girlfriend shows back up, tell her we live in a civilized country, all right?"

"Got it."

The cops left, followed by the prancing night manager. Ritter shut the door.

Silence.

He couldn't make his brain work. Had she simply run away? Had someone tracked her down?

He flopped down on the sofa, bad leg raised and dangling over the end. What the fuck? he thought. What do you do now, ace detective? The pizza smell conquered the room and he finally got up, bullying his bad leg, and shoved the cardboard box and the salad container into the refrigerator.

The refrigerator's order had been disturbed. A pack of pressed turkey had been opened, half-emptied, and half-heartedly resealed. Same for a block of jack cheese.

A woman of serious appetites, he told himself.

Ritter felt as though the entire world were making an ass out of him. On the rare occasions when he read thrillers, he could invariably predict the plot in advance. But real life was just so damned sloppy.

No disturbance, no blood, no drama. Maybe she had just gone home. Without her things. Ritter limped to the coat closet by the front door.

Nadya's winter coat was still there.

Ritter meandered back toward the sofa and clicked on CNN. Curious about how Charlee would handle the press.

His timing was perfect. Charlee stared out at him, Joan of Arc on a bad hair day. She spoke brilliantly and dishonestly. Even as it was being asked, Ritter wondered if the second question from the press had been set up in advance.

Charlee's reply was evil. Absolutely shitty. She knew damned well that nobody in uniform had bombed her office.

Just when he had begun to trust her, to believe that they might share some of the same concerns after all.

But she was good. He had to admit it. Throwing out a red herring the size of a whale.

Keep the press occupied.

He watched her walk off camera, wondering what she was really hiding.

Ritter felt a burst of powerful anger. Toward Charlee. Toward Bates. Toward his knee and toward the Russian woman who couldn't even figure out how to close a pack of cold meat properly or just didn't care.

"What a mess," he said, not quite sure whether he was referring to the POW/MIA business or to his entire life.

Why on earth were people dying over forty-year-old photographs? What was going on?

Something was wrong. There was more to it. There had to be something bigger, some monster hidden under the surface of the water.

Christopher Ritter, detective to the defective. No problem too senseless.

He went into the bedroom, fetched the photo of his wife, and placed it on the coffee table atop a book on Armenian ecclesiastical architecture. He stared at her. Angry at Lena now, too. Furious with her.

"You just had to bail out on me. Didn't you?" he said quietly. He stared at her as though he could force the snapshot to answer. But he could not concentrate on his dead wife. He found himself thinking of the Russian woman.

Behind his back, the sliding door to his balcony began to open.

SEVEN

IT WAS NADYA. SHE WORE A TOO-BIG PAIR OF RITTER'S CORDUROYS and an old chamois shirt pulled from the back of his closet. Insufficient protection against the late-autumn cold. And she was barefoot.

She kept her distance, as if expecting violence.

"Can I come in now?" she asked in English. "I am cold."

"What in the name of Christ were you doing out there?"

"Should I go back outside?"

"You're lucky I don't carry a gun."

She shut the sliding door, digging frozen toes into the carpet. She tried to smile. "You will not shoot me."

"Just tell me why you were hiding on the balcony."

"I was afraid."

"It wasn't just that the music got too loud for you?"

"What?"

"Never mind. Listen, do you always play music that loud?"

She smiled more confidently. "Oh, yes. It is very nice like that."

"Well, you can't play music at that kind of volume here. In fact, don't play any music at all."

"You're mad at me."

"Yes. I am. Why did you hide? I thought you'd been kidnapped."

"Someone hits very hard on the door. They are shouting. I am afraid. I will have a cup of tea now, yes?"

Ritter peg-legged into the kitchen. Nadya took his place on the sofa. She shivered exaggeratedly, then tucked her feet up under her rump, massaging her toes with an idle hand.

"That was the police," Ritter said. "Banging on the door."

"Oh. Do they come here often?"

"No."

"They were looking for me?" A note of sudden alarm.

"The music was too loud."

"It was not *so* loud."

"It was. I could hear it from the elevator." He snapped on the front burner, parked the kettle.

"Is this a prison?" Nadya asked indignantly. "Where you cannot play music?"

"The neighbors don't like it."

"And what kind of neighbors are they? *My* neighbors never complain."

Ritter shook his head, snatched down a box of tea bags. "Different neighborhood. Listen, when I saw the police, I was afraid that something had happened."

"I could not live in such a place. You mean you were afraid for me?"

"Yes."

"That is very nice. I was afraid, too."

"Of what? Exactly."

"I am afraid they will make me go back to Russia. Do you know that your apartment smells to me like pizza?"

"I brought you some back. It's in the fridge. Who would want to send you back to Russia?"

The kettle made its first sparkling noises.

"Then I will eat this pizza, thank you."

"Why would somebody want to send you back to Russia?"

"I like the things you have. You have nice clothings, I think. And you have many books, for an American."

"Nadya, who wants to send you back to Russia, the INS?"

"But I don't like this woman."

"Charlee? You already said that."

"No. I don't like her, too. But this woman in the photograph. I don't like her."

"That's my wife."

"Oh."

The kettle howled. Ritter clicked off the stove and drowned an English tea bag.

"Well," Nadya said slowly, "then I think she is a very nice wife."

"She was. A very nice wife."

"Oh?" Nadya said brightly. "You are not together now?"

"No. She died."

"That is very sad," Nadya said happily.

"You want the pizza heated in the microwave?"

"No. It is also very good cold. Has your wife died because of the many murders in Washington? A woman is murdered not far from my apartment one week past."

"No. Cancer."

She brushed a finger across her lips. "That is terrible, too."

Ritter retrieved the pizza from the refrigerator. It still gave off a ghost of warmth. He decided to let her eat it that way.

Nadya moved to the breakfast bar with startling quickness. She ignored the plate he had set out and drew the pizza box toward her.

"You have loved your wife?"

"Immensely."

She ate and spoke. "I loved my husband like this, too."

"And now?"

"Not so much now. He is making a divorce. That is why I am afraid I must leave America. I am here because of him. Now he does not want me. So I think they will make me go back."

"I don't think it works that way. As long as it was a legitimate marriage. But I'm no lawyer."

"I do not want to go back to Moscow. Maybe I will kill myself before I go back to Moscow." She bit into the pizza crust with little white teeth. "I see you have books of Bulgakov. You like to read Bulgakov?" She lifted the broken triangle of pizza back to her mouth.

"He's all right."

"No," she cried, interrupting her bite. *"No,* you must *love*

Bulgakov. He is the only one who understands women." She clamped her teeth down hard. With a look of determination and finality.

"I thought Chekhov understood women pretty well."

She hastened her chewing. Nodding to him: "Wait."

It struck Ritter again how remarkably beautiful she was. Even eating cold pizza in one of his old shirts.

She swallowed, then spoke with a husk of crumbs in her throat. "Chekhov understands women who are not interesting. Bulgakov understands interesting women."

"And Tolstoy? Anna Karenina seemed pretty real to me."

Nadya raised her chin. Slight gleam of pizza oil. "She is only how the man wants a woman to be. Maybe an educated man. But she is too good, you know? Do you think I should throw myself over a train because my husband does not want me now?"

" 'Under a train.' We can speak Russian, if you want."

"No. It is better to speak English. So I can be an American. If they don't send me back. You see, I am not like these silly women of Tolstoy. Or the little dolls of Mr. Dostoyevsky. You see how writers are? They are such unhappy men. They must make up fantasy women because the women they meet in life are not perfect. I could never make love with a writer. That is what I think."

"Except Bulgakov."

"Well, he doesn't understand women, either. Not really."

"Is there any author who truly understands women? In your view?"

She ground cheese and crust between her teeth and thought deeply. Her eyes ranged through the kitchen wall.

"Jack London."

"You can't be serious. He didn't even have women in his books. Except as occasional background noises."

"You see? That is how I know he has understood women. He does not put them in his books. Because he knows it is impossible to describe them. But I will also tell you that I think Margaret Mitchell understood women very much. She is the greatest American writer."

"I'm not sure the majority of critics would agree with you."

She waved away a century's taste, swallowing the last of the pizza. "But she was very wise, this Margaret Mitchell. I will tell you why: she understands that intelligent women always make the wrong choices."

"Do you always make the wrong choices?"

"Sometimes." She cradled the teacup in her fine hands. Her face saddened. "It was a great mistake to bring my father here. I have killed him now."

Tears grew in her eyes.

"Why did you bring him here, Nadya? Why did he come?"

She began to cry. Ritter resisted the urge to take her in his arms. "Because he has loved me. Because he has no one else. Because all of his friends forget him. Because I am the only one he can love."

"So you and your husband sponsored him?"

"My husband was against it. He is not a nice man. He does not like my father. But he helps me, I don't know why. Now he makes a divorce. And my father is dead."

Ritter held himself in check. Listening.

"I have killed my father," she said, weeping. "You know, I forget he is dead for some minutes. Do you know it is such a terrible thing to kill your father?"

"You didn't kill him."

She looked at him. *"I did."*

Ritter could not bear to look at her sorrow. "Where's your husband now? What does he do?"

"He's here. Very close. He makes software. For a big telephone company."

"So he's doing well? Financially, I mean. Doesn't he help you?"

"Him?"

"I mean, your apartment . . ."

"I have no money. I cannot make a good job until my English is better."

"What do you do? I mean, what was your profession in Russia?"

"I am a psychologist. But it is different in America. They say that in Russia our standards are too low. So I cannot be a psychologist in America. This is sad, because I have worked with people and helped them. I am very good at helping people."

Ritter would never have guessed her for a psychologist. Maybe a model. He thought for a moment.

"And your father—was he in America very long?"

"Only some months. It was very hard on him. He did not speak English. Only some words. My husband hated him."

"Nadya, my friend—the woman you don't like—told me that your father was a general in the KGB."

Nadya nodded as if it were the most natural thing in the world. Then her eyes darkened, amber sinking into night.

"You believe that I am a spy?"

Ritter laughed softly. That had never occurred to him. He knew how the Russian security-service types tried to shield their children, pampering them. There had been KGB dynasties, but they were the exception, rather than the rule. The biggest family problem the modern security-service people had with their offspring was spoiled children going bad.

"No. I don't think you're a spy. You may be a lot of things, but I don't think you'd make a very good spy."

Nadya stood up and marched across the small living room. She stood by the balcony door, sulking and peering out between the vertical blinds.

"Perhaps I cannot trust you. Perhaps you are an agent of the CIA."

Ritter laughed again. "I've been called a lot of things in my life, but that's about the worst."

"I think I do not understand men," Nadya said, wallowing in the idiotic pout that Russian women routinely affected. "I am a psychologist, you see. I understand only the problems of others. But I have never solved my own problems." She turned and looked into his eyes, a gorgeous ragamuffin. "Maybe *you* will send me back to Russia."

"Not in my power."

She was serious, though. "You could tell them."

"Tell them what?"

"About my father."

"That he was a KGB general?"

"No. The other thing."

"What 'other thing'?"

She stepped back toward the sofa and sat down resignedly. A beaten woman at the end of a butchered day. Even in defeat, her profile showed wonderfully. Ritter warned himself that she must have given her husband a damned good reason to leave her.

"What 'other thing' about your father, Nadya?"

She lowered her face into hands held up for prayer. All of the coquetry had been vanquished.

"In the photograph. Of the dead American. I told you that there was a Russian officer. It was my father."

The maid had already gone home by the time Charlee made it back to her row house on Capitol Hill. The house was a three-story brick Edwardian, its interior entirely renovated to her specifications. She let herself in and the foyer lighting came up automatically, illuminating a row of African masks facing off with a pair of Käthe Kollwitz etchings. Charlee went immediately to her second-floor study, winding through exact antiques and third-world artifacts. In the quiet, she flipped out a false front of classics and pressed the combination into the keypad of her safe.

Gently, she drew the photograph and the key from the deep hip pocket of her dress. The light was poor, but it was easy to recognize Morozov standing over the dead, unexpectedly aged prisoner. She could not read the Cyrillic inscription on the margin, but that wasn't important.

She thrust the photo and the stolen key to the Russian woman's apartment into the safe atop a stack of papers and velvet jewelry bags. Then she closed the panel and sat down at her desk for a moment, waiting for the nausea to leave her stomach. She did not understand why fate had chosen her to face this.

The turbulence in her stomach began to ease and she stood up. Before going downstairs, she flipped through her Rolodex until she found her analyst's number. She left a message on the answering machine booking an appointment. She had not been to see the woman for a couple of years. But it was time now.

She fetched an open bottle of Sonoma chardonnay from the kitchen, picked out one of her favorite stems, and went into the dining room to go through the day's mail. But she found she needed to sit for a moment, sipping the wine with her eyes closed.

It had been a horrible, horrible day. She knew that the bombing had not fully reached her yet, that the impact was still coming. Then, going through that little Russian tart's drawers, she had come upon the photograph. She had immediately realized what it meant—she was the first American to possess proof of what the old Soviet regime had done. It had almost made her throw up over the ill-folded underwear in the drawer.

She wasn't as hard as she had believed. Every day it was more difficult to carry on. She didn't want this test. She had always managed to keep her personal problems at a remove.

And Chris. The poor bugger had nearly made her lose it over a plate of cheap Chinese. He had not even noticed. Speaking so casually. And suddenly it had all fallen into place for her. Why Ollie was being so secretive, why he did not want to work it through his senatorial staff.

Ollie really was a bastard. She understood that as clearly as she had ever understood anything.

So what's new? she asked herself.

No matter what course of action she chose she was going to be the great loser in this affair. There was no way to win.

She wished Chris hadn't been so damned smart. He was smarter than he knew. Maybe he'd be smart enough to extract himself from all this before it was too late.

She felt an impulse to phone him, to tell him to stay away. But it died. She needed him. Needed his help. No matter what. There was no one else now.

She poured herself another glass of wine and cut open a letter from her mother with an inlaid Persian dagger. She forced herself to read:

> Charlene, my dearest,
>
> Your stepfather and I were utterly crushed to learn that you won't be joining us for Thanksgiving again this year. We miss you so terribly much. But we've decided to make the best of it. We've accepted an invite from the Andersons to join them in their little villa down in P.V. Just for the

week—you know how Larry feels about the Mexicans. Anyway, we both have to rush right back to play in a tournament. Larry's up in arms, by the way. He believes the Japanese are ruining golf out here. They really are buying up all the best courses. I mean, you just about have to fly to Scottsdale to get a tee time. Which reminds me, darling, when you see Ollie next, please tell him your stepfather's counting on him for the Oilmen's Open. Just between us, I think Larry wants to give him a good talking to. Larry feels that Ollie's spending entirely too much time with some of those foreign oil people of whom he does not approve. I've told Larry that you don't see much of Ollie anymore, but he simply won't get it through his head. Which reminds me, darling—could you please sign those papers Larry sent you and send them back to us? He just wants to do something nice for you. He's always loved you as if you were his own daughter, you know. Anyway, we simply must transfer those properties to you before the new tax code comes into effect. You know, I don't recall your stepfather ever so despising a president. He won't even say the poor boy's name. He just calls him "that man." But I suppose you like him. Who would have thought that our daughter would turn out to be one of the enemy? (Just joking.) Did you know that Sussee Wilder's getting a divorce? With all of those children? Sometimes I just say to myself, "Our Charlene made all the right choices, after all." Anyway, we love you. The Andersons say how-do, and so does Vixen (Bow-wow). Don't forget to send Larry those papers. He's promised me he'll take care of the management end, so the properties won't be a burden to you. He does worry about you so. He really loves you, dearest. Did I tell you I won the "Old-Timers" up at the Beach? Isn't that something? Larry was so proud, he flew me down to Wolfgang's just for dinner. I had the shrimp the way you like them, but the place was full of those awful movie people who really can't afford to eat there. Don't you just hate people like that? Wolfgang says he always watches you on TV. He thinks you need a new hairstyle. He's such a sweet man. I just have to run. I have a million things to do.

Buckets of love,
Ronette

The rest of the mail was just mail. There was a courtesy copy of a book for which she had written an introduction without reading the deadly dull contents and a calendar of events from St. Mark's. God, she hadn't been there in so long. She glanced over a mailing reminding her about the big pro-choice rally coming up on Saturday. The goal was to get half a million people on the Mall, and she was expected to be one of them. There was never enough time to do everything that needed to be done. She poured herself a last glass of wine and headed upstairs.

She kicked off her shoes as she transited her bedroom, went into the bathroom, and unleashed the hot water into her over-size tub. She had designed the bathroom herself, it was one of her greatest indulgences. The tub was wonderfully contoured, beautiful and deep, and sometimes she wished she could just live in it. Her one clean place.

She worked her way out of her clothing, smelling herself and dropping each item wherever she stood when she took it off. She caught herself thinking that it was amazing that Sussee Wilder's marriage had lasted as long as it did, since none of the kids looked like the father. Poor Josh. In his Zegna suits, with his idiotic smile. The thought of such mundane concerns made her laugh, mostly at herself. Poor Josh, poor Sussee. Charlee had had a very brief affair with him before Sussee had decided to mend her reputation through marriage, and Charlee always thought of him as the only man she had ever met who began to snore even before he ejaculated. He was convinced he was God's gift to women, of course.

Naked, Charlee tested the bathwater and adjusted the tap, belatedly pouring in a generous portion of oil. Then she saw herself in the mirror.

It was odd how you could see yourself day after day without being much affected by it, until, one day, you caught a glimpse of yourself with different eyes and it was as if years of changes had happened overnight. Charlee hardly recognized the woman in the mirror.

She had never had a perfect body. But it had been all right. And she had grown up knowing how to use clothing. Even in her denimed campus days, she had understood the dos and don'ts. She had been able to attract men, and she had not been ashamed to lie naked beside them or to stand in the light. But the body she saw in the mirror was not meant to lie uncovered or stand revealed any longer.

Charlee smiled bitterly. Her body looked exactly the way she felt at the moment. Then her smile faded and she stared at herself with a level of comprehension that somehow could not progress.

I'm not that old, she thought.

She remembered the water in time and shut the gold taps tightly. She ran her hand through the hot velvet. She always used a lot of oil. A small indulgence to keep the other systems running.

She began to step into the tub, then stopped. She turned bravely to face the mirror again. Calculating, she reached for one of her big white towels and robed herself in it so that it covered her quitting breasts and flowed just down to her crotch.

Not so bad now. She could still get away with an off-the-shoulder gown. Her thighs had thickened a bit, but she still had good legs. No ruptured veins. And the skin tone was good. Really, her problems centered on just a few specific locations.

But so did men.

She resolved, again, to begin an exercise program and stick with it.

She had not made love to anyone in months. God, was it almost a year? And even that wasn't quite right. What she meant was that she hadn't fucked anybody in almost a year. She hadn't made love for a much longer time.

Ultimately brutal with herself, as always, she let the towel fall away. Considering the devastation between the upper slopes of her breasts and the coppery mush between her legs.

Perhaps it was instinct, intuition. Or perhaps she caught a hint of movement in the mirror. She might have heard a footstep on her bedroom carpet. Whatever the cause, Charlee suddenly realized she was not alone.

"Ollie, you bastard."

Sen. Oliver Cromwell pitched his shoulder against the doorframe. "You're still a fine-looking woman, Charlee."

She had been his lover long enough to gauge precisely how much he had been drinking, and the range of feelings he excited in her was broad and each feeling was bad. Watching him watch her in the steam-clogged air, she believed that she hated everything about him. His eyes settled unashamedly on her crotch.

Charlee picked her robe from its hook and covered herself. "How did you get in?"

Cromwell smiled. He had a grand smile, warm and ageless. He held up a key.

Charlee strode across the tile and ripped the key from his fingers. He reacted slowly, as though everything gave him direct physical pleasure and he was in no hurry to move on.

"How did you get past the alarm system? I changed the code."

He showed teeth, a happy carnivore. "You didn't set it, my sweet. I've told you about that."

"You're drunk."

"Yes."

"You said you'd given me all your keys."

His eyes followed her as though he were aiming a weapon at her. She had learned, the hard way, to respect and distrust those eyes. Even when he was filthy drunk, Ollie saw things with astonishing clarity. And he remembered what he saw.

He reduced his grin to a flirty smile.

"Do I have to change the locks?"

He shook his head. Very slightly. And he slipped his hands into his trouser pockets. "Last key. I just couldn't bear to give you up entirely, my sweet."

"Get out of here, Ollie."

"Is that any way to treat an old friend?"

"Just get out."

"Bad day, my love?"

"Ollie, you're being tiresome."

He raised his eyebrows, pulling a face that played to an invisible audience. "Now *that,* my darling, is an insult worthy of your intellect. I have been called many things. But never 'tiresome.' "

"What do you want?"

He stepped fully into the room, bringing his alcohol smell into the moist perfume off the bath. His shoes clapped on the tile. He wandered through the little space, then parked his backside against the lip of a counter, drawing his hands back out of his pockets and folding his arms.

"Maybe business. Or maybe I just have not been able to get you out of my mind."

"What business?"

The persona cracked slightly. The studied voice grew briefly impatient, and a grimace brief as love passed over his face.

"You know damned well what business, Charlee. It appears to me that a signal investment of ours may have gone a tad sour."

"Fuck you, Ollie. I was nearly killed."

"And I am grateful that you were not. The world would have been distinctly poorer without you. What about the photographs?"

She looked at him, imagining for an instant that he could see into her and register what she knew, what she had learned inadvertently from Ritter. It struck her that this man to whom she had so long given her body and her talents just might be the most repugnant human being she had ever met.

She had considered confronting him with what she knew, with the full, revolting design of what he was up to. But she restrained herself, recognizing that her knowledge brought her latent power. There would be a time for truth. But it wasn't now, with Ollie's drunken ass nudging back into her toiletries. "I don't know," she said. "I can't make sense of it. But I can't believe he had the photos with him. Maybe somebody swapped packages on him." She clutched her robe more tightly around her, suddenly cold in the overheated room. "Ollie, who tried to kill me? And why?"

Ollie shrugged.

"What's going on, Ollie?"

"My darling, you have to realize how sensitive this is. People have interests . . ."

"This is bigger than you told me. Ollie, what happened today scared the hell out of me. And I don't scare easily. People *died.* People who had no role in this. They're *dead,* Ollie."

He moved toward her, a bit unsteady, opening his arms to comfort her. Charlee stepped aside, turned away.

Cromwell dropped his hands to his sides with an exaggerated sigh. "Charlee, we need those photographs."

"You need them."

"No," he said calmly, "we need them. You know the deal. I get the photographs, you keep your job."

"You're such a shit."

He sighed again, a disappointed teacher this time. "My love, you just have to keep your eyes on the goal. Don't be so damned virginal."

"And what's the goal, Ollie?"

"The goal is for you to put those photographs into my hands. So that you may continue to save little brown babies."

Recinching her robe, she said calmly, "And your goal?"

"To serve my country. In bad times and in good."

Charlee sat down on the side of the tub. A flap of her robe fell away from her thigh, but she covered herself again.

"Now," Cromwell said, "about the money."

She looked up at him, weary and not quite comprehending.

"The *money,*" he repeated. "One million dollars. Remember?"

Charlee shrugged. "It's gone, I guess. It was in the office. Everything's gone." She felt shrunken. His voice, asking about the money, had taken on a seriousness that had been absent when he commented on her personal survival. This man whom she had taken into her body, her life. Whom she had even loved.

"You can't just guess, Charlee. I'm accountable."

She looked at him in wonder.

"Charlee, a million dollars in cash is not to be taken too lightly. A million is just about the amount where people start getting concerned."

He really had surprised her. Ollie could be a shit. But he had never been one to worry about money. The men who buoyed his career had so much money they could play with continents.

"It's gone. Sue me."

"Charlee, you have to understand. It's not just the money. It's the principle of the thing."

She laughed out loud. "Ollie, sometimes you make me want to vomit."

"You're not being fair, Charlee."

She laughed again. "If it's so damned important to you, I'll get it from Larry."

Cromwell recoiled. It was a faint gesture, the ghost of a retreat, but Charlee caught it.

"I don't want your stepfather involved in any of this," Cromwell said sternly.

"But he *likes* you, Ollie. Birds of a feather."

"I'm serious, Charlee. I don't want your stepfather within a thousand miles of this."

Charlee looked up at him. "What the fuck is going on, Ollie?"

He tried a more businesslike tone. "Charlee, it's just that Larry's a dinosaur. He's stuck in the past. Christ, he can't see across the Rio Grande. He's living back in the days of John Foster Dulles. I can't have anything to do with a clown like that."

"He was always there when you had your hand out."

"And he didn't lose anything in the process." Cromwell dipped his hands back into his pockets. "For God's sake, times change. You have to change with them."

It amused her to listen to him. She was putting more of the scenario together now. Ollie was a slimeball on a transcendent level.

"Mind if I fix myself a drink?" Cromwell asked.

"I don't keep liquor in the house now."

"A glass of wine then. One glass and we'll call it quits on the million."

"We're already quits, Ollie. Somebody tried to kill me."

She saw it coming, knew his alcohol moods. His face turned to stone as the inner rage started. He was a man accustomed to having his own way.

"You're wearing on me, Charlee. We made a deal. You fuck it up, and you're history. You'll be giving sob-sister lectures at community colleges."

"We didn't 'make' a deal, Ollie. You dictated one."

"Same difference. You *owe* me. Everybody has to pay their bills."

She shook her head. "You really do make me feel dirty."

He looked down at her. "You *are* dirty, Charlee. That's the price of doing business. And speaking of business, the bombing rather complicates things. We're going to have to play this very close to the chest—your press conference was brilliant, by the way. You're a tactical genius, my love."

"I hate this."

"I know you do. Just another good girl gone wrong. So how's your loverboy? Is he on board? He didn't get himself blown up, too, did he?"

It took her a moment to understand him. Then she said, "He's not my 'loverboy.' "

Cromwell smiled. "The past is always with us, Charlee. It is the one thing we never escape." He laughed, clearly wanting a drink. "I'm here, am I not?"

She looked at him earnestly. "Ollie, please. Tell me the truth just once. What are you planning to do with the photographs?"

He put on his official mask. "I'm going to share them with the American people, with the family members."

"Is that the truth?" She knew he was lying. She had it down now. Just about all of it. The photos were never going to go public. And she would not be able to do anything about it.

"Ollie . . ."

"So tell me about your soldier boy."

"What about him?"

"Is he going to help us?"

Charlee thought of Ritter. With immeasurable sadness and a great deal of shame.

"Yes."

"Good."

"He'll get the photos. If it's humanly possible. He'll do it because he believes it's the right thing to do. He'd give his life to do the right thing."

Cromwell nodded solemnly, very much the senator. "Well, our country needs people like that. My hat's off to them. So have you developed any contacts beyond the old man?"

Charlee answered, but her mind had gone elsewhere. "Only his daughter. And I don't know how much she knows. I don't trust her."

"Find out. How much she knows."

"I want to go a little slowly. Ritter can handle her." She smiled at the unintended private joke.

"Ritter?"

"My 'loverboy.' "

"All right. Good. But don't waste time, Charlee. If you need to hammer that little cunt to get things done . . . I mean, she's disposable."

"Damn it, Ollie. Don't talk to me that way."

He walked up to where she sat. Slowly. Just keeping his balance. He stood in front of her, too close, and she could smell alcohol, the day's wear on him, and a hint of urine from the crotch of his trousers.

"We're all disposable," he said.

Ritter lay on a bed of sofa cushions, feet thrusting out into space, the ache in his knee a dull, constant thing. The Russian woman lay in his bed, a thin wall away, and he could hear the occasional movements of her body under sheet and blanket. Odd how a hundred women might be utterly uninteresting and one a spur to immediate desire. Nadya. He could think of plenty of reasons not to think about her, but found himself imagining the bluntly physical.

So strange. That no other woman had reached him like this since Lena. The Russian woman certainly did not bear comparison with her. His Magdalena. The word *lonely* seemed too simple, too weak, for what he felt, yet no other word or combination of words expressed it better. He was lonely. Without the one woman he had loved truly out of all the girls and women he had fixed to a bed.

Was it fair, was it even sane, to forever compare other women to Lena?

He remembered his wife with that infrequent vividness that

leaves the soul powerless to resist: one of their early meetings, on the terrace of a student bar. On a silken evening. Lena sat across the table in the twilight, *dark* brown hair heavy in the late heat, and he watched her full lips shape words, now and then showing straight white teeth and the oblivion beyond. She was telling him about religious poetry from the Spanish colonial era and about her master's thesis, when she suddenly asked:

"Are you the type who repents when he gets what he wants?"

Then she laughed and wrapped her lips around a long-necked beer bottle. That night, she tested him, and in the morning, he offered her not repentance but an unquenched animal hunger.

He heard the unmistakable sounds of the Russian woman rising. Footsteps on the carpet. For a moment, he imagined she was coming to him, and he longed for it. But she paused in the hallway, a light flashed on, then she closed the bathroom door behind her.

He was left on his uncomfortable bed, listening. She ran the water in the sink for a long time.

She stumbled a bit when she came back out into the darkness. Searching for the way. But she did not go back into the bedroom. She came—slowly—out to where he lay, hunting for him with light-ruined eyes. He could see her very clearly. Night in his apartment was ever slightly tainted by the glow of the boulevards. He saw that she was naked, finely outlined. She got the sense of him and knelt down.

"You are not sleeping," she said.

"No."

"And I am not sleeping."

"Yes."

"Let me stay with you some minutes."

"Yes."

He lifted the sheet and blanket, welcoming her to the improvised bed. She arrived against him with a shock. Warm, warm flesh.

"I am crying," she said.

He held her against him. She was so slightly built it was

almost like holding a child. But her lean muscles were far from powerless.

Her face pressed damply against the top of his chest. He savored the wonderful lines of her. His response had been immediate, but they both ignored that for a minute. Then she reached down and closed her hand around him.

"I think," she said, "there is one very good help for sadness."

Charlee told herself that it didn't matter, that she needed the physical release. And Ollie, for all his faults, had not been the worst of lovers. He knew her so well.

Revolting that it took a bombing to bring him to her bed. Or perhaps he and his Lolita were having a spat. But it did not matter. She loved feeling a man inside her, against her, on top of her—until that shattering instant. Then she wanted him to finish and let her be. And Ollie had always been okay with that. He wasn't an *après* kind of guy.

She felt herself starting to go.

"Harder," she commanded.

Ollie, unspoiled by drink in this sense at least, firmed up the rhythmic pressure of his finger, pushing himself into her with a kindred motion. In the moment when she was on the edge of dying, it wasn't Ollie, of course. She screamed. Shocked back to life. Then she failed wonderfully, as if her bones had melted. Ollie finished with her, a vulgar, capable man.

She wondered if it was going to be like this for the rest of her life.

They lay in a careless, uncommitted embrace, unspeaking. Charlee thought of all the things she had gotten wrong, of how lies became necessary. Then she turned onto her side and shrugged. Nothing you could do about it.

Ollie followed her with a dead arm, but he was already asleep. Nothing ever touched Ollie Cromwell.

He smelled his age, though.

She rolled out from under his arm and rose. Scavenging her robe from the floor, she went downstairs. In the kitchen, she lifted the phone from the wall, then realized she didn't know the number. She drew out a northern-Virginia phone book, but there was no listing, the connection was too new. Finally, she called information.

The phone at the other end went unanswered for a very long time. But she waited. At the moment, she had nothing else to do with her life.

The two new lovers lay drained. Clinging. Then Ritter kissed the woman gently, but with an implicit desire that could not be mistaken for innocence. He moved his lips over the planes of her cheeks and jaw, into the recesses that gathered salt, and down to where strands of damp hair softened the skin still more. He kept his eyes closed, seeing her with his lips and, less often, with his tongue, following the lines of skittish tendons in her neck down onto shoulders slight as porcelain. He had always loved the complexity of women's bodies, not just the magnetic, explicitly sexual parts but the bow-trace from shoulder to outstretched arm and the hollow at the base of the spine, the sweet flesh of a woman's biceps and the tenderness inside the thighs . . . and the burnt smell of hair when they were tired and you held them against you. Sometimes the women who had been ruined by too much sex with too little feeling failed to understand him at all, but more often, the women he touched reveled in the unaccustomed attention, falling in love with him not so much for the animal stamina that impressed them at first but more for the kindness resonating in his touch at the times when another man would no longer have bothered to touch them at all.

The Russian woman lay receiving his kisses, stroking him now and then, and giggling opaquely. She smelled of fruit gone slightly off.

Somewhere in the waking dream, the telephone rang. Ritter did not want to answer it, didn't intend to answer it. But the caller would not relent, and he began to worry that it might truly be an important call.

He lifted himself away from his new lover, brilliance trailing between. He felt their mixed wetness on him, not the injury to his knee.

"Ritter," he answered.

"Chris? It's Charlee."

"Something the matter?"

"No. No, nothing. I thought there might be something the matter with you."

"Charlee, are you all right?"

"Yes. Listen, I'm sorry I called. I just thought . . . I thought that maybe we don't realize how dangerous all of this is. Sometimes it hits me all over again, the bomb and everything."

"You've handled it like a soldier."

He sensed a laugh. She said, "Is that supposed to be a compliment?"

"Charlee, what's this all about?"

"We'll talk tomorrow. I'll call you at a decent hour. So how's Miss Moscow? All tucked in?"

"Yes."

"Don't let the bedbugs bite." She hung up.

Ritter limped back to his makeshift bed. He got down on his knees and took up his new lover in his arms. She weighed nothing at all. It was like lifting a ghost.

He carried her into the bedroom, feeling her small and warm and marveling again at the raw sexual power she had brought against him. He dipped his head to smell her, kiss her, drinking her taste to deaden the pain starting up in his leg again. She moaned and let herself hang limply from his arms.

He nudged back the disordered covers and let her down onto the sheet, wondering at the different palenesses, at the beauty of her. He kissed her where her belly declined, smelling her, him, *them.* Then he lowered himself along her body and she shaped herself to him.

"She called because she knows," Nadya said suddenly.

"What?"

"She knows. That is why she telephones."

"What does she know?" Ritter asked absently, in mild, tired amusement.

"Too much."

EIGHT

RITTER RETURNED FROM THE DEAD, WITH NADYA IN HIS ARMS. HE wanted her again, but she was sleeping soundly, a questionable woman whose father had just died and who had spent the night in a stranger's arms. He decided not to disturb her. Yet. Then he heard the thump of a newspaper falling against his door. He rose, pulling on a T-shirt and undershorts, and carefully closed the bedroom door behind him. He brought in the paper. Then he ground coffee beans and unfolded the world on his counter.

He scanned the front-page article about the bombing. Charlee's politically lascivious comments figured prominently. But there was no mention of a retired KGB general. No photographs of murdered U.S. POWs. Without waiting for the pot to fill, Ritter poured himself a first cup of coffee. Alerting to the heat and bite, he thought again of the woman sleeping in his bed, and he felt anxious for the next hour to pass so that he might lie back down beside her and kiss her back to life. He turned to the world news section, his section. And the photograph in the top center of the page woke him completely.

It was Rakhman. Smiling, with his arm around a general officer from the Russian security services. The accompanying article's headline announced, "New Government in Central Asia."

Ritter began to feel sick as he plunged down through the

paragraphs. The new country's capital had fallen to a lightning blow delivered by a coalition of regional interest groups and "reform" Communists. The democratically elected government had fled, and the president's whereabouts were unknown. Retired general Ali Ali-Rakhman had been appointed provisional head of government. A Russian security-service colonel general named Virov had been appointed as Moscow's special representative to the new government, and he had issued a statement of confidence in Rakhman, anticipating a rekindled relationship that would be of benefit both to the region and to Russia. General Virov would also be responsible for security along the oil pipeline that gave Russia a continuing share of the regional economy. Meanwhile, fighting continued in the eastern provinces between fundamentalist rebels and the government troops who had pledged their allegiance to the new men in power.

Ritter felt beaten. He had hoped that, somehow, Rakhman would be brought to justice, that he and the white-haired thug would pay for Ben's death. But that wasn't the way the world worked. Ben's bones lay somewhere in the desert where they had been picked over by animals less and less discriminating, and the man who had ordered his death was the ruler of a private khanate.

Maybe Charlee was right. Maybe you had to fight against them with every last weapon. Maybe pragmatism didn't work. Perhaps it truly was a struggle between good and evil.

He was sorry to be in Washington, where he made no difference. Chasing ghosts. He wished he were in the embassy in Rakhman's capital, where he could at least send off honest cables and from where he could launch himself into the tide of events. He took another sip of coffee, found it bitter, and turned the pages, moving through the sections, passing inconsequential sports scores and a style feature about activist women who were organizing an ambitious pro-choice rally on the Mall on Saturday. Then, on page three of the business section, he got his second shock of the day.

This time it was an article about a mammoth oil-and-gas joint venture whose terms had just been concluded between Argent Oil, a U.S. consortium, and several Central Asian governments. Argent Oil had pledged to use Western technology to develop vast, untapped fields in a manner that was efficient and ecologically sound. The reason the deal included more than one government was that the deposits were so huge they spilled across three borders. But the main reserves lay in the country that had only just undergone a change of government. The provisional head of state, Ali Ali-Rakhman had already assured the business community that he saw the deal as beneficial to his people and that he intended to honor it without amendment.

In a sidebar, Sen. Oliver S. Cromwell told a reporter that "this agreement is not only of tremendous potential financial advantage to the United States, but it also marks a new spirit of enlightened cooperation with fledgling states struggling to find their way into the family of nations." The sidebar noted that Senator Cromwell's support had been instrumental in securing the contract for the U.S. business community against stiff European competition, and that Cromwell had pledged to do all he could to help American businessmen overcome outdated bureaucratic hurdles to trade with exciting new partners abroad.

"Maggot," Ritter said. He closed the paper and just leaned down over the counter, head resting on his right hand. He could not help thinking of Ben with his brains splashed all over a mountain road. Someone with the gift of perspective would say, with no disrespect intended, that diplomacy on the world stage had unavoidable costs. But, to Ritter, it seemed now that Ben had died so that rich men could get richer. He knew there was no direct tie-in. But it didn't matter. In his world, Argent Oil had Ben's blood on their hands.

And Rakhman. The bastard would get enough money over and under the counter to keep the locals happy with bread and circuses *and* to send billions to Switzerland. Ritter laughed. For the Americans involved, what the deal really meant was a chance to turn back the clock to the days of low labor costs, no pollution controls whatsoever, and accounting procedures no single government would ever unravel. It was a deal no patriotic businessman could pass up.

Ritter sat down in the gray light, soul hurting far worse than his stiff knee. After all he had seen, he still wanted to believe there was justice in the world. But he couldn't find it anymore.

Rakhman and his white-haired, white-faced henchman would never pay for what they had done. They were far away, with an entire country at their feet. In all their bloody glory.

Ritter drank his second cup of coffee without tasting it, wondering if Charlee was right, if he hadn't wasted his life after all. Perhaps, in the end, there just wasn't much a single man could do. But, if he had been able to choose one thing to accomplish in his life, it would have been to avenge the death of Ben Williams.

Two men stood in an abandoned roller rink on Long Island, eating fried chicken from a cardboard bucket and watching a third man who was bound to a pole. The third man's head slumped forward as though his spine had been removed, and his hair, skin, and clothing were painted with blood.

"That little shit-breath," Mitya said. "I hate men like that. No pride whatsoever."

Zhan chewed off a moist, wonderful piece of meat. He had never eaten chicken with so much flesh on the bones. He let his Russian colleague ramble and complain.

"You know, we're not eating enough," Mitya said. "I'm not getting enough food to keep up my strength."

"You're getting enough food. Everything's expensive here."

"We have to eat. And I need something to drink."

"All of our expenses must be accounted for," Zhan said flatly.

"Shit. And more shit. A man has to eat."

Zhan looked down at the nearly empty bucket. "We have plenty of food."

"Maybe for you. You fucking jailbirds are used to starving."

"You're not a jailbird?"

"I didn't grow up in the fucking camps. I had a normal childhood."

"It's Rakhman's money. Your people are bankrupt. You're lucky to be eating at all."

"Shit."

Zhan let it go. He had already spoken more than he liked to. He did not want to establish any human bond with the Russian, since the odds were good that he would have to dispose of him at the end of the mission. He had killed friends before, but he didn't care for it. In any case, the Russian would never be a friend. He was too stupid and crude.

"You and your camel-fucker friends," Mitya said.

On a shared impulse, the two men turned their attention back to the man they had tied to the pole. The pole served as a support for the sagging roof. Something about the slovenliness of the whole arrangement bothered Zhan. He much preferred working in his own country, where he was entirely in control. It was interesting to see America, but he didn't like operating like this.

"Think he's hungry?" Mitya asked with a smirk. He scooped up a chicken leg and walked over to the prisoner.

"Hey. Shit-breath. You awake?"

No response.

Mitya teased the food under the man's nose.

Slight movement. Nothing that was any fun. The chicken leg had picked up a trace of blood, but Mitya ignored the stain and bit into it.

"I don't think this shit's going to give us anything," he said. "We need to get to Washington and deal directly with that son of a bitch and his daughter."

"I'll decide what we do and when we do it," Zhan said calmly. But he knew his companion was right.

Without warning, Mitya slapped the prisoner with his free hand. It was a very hard blow and the sound sent a small bird fluttering in the eaves.

"You waking up for me, you piece of scum?"

Zhan sighed. "Get out of the way. Eat your chicken. I'll do it."

It was time to finish and go.

Zhan cradled the prisoner's head in his hands as though he were about to kiss him. The young man's eyes were open, but dulled.

"Listen to me," Zhan said. "I want to help you. I know you want to live. All you have to do is tell us where the photographs are."

Zhan could not tell whether his words made any sense to

the beaten man in front of him. He reached into his pocket and pulled out a cigarette lighter.

With the quickness of a boxer, he grabbed the prisoner by the hair and yanked so that the young man's skull stretched away from the pole. With his other hand, Zhan snapped on the lighter and held it under the prisoner's lower lip. His victim came alive with a nightmare scream and instantly fought to free himself. But Zhan clutched him by the hair.

"That's good," Mitya said. "That's real technique."

Zhan covered the lighter and released the prisoner's head. The young man groaned and sobbed.

"I'm glad you're with me now," Zhan said. "You really must listen to me. We know all about you and General Morozov. He's a bad man, a traitor to his country and his friends." Zhan softened his voice even more. "But you . . . you're just a helpless victim in all of this. We know that Morozov talked you into bringing out the photographs. It's natural enough. We understand. Everybody wants to make a little money, to get a new start. You made an honest mistake. But you must tell us who else is involved and where the photographs are right now. Otherwise, I'm going to kill you." Zhan sighed. "Who else was part of this operation?"

The prisoner tried to speak. His lips stank of ruination, and it clearly pained him to move his mouth even slightly. Zhan began to feel sorry for him. What kind of life could such a weak man have had? A man who was no man at all?

"Nobody," the prisoner said finally. "Nobody."

Zhan stroked the side of the young man's head as if he were petting a beloved dog. "All right. If nobody else is involved, who has the photos? Does Morozov have them personally, or are you holding them for him? Where are they?"

The prisoner wanted to speak, ached to speak. His eyes reminded Zhan of the eyes of a young girl who had been put into a boxcar full of criminals, of which he had been one, on the line from Vladimir to the Urals in the good old days. By the end of the trip, the girl's eyes had looked exactly like this. A good-natured, laughing guard later told a friend of Zhan's that the girl had been the daughter of someone who had crossed

Brezhnev's son-in-law, and Zhan had been dazzled by the incisiveness of the punishment.

"Don't know," the prisoner mumbled. "If I knew . . ."

Zhan shook his head. "Why are you so unreasonable? Consider this from our point of view. You've been in America for months, you're almost an American. So let me explain this in a way you can understand. Think of our superiors as businessmen who are trying to protect their interests. They're good people, the salt of the earth. And Morozov betrayed them. With your help." Zhan laughed softly. "Did you really think we wouldn't find out? Or that America was so far away you'd be safe? You silly man." Zhan shook his head. "Do you know how much damage you've already done? You have everyone excited. Everybody wants those photographs. Not just the Americans. Even the no-good Russian government bastards who just can't leave well enough alone, the fucking so-called democrats. Do you know what might happen if that wicked man in the Kremlin ever got his hands on those photographs? He could use them to embarrass good people, to blackmail men who gave their entire lives to serving their country. He might even give them to the Americans. And then where would we be? Careers ruined, families destroyed, great opportunities missed. And you and Morozov were willing to do that for money. What a small man you are. I really don't believe you understand what a mess you've made. Do you?"

The prisoner didn't respond. His eyes remained open, but his mind, his soul, seemed to have escaped. The thought made Zhan furious.

"Just look at you," he continued, speaking softly, in a voice that might have been telling stories to children at bedtime. "I'm afraid fate has not been very kind to you. Such a well-educated young man. Even working in a bookstore. And ambitious. A waiter on the side. But I wonder if right now you don't wish you had stayed home in Moscow with your safe little job in your cozy little archive. Where you could read all you wanted—you like to read, don't you?"

Zhan grabbed the young man's hair again. The prisoner responded with a grunt. In an instant, the cigarette lighter reappeared, alive with flame. This time, Zhan positioned the young man's head so that his downturned face paralleled the floor.

Zhan centered the lighter under the young man's left eye.

His prisoner jerked so violently that the roof of the building quaked above the pole. His scream was unique and surprisingly powerful.

Zhan held tightly to the prisoner's scalp, cooking the eye. When he felt satisfied, he closed the top of the lighter again. He stepped back and folded his arms.

The young man sagged and groaned.

"See what you've done?" Zhan asked. "Now it's going to be harder for you to read. I don't understand why you're being so unreasonable." He shifted his weight from one leg to the other, a habit left over from standing in endless lines and formations in the camps. "Don't you want to help good people fix the mess you've made? Do you really want the Americans to become angry at honest men who are just trying to do some honest business? Morozov's such a bad man. It's a shame you ever fell in with him. He's using those photographs to make good men look like murderers. When they were only trying to do their duty. And you know Westerners don't like to do business with men who might be seen as murderers. It's just so embarrassing for everyone. And it's your fault."

Mitya stepped up, licking his fingers and scratching at his nose. "Hey, let me try that thing with the lighter."

Zhan ignored him, stepping in closer to the prisoner. Something brown was seething from the young man's mouth, dripping down over his clothing. It looked filthy, revolting.

"This is not my nature," Zhan said wistfully. "But you're forcing my hand. Where are the photographs?"

"I don't know," the prisoner said with astonishing lucidity. "I gave them to Morozov. I don't know where they are now." His cooked lip split and bled.

Mitya fetched himself a last piece of chicken. Between bites, he told Zhan, "Ask shit-breath about Bernshtein."

Zhan bent closer, smelling the young man's dissolution. "Could you answer my colleague's question? What about the talented Mr. Bernshtein? Is he involved in this with Morozov?"

The prisoner seemed, inexplicably, to have returned to a

higher level of cognition. His spoiled eye spread egg white over his cheek and the side of his nose.

"Bernshtein . . . ," he said, "just a fool . . . he didn't know . . . never knew anything . . . the girl . . ."

"Yes," Zhan said. "Tell me about the girl. She knows everything, right?"

The young man moved his head slightly. He might have been trying to shake it. "He protected her . . . her father . . . do anything for her . . . doing it all for her."

"He's going to make me cry," Mitya said. "Wait till you see how I protect that little slut."

Zhan began stroking the young man's temple again. But his hand was heavier this time, at the edge of a threat.

"Tell me. Does the girl know anything or not?"

"Father didn't want her to know . . . he . . . would've died for her."

Mitya tossed the last gnawed chicken bones on the floor. "This guy's worthless. He was probably fucking her, too. Were you fucking her, shit-breath? That little whore? I'll bet you were." He spat into the shadows. "Let's get it over with. It's getting cold in here."

Zhan looked at the young man. It was disgusting how low the human animal could go. A man needed to cultivate his strength, his dignity. Or he ended up like this.

For the sake of symmetry, Zhan burned out the young man's other eye. He took his time, practicing his skills, making the best of things.

Mitya watched in open fascination. "The cruelty of the fucking Orient," he said admiringly.

Zhan snorted. "I learned how to do this from a Ukrainian."

The young man screamed himself into unconsciousness. His body retained only the form enforced upon it by the rope fixing him to the pole.

"Wasted effort," Mitya said.

But it wasn't a wasted effort from Zhan's perspective. It was important to be thorough, to do everything right, not to make any mistakes. He knew that, if anything went wrong, he would be killed, his years of good service to Rakhman notwithstanding. It was the way of things, and a man accepted it. But it was, in the end, better to live than to die.

His sole worry was that Morozov would sell the pictures to the Americans before he could get his hands on them. When he had last spoken to his contact from the Russian embassy two days before, the deal still had not gone through. But the embassy man was afraid. And unwilling to do the manly thing and approach Morozov directly. Or just kill the bastard.

So Zhan followed his orders precisely. But he was anxious to get to Washington. He had suspected all along that this young man was nothing but a tool that had already been used and set aside.

He reminded himself to phone his contact again as soon as the opportunity presented itself. To find out if there had been any new developments. And for the pleasure of making the weak-voiced creature from the embassy cringe. He despised all forms of weakness.

Zhan drew a 9-mm pistol from beneath his coat, primed it, and casually put a bullet through the young man's forehead. The shot made the old building quiver, and a panic of birds careened overhead.

"You should've let me wake him," Mitya said. "I like it better when they're conscious."

The two men looked at the corpse. Both of them had seen more impressive deaths. But there was always something about killing that reached you on a higher plane.

Col. Jeb Bates sat in a Pentagon men's room in a splendid mood. He had not come to the men's room out of any pressing need, but it was the nearest spot where he could spend a few minutes in peace and privacy, away from the hubbub of his office. And he needed a little time to think through the implications of his remarkable good fortune.

Charles Turner, the individual Ritter had asked him to trace, had come up immediately as an unaccounted-for service member from the Korean War. Air Force first lieutenant and a navigator on a B-29 knocked down near the mouth of the Yalu. No confirmation of death, no body ever recovered, and he had not been one of the returned POWs. It was a classic MIA case.

Ritter was turning out to be a giant rabbit's foot. Although Bates didn't know what else Ritter knew at this point, the younger man was obviously headed in the right direction. And, as the Vietnamese said, a lucky man spreads luck. Thanks to the quest for information about Charles Turner, an archivist from Bates's office had struck gold. The man had been so excited he had lifted his snout from his research long enough to run to a public telephone and report to Bates in a voice of wonder that he had uncovered something they had all missed, the sort of thing you had no reason to anticipate and that you learned only through serendipity:

The case of Capt. Luther Schwartz.

Captain Schwartz had been a hot-dog F-86 pilot in Korea. Until the morning he overstayed his welcome near an antiaircraft artillery emplacement. Schwartz had been declared dead on evidence that had seemed convincing enough at the time, and his wife had remarried. She was currently Mrs. Lawrence Whyte of Pebble Beach, California, and her daughter from her first marriage had been given the second husband's name as a child. The daughter had come a long way in the world.

It was a connection of which Bates would never have dreamed, and it gave him a very different perspective on Charlee Whyte: the little girl whose daddy didn't come home. It was classic, and it reminded Bates, for perhaps the thousandth time in his career, that knowledge truly was power. The Honorable Ms. Whyte was *not* going to beat him.

It was time to get back to the office. There was a great deal of work involved in raising the dead.

NINE

Nadya walked the rain-pecked streets, wary of human contact. This neighborhood was markedly worse than her own, and she always felt afraid when she came to visit. But she never hesitated to come.

As soon as the American had gone off in his uniform, trailing reassurances, she had borrowed an old trench coat from his closet. Now she lofted it higher onto her shoulders, hoping to appear as inconspicuous and unfeminine as possible. Black people frightened her. She did not understand their smiles, and she had learned quickly not to trust their male willingness to help her. In her own neighborhood, which she aspired to leave as soon as things were in order, she at least felt that her cries for help might be answered. But here, in these depths, she sensed a casual evil that made the worst streets of Moscow seem soft and humane. America was a place of immeasurably powerful contradictions. The trick, as she understood clearly, was to end up on the right side of those contradictions.

On the corners, young men, garish and jobless, called to her in a language that only faintly resembled English. Cars slowed and men in dark glasses watched her. Sometimes they lowered a window and called out, otherwise they simply drove off with fantastically loud music thumping the world like a big fist. Even the children spoke in mammoth, swaggering obscenities.

You had to end up on the right side of the contradictions, no matter what it cost.

A man in a fine topcoat and a hat that reminded her of the hats African dictators wore in photographs watched calmly as two other men dragged a huge-eyed boy into a playground and began beating him in the stomach and face. Nadya lowered her eyes and crossed to the far side of the street. Behind her back, a woman's sudden voice howled rage. She might have been accusing the boy's tormentors, but not one word was intelligible.

You had to end up on the right side of the contradictions.

She crossed a broader street and entered a building that she would once have assumed to be uninhabited. Before her eyes had been educated by this new world. All of the building's ground-floor windows had been smashed in, and the upper floors showed cardboard and rags in place of curtains.

In the hallway, she stepped over a snoring woman in a fur coat. A wig, golden with chemicals, had slipped from the woman's cropped scalp and lay in her waste.

Nadya climbed the stairs, passing histories of desolation. Even with her uneven command of English, she recognized that much of the graffiti was misspelled. But the messages were generally clear.

She knocked on a door at the back of the top floor. No one answered, there was no feeling of life here. She rapped again, harder, concerned because the American officer, Chris, and the horrible woman had made her come away without all of her keys.

No answer.

On impulse, she tried the door and found it unlocked. She shuddered. She had told him countless times about leaving the door unlocked. But he never felt the least fear. And, when he was drunk, he never felt anything at all.

She could tell he had been drinking hard as soon as she stepped into the apartment. His smell had been doused with alcohol. A dirty window gave light, and she wandered past a shoe and a table cluttered with a chemist's paraphernalia. She noted that the radio–tape player was gone and wondered whether he had sold it for more drinking money or if it had been stolen while he lay passed out.

She sensed him now, knew that he had made it as far as the bedroom this time. But she did not go to him immediately. She went into the kitchen alcove and began to clean up. She was not particular about the details and the effort did not take long. She did only enough to bring him back to the edge of civilization. Then she sat down at the tiny kitchen table—the one thing reminiscent of Russia—and wrote out careful instructions in a clear hand. She sighed and went into the bathroom for a moment. He had fouled it, but that could wait. She finished and sought the bedroom.

He had not gotten to the bed. He lay on the wooden floor in light the color of ashes. As she stepped closer, a dark living thing the size of a coin hurried away from him and found a gap between the wall and the floor.

Nadya stood over him for a moment, calculating how long he had been this way. She had not seen him for two nights and a day. He had been worried about everything and she had knowingly given him money. Assuring him that everything would be all right.

The gray that had come early to his temples spiked his beard now. He had a heavy beard, a man's beard. Gently, she sat down with her back to the bed and cradled his head on her thigh. He did not awaken.

"It's all right," she said in Russian, speaking to a hurt child. "I love you, and you love me, and everything will be all right." She stroked his hair, looking down at the near-ruin of the only man she had ever loved, the only man she would ever love. The man for whom she had done everything and for whom she would do anything.

"Don't worry," she told him. "We're smarter than they are."

He murmured once, but never woke during her stay. She remained by him as long as she could, then substituted a pillow for her thigh. She took half of the money still in her purse and worked it deep into his pocket, just as she had always done in Moscow. Then she kissed him on the lips, drinking in the taste

of him that was real and true and that steeled her for everything else.

She was about to leave when she felt a sting of worry. Stepping over Volodya's heavy body, she opened the closet door
and bent to pry behind his clutter. Glancing backward to ensure
that they were alone, she used her fingernails to loosen the
board that hid the private place they had built together.

The envelope was still there, wrapped in double layers of
plastic. She did not bother to check its contents. She could tell
by the look of it that no one had disturbed it. Squeamish of
the creatures that lived in these walls, she tested her fingers
down under the packet until she felt the unmistakable metal
cold of the pistol, then rapidly withdrew her hand, relieved.
She feared that he might one day sell the pistol when he ran
out of money. Carefully, she relaid the board and massed her
beloved's possessions above it again.

The light shifted and covered Volodya like a layer of water.
His face looked peaceful now, and it made her think of the
American officer whose face was at once fresh and disturbed.
The American was decent and foolish and typical of intelligent
men in mistaking sexual energy for passion. Volodya wouldn't
care about that, if he ever found out. He had not even minded
when she married Bernshtein. He knew that it had all been for
him. He understood what it took to survive.

"Where is she?" Charlee asked. Her face merely looked disappointed, too tired to be angry.

Ritter took one last discreet look out onto his balcony: concrete, brick, iron rails, but no flesh.

"No idea. She promised me she'd wait here."

Charlee almost smiled. "I suppose neither of us is as magnetic as we used to be." Then the smile crashed. "Oh, God,
Chris. I've got to find her. This is serious."

"I know it's serious," he said, hobbling through his rooms.
"Her stuff's still in the bedroom. She'll probably come back."

"I wish I knew where she went." Charlee looked terrible,
deprived of sleep and all joy. "Chris, you've got to watch her.
Don't let her out of your sight from now on."

"Charlee—"

"Got anything to drink?"

Ritter shrugged. "There's some Orvieto in the fridge."

Charlee shook her head and grimaced. "You really live down-market. Don't you?"

The phone rang. Ritter hastened to answer it. His leg felt as though splinters of bone were stabbing up into his brain. It was getting worse, not better.

"Ritter." He waited to hear Nadya's voice.

"Is this Maj. Christopher Ritter?"

"Speaking."

"Major, are you aware that you had a therapy appointment at two o'clock? You know, if you miss two appointments in a row, we'll have to report you to your commanding officer."

"I'll bear that in mind."

Zhan and Mitya sat in a fast-food corral along the Garden State Parkway. Their meal was finished, and stained paper and slops covered the little tabletop between them.

"Let's go," Zhan said. "I need to make a phone call."

"I'm not done with my cola. Can't you relax a little? Look— this is a great place."

Zhan didn't reply. He despised his Russian colleague more with each passing hour, contemptuous of the other man's indiscipline and self-indulgence. Besides, Mitya was unbearably vain about his knowledge of America, which was based on a single previous visit. He was, finally, too Russian.

Zhan suspected that he had Russian blood himself. Based solely on his partly Slavic features. But he had no inkling as to the precise identity of his parents. He had grown up in a series of orphanages that were nothing but schools for apprentice criminals, then he had been hastened to a prison camp for underage offenders. For participating in the rape of a younger boy who died of internal hemorrhaging. Among other things. Zhan had genuinely not realized at the time that such a thing was wrong, since, when he had been younger, he had in his turn been the victim. Now, of course, he wouldn't think of doing such a thing. But he accepted his past without shame. It meant nothing.

He would have liked to know the identity of his parents,

though. Out of simple curiosity. He hoped that his Slavic features, evident under the snowstorm of his hair and skin, were Ukrainian. Or anything else but Russian. Perhaps one of his parents had been a Balt. Plenty of them had been sent to the camps. Maybe he wasn't a Slav at all.

He hated working with the Russians. But it was still necessary. When you had to reach out into distant places, only Moscow had the means and expertise. The Russians knew how to bring people in from Canada, how to arrange for vehicles, how to move within the American system. And that meant that even the deputy of a man as powerful as Rakhman had to endure slights and insults. For the present.

Mitya did not have the manners to chew with his mouth closed. Even camp orphans learned that. Painfully.

"Look at that one," Mitya said disgustedly. "Just look at her. You know that the Americans make fun of Russian women? They think Russian women are all big and fat. But did you ever see a Russian woman who looks like that? It's a disgrace. Her husband ought to take her out and shoot her."

Zhan followed Mitya's stare. The woman in question was huge. She had covered her shame inadequately, and great tides of flesh rolled forward as she walked, her terrible secrets exposed by the clinging fabric she wore. Her hair was unwashed and the expression on her face as she lofted her tray of food was that of an animal about to feast on carrion. One of the immediate surprises America held for Zhan had been the frequency with which he encountered such women. He had believed that all American women were proud, lascivious, and fine, like the great Miss Julia Roberts, whom he had never tired of watching on videotape. He was ashamed of his naïveté now. He had believed that the women of America, sculpted and magnificent, wore excellent clothing and jewelry even to perform household tasks. But it was clear that the glorious Miss Julia Roberts was only a tool of American propaganda.

Reality was sometimes not a very nice thing.

"I think," Zhan said, "that the husband of this woman must be very sad."

Mitya snickered. "It'd be like fucking a corpse that's been bloating in the sun for a week."

But not all of the women of America were so terrible. Zhan liked the way the young girls behind the counter smiled pleasantly and exhibited a deep desire to please. The girl who had taken their order might have become a great courtesan.

"Some American women are attractive," Zhan said.

Mitya grunted. "They're all whores. Like the Morozova slut. Except that she's better looking."

Zhan, too, had seen the photographs of General Morozov's daughter. She was a dangerously attractive woman.

"I'll bet she made a bundle," Mitya went on. "When she was working the hard-currency hotels."

Zhan breathed deeply. He was always disappointed in his fellow man. No man could be trusted fully. And no woman could be trusted at all. There was nothing on this earth but disappointment and betrayal, and a man had to live with that expectation.

"I'm going outside to call our contact," Zhan said, rising. "Don't be long."

"I'm still hungry."

"You've had enough to eat. We've spent the entire food allowance for today."

"Don't be such a shit."

"No more. It's time to go. I'll meet you at the car."

Mitya stood up, too. "You go ahead. I've got to piss."

Zhan turned from his companion and walked past the impossibly fat woman. Her rat-faced husband wore a baseball cap and a handsome satin jacket with script across the back. A faded T-shirt stretched over the woman's consequential breasts. The great block letters were legible even to Zhan: I'M WITH STUPID.

The brazenness of it jolted him. Any man who would allow his wife to wear such a message was no man at all. Zhan wanted to slap the husband, to demand an explanation for such folly. And the woman deserved no less than death.

Americans, Zhan thought. It bewildered him that such a vulgar, unappealing people could be so powerful and rich as a nation and that they could live so well. He went out into the cold air, already attuned enough to know that the indoor phones would be occupied or at least insufficiently private, but that, in such weather, an outdoor telephone would suit his needs perfectly. He went around the building, past the metal splendor of the parking lot, to the service station, telling himself that the Americans were almost as hopeless as the Russians.

But the phones worked. He got through on the first attempt, careful with the instructions he had copied down. The voice at the other end sounded as if it had been waiting for him for a long time.

"Is there news?" Zhan asked.

The voice hesitated the way men sometimes do when they are overly anxious to speak. Then it said:

"There's plenty of news. Too much news. Morozov's dead. And nobody knows what happened. Somebody planted a bomb in an office."

"That's bad news."

The voice laughed. With a mean little laugh. "Well, not for you. Morozov was apparently on his way to sell the photographs."

Zhan was quick. "Did he have them with him?"

The voice hesitated, then said, "We don't know. Maybe not. Anyway, you'd be dead if he'd handed them over. Now you've at least got a chance."

"I thought you were supposed to be working an angle of your own."

The voice waited again, choosing words carefully. Zhan had a strong sense of the man he had never met: self-important, officious, and finally, weak. A man who could be moved by just a little fear.

"It hasn't worked out. At least not yet. You still have the responsibility."

"What about the daughter? Is she alive?"

"The daughter. Well, she's a problem, too."

"Why?" An enormous truck rolled by, its motor-sound solid and rich.

"She's disappeared. She's not at her apartment. We don't know where she is."

"We'll have to find her."

"*You*'ll have to find her," the voice said quickly.

Zhan paused for a moment, thinking. Then he asked flatly, "Do you have anything else?"

"No. We don't know where she is. She hasn't been back to her apartment. There's no information."

"I'll have a look for myself."

"You have to find her." The man's growing anxiety made it clear that, if they failed, Zhan would not be the only participant to suffer.

"I'll find her," Zhan said finally. "And I'm sure she'll cooperate."

Mitya stood at the urinal for several minutes, waiting for the stars to line up. The rest room made him smile and shake his head. It was ridiculously, needlessly clean, as though Americans were so ashamed of what their bodies did that they had to make a toilet area into a miniature resort.

He tracked a pair of likely targets, but neither of them worked out because there were always others in the room. Only when the third prospect locked himself into one of the little stalls did things begin to look promising. Only one other man was in the room, and he stood at the row of sinks, washing his hands.

The extraneous man pushed out through the swinging doors and Mitya listened to the universe. He heard only the pathetic noises of his target, an elderly man, dressed well enough to have a full wallet. Mitya positioned himself, waiting ready, hoping no intruder would come to interfere.

The toilet flushed and moments later the old man unlocked the stall door. Mitya moved with hard-learned speed. He shoved the man back into the stall, knocking him rearward so that he fell awkwardly onto the toilet. His aged eyes spoke wonder.

Without a break in his movements, Mitya closed one paw behind the man's neck and smashed the other into his victim's forehead with a tremendous thrust. The old man's neck cracked with the sound of a plank snapping in two. Mitya released him.

His victim slumped sideward, almost fell. But Mitya had control of him again, gripping him differently, hunting for his wallet.

The pockets were empty except for a bit of change and a handkerchief.

Mitya was about to beat the corpse in his rage when his hand grazed a bulge at the man's waist. Quickly, he yanked out the man's shirt and undershirt.

The old bastard had strapped a money pouch under his clothing.

The item was secured with some new gripping material that parted with a tearing sound. Inside, green-and-white U.S. currency had been tucked neatly behind a stack of plastic cards. Mitya pocketed the money without counting it. It felt like enough to give him a margin of freedom from his companion's stinginess.

He moved with great speed, not particularly wanting to expand the range of violence to include any intruders. He propped the old man up on the seat, leaning him backward and balancing him so that he wouldn't collapse on the floor. Then he locked the stall and climbed over the top with an agility that would have surprised anyone who had only seen his bulk.

He pushed out through the swinging doors just as a father and son entered.

Lucky shits, Mitya thought.

He strolled back over to the food counter. His turn came in a moment and he spoke to the smiling girl in his very best English:

"Big hamburger, big potatoes, big cola, okay?"

Sen. Oliver Cromwell brushed his hand over the mane of the wooden horse the decorator had installed in his living room and looked out over his city. The roof of the National Archives cut a near horizon behind which the dome of the Capitol bulked white against the gray sky. Occasional raindrops tested the floor-to-ceiling windows and spotted the marble balcony. This glassed edge of his suite was a commanding place to stand, a spot to which you could lead a woman with a wine-glass in her hand, where you could settle your hands upon her shoulders and test her reaction without overly compromising yourself. This small, spectacular corner of the world belonged to him, and it echoed power and money.

In the end, of course, money was the key to power. Money was the most powerful living thing—and so few people even realized that it was alive. Or that it could betray you as easily as could a woman.

The senator had begun life as a grocer's son in a desert town a few miles beyond the end of the world: a son of the American Southwest. Easterners thought so highly of his home earth now, making a cult out of its cooking and furniture the like of which his childhood had never enjoyed. But he had known early that he was destined to leave the sand and dust behind.

He had worked hard from an early age. He could smell the world beyond the world he knew, like the mark of someone else's woman left on the sheets. Aproned, he smiled mightily behind his father's counter, making change for oil-field roustabouts in town to stock up on snuff, canned peanuts, and beer. He studied diligently because of what he might gain and played sports for the same reason. He chose his life's course so early that he could never pinpoint the inspiration. He thought he might, perhaps, be president one day. He was certain he would be at least a U.S. senator.

He interrupted his studies at the state university to volunteer for the Korean War since, in those days, a shirker could not build a political career. Tapped for officer candidate school, he went gladly, since an officer's rank would better suit his résumé and the course also meant a delay of several months in shipping out for Korea, where things were going badly. In the end, he didn't go to Korea at all, but found a comfortable job at Far East Command in Japan. He worked intelligence, counting Chinese Army units, and he counted among his friends and mentors a number of officers with the wherewithal to lift an earnest, talented young man out of the dusty world of the state university system. First Lt. Oliver Cromwell left the Army with ribbons and GI benefits and a place at William and Mary for the completion of his undergraduate degree, from whence he rose to Harvard for his degree in law. William and Mary softened his accent, and Harvard hardened his will. He made friends handsomely.

Then he almost lost it all. He married an only daughter from an oil family back home, convinced that her beauty would adorn his life as richly as would her means. It quickly turned into a hellish marriage, cankered with embarrassments, that sickened for two decades—until his career was secure, the times more liberal, the children grown, and he had amassed a fortune of his own. His wife, who imagined herself a star in the Washington sky, had lugged into town every regional crudeness, and she had merely provided comic relief for those whom she sought to rival. Now, remarried to a rancher, she lived well—and blessedly far away. She only rarely visited the house in Chevy Chase from which her lawyers had driven him.

Life after Rose had been a marvelous thing for a time. Divorced, he found his eligibility celebrated, and he exploited the situation with appetite. He had a good ride. Until the past few years. In the last election, a steely, unfathomable woman had almost unseated him, accusing him of nearly everything he had ever done. It was a witch-hunt atmosphere in which once-minor derelictions received attention as undue as it was ungracious. It was only his years with Charlee that had finally allowed him to sense the woman's weak spots and bring her down.

But he had come damned close to losing the election. And he found himself teetering on the edge of bankruptcy at the same time. He had grown too relaxed, too trusting. He had taken his power, in all of its forms, for granted, certain that no one would ever try to cheat him. He had believed that the men with whom he played golf and flew down to Mexico for the occasional interesting weekend would take care of him. Then, one after another, the insider tips had gone sour. Friendships curdled. And he had missed the warning signs, smitten by a smart, sexually incandescent young woman who made him feel half his age.

He had come home a day early from a failed attempt to beg a loan and found his beloved's lover sitting naked in front of his television, drinking his Biondi Santi Brunello from the bottle, while the young woman lay sprawled on the senatorial bed, pornographically stained and snoring.

It had been something of a low point.

But he had been tough. He had scrambled—effectively—to hold on to his essential properties, and he learned a hard lesson in the process. In order to survive he had had to do things he had always scorned for men whom he would once have black-balled from any club to which he belonged. He began to choose his friends and business associates differently, and in time, he recovered a bit financially. But the days of happy extravagance were behind him, and it hurt his nature. He had spent his entire adult life serving his country, and what did he have to show for it?

Sen. Oliver Cromwell stared out over the city that had loved and betrayed him. He lifted his hand from the silly Chinese horse that was supposed to hint artfully of his Southwestern roots—the horse didn't even look like a damned horse—and he poised the hand before him as though holding a glass of whiskey. But the gesture was one of habit. There was no whiskey at the moment. He was sober, hangover transcended, and he was determined not to have a drink until after his next guest had departed.

It was terribly bad timing. He was in danger of missing a health-care vote on the Hill, one his constituents would be watching. But the meeting was, in the end, more important.

Oliver Cromwell knew that, if he blew this one, he would not have to worry about the next election. When you played for top stakes, you paid the top price. Lost billions meant lost life.

It staggered him a bit to think about it. Amazing to be in such a position. A U.S. senator. And all that. How complex life was. And how miserably disappointing, in the end.

Money. It brought all the worthwhile things in its wake. Power. Women. Deference. Convenience. If money could not buy love, it could certainly excite adoration. And Cromwell had never known a woman whose affair with one of those marginal artist types had lasted beyond a few splashy orgasms. The women who could not be reached by the proper application of money were statistically insignificant.

Had he had it all to do over again, he would have aimed first at fortune, then at political power. He would have been more concerned with the essentials, and less with the superficials.

And then there was Charlee. Odd woman. Prickly as a cactus,

hungry as a coyote, and blind as an armadillo. He might have called her queer, had that word not been so unfairly disfigured. Charlee genuinely did not care about money. But then she didn't have to. Her stepfather could have written her a check to buy the third-world country of her choice. And he would have done it, too, had Charlee asked. Childless, the old bastard doted on an adopted daughter who despised him.

But wasn't that the way it always was? The men and women who had that kind of money didn't have to care about it. It was hateful to find oneself an outsider, after so many years of imagined insider status.

Cromwell looked at his watch. Bound to miss the vote. Where was the insolent Russian son of a bitch?

The phone rang as if willed to life.

It was the front desk.

"Excuse me, Senator. There's a Mr. Black here to see you."

"Send him up. And thank you, Custis."

Cromwell clutched his imaginary drink and closed his eyes. When you lie down with dogs, he told himself, you are apt to get up with Republicans. Or worse.

He answered the door. Chorney came in without a word. Looking dark and miserable, as usual. Gene pool all shot to hell over there. Killed the best, didn't they?

"You know, Dan," Cromwell began, "I am uncomfortable with meetings under circumstances such as this."

The Russian ignored him, taking a seat on the long sofa covered in Belgian tapestry. The little creep who had done the room had combined the sofa with mighty leather chairs and a room-size Farahan that gave just the manly, resourced look Cromwell wanted.

"Sometimes there's no substitute for a face-to-face meeting," Chorney said. He no longer bothered addressing Cromwell as "Senator," and his English was that of a tough, educated businessman.

"Start talking. I'm needed on the Hill."

Chorney looked at him with intolerable condescension. No people skills. "I assume you have not recovered the photographs?"

"I'm working on it," Cromwell said, annoyance plain in his voice.

Chorney nodded. "The bottom line is we can't afford to fail in that regard. So we're taking other measures."

Cromwell looked up in alarm.

"You go on with your quest," Chorney continued. "All in all, it would be better for you if you came up with the photos. Your stock's down, at the moment. But we're putting a backup system in place."

"What 'backup system'? What're you talking about?"

Chorney folded his arms. "We've brought in some people of our own."

Cromwell turned on the man. "Now wait a minute—"

"Researchers, you might say. Specialists." Chorney unfolded his arms and brushed a hand over the fabric of the sofa, as if considering its purchase. "The kind of people who can uncover secrets."

"You just wait one minute. If we're talking about some kind of goons, I'm not going to stand for that sort of thing."

Chorney looked up from the sofa. Calmly. "You have no say in the matter." Then he smiled, indulging a child. "You have to understand the role you play in this. You are not unimportant. But you are not indispensable. Our relationship would be more functional if you were to grasp that."

"Without me . . . ," Cromwell said, struggling to keep his temper, "without me you'd never get the government to approve the provisions of this deal. *I* put the package together for you. *I* brought the right people together. I'm the one who knows—"

"I know, I know. Every man seeks recognition. Hegel, you know. Marx took the wrong bits, all the wrong bits. But that's hardly pertinent." Chorney sighed, as if longing for books and a respite from this harsh world of deeds. "Try a bit of humility. Think of yourself as what you are: a paid employee. Well paid, I grant you. But no more than that. You control neither the money nor the resources. You are simply a facilitator. You add no value."

"I will not have foreign thugs running around here. You'll

only make things worse. Now *you* tell *me*, damn it, who killed Morozov? And who tried to kill my protégé? What's going on?"

Chorney held up his hands. He had a different way of holding up his hands for every situation. This time, the palms extended vertically toward Cromwell in a gesture of pushing something away.

"I thought perhaps you would tell me. *We* didn't do it. *My* people were shocked. And alarmed. It raises many questions. To say nothing of bringing us unwanted attention."

"An understatement." Cromwell wanted to gain control of the conversation. But Chorney was such a bastard, and getting worse every time they met. Cromwell did not think much of the New Russia. "Every damned federal agency with badge-carriers is nosing in on this. It was the most stupid damned thing I ever heard of."

"I told you—*we* didn't do it. But my people want to know who did. And what's the connection to the photographs? Why isn't there anything about Morozov on the news?"

"Charlee's kept quiet about it. They're still sifting through the wreckage."

"Yes. Your Miss Whyte. And she has the daughter?"

"Essentially, yes."

"And what does the daughter know?"

"I don't know. Charlee doesn't know. Not yet." Cromwell made a disgusted face. "She says the girl's in shock. Anyway, you told me you didn't think the girl was in on this."

Chorney leaned back, thinking. "I don't know. I thought I understood Morozov. I thought it would be very straightforward. His type generally tries to keep their families out of the line of fire. But who knows?"

Cromwell turned and looked out through the great windows. A jet descended toward National Airport, lights on against the darkening weather. He wondered if his life was finally going to fall apart irremediably.

"I don't trust anyone anymore. Not even you, Senator. And I'm a bit concerned about our army attaché at the embassy. He asks the wrong questions. About things not in his area of responsibility. And, like so many of the idiots who join the military, he's a bit too much of an idealist for his own good. I find him excessively supportive of our president and insufficiently partial to the people to whom you and I owe so much. I'm concerned that the factions in our government to which he seems so drawn might covet those photographs. *If* they knew about them." Chorney paused. "The photographs could be very bad for business."

Cromwell looked at his watch. Certain that he had missed the vote. He dropped wearily into one of the big leather chairs, forgetting his posture.

"You damned Russians. You know, I just don't understand all the fuss, when you get right down to it. Sure, the photos would be embarrassing, if they ever came out. I mean, I'm a veteran of the Korean War myself, and I'd be mad as hell. But it'd blow over. And business is business. I mean, I don't understand why Rakhman and Virov are so damned nervous. Dead POWs would be an embarrassment. But it's a forty-year-old embarrassment. There's a public outcry, it dies down, the deal goes through. And everybody counts their billions. What's the big deal?"

Chorney let his hands go dead in his lap. It was clear to Cromwell that the Russian was thinking about something. The silence hinted at bad news.

"My friend," Chorney said at last, "I can see I need to reignite your enthusiasm."

Cromwell waited, sunk in the shadows of his mighty chair, a great gray world behind him.

"I've told you that these photos depict the execution of U.S. prisoners of war from Korea. I told you honestly that these are security-service file shots of very high quality. But there is another small detail it was not necessary for you to know until now."

The dirty bastard's going to shit on me, Cromwell thought.

"These men were *captured* forty years ago. But they weren't *killed* forty years ago. The photographs . . . are not of young men."

Cromwell felt invisible insects hustling over his skin.

"When were they killed?"

Chorney met his eyes again. "A few years ago."

"When?"

"Nineteen eighty-nine."

"No one knew what to do with them," Chorney said. "Only a handful of security-service insiders even knew that they existed. If Stalin had lived a bit longer, they probably would have been eliminated in a more practical and timely fashion. But Stalin died. And the prisoners were the least of our concerns. And—well, what could we do? Just give them back? We weren't even supposed to have them in the first place. Officially, we weren't a belligerent power. It would have been terribly embarrassing. And . . . we Russians are a bit sensitive to embarrassment. Anyway, the prisoners became a secret within a secret. No one wanted them, but no one was willing to take the responsibility for getting rid of them. It's a very Russian situation. Then came 1989. It was clear that a world was coming to an end. Perestroika and all that had just seemed like another phase, a sort of fashion, to the security services. Then, out of the blue, walls started tumbling, borders were opening, and the men who knew the secret saw that it was time to . . . take out the garbage. We're talking about responsible men who understood their duty."

"You *shot* American prisoners? In 1989?"

"Yes."

"Christ."

"It gets worse, I'm afraid. You see, the executioners themselves appear in some of the photographs."

"And?" Cromwell was thinking and not thinking, trying to separate his emotional reaction from the real potential damage.

"The executioners were Rakhman and Virov. Our deal-makers. And a third man."

Cromwell looked up in black wonder.

"Morozov was the third man. But that doesn't matter now."

"Morozov? And Rakhman? Virov?" Cromwell sensed that his voice sounded unforgivably stupid.

"Morozov was their teacher. Eliminating the American prisoners was his swan song. He retired just after that. Actually, he was forced to retire, but that's another story. Security-service generals can't have their daughters working as hard-currency prostitutes. Of course, even then no one dreamed she was going to find her way to America and bring her father after her."

"Doesn't sound terribly efficient on the part of your security boys."

Chorney shrugged. "When your world's collapsing, some things get away from you. A whore with an exit visa was not a priority concern. Father and daughter slipped through the cracks."

Cromwell snorted. "How on earth could Rakhman, or Virov for that matter, be so goddamned stupid? I mean, to have themselves photographed in a situation like that . . ."

Chorney's mood swung back toward nonchalance. "Why do politicians let themselves be photographed with their harlots? Really, what man is always wise? And you have to realize, shooting prisoners was great sport for men like that. They took photos of each other as though they were on safari. You know, posed over the carcass of a lion. Americans would have been the biggest game of all."

"But the risk?"

"We forget how quickly the world has changed. Even in '89, no one thought the inner recesses of the KGB would be penetrated, let alone that the institution would be dismembered. Those photographs were kept in very secret archives."

"My God," Cromwell said as the implications hit him again. He saw a deal worth countless billions collapsing. Because of stupid, gruesome vanity. He felt the need of a drink with unaccustomed intensity.

"But how . . . ," he asked the Russian, "how could Morozov do something like that . . . and, just a few years later, come peddling photographs that would incriminate him and everything he'd valued all his life, everything."

Chorney laughed. "Perhaps Russians and Americans are really very much alike. At least some Russians and Americans. Perhaps he did it for the money. He could have just culled the photos in which he was visible. Easy enough."

"But to turn his back on everything . . ."

"Well, the system turned its back on him. Overnight, he turned into a nobody. And then there's something else."

Cromwell looked up.

"I have a personal theory about why Morozov pulled this stunt with the photos," Chorney said. "Oh, I mean it was for the money, all right. But what does a sick, old man want with money?"

"You tell me."

Chorney smiled whimsically. Amused at his fellow man. He looked at Cromwell with tiny points of light in his eyes and said:

"He wanted to buy his daughter's love."

TEN

COL. JEB BATES HUNG UP THE PHONE. HE HAD WAITED LATE IN HIS office, hoping for good news, with the great building settling into its evening doze around him. But Schwaitzar, the Russian Army attaché, had disappointed him. Schwaitzar had not forgotten to call, and he offered enough information to earn his keep. But the news was all bad.

Bates liked Schwaitzar. The way a man might like a dog who did amusing tricks. The attaché was one of those wonderful ex-Soviets who could take regular payments from U.S. intelligence agencies and still convince themselves they were Russian patriots. In a career full of counterintelligence experience that had taken him from Southeast Asia to Central America to the Middle East and back again, Bates had never encountered any other people whose genius for self-deception rivaled that of the Russians.

But Schwaitzar's information rang true. The Russian security services—and that shabby bastard Chorney—had imported a couple of hoodlums to do their dirty work so that none of the agents working at the embassy would be PNGed—a persona non grata banishment from the United States was the last thing a Russian wanted these days, with conditions gone to hell back home in Moscow. It was truly bad news to Bates, since it left him no choice. He would have to notify the FBI. Army CI had no jurisdiction when it came to purely criminal matters within the United States.

Well, the FBI were good folks. It was only that he had wanted the Army to do this job, and to do it right.

Then there was the business with Cromwell. The U.S. intelligence services had always giggled over the way the old Soviets tailed one another, often devoting more energy to their own staff security than to offensive intelligence work. But, today, Bates found beauty in the holdover system.

Schwaitzar's GRU military intelligence man had tailed Chorney, who was Foreign Intelligence Service—former KGB—and who worked under the cover of an economic-affairs post. And Chorney had gone directly, shamelessly, wonderfully, to the apartment suite of Sen. Oliver Cromwell.

It was unforgivably sloppy on Chorney's part. And stupider than anything Bates might have expected from Cromwell. But you saw that sort of thing go down. Things got hot and people got nervous. They broke their own rules.

Schwaitzar was funny, really. He still didn't get the connection. But, the moment the Russian told him that Chorney had gone to Cromwell's apartment, things had fallen into place for Bates.

That was why Charlee Whyte knew so much. Cromwell was feeding her. And Cromwell was being fed by the Russians.

That changed all the rules. The FBI would have to pick up that ball, too. A U.S. senator. Bates shook his head. The Army was just a bit player now, a junior partner at best. Helping other agencies where the law allowed, offering occasional expertise.

Well, as long as they didn't blow it. Maybe it was even better this way. By spreading responsibility, you also spread knowledge. And it would be that much tougher for some political son of a bitch to suppress any POW-related information that might emerge. There were more options for working the system to ensure that the truth came out. Whatever that truth might be.

Bates leaned back in his chair, listening to late footsteps tapping far down the hall. He liked the Pentagon at night, when you could think, or work, without being disturbed. Where you could walk miles of corridors and see no one, or perhaps a sluggish janitor. The round-the-clock activities were hidden away down in deep basements and sealed chambers. At night, the building was full of ghosts.

Ghosts. POWs. Phantoms. Misery enough for all. The issue consumed you. Possessed you. The lost men. And the need to bring them back. Dead or alive.

The lost brothers.

When Schwaitzar had tipped him to the existence of the stolen photos a few weeks before, Bates had been as excited as a child on Christmas Eve. The attaché had not been able to offer many details. Only that these vaguely described photos had been brought to the United States. Schwaitzar pointed him at Morozov and several other émigré suspects. And Bates moved quickly to set up legal surveillance operations against foreign nationals involved in possible espionage against the U.S. Army—although that was stretching it a bit. Then he waited.

At first, it looked as though it were all a mistake. None of the targets paid off—the émigrés were just typical ex-Soviets, involved in a variety of tawdry criminal activities. Morozov was exceptional only in that he seemed to be the most upstanding of the bunch. Bates had been ready to call off the surveillance operation, to write off Schwaitzar's tip. When Charlee Whyte marched into the late Mr. Morozov's life.

Bates knew he was on to something then. And, in an act of sheer serendipity, Charlee Whyte had put in a by-name request for Ritter as her military aide. Bates had felt the hand of God upon the waters.

He frankly welcomed the chance to take down Charlee Whyte. She did a great deal of harm and little good, and if she landed on her ass, he would be glad. His first priority was the POWs. Knowledge. Proof. But he figured he had a little energy to spare for the Honorable Ms. Whyte, as well.

He did not want to hurt Ritter, though. The man was a good officer. Bates fingered the day's surveillance reports, reminding himself to put them in the safe before leaving, and wondered if Ritter had slept with the Russian woman. The man he had put on Ritter's apartment had confirmed that she stayed the night.

Bad medicine, Bates thought. The Morozov woman was definitely one gal with more history than future. But she was a beauty, you couldn't deny that. Not just born to be a tart, but born to be a successful tart. Well, Ritter was a big boy.

It was just that Ritter was such an inept judge of the ladies. Bates was convinced that the younger officer would draw a losing hand if he tried to play with the Russian woman.

But that was the whole point, wasn't it? To force every player to show his or her cards?

And Ritter had plenty of history himself. Charlee Whyte. Bates shuddered at the thought. And then there was the awful business with Ritter's wife.

Ritter was the kind of officer who was scrupulously honest, no matter the personal cost. Yet he went around telling one great lie. Telling everyone that his wife had died of cancer.

Bates had seen the Criminal Investigation Division's file on the case. Oh, Magdalena Ritter had certainly had cancer. And she had been dying of it. But she didn't wait. She shot herself with a pistol registered in Ritter's name.

She left him a note. A photocopy was in the CID files. Bates knew he would not forget the contents of that note as long as he lived:

> My dearest Chris,
> In our years together, you have given me more joy and beauty than any other woman could feel in a dozen life-times. Now it's time for you to get on with your own life.
> With undying love,
> Your Magdalena

To a man with a different background, such a last message might have seemed like an act of utterly selfless love. But Bates had seen too much in his life, and he had to ask himself whether a woman who really understood a man like Chris Ritter would leave behind such a note out of love or out of immeasurable hatred.

"Can I trust you?" Nadya asked in a fragile voice. She sat up against the headboard of the bed, sheet drawn lackadaisically up to her belly. From where Ritter's head lay, the contour of her far breast showed orange against the lamp, her skin drinking the light and mixing it with the blood just below the skin. She looked inhumanly delicate.

"Can I trust you?" she repeated.

Ritter knew only that he did not trust her. The woman who promised to stay in his rooms, then disappeared, only to return late and fall through the doorway into his arms, destroying his resolve to postpone any further sex until the world came back into order. He did not trust her and did not even think that he liked her. But he wanted her.

He took the coward's path and did not answer, feigning a satisfied drowsiness when he was neither drowsy nor satisfied.

"I am afraid," she said in a reduced voice, allowing him to listen or not. "I think that people cannot trust each other so much."

He could smell their lovemaking on her, on him, on the crumpled sheets. It was a good, reassuring smell. A gift of reality and life.

"Has something happened?" he asked softly. "Where on earth have you been? I was worried about you."

She moved closer so that her flank cushioned his face. He kissed her lightly and retreated.

"I went back to my apartment," she said, choosing to speak Russian now. "I don't even have any clothes here."

"But . . . you didn't bring anything back with you."

"No. Because of what happened."

Ritter tensed. "And what happened?" Her flesh before him looked as perfect as if it had never been touched. She was, literally, a flawless woman. In the physical sense, at least.

"I thought I would only go for a few minutes. So that you would not even see I am gone. But, when I go there . . . I feel surrounded by my father. Everything makes me think of him. The old shirts he doesn't throw away. He wouldn't let me buy him new American shirts. And his razor. There are still whiskers on his razor. And there was another thing. I thought perhaps I could find the photograph. The one I told you about. I wanted to bring it to you. So I had to go through all of his things. And it's so sad. He had a magazine. He'd hidden it away, so I wouldn't find it. It had photographs of naked women. Don't you think that's sad?"

Yes. Ritter thought it was sad. There were few things sadder than magazines that specialized in pictures of women pretending to entice. Sex was not a spectator sport. You had to be a player. Nor could true sexuality ever, ever be reduced to the purely visual.

"So I found this magazine. But I didn't find the photograph I told you about. It's gone, I don't know where. I was crying. Sitting on the sofa and crying. For I don't know how long. And the telephone is ringing."

She reached out a hand and stroked him. With unbearable gentleness. "I thought it was you. Trying to find me. But I couldn't answer. I needed this loneliness. Even you could not help me, and you are such a sweet man. I could not answer the telephone. But it is ringing and ringing. And I thought again, That is Christopher. He is worried about me. So I answered it. But it wasn't you."

"Who was it?"

"I didn't recognize the voice. But the voice knew me. It was a very hard voice, the voice of a man no woman wants to meet. The voice began talking to me. I felt as if whoever it was could see me through the telephone, could see me crying and weak."

"What did he say?"

She drew closer to him, lowered herself, seeking the false protection of his arms.

"He told me I must meet him. Tonight. In Georgetown. I know the place. It's a Russian restaurant, the Muscovy. It's not for good Russians. I never go there."

"Why does he want you to meet him?"

"He said that I *must* meet him. That my father started something and that now I must finish it. He said that . . . if I don't meet him . . . he'll kill me."

Ritter placed his arm between her and the world like a bar.

"Nobody's going to kill you. And you're not going to meet him. This is all crazy, Nadya. It's time to call the police."

It struck him that they were all in the wrong—Charlee and Jeb Bates, he himself. Playing games. With a woman's life.

Nadya made herself very small against him. "No. Please. We must go to meet this man."

"You're not going anywhere."

"Christopher, listen to me. My father is dead. And I don't understand. He was all that I had in the world. And I at least want to know why. I want to know why my father is dead."

Ritter held her more tightly. As though he would never let her move from the bed.

"He agreed to meet me outside. On the sidewalk. He says that he has something for me. You will go with me. You can stay just far enough away so that he doesn't see you. Then I will be safe. And you will see this man. We'll both see him."

"Nadya, I can barely walk. If anything happened . . ."

She slipped from his enfolding arm. Too easily. And curled down to kiss his ruined knee. He felt nothing, a ghost kiss.

Instead of coming back up to him, she laid her head on his thigh and held to his legs.

"I'm sorry," she said softly, and he could hear that she was weeping. "I want to please you, Christopher. But I have made up my mind. I am going to meet this man. Perhaps he is even the one who has killed my father. Perhaps I will know when I see him. I ask you to come with me, to watch over me. But I am going, whether you come or not."

"It's time to call the police."

She erupted. At first, he thought she was going to strike him with her fists. But she only hit the bed. Pummeling the mattress and her vacant pillow, raging.

"No police," she cried, *"damn you, no police."*

She pounded the bed ferociously, utterly animal. More animal than she had been in the hardest grip of sex.

"No police. They'll make me go back. No police . . ."

The terrible energy began to fade. Then, suddenly, she collapsed beside him and curled up as though it were her turn to be beaten and she was afraid.

"I hate all of this so much," she said, weeping. "You cannot know how much I hate this. I hate it and hate it."

He moved to take her in his arms, but she transmitted an animal signal to keep away. At least she looked at him now. With eyes stripped of all socialization, even of decency. *"You* couldn't know what such a life is like. How you must give up so many things, how you must give up your pride, your being, until there is so little left. I'm never going back to Russia."

Yet it struck him that her eyes, amber lit by the fires of Genesis, were those of the God-gripped men and women who had burned themselves alive in the Russian wilderness rather than imperil their faith. "There must be dignity for a person," she said, with immeasurable bitterness. "A person must receive the means to live. All of my life, I have only wanted to live the life of a human being. Only the life of a human being, can you understand? But it's all so degraded. Everything in Russia is made to humiliate you, to break you down, to pull you down so that you are like all the rest, and so that everyone is equal to the lowest of the low."

"But you're in America now. And you can stay. But not if you get in trouble with the police."

"No police," she shouted, easily loud enough for the neighbors to hear. Her tiny face had reddened as though terribly sunburned. "Do you know how I came to America? To come to America, I married a man I didn't love. I *paid* him to marry me." She laughed, poisoned by memory. "I'm not an ugly woman, but I had to pay this bastard to marry me. Just so that I could come to a place where I don't have to be ashamed. Isn't that funny? That I had to humiliate myself so fully just to reach the edge of a decent life? You say you've been to Moscow. Could you live a life of dignity there, as a Russian? So I paid this man to marry me, and I let him use me as his wife, besides. So that he wouldn't turn me in. I can't tell you everything I've done. But I told myself that it wouldn't matter in America, that I could start again. A new life. The life of a human being."

She wept, and Ritter tested her shoulder with a hand. She did not fight his touch and he petted her gently.

"I want my American life," she cried. "But the past is a smell you cannot wash away. The police will ask one question, then another. And there will be nothing I can do." She broke down again. "I'd sleep with the devil himself to stay here. But you could never understand that."

He let her cry. Wondering if he were the devil. He knew he was going to go with her. On her terms. To Georgetown and to her bed. And he was not going to call the police. Or anyone else.

Mitya watched the girl with professional concentration. Standing in the uneven shelter of a billboard, she and her backpack were doused. She was certainly no beauty. But she was not without appeal. She smiled at each car as it pulled out of the service station, lofting a placard that said PRO-CHOICE RALLY. To Mitya, the words were arcane and exclusive. But words didn't matter in the end.

They had time. Zhan wouldn't like it, but Mitya was sick of his colleague's endless tyrannies.

Zhan returned from the little food shop that was part of the service station, counting his money in the drizzling rain. Worse than a Jew, Mitya thought. Let a man fall in with those Asian bastards and, before you knew it, he was acting like them.

Zhan seemed to sniff the air, then he got into the passenger's side of the big car. The drizzle-ass snowflake's afraid to drive, Mitya told himself. It pleased him. To grasp his counterpart's weakness: afraid of America.

Mitya wasn't afraid of America. He drove right up to it and lowered the window, smiling and looking out at the drenched girl in the parka, her wet hair straggling out from under the hood. Up close, her skin was broken. But Mitya had seen worse.

She lowered her sign and her smile began to fade.

"We are going to Washington," Mitya said in his most inviting voice. "You are going to Washington, miss?"

The girl looked into the depths of the car, looking at Mitya, then past him, then back into his eyes. Then she dropped her sign in a puddle, grabbed her backpack, and ran for the brilliant lights of the service station.

Charlee stood with her hands in the pockets of her raincoat, fingering the key to Nadya Morozova's apartment and staring up at the great statue of Lincoln. She despised most of the city's monuments as nothing but tasteless tributes to bloody white males. The more you killed of your fellow man, the more likely you were to be immortalized in bronze. But Lincoln . . . was the great exception.

She liked coming to the Lincoln Memorial at night, when the crowds were gone and the public place became her secret place. She believed she felt the man's presence in those hours. Especially at times like this, when the rain had swept the streets clean of people and the washed air let you think clearly.

Down on the Mall, a last team of workers were knocking together a speakers' platform for the next day's pro-choice rally, but Lincoln, forgotten, sat alone. She loved Lincoln, cherished the thought of him. An ugly man, to whom nothing would have come easily. He had loved the law, yet recognized its limitations. He had been willing to break the law to achieve a higher end. He had understood the purpose of power, the need to enforce good on humankind. More than any saint, he had grasped the trivial venality that defined the common man. Possessed of a common touch that Charlee knew she would always lack, he had gloved the steel of his will in muslin humor, and he had changed a world that did not want to change. Lincoln . . . had understood that all men truly were brothers, whether they liked it or not.

And that was the key. Lincoln had been no trivial, Constitution-thumping patriot, no vulgar nationalist. Lincoln had not belonged to the United States. Lincoln had belonged to the world, and his legacy of respect for human rights, for freedom and simple decency, his willingness to struggle against the selfishness that spawned so much of the world's daily evil, were transcendent—you could not wrap Lincoln in a flag and use him to club men and women into approved behavior.

Charlee believed that her understanding of history was deeper and richer than that of any historian. Historians blinded themselves with facts. Lincoln, to Charlee, had not preserved a union. Lincoln had *destroyed* the filthy, slave-holding, patriarchal America into which he had been born. Lincoln, she believed, must have hated America as he found it, and he had leveled it, North and South, ripping off its mask of self-serving gentleman's laws, stripping off its dress of privilege, and lashing the naked thing into modernity. Lincoln killed feudalism.

Lincoln murdered the United States that had been created to protect well-to-do Virginia tobacco farmers and their sons. Lincoln forced multiculturalism upon his recalcitrant countrymen a century before academics stumbled upon the word. To call Lincoln an American was to disgrace him, to make him too small.

Charlee wished she could have had a father who was a little more like Lincoln. Instead, her father had been an overgrown boy who had deserted his pregnant wife to fly airplanes in a war. A loathsomely typical male, refusing to grow up. She had hated his memory at first, then she had simply pushed it away. And now, after so many years—why, after so many years?—his grinning, boys'-club ghost had come back to haunt her.

It was like a punishment from God. There was no logical reason why she should have become involved with the whole business of the POW photographs. It was an infuriating cosmic accident, or the deed of God the Joker.

She feared, terribly, that one of the photographs would show a man whose identity as her father could not be disputed. And then she would be forced to confront him, to imagine his sufferings, to accept him as worthy of regard.

Of all the photographs her mother treasured, Charlee always recalled the one of a boy in a pilot's getup, grinning idiotically beside his silver jet, an eternal adolescent in possession of a splendid toy. She could not understand how her mother could ever have loved him, how she could have taken him seriously enough to draw him into her body. Even her stepfather was an enormous improvement.

And yet. Charlee could not stanch the wound of curiosity. Emotions sneaked out of corners. And she feared that she would not have the strength to do what was right—to get the photos and hand them over to Ollie and keep her job, where she could make a difference, have an impact. She sensed a danger in herself, a budding weakness, a possibility of self-betrayal. Because a part of her had begun to imagine that the fate of those dead boy-men in the photographs might matter.

It was all so revolting. She wished she had never seen a man in uniform in her life.

Lincoln had seen no great need to wear a uniform. But he

had tolerated the military peacocks around him, because he recognized that he needed them. To change a world the generals did not even know they were changing. Lincoln had understood the need to employ even the basest tools for the common good.

She had spent too much of the day involved in condolences and funeral arrangements for her staff members who had died in the bombing. Feeling only exasperation and impatience. She did not feel genuine sorrow for them, and it troubled her. It was that, above all, that had driven her to make fifteen minutes for Lincoln. She looked up into the face that was so pathetic it could not be properly idealized, then at the strong, gripping hands. Lincoln surely had not felt the loss of each last soldier in his war. He had retained his vision, accepting the necessary casualties. He had not allowed himself to become distracted by transient individual suffering. He had, above all, understood the need to sacrifice for the greater good. She was certain that the immature, schoolbook version of America with which the middle class associated him had meant nothing to him. His vision had been of mankind, of the greater entity. Charlee suspected that Lincoln, in his heart, had despised the very notion of borders, flags, and citizenship. The United States of America, in and of itself, would have meant nothing to him, would have been ultimately contemptible.

Charlee heard footsteps on the marble floor and turned about. It was, after all, an unsafe city at night.

An aged caretaker in a service uniform stopped and stared at her. He held a worn mop over his shoulder like a gun.

The old man smiled softly and came a bit closer, testing, not wanting to threaten her. He looked worn, the end product of a life of chronic underpayment. Yet his smile was beatific.

Charlee did not want to be bothered. She turned back to the statue, staring up at the face that did not change, that never let her down: the face of her spiritual father.

The old man lowered the mop, and the movement tugged at her eye. His smile was so unyielding that she wondered if he might be mentally disabled.

"Isn't he just wonderful?" the old man asked her.

They both looked up into Lincoln's face.

"Yes," Charlee said after some delay.

The old man laughed softly, unreasonably delighted with his place in the world.

"Yes, ma'am. He sure is wonderful." He leaned on the handle of his mop. "Now you tell me—you just tell me—what other country in the world could have given us a man like that?"

ELEVEN

"MR. BERNSHTEIN?" JEB BATES ASKED, MOVING SO THAT THE MAN could see his uniform through the chained, cracked-open door. "Could we talk for a few minutes?"

Bates had no legal means to force an interview with the Russian woman's husband or ex-husband or whatever he was at the moment. But Bates knew émigrés. He was sure that his uniform would be sufficiently intimidating to persuade Bernshtein to talk voluntarily. Whether the man would tell the truth or not was a different matter. Bates knew that side of émigrés, as well.

The man behind the slightly opened door was handsome in a harried, indoor way. He wore made-in-the-West gold-rimmed glasses that framed wounded eyes, and his lips were eternally parted, forever on the verge of speech. Early thirties, Bates figured. He judged that Bernshtein was the kind of guy who took the wrong women far too seriously.

"Are you . . . a policeman?" Bernshtein asked.

"No. I'm from the United States Army."

Bernshtein was a very intelligent man, and in at least one respect, his intelligence was so incisive that it could even surprise an old CI agent like Jeb Bates:

"Oh. Then you must want to talk about my wife."

*   *   *

Ritter and Nadya took a taxi to the heart of Georgetown, getting out far enough from the Muscovy Restaurant to avoid being seen together. Ritter dreaded the walk ahead of him. His knee was deteriorating to the point where he was afraid it might refuse to go on. The reconstructed mosaic of bone felt as though it were made of thin glass.

The rain had stopped for the time being, and the damp, late evening bloomed with grunge-look university students, with homeless beggars and bureaucrats out for a beer or an ethnic meal, with little mobs of concerned-looking women in denim, and a few last, insatiable tourists. Ritter, in jeans and an old bomber jacket, was as invisible as a limping man could be. But Nadya would never be invisible. Even buried in the old trench coat she had adopted from his closet, she burned the street with beauty. Men looked at her, startled. Women looked, too.

"Sure you want to do this?" Ritter asked.

"It is necessary."

He shook his head. The air moistened their faces, making Nadya's skin glow. "All right. The restaurant's about five blocks up."

"Yes."

"It's on the other side of the street. I'll stay on this side, a block behind you."

"Yes."

"And pay attention. If the situation feels dangerous, just get out of there. Scream. As loud as you can. And run."

"Yes. I know you will take care of me."

Ritter closed his eyes for an instant. "I can hardly walk. Nadya, I won't be able to come running to your rescue."

"You will take care of me." She looked at him with an expression blank enough to allow him to fill in any meaning he wanted.

"Go ahead," he told her, before she could turn away from him on her own.

She kissed him on the cheek, a quick good-bye kiss, airy with innocence. He watched her as she dashed across the street, dodging cars as though it were a game.

As soon as they separated, she seemed to forget about the

limitations of his leg. She walked briskly, forcing him to struggle to keep the right tactical distance. He lurched up past his favorite bookstore, past burger bars and a beat French restaurant, hurrying by exotic boutiques and student-staffed junk shops selling glow-in-the-dark condoms and T-shirts celebrating society's fractures. He tried to walk with an appearance of normalcy, but that broke down in seconds. He could not maintain control either of his leg or of his facial muscles. A plump girl in harem pants watched his approach as though he were coming to attack her.

He could not keep up. Nadya surged ahead. He could barely see her. With the traffic noise, she would not even hear him if he called out a warning.

He could just follow her head and shoulders, proud in beauty, bobbing along the pavement behind a barrier of parked cars.

She stopped in front of the restaurant, alone. No one was waiting for her.

She had a two-block lead on him and he hurried to close the distance. Rapt, he stumbled into another pedestrian, a sad man who looked like an eternal victim. Ritter apologized.

In that instant, a figure appeared beside Nadya.

Ritter dropped the apology and staggered on. The man who had emerged from the restaurant was tallish, dressed in a dark, nondescript coat. He stood with his back to Ritter, facing Nadya, standing too close to her.

The stranger reached out and grabbed Nadya by the arm. She recoiled. The man responded by challenging her with both hands, shaking her.

Ritter tried to run. And his leg quit.

He tumbled to the pavement.

The pain in his knee left him gasping. Passersby stared, even as they avoided him.

He raised himself up with the aid of a parking meter.

The man with Nadya began dragging her off, pulling her into a side street. She didn't really seem to struggle, didn't scream. Ritter wanted to shout at her, to tell her to run for her life. But the pain left him breathless. In seconds, the stranger had dragged her out of sight.

Ritter struggled up the sidewalk, stumbling from parking

meter to parking meter, sliding along the flanks of parked cars. The pain forced tears into his eyes. He felt pathetic in his helplessness, unspeakably ashamed.

He drew even with the corner beyond which Nadya had disappeared and he stopped, breathing as though there was not enough oxygen in the world. He felt dizzy and nauseous.

The side street was empty. And the woman of countless faults, who had just coaxed him back to life, was gone.

Ritter collapsed against a pole, sliding down until his ass hit concrete. It started to rain again.

"Grab me by the arm," Nadya commanded, staring up into the face of the man she loved.

Volodya responded. But he was far too gentle.

"Don't be an ass. Use both hands. Make it look rough."

Volodya obeyed her to the extent his love for and awe of her would let him. "Is that all right?"

"No. Pretend I'm a man. Someone you hate. Push me around the corner."

He began to guide her.

*"Har*der," she commanded. "Be a *man,* for God's sake."

She could tell he was still rising from the depths of his hangover.

At least he had read the letter, done as he was told.

"Should we hurry more than this?" he asked.

She pulled him around the corner.

"This is just fine. Now we can walk." She laughed. "The poor idiot's going to be down on his hands and knees crawling in a minute. He's God's gift."

"Do you like myths? Fairy tales?" Bernshtein asked.

"I don't dislike them," Bates said. But the answer did not matter. Bernshtein was talking to himself, for himself. The mathematician sat in a small apartment littered with software manuals and journals and the remains of a bachelor's dinner.

"She is a woman from these myths." Bernshtein smiled as though he had stumbled into a specific memory. His eyes looked away from Bates. "Perhaps she is the last one, but I do not think so. I fear that we will always find such women. Helen of Troy. Salome. Circe. You know that the stories of the Caucasus, the epic poetry of the Persians ... all this is full of her? Tamara ... Shirin ... Leila ..."

Bernshtein lit another cigarette. He had smoked half a pack in the short time Bates had been in the apartment. "It's funny, you know? This has been a hobby of mine. The fairy story and the great old poems, all this telling that is not quite history but that reveals so much about us. Think of Delilah. Or imagine how powerful was the beauty of the woman who made King David sick. In Russia, we have folktales of marsh spirits and river demons who lure men to their deaths with the false beauty of a woman." He sucked on his cigarette as though it were his source of life. "Who would ever think that such a woman would come into my life?" He ran a hand back through his thick hair. "Sometimes I think that I have summoned her, like a devil."

Bates had long ago lost count of the interrogations and interviews he had conducted during his years of service, but he had been through enough of them to know when to shut up and let the subject talk.

Bernshtein laughed abruptly, like a drunk. But there was no trace of alcohol in the air. And his speech was clear. He held his cigarette stub loosely over the carpet. "She is brilliant, you know. Much more intelligent than I am. I did not know that, of course. It is a fault of the well-educated, you know? When another is not so well-educated, we think they must not be so intelligent. Oh, Nadya had been to school. But I think it was not so good for her because she is too alive. She was going to be a psychologist, a specialist in behavior, which is not the same in Russia. I think maybe she has a real talent for this. But she gave it up. And she did other things. She fell in love with a man who was very bad for her, I think." He grimaced and reached for his little box of Marlboros. "I still don't know what is true or false about her. She always tells you some of the truth. It's a very good technique for lying, you know?" He fueled himself with more tobacco, drawing the flame from the lighter so powerfully it scorched the white paper for half an inch. "I think she is the most honest liar I have ever met. Certainly, she's the best one."

Bernshtein stood up suddenly. He strode into the depths of the apartment. Bates waited patiently, listening to the sounds of a search.

When Bernshtein reappeared, he had a photo album in hand. With exaggerated callousness, he flipped through it until he found the desired page, recoiled slightly, then tossed the book into his guest's lap.

It was a portrait-size photo of a woman. Nadya Morozova. Nadyeshda Bernshtein. Perhaps there were other names, as well. Bates did not know and did not care beyond that which might be pertinent to the case.

She had been photographed by a semiskilled friend or perhaps by a clumsy official photographer. The photo had a crudity the subject did not. The portrait showed a young woman of perfect beauty, with the sort of exactness in her features that top models labored to achieve. And there was something else, too.

Magic.

Bates closed the book, unwilling to risk her spell even at a remove.

Bernshtein dropped back down on his discount-store sofa, scratching at his hairline. Then he slapped his hand down on the fabric. "I *believed* her, you know that? She was so clever. She told me of so many things that she had done that I could not believe there was more. I believed that she had changed. Men always believe that women can change. I believed that she had changed for me. Because she loved me. I cannot tell you how much I believed her. Oh, I knew I was to be desired. I am a skilled man. But, most of all, I am a Jew and I could come easily to America. I thought of all these things. And my family, my friends, they told me this is what she is after. But then I would see her again and I would forget everything." He leaned back, slumping, drained by the power of memory. "I think a man who has not experienced such a love—such a passion—cannot know what it is like to feel in this way."

Bitter-faced, the émigré retreated into his memories. Bates waited out as much of the silence as he could. Then he decided to toss out a firecracker to get things going again:

"You still love her?"

Bernshtein's smile became a death's head. "I think of her. Of her body. Of sex. I think that I can never forget her. I think of her beauty. But I do not love her. I can become sick if I think about her too much. But I think that it is the body's desire only. How Circe has made men become pigs—you see how much truth there is in these stories? We cannot say that no one has warned us." He closed his eyes, a man bitten by a parasite in his belly. "No, I do not love her. I think I hate her." For a moment, he managed to meet Bates's eyes. "But it does not matter whether I love her—I will not forget her. Cigarette?"

Bates told him, for the third or fourth time, that he didn't smoke.

"She thinks so far into the future," Bernshtein continued. "She could be an officer of the general staff, the way she plans. And she understands people. She has a genius for it. With me, the plan was not such a long one. Only a few steps. First, I must marry her. Then we go together to America. Next, I find a good job, where I can use my mathematics. Then, only then, does she tell me that her father is sick and that he must come to America as part of our family."

"You didn't get along with the father?"

Bernshtein coughed with the intensity of his laughter, exhaling a little fog of smoke.

"With him? General Morozov? When Nadya told him she was getting married, he would not even meet with me. The idea of his pure Russian daughter marrying a Jew ..." Bernshtein made a sudden retreat into his thoughts, crumpling his eyebrows behind the gold frames of his glasses. "Of course, thinking back—maybe she didn't want us to meet. Nadya always had the angles on things, you know? Anyway, I really did not wish to meet him. He had a reputation, you know. He was one of the KGB's champion murderers—this is the man Nadya brings to America. Because he is old and sick."

"But you sponsored him?"

Bernshtein milked the cigarette. "Yeah. I sponsored him. For Nadya." He flexed the muscles around his eyes as if struggling to wake up from a long bad dream. "We fought. And she won. Nadya always wins. In the end, I did everything for her, you know?"

"And then?"

Bernshtein spit smoke. "And then the old man comes. Welcome to America, Mr. General of the KGB. So many lies, he must have told them. To come to America. And I tell you truly, I did not volunteer the information that was known to me. I did not lie to the immigration officers. But I did not tell all that I knew—did I break the law?"

"I don't know," Bates said. "Probably."

Bernshtein looked down, smirking. "That, too. For her." He shook his head in boundless disgust. "Anyway, he lived with us. In this apartment. And, you know, he is different from what I expected. Like an old whore who has gone to religion. I don't mean he is religious. But he is very nice to me. And to his daughter. He loves her I think more than I do." He smiled bitterly. "Everyone loves little Nadya. So. I am working hard. And this sick old man is good enough even to go away to walk in the evening to give us privacy to love one another. I think that maybe even this will work out, you know? I plan to find him a small apartment sometime. I tell Nadya she must work, too, because we need the money for his doctors and hospitals, because he is sick in his liver. But she will not work. She says she must go to the libraries, that she must study better English to have a good job, that she must do a thousand things. Then, one day, I am invited to eat lunch with people from California who are also writing software for my company. We go to a restaurant in Alexandria, a nice one. And there is Nadya, working as a waitress. She has been working, but she cannot tell me, you see. Because she keeps the money. Anyway, it is a strange event. She pretends she does not know me. And I pretend, too. And the other men are flirting with her and making jokes about what they would like to do to her. But I understand this, too, you know? But, what I do not understand is that I come home from work and no one is there. Nadya is gone. Her father is gone. The television and video machine are gone. The next day, I go back to the restaurant. But she is gone from there, too. She—do you know where she is now?"

"More or less."

"And you will tell me? I need to talk to her, there are things . . ."

"I'll tell you. But I can't tell you tonight."

"She is in trouble? Because of her father?"

"Not exactly."

"But she is in trouble?"

"I'm not sure."

"No. She is in trouble. She will always find trouble. Does she need someone to help her?"

Bates thought about Ritter. And about everything he knew thus far about the woman.

"No."

"If she needs someone to help her, you must tell me." The tip of Bernshtein's cigarette glowed fiercely.

"Listen. When her father came here—did he bring anything special with him? Anything unusual? Did he seem to be trying to hide anything?"

The look of bafflement on Bernshtein's face was answer enough. But the man said, "I don't know. Not that I remember."

Bates was tired. He glanced at his watch. Thinking of his wife and another dinner missed. Both of the kids were off to college, and his wife needed more of him now in order to endure his country. How odd it was that one woman would do anything to come to America, while another had to be half-kidnapped. He had promised his wife she could go back to Vietnam again in the spring, to visit her family. It was going to involve some penny-pinching in the meantime, with the girls in school. Someday, he thought, after he took off his uniform, he might go back with her. For a little while.

"I'm trying," Bates said, "to get a clearer picture of your wife—does it bother you when I call her that?"

"No. In the law, she is still my wife."

"I'm trying to make her come clear. Now, it sounds as though, if nothing else, she genuinely loved her father. It sounds—"

Bernshtein howled. It was the joke of the century. Then he flicked his cigarette butt into a crowded ashtray.

"*Loved* him? That's a laugh. She *hated* him."

"But you said—"

"I said that *he* loved *her*. Every man loved her. Even her father. He would have done anything for her. *Any*thing. He would have died for her."

"But—"

"She *hated* him. You would not believe, if I told you the things she has said about this man. She even believed he has the guilt of her mother's death." Bernshtein put his smirk back on, lips poisoned by cigarettes. "That's why I was so shocked when she told me she wanted to bring him to America."

The two men sat apart, coffee table and a heaping ashtray between them. For a long time, Bernshtein did not even light another cigarette. Bates sensed that, for all his years of service, he had not even begun to exhaust the infinite variety of humankind. There was no end to the mystery of men and women.

Finally, Bates asked, "Well, what do you think? Why did she bring her father to America?"

Bernshtein smiled, eyes toxic. "Nadya always had a plan."

Vladimir Antonovich Lyubovsky was born in the year of Stalin's death. By virtue of his success as a physicist, Volodya's father had become a minor aristocrat in the Soviet system. The elder Lyubovsky, a patient, good-natured man, worked in the atomic weapons program. His work was largely theoretical, conducted in the insulated world of scientific cities and settlements, where those who served the system well or at least vocally were pampered with goods and medals. Volodya attended elite schools, and the kitchen table in his parents' apartment shivered under the weight of genius as thinkers of stature brought down their fists to emphasize each hypothesis.

Volodya's mother was always in the other room, ever at a slight remove, playing the piano until it shook the china in the enormous wooden cabinet she had salvaged from the destruction of her family in the Civil War and the Purges. She was an oddly vacant woman, alive only at the keyboard, which she attacked gracelessly, face impassive, fingers swollen with anger. Even when she took Volodya in her arms and kissed him, a vital part of his mother was elsewhere. In later years he thought that it must have been a great surprise to her to one day find an infant struggling out between her thighs.

His mother gave birth to a second child, a daughter, but the speechless being died of polio before Volodya could learn her well enough to miss her. Otherwise, the prime of his childhood passed happily, occupied by youth organizations, books his mother dropped in her wake, and sports. His body developed quickly, his strength a wonder to his father, whose profession had rotted his muscles and softened his bones. His mother, thin as honor, barely seemed to notice the change in Volodya.

But the men charged with turning children into healthy citizens of the Soviet Union noticed him, and they helped him discover a talent for wrestling. Volodya loved, inarticulately, the collision of fine, living bodies, the brilliant tension, and the immediate, wonderful reality of the struggle. It only astonished him when his opponents brought anger, even hatred, to a match. To Volodya, each bout was a celebration. He won thoughtlessly.

And then a girl smiled. Irina Mikhailovna, with braids the color of honey and a mildewed book of poetry in hand. They enjoyed each other in extreme chastity, shepherded by the presence of others on summer camping trips and school excursions to the museums in the regional capital. She read to him in a grown-up voice, demanding that he listen, her face rehearsing womanhood. Then he would see her laughing in the middle of a child's game, surrounded by the shadows of other girls. When her father transferred to another nameless research settlement whose existence was confirmed only by a postal code, she cried and kissed Volodya once, solemn as though sacrificing her virginity, and made him promise to love her forever. Next term, a rather different girl strutted into his life and gave him his first lessons in applied biology.

Biology in all its forms appealed to him. What made life happen? How could his girlfriend Luda's body make him feel the way it did? Biology seemed a wonderful path, too, because he did not want to follow his father into the hermetic world of weapons research. By the waning years of the 1960s, the revolution in human awareness that had crazed the West had reverberated as far as Siberia. Science, he and his closest schoolmates whispered, should serve peaceful purposes. Science should better the lot of men.

Volodya began his university studies with one eye on a future in the field of biology and the other fixed on the girls who sat out in front of the academic buildings, sunning themselves in the breaks between classes. But he could no more bind himself strictly to one discipline than he could remain faithful to one female. He had an intelligence, an appetite, that moved faster than the thought processes of all but a few of his professors. He touched chemical engineering and statistics, did enough physics to confuse his listeners, then split off into genetics—a field undergoing a sharp reevaluation in the Soviet Union. Professors fought for his allegiance. And, in the end, he returned solidly to biology, to the dependable miracle of life itself.

Upon graduation, he was due for military service. But, he was told, that could be arranged away if he would serve a few years in a military research laboratory.

Where?

You'll find out.

Doing what?

You'll see.

After some soul-searching, he agreed. After all, it would be a temporary arrangement. And it would be better to work as a scientist than to endure the drudgery of a soldier's life.

The state sent him to a site in the Urals. To his delight, the work turned out to be fascinating. The laboratory to which he had been assigned did work on animals that had been sent into space. And on astronauts, too. He joined a team investigating the effects of weightlessness on muscle tissue and found himself enmeshed in questions of how cells and their component parts metamorphosed given different variables. The only problem with the work was that there were few women at the remote installation, nearly all of them married, and the notion of affairs with the wives of his colleagues offended Volodya's sense of morality.

Near the end of his term of assignment, the site director called him to his office. Volodya had been expecting and dreading the call. He assumed the director would offer him a permanent position—and the work could not have been more to Volodya's taste. But the isolation told on him. He saw his best years slipping away in helpless monasticism. He had even begun to suffer depressions, and he attended his equally celibate colleagues' drinking bouts with ever greater frequency.

Volodya could not make up his mind what to do. He suspected that he would decide in front of the director's desk.

The director surprised him. There was no talk of a permanent job. Professor Dimenko wanted only to invite him to a party for his daughter, who was home for a visit. The daughter, Yekaterina Ivanovna, whom her literary-minded parents called Kitty, rarely came home, but her infrequent visits were enough to make her a legend in the lab. A great beauty, with her mother's southern cast, Kitty was reputed to be as cold as winter in Magadan. Yet every young scientist within sniffing range tumbled over his coworkers trying to meet her. She was intelligent, too, working as a pathologist at another site in the middle of nowhere.

Volodya understood the invitation. He was being examined as a potential son-in-law. It made him feel a bit like a lab specimen. But it made him smile, too.

Later that night, after all of the other party guests had staggered home and her parents had gone to bed, he and Kitty made love standing up in the stairwell of her parents' apartment building. As quick and violent as she was small, Kitty stopped herself from screaming by chewing into his neck until he bled. They married two weeks later.

The facility where she worked had a vacancy for a biologist. It was a heaven-sent opportunity. She was not allowed to tell him much in advance. The work was highly classified. But they were doing fantastic things with disease mutations. She was sure he'd love it.

When all of the forms had been stamped and the permissions received, after his personal and family history had been reviewed yet again, Volodya found himself stepping down from a small military passenger plane onto an airstrip not far from the Aral Sea. The plane never cut its engines entirely, and soon it was taxiing about, groaning and lifting back into the sky. Volodya put down his suitcase, staring at an empty hangar whose doors had gone missing and a cement-block building with the windows smashed out. Around the strip lay lifeless, salted desert.

He began to fear that the pilot had made an error, that he had been deposited at the wrong location. He had no idea where he was. He did not know in which direction he should start walking. He sat down on the suitcase that held his life.

After perhaps twenty minutes, he spotted a dust cloud. It grew. In another quarter of an hour, a sunburned officer in hot-weather dress stepped out of a range car and said:

"Vladimir Anton'ich? Yekaterina Ivanovna sends her greetings. She's in the middle of an important experiment and couldn't come herself."

The important experiment involved killing mammals quickly with enhanced toxins dropped in bomblets. It was successful. There was a party in the housing area that evening, partly to welcome Kitty's husband and otherwise to celebrate the culmination of an entire cycle of experiments.

The facility was the leading research and experimentation center in the Soviet Union for biological warfare.

Volodya's work—and his marriage—quickly became a nightmare. Far from the mysteries of life, he found himself bound to the mysteries of death. The imperialists in the West were marshaling their forces. The military and industrial factions in the United States wanted revenge for their humiliations in Southeast Asia. The worldwide struggle was intensifying, and it was the duty of every Soviet citizen to help the Motherland prepare. In Volodya's case, this meant working with refined strains of typhus, anthrax, and various septic materials. The goal was to identify those strains that were the most efficient and that were robust enough to be delivered by military means. In front of the administration building, a statue of Lenin extended a hand in the direction of the test ranges, one of the most poisoned areas on earth.

Kitty continued the long-term affair she had been enjoying with the facility's married director. Confronted by an outraged husband, she shrugged and said that she didn't see that it mattered, as long as she could physically satisfy both of them. Then Volodya began to detect signs that she was having sex with other members of the staff, as well. But he wasn't certain. He began to think he might be slightly mad, that he was imagining things, making his life worse than it already was.

After a year, in the course of which his wife became pregnant and his drinking increased markedly, Volodya managed a transfer to an adjoining lab working on vaccines for the same diseases he had been working to sharpen. The soldiers of the Soviet Army would need to enter infected areas, so they would require dependable immunity. Even if the research still concerned war, Volodya much preferred working on immunizations and potential cures to perfecting the ultimate virus. A mere building away from his former work, the new lab seemed like a distant paradise.

His son was born with no eyes. The chief physician, consoling him, told Volodya that such things happened with increasing frequency in the Aral Sea region and that, really, it was no place to have children. Kitty refused even to see the baby, and it disappeared into the medical system.

Six months later, the facility's Party committee summoned Volodya. The panel members were gentle, but firm, with him. Other comrades had complained of his drinking excessively during the workday and of disturbances he and his wife caused in the housing area. Was there any way the Party could help? They understood that it was a difficult time for him. Perhaps he needed someone to talk to? In any event, it was his duty to take his life in hand. Reagan, the American president, was bent on war. The world situation had never been so threatening. The country and the Party had to be ready. The laboratory had urgent work to do.

Volodya swore off alcohol and received a room in the bachelors' dormitory. Shocked, Kitty wept and swore she loved him, accusing him of deserting her because she had given birth to a deformed child. She amazed him with her inability to conceive of penalties for her own behavior. Sometimes she visited him in the dormitory for sex. Often they did not even speak. Twice he saw her go into the rooms of other young scientists.

But he stayed away from vodka. And he worked hard. He slowly began to feel capable again, to relish his intelligence and what it could do. Working with a veteran of many years in the lab, he developed a promising vaccine against anthrax— one that could be administered only days before intense exposure.

To his astonishment, the vaccine was scheduled to be tested directly on human beings. The international situation had grown so precarious that drastic measures were excusable. A company of construction troops, mostly Central Asians, arrived and bivouacked at a remote range. Even their officers were not told the purpose of the deployment. Each of the soldiers received a shot, but the doses were varied and carefully recorded to test the vaccine's power. Five days later, a slow-moving aircraft passed over the bivouac site, trailing vapor from a tank fixed under its fuselage.

Every soldier died of anthrax. If anything, the vaccine appeared to have accelerated the disease's progress.

Wearing a suit that might have been designed for outer space, Volodya visited the bivouac site. Not all of the soldiers were in or near their tents. A number of them, as soon as they realized that something horrible had begun to happen in their midst, had tried to escape on foot. The corpse of one lieutenant was found a dozen kilometers away. Other bodies were never recovered. The desert swallowed men whole.

The corpses remaining at the test site were enough for Volodya. He inspected every one of them. And it was evident that each man had died in a private agony that words could not express.

He was to blame.

Yet, no one blamed him. The project leader took him aside and explained that, while no one liked to squander human lives, you sometimes had to look at the bigger picture. And the increased lethality the vaccine had lent to the disease just might constitute a breakthrough—this might be the key to developing the powerful strain of anthrax the facility had been seeking.

His wife came for sex and laughed over the whole business.

Volodya begged to be released from the project, from the research center, from military-related work in general. The Party representative was very understanding. He acknowledged that Volodya had certainly had a run of poor luck. But think of Lenin in Zurich! How much he had needed to endure before he was able to return and rescue the Motherland! The Party was prepared to help Volodya through his time of troubles. But he was *needed* here. Didn't he know that the U.S.A. and NATO were undergoing the biggest peacetime military buildup in history? Hadn't he read about the invasion of Grenada? Next, the

U.S. Marines would be landing on the beaches of Cuba. War might be imminent. Surely, Volodya wouldn't think of turning his back on the Party and the Motherland at a time like this.

Volodya wondered at the speed of his deterioration. He drank. With an appetite that put off even the most notorious alcoholics on the research staff. And he decided to write letters of condolence to the families of the soldiers he had killed.

This time, the Party representative was less genial:

"Are you *mad?* Don't you realize that there isn't a single facility in the entire country more secret than this? And you want to write letters to families? What do you intend to say? 'Sorry, your son died of anthrax in a biological-warfare experiment'? Are you a lunatic?"

He was forbidden any alcohol. The Party apparatus put out the word that no one was to supply him with drink.

Volodya began to write poetry. He didn't know where it came from, couldn't judge its merits. But it poured out of him like blood from a wound, as dark as death.

He found alcohol. You could always find alcohol. Such a research facility could not exist without it.

His wife received a divorce.

The Party, with its caring heart, brought his father to visit him. The old man was helpless and bewildered to find that his son could hardly speak rationally. His father went home, shattered, to a wife who had stopped speaking at all and who played the piano until her fingers locked in agonized spasms.

Kitty's primary lover came to Volodya's rescue. Volodya never understood it completely. Perhaps the man thought it was a great joke, or maybe his conscience troubled him. It might even have been just as he explained it—that he believed in Volodya's potential as a scientist and that it was clear that his environment was ruining him. The director arranged for Volodya's release from military research. He also found him a research assistant's job.

In Moscow.

Volodya's colleagues were outraged when the news got out. Everyone wanted to go to Moscow. Nobody wanted to remain in a hellhole in the middle of the desert. And who was allowed to go? An alcoholic who didn't show up in the lab for days on end. A delegation complained about the injustice to the Party representative. But the Party representative saw what was for the best. Plus, Volodya figured, the Party man wanted to be rid of his paramount problem case.

In Moscow, Volodya fooled himself into believing that he might make a fresh start. But he soon found that he could not do without alcohol. Most of the time, he worked quite well on half a bottle of vodka. He didn't need so much. But, on days of forced abstinence, his head imploded and he could not force himself to come fully alive, let alone to work.

Robotlike, he sent off some of his poems to a journal. And a miracle occurred. An editor decided that their raw honesty fit the times and the new spirit of glasnost. The poems found other outlets, as well. For a time, Moscow's broken-backed intelligentsia made love to him. Until the plain, serious women and the small men in their home-knit sweaters discovered the violent streak that had begun to emerge in the former wrestler. For no reason that anyone could identify, he severely beat a playwright who had tried to befriend him. And he threw a woman down a flight of stairs. But he hardly remembered any of it. It was as if another person had done those things while he watched an out-of-focus film. He smashed up the office of an editor who refused to publish one of his poems and found himself in a cell.

But drunkenness excused almost anything in Moscow. With a swollen face, courtesy of the militia, Volodya found himself back on the street. He had not been to work for days—he could not remember exactly how many days—and he had neither money nor food in his sliver of a room. Shameless, he began working through the addresses he had collected over the past months. But it was the middle of the day and no one seemed to be home. Until he got to the apartment of a woman whom he had met at a party a few weeks before. He remembered only that she had looked at him with eyes that were almost frightening in their steadiness and that she had surprised him with her ability to talk about science. She had been studying psychology or something of that nature. He had wanted to pursue her, but had fallen into a long drunk with two new friends.

Nadya took him in without question. It was as though she

had been waiting for him all her life. She drew him a bath and he passed out in the bathtub.

She had it good—a Moscow apartment that belonged to her father, an absent general of some sort. It struck him that she had the same hair as his childhood sweetheart, the poetry girl who had left him with one unforgettable kiss.

She woke him, dried him, and dressed him in a robe. Then she fed him bread and jam with tea. She made him shave with a razor her father had left behind. Then he fell asleep on her sofa and did not wake until the next day.

He had never met a woman like her. She was sexually splendid, and frank about her desires. Yet there was something else, a quality for which there was no word, that distinguished her from all other women. He felt as though ho had no choice but to do what she told him. And what she told him unnerved him at first.

She had a plan. Her own five-year plan. Moscow, she said, was nothing but a mass grave for the living dead. She was going to go to America. No matter what it took. And one of the things it took was money.

She told him openly that she had been working as a prostitute. Only for Westerners, usually for Scandinavian or German businessmen staying in the Cosmos or the Inturist. But there were problems. With pimps. And street thugs. With the mafia. She needed a protector. Someone who was strong and who wasn't afraid.

Volodya laughed at the offer. Of all things he had thought he might become in life, he had never expected to become a pimp.

But he did. He guarded her. And waited for her. He rubbed shoulders and drank with men whose life stories would have been impossible to believe had they not carried the scars and tattoos to prove them true. Everyone had a nickname, and his was the Scientist.

Some of the other "protectors" had a naive respect for education and intelligence. The rest respected Volodya's readiness for violence. As long as he and his girl paid their commissions into the right hands, there was no real trouble. Except when one German executive refused to pay what he had promised, trying to brush off Nadya with a couple of rubles. Everything had to be in dollars or German marks, as the German learned painfully.

Volodya even managed to put his technical skills to good use. Although theoretical biology wasn't much in demand in his new circle, his ability to work with chemicals stood him in good stead with some very powerful people. Making car bombs and incendiary devices was child's play, and the work made him feel less of a parasite. The sort of men who needed his help were the sort who held hard currency, and he was able to add to Nadya's savings now and then.

They lived like a married couple: decently, frugally. Then, one night when something ugly happened to her in a hotel, he realized that he loved her with that unrivaled adult love that consumes the soul and can never be explained. And he believed, against all reason, that she loved him.

She loved sex, liked men, but utterly hated her father. Volodya didn't see that it made sense. But then, none of it made sense. She spoke about her father as though he were a combination of Beria and a fool. She referred to him casually as a murderer, as though the whole world knew. When the general called to say he would be in Moscow for a few days for a conference, Volodya went with her to meet him, imagining that he was along for her protection. Instead, he met a smallish, plump old man in a general's uniform, a man with big cheeks who seemed to be forever smiling. He was openly delighted to see his daughter, who simply glowered at him and cut him off.

Old Morozov was endlessly apologetic. He hoped that he had not disturbed his little Nadinka. He had wanted only to see her for a little while. And who was this fine young man with her? He had decided to stay at the military hotel, since he didn't want to disrupt her life. And how was that life? When would she complete her degree? Did she need him to call anyone for her?

When old Morozov commented that Nadya looked just like her mother, she asked him icily if that meant he was going to kill her, too. And she turned her back and left the two men standing there.

The old general apologized to Volodya for the scene, telling him that Nadya tended to say things she didn't really mean.

When Volodya caught up to her in the street, he asked Nadya why she was so hard on the old man.

"Shut up," she said. "It's none of your business."

That night she asked him to do things to her that he had never done to any woman, and when he hesitated, she began to weep and shriek and strike at his face. He did everything she asked, leaving her moaning and semiconscious, with blood on her mouth and legs.

He woke in the middle of the night to find her clutching him, her arms tightened around him like leather straps. When she realized that he was awake, she grasped him even more tightly, with incredible strength, begging him:

"Don't ever leave me. Tell me that you'll never leave me."

He promised her that he would never leave her, frightened because he realized that it was true.

Not long afterward, she began going out alone. When he finally asked her what was going on, she said:

"I think I've found a husband. One who can take me to America."

He must have shown the shock and terror he felt, because she hurried over to him, sat down on his lap, and kissed him, saying, "Don't worry. It's all part of the plan. You're coming, too." She smiled at him. "Why do you think I need so much money?"

It was all true. She found a husband, a clean-looking Jew who intended to take advantage of the times to go to the United States. Volodya, who had been shifted to an apartment of his own at Nadya's expense, started drinking seriously again, although he tried to conceal it from her. When she received her U.S. visa, he felt his insides collapse. He knew she had been lying about taking him with her. Why would she want him? He decided he would not—could not—reproach her. After all, he had been living off her body, rewarding her only with the occasional poem and sex when she wasn't too tired. He had nothing to offer her, really.

One morning—late one morning—he woke to find his internal passport missing. Other papers were gone, as well. He tried to remember whether he had come home alone or if some companion might have stolen them. He decided he must have lost them somewhere. He had not seen Nadya for days. He had been drinking with some acquaintances from his most recent life, and he was not even certain of the day of the week. He felt sick, without knowing why. He went out into the hallway and threw up in the toilet he shared with the inhabitants of four other one-room apartments. When he emerged, a little girl with a bow in her hair looked at him disapprovingly.

He went back into his room and sat down on the bed, clutching his stomach. He was still sitting there when Nadya arrived.

She looked at him and smiled timidly. Then the smile grew until it became the grin of a child wild with joy. She reached into her bag and produced a fistful of passes, papers, and vouchers, letting them fall on the soiled bed. And she hugged him wonderfully.

"The Americans were easier than the Russians," she said. "I didn't know the Americans were so corrupt."

Volodya idly sifted through the papers. Then he stopped. There was a passport in his name, valid for travel abroad. And there was a U.S. visa. Also in his name.

It was an immigrant visa.

He looked up at her in awe.

Nadya threw herself down on the bed, laughing. "You owe me six thousand dollars," she cried. "And a kiss."

A moment later she jumped up again, a happy, happy girl, and produced a bottle of Crimean champagne from her just-in-case bag. She fiddled with the plastic cork until it shot against the wall and champagne foamed from the bottle. She handed the drink to him.

"Here's to a new life in America."

"I told you to pack your things," Nadya said savagely.

Volodya looked around the tiny Washington apartment, amazed at how much remained undone. He pointed abjectly to the little plastic travel bag by the door.

"I have the photographs. And the gun."

Nadya lost the last of her patience. She tore through the stacks of paper he had left behind, ripped through drawers. His laboratory equipment slept on its table.

"What about this? And this? I told you to pack everything that could identify you."

"Nadya—"

"You're like a child—you know that? You're supposed to be helping me. And you can't follow simple instructions."

"There wasn't time," he said sadly.

Her anger passed into disgust. "Just help me. Come on. We've got to get out of here."

"But where will we go?"

"Don't worry about that. Just help me."

He imitated her. Dropping his life's humble accessories into a paper bag. Then he stopped and stood upright, looking at her.

"What is it?" she asked, brushing back a strand of hair. "What's the matter now?"

He stared at her: the sum of his life. A hasty angel, with spun honey falling down around her face. Her eyes showed immense depth under the dark curves of her eyebrows. Beauty in bad light.

"Nadya . . . maybe your father was right. Maybe we should just give them the photographs."

She straightened her back. Slowly. As if pushing through water. Her expression balanced between fury and wonder.

"Are you *insane?*"

He smiled. It was a paltry smile. But it was the best he could manage in the face of her scorn. She was always so . . . overwhelming.

"Maybe it's all bad luck. Too much blood. Maybe your father was doing the right thing."

"You're crazy," she said in a low voice that frightened him. Then her words gathered momentum, her pitch climbed. "That stupid old bastard. He would've ruined everything. Do you understand what a million dollars means to us? One million dollars? And that perverted old scum starts talking about his *conscience?* When did he ever have a conscience?"

"Nadya—"

"He *owed* me that money. Why do you think I brought him to this country? Do you know what it cost me? I didn't pay for him to have an attack of guilt—you think I laid on my back under all those men just so that bastard could try to wipe the blood off his conscience with some kind of grand gesture? At our expense? He was going to destroy everything we worked for."

Suddenly, she softened. Out of breath. She approached him, motherly now. "Volodya . . . we'll never have a chance like this again. It only comes once."

He tried to hold his ground. "But . . . perhaps it really is immoral. To make money off of death, off misery."

She laughed. With the laugh she reserved for the folly of men.

But he could not let it go. He forced his mouth to speak. "Perhaps we should just give them the photos. Maybe they'll leave us alone. Maybe they'll even help us. We could start new lives."

She grasped him by the biceps. With her hard little hand.

"In *this* country? Look around. Do you want to live in this filth? Do you expect *me* to live in this filth? In this country nothing counts but money." She laughed again, with the sound of a bag of shaken stones. "Even alcohol is expensive here."

"And if they arrest us? What kind of life will that be for us?"

"They won't arrest us." Her eyes showed a diamond certainty.

"But if they did? We're murderers."

She slapped him hard across the face. Very hard. She was remarkably strong.

"Don't *talk* like that. *Don't* say that. Don't think like that."

He looked down at her, a giant set upon by hounds.

"But it's true. We're murderers."

She slapped him again.

"We killed your father."

She screamed at him. Without words. It was a howl of animal desperation. She turned from him and swept her hand across the top of a dresser. Then she lunged for the table where his chemist's toys waited purposeless. She smashed the glass and metal to the floor. Shrieking. Until she cut herself and stopped.

She pressed her left hand over her wounded forearm and looked at him from amid the wreckage.

"He killed himself," she said, "he killed himself."

"He trusted you." The speech came on its own. "He *loved*

you. He knew the photos weren't in that packet. He *knew,* Nadya. He would have done anything for you."

"Shut up," she said coldly, quietly. "Shut your mouth and pack your things."

"Just stay put," Bates said over the telephone. "I'll be right over. I've got it figured out."

Ritter did not even have time to reply. Bates hung up.

Ritter realized that the call should have put him in better spirits. He had been trying to reach Charlee or Bates for two hours, and he had finally left a harsh message on the colonel's answering machine, threatening to go to the police with everything he knew if he didn't get a response quickly. It had been a childish thing to do. But he was sick with worry about Nadya.

He realized there was nothing much between them, and that there never would be. He would barely be able to tolerate her for a long weekend. And his desire for her had a tinge of viciousness. He did not trust her. Even after watching some thug drag her off. But he worried about her. And he wanted her in his bed. At least one more time.

He took two more painkillers for his knee, lurching around the apartment with the help of the cane the physical-therapy clinic had forced upon him. Even with its aid, he could barely make himself go.

He sat down and looked at the picture of his wife. She no longer seemed to belong to the same lifetime: the woman with whom he had crossed the border at Nogales to eat shrimp in La Roca and drink the small, atomic margaritas, while a fat guitarist strained his back to sing to her. The Catholic girl who, in her final days on earth, had taken to reading the works of a Protestant mystic dead two and a half centuries. She was as distant as Byzantium. He took up the frame, and the photograph was only a pottery shard in an archaeologist's hand.

His wife. With her inscrutable smile that might not have been a smile at all.

"How could you do that to me?" he asked her.

TWELVE

"KNOW WHAT I HATE MOST ABOUT SURVEILLANCE?" SERGEANT LOPEZ asked. Without pausing to give his partner an opportunity to reply, he answered his own question. "You get soft. No exercise. Just sitting around on your butt. I hate the porked-out feeling you get."

"You eat too much junk," Nolan said. Nolan was a fifteen-year veteran of Army Counterintelligence, a sergeant first class, and a disciple of Jeb Bates, for whom he had worked in Germany, El Sal, and on the home court. He liked Lopez, who had potential. But the kid really did put garbage in his gut.

"A man's got to eat," Lopez said. "And I don't see any salad bars around here. This neighborhood's like suicide by malnutrition. It's worse than San Juan. If you can't fry it, they won't buy it."

"You could bring some fruit."

"I don't like fruit. I mean, not all the time. Anyway, my theory is that exercise is the most important thing. You got to keep the engine tuned."

Nolan nodded. Lopez peered out through the surveillance scope as he spoke. Whenever Lopez wasn't on watch, he was either doing push-ups or sleeping. Or eating.

"It could be worse," Nolan said. "We could still be in the van."

The mission had started in the back of a marvelously equipped van, the outside of which was bland and artfully battered. Inside, beyond the magic spook gear, the vehicle was constructed and stocked so that two agents could stay inside for five days without showing their faces on the street. On city jobs, you set it up with the local police so that they just kept putting tickets under the windshield or booted the van, but didn't get carried away and tow it. The van was an extremely effective tool. But you *really* had to get along with your partner.

This time, they had picked the wrong neighborhood. On their first night out, two kids had tried to steal the vehicle. There had been plenty of commotion and embarrassment, but fortunately, neither of the Russians who lived in the target apartment seemed to notice.

After that, Bates had plugged into one of his D.C. connections and set them up in a condemned building. What the site lacked in amenities, it made up in atmosphere. On top of which, the mission was a snoozer. The old Russian went off and didn't come back. Then Charlee Whyte and some limping major had taken the girl away—which was a downer, because, when the light was right, they had been able to watch her doing aerobics in her apartment. And the girl was serious about her exercise.

Both Nolan and Lopez had been fascinated by the Russian girl. Lopez, who could do back-on-the-block with the best of them, said that any squeeze who looked like that and survived in this kind of hood had to be a serious player. Yet the girl looked beautiful and clean, almost too delicate to lift a quart of milk. She certainly didn't look like a hard case.

One of life's little mysteries, they agreed.

"Spell me for a while?" Lopez asked. "Tired eyes miss the prize."

"Got it." Nolan moved in on the scope.

Lopez got up and stretched, a black shadow in a dark world. "God, this one's dull. So, you think now that the Bureau's in, they'll pull us?"

Their supervisor had checked in earlier in the evening and had mentioned that Bates was bringing in the FBI. Something was going down in shaky-town.

"Don't know." Nolan watched the street through the optics, but he could sense his partner behind him.

Lopez was a good guy. But he was comparatively green. He didn't know what dull was. But Nolan knew. Dull was a full year of all-day-every-day alone in a room that had been a cell, going through the files of the dissolved East German Ministry of State Security, courtesy of your West German colleagues who were bending their own government's rules to pay a big, big debt. Dull was a month in the jungle during rainy season, talking to the monkeys and waiting for a mark who never showed.

"You never know," Nolan said. "You go through a dry patch and you figure the mission's a bust. Then a car pulls up or a door opens and you've got the battle of Gettysburg on your hands." He shifted on his chair. "You might as well get some sleep."

"Maybe later. I don't much like the idea of sleeping with all the wildlife around here. Ever been bit by a rat?"

No. Nolan had never been bitten by a rat. But a monkey had almost taken off one of his fingers.

"I hate rats," Lopez went on. "Growing up, we had rats. They'd come in from the dump. Sometimes I think I joined the Army just to get away from the rats."

A moment later, Nolan heard the sound of Lopez flopping down on the cot they shared. Nolan relaxed into his low-rpm watcher mode. Lopez had made him think of a suspense movie he and his wife had just seen. Entertaining and all that, but it had only been some Hollywood weenie's notion of how things went down. Not that that wasn't typical. Nolan was a student of films that pertained to his calling. He went to or rented every crime or spy movie he could locate. He looked on it as his professional development program. Sometimes you really picked up a good idea. But mostly Nolan was just disappointed. The films tended to fail in three areas. First, they never showed the incredible amount of paperwork that went with law enforcement or any variant thereof. Second, they never captured the boredom, the routine, the need for superhuman patience. And finally, they never caught the squalor of it all. Even when a film tried to shock you with ugliness, it was picturesque ugliness. After all, when movie stars played hookers, the hookers were going to look like movie stars—not like the needle-marked slabs of AIDS bait who came out only at night for good reason. Someday, maybe when he retired, Nolan planned to write a book they could make into a *real* movie.

Thinking about the book he would one day write was a dependable pastime when nothing else was on the mental burner, and Nolan had gone back to the game of casting the film that would come of it when he saw something that made him straighten his back and clutch the surveillance device with both hands.

Yes.

No question about it.

"Tony," Nolan called in a power whisper. "Come have a look."

Lopez rolled off the cot and came creaking across the floor.

Nolan made room behind the optics. "Catch her going in the door. Quick."

Lopez locked his forehead against the machine.

"America's fucking sweetheart," he said after a moment. "That's my baby."

"See anybody else?"

"No."

"Charlee Whyte's got guts, I'll say that for her. Coming to this part of town alone after dark."

Lopez shrugged. "This ain't bad. I'll take you up to Northeast some night and show you bad."

"She go in?"

"Yeah. She's inside. You figure it's a meet?"

"We'll see." Nolan didn't want to get Lopez too excited. But fifteen years of on-the-job instinct refinement told him they had action-front. Either Charlee Whyte was looking for something in the apartment, or she was going to meet someone. She hadn't come strictly for the entertainment value.

"Think we should call it in?" Lopez asked.

Nolan chewed his lip, figuring. Then he said, "No. Not yet. We don't want to cry wolf."

*   *   *

"That was it," Mitya cried. "That was the street." He glanced bitterly over his shoulder, then turned back to the task of guiding the big automobile through the streets of Washington. "This city doesn't make any sense."

Even when Mitya did not use his customary foul language, his voice echoed old obscenities. The Russian's exemplary and comprehensive vulgarity fascinated Zhan.

"And now they're all one-way streets." Mitya punched the dashboard. The act seemed to make him feel better and he said, almost happily, "At least now we know where it is."

"Just take us there," Zhan said coldly. "We have no more time to waste." It was clear to him that Mitya did not fully grasp the penalties for failure in such an important affair. And Zhan did not want to die just because they had gotten lost in traffic. He did not want to die as cheap and foul a death as the men he had killed.

He looked out of the side window. Following the wet streets. They were in a very different America now. Somewhere along the way they had crossed an invisible border to enter a bleak, miserable, and dangerous new country that Zhan could not believe was part of Washington, D.C., capital of the world.

"This is a terrible place," he said suddenly. "This is worse than Moscow." He could think of no greater insult for a Western city.

Mitya laughed. "This is nothing."

Zhan understood his fellow man. It had enabled him to survive. And he knew that Mitya was thinking about sex. With the Morozova woman. Zhan had decided to let Mitya have her. He personally found the Russian so repulsive that he had no doubt that Morozova would share his antipathy. Despite her scarred past. And she would be intelligent enough to know that she would die at his hands if she failed to cooperate. Of course, she would die anyway. But she would hope that, by giving up everything else, she just might keep her life. The human animal was disappointingly predictable.

The damaged streets of Washington hurt Zhan in a way he could not fully explain to himself. He could not imagine how any country that looked like this had managed to bring down the Soviet Union. The car passed a clot of black men on a corner, splashing them with leftover rain. A moment later something thumped against the back of the car.

"This is not America," Zhan said firmly.

Charlee tossed her purse and raincoat on the sofa and hurried into Nadya Morozova's bedroom. She felt rushed and uncomfortable, although she could think of no rational grounds for her nervousness. She felt as though she carried her own private darkness with her wherever she went now. And here, in these strange rooms, the darkness thickened. As though something terrible was about to happen, as though a vicious animal was about to snap its leash and come silently for her back. The Russian woman's apartment, on the edge of civilization, was a long way from Lincoln and the pathetic, self-satisfied old man with the broom.

She went through each drawer thoroughly. The Russian woman's wardrobe basics were Lycra spandex tights and candy-colored underwear with labels Charlee had never owned. There was no need to worry about disturbing the order of things. The fuck-me outfits were jumbled together with street-vendor jewelry and cheap sweaters. But there was no sign of anything resembling photographs of American POWs. There were not even any letters from home. It seemed as though the woman had cut all ties, or tried to. Charlee did not find even a single personal snapshot.

When she finished with the drawers and the equally depressing closet, Charlee sat down on the edge of the bed. There *had* to be *some*thing. Because she willed it. Because she needed to find something. Because her world depended on it.

A tall stack of magazines sat beside the nightstand. Idly interested in what such a woman would read, Charlee picked up the top issues. They had the look of having been salvaged from someone else's trash or slipped under a coat upon leaving a hair salon. But the titles surprised Charlee:

Lear's, Vanity Fair, Gourmet, Elle, another *Vanity Fair, Fortune, Cosmo*—well, at least that one tracked, Charlee thought— then *Architectural Digest*.

The assortment struck her as pathetic and absurd, given its environment. How to marry a millionaire, Charlee figured. The immigrant bimbo's dream.

Charlee went back into the front room and continued her search. She wished Ritter were with her. She was weary of doing everything alone. And Ritter understood these people. But she just could not bring herself to trust him enough.

She found a small plastic suitcase behind the sofa. It held a few cheap men's shirts and two ties a charity wouldn't have, underwear the color of dishwater, and socks that looked as though they had been mended by male hands. At the very bottom lay a collection of ribbons and medals that would have done a dictator proud.

God, what lives, Charlee thought. She went to the bookshelf. Foreign alphabet, cheap bindings. Dust. She leafed through each volume, anxious to discover secrets between the pages.

More dust.

Charlee began moving the furniture, wishing again that she were not alone. She felt as though enemies were coming at her from all sides now. The way they had come at Lincoln. They all wanted to stop her. There had been a message on her answering machine from a U.S. marshal. Asking her to call as soon as possible.

But none of them were going to stop her. She was needed. If she gave up, no one with the necessary vision would be left to carry on the fight. The military would go back to its comfortable little routine of parades and promotions, contributing nothing of worth. And the craven little creatures from State were as bad. With their willingness to sacrifice entire populations to preserve the diplomatic peace and quiet. They needed to be shaken. To be shocked by the suffering of the world.

Someone had to stand up and shriek.

To shame them into action.

To shame them into simple human decency.

Someone had to be willing to play the fool.

Why couldn't Chris see it? Why wouldn't he help her? She needed someone. Not a man for the sake of having a man. An ally. Someone to carry on the fight when she grew tired. Someone—just one other human being—upon whom she might depend.

A friend.

Even Chris just wanted to be rid of her. He was just another man, gone the minute some little tart shook her ass.

She had made a fool of herself. And it wasn't even for a good cause.

No.

It was all right.

It was always all right to be the fool.

Only fools ever accomplished anything worthwhile.

The generals in their star-studded polyester suits never risked being seen as fools. Nor did the twits from Foggy Bottom, who kept their spines erect only by starching their shirts. And they never accomplished anything worthwhile.

But Chris had disappointed her. All of their adult lives, he had disappointed her. It was as though he had chosen his path for spite. She thought again of how the Russian woman had fallen into his arms and laughed at her folly as she strained to move the ancient refrigerator away from the wall. She laughed and tilted the gurgling machine, shifting its weight by inches. Glass clinked, something fell. Everything was a struggle.

She managed to move the appliance out far enough to see decades of filth behind it. But she had no time to indulge her revulsion.

Someone was at the door.

"Now who we got?" Nolan asked himself.

"Let me look." Lopez was as anxious as a child.

Nolan leaned to the side to allow his partner to check out the two men who had paused in front of the target building. The taller of the two was trying to read a slip of paper in the poor light, probably confirming the address.

"Out-of-towners," Lopez said. "Definitely from east of Eden. Just off the jumbo. Get the old guy with the white hair."

Nolan took over the optics again. But he had already seen more clearly than had his partner. "He's not old. Watch the way he moves. He's just some kind of pale blond. Strange-looking sucker." He tensed. *"They're going in."*

"You think these are the guys Charlee Whyte's expecting? We got a meet going down?"

It was a reasonable conclusion. But Nolan had learned the hard way to trust his instincts over logic:

"No. I don't think she's expecting these guys at all."

"I heard somebody." Mitya cocked his head toward the apartment door, pistol ready.

"Good," Zhan said. "We won't have to waste time waiting."

Mitya looked at the smaller man in the twilight of the hallway. The albino was beginning to make him feel uncomfortable. Mitya had known a lot of hard men. But his current partner was the first one whom he had ever suspected of having no human feelings whatsoever.

Mitya knocked with the butt of his pistol.

The noise inside the apartment stopped. Downstairs, a recorded voice jabbered over drums.

"Let me do this." Zhan bent to the door, applying a tool that looked like a small piece of modern sculpture. In seconds, the lock clicked and the door began to ease.

Mitya shoved it wide and went in, pistol ready. He didn't see anyone at first. He twisted deeper into the room, scanning.

Through an open archway, he saw a blonde standing with her mouth open, her body half-hidden by a refrigerator.

It wasn't the Morozova woman.

"Come in and shut the door," Mitya told his partner. The presence of a woman, any woman, made him feel physically confident. He knew how to handle women.

This one looked terrified.

"That's not her," Zhan said from behind Mitya's shoulder. It was the first time Mitya had heard his partner sound genuinely surprised.

Mitya looked the woman up and down. Sensing him, she moved to cover herself more fully with the appliance.

"No," Mitya said angrily. "This cow is definitely not Morozova."

But she'll do, he thought.

"Take care of her," Zhan said, making a gift. "I'll check the other rooms."

Mitya stepped toward the woman. She looked wonderfully afraid of him, trying to make herself small. Mitya liked it when women were afraid of him.

With a quick lunge through the archway, he grabbed her by the arm and pulled her away from her imaginary protection. Then he slammed her back against the side of the refrigerator with enough force to let her know who was in charge. The machine's insides jingled.

"You speak Russian?" Mitya asked.

He loved her eyes. So full of fear. Wondering what would come next.

He moved closer and placed a hand over one of her breasts. In a reflex action, she tried to knock it away.

He punched her in the stomach, dancing back to let her fall. She hit the floor heavily and, several seconds later, made her first attempt at speech. But he could not make out the words.

He straddled her, waiting for her to regain just enough control of herself to rise back to intelligent fear. Then he dropped to his knees, sitting just below her chest.

"Who are you?" he asked in English.

She would not, or could not, answer. He examined her more closely. Older. But really not so bad. Expensive stuff. He rubbed the flat of his pistol into her chest, testing the fabric of her blouse and the pattern of her bra underneath.

"Tell me who are you."

She responded with words he simply could not understand. His inability to get her meaning enraged him, and he slapped her with his left hand. Then he grasped her by the throat and brought the pistol barrel to her eye. He watched the first drop of blood form at the corner of her mouth.

"Talk slow."

"*Please*," she said, offering the first word he recognized. "Please."

"Yes. Please. Who are you?"

"Important," she said slowly. She had to struggle to control her voice and it delighted him. "Important person. U.S. government."

Mitya couldn't quite get the meaning. But he felt that he

should and it plunged him back into anger. He leaned down so that his face covered her features with its shadow.

"You have photographs?"

Zhan called from the next room. "What does she say?"

"She's making problems. I'll have to teach her a lesson."

"Don't kill her before you find out who she is," Zhan said matter-of-factly. Then he went about his business.

The woman lying under Mitya turned her head to the extent his grip allowed.

"No photographs," she said. "No photographs."

Mitya had been concerned that Zhan might try to interfere with him. But his partner had made it clear now that the woman was his. Mitya relaxed and let himself enjoy the situation.

"Miss, you must help us."

She looked up at him with despair in her eyes. He did not like that. It was too soon for despair. She was hurrying him.

He got into a crouch and grabbed her by the hair, yanking her halfway to her knees. She had beautiful hair, thick in his fist.

She reached out to grab his hand, then caught herself. But she could not hold back the cry of pain.

Fear was a gorgeous thing in a woman. Much better than fear in a man. There was always something a bit embarrassing about the cowardice of a fellow male.

The woman began to plead. He could not understand the words. But the message was clear.

He began to drag her across the floor, heading in the direction where he sensed there would be a bed.

Suddenly she began to resist. She fought to break free, screaming, kicking, punching.

Mitya struck her so hard on the side of the head he heard bone snap. She landed against a wall. He grabbed her by an arm and yanked her toward the bedroom.

"Just shut up," he said in Russian, forgetting that she could not understand his language. "Just shut up and get in there."

She stumbled and fell, looking up at him with enormous eyes and blood streaming from one ear, straining through her hair.

He grinned and lifted her up to her feet. He kissed her, holding her against him with his left arm while the hand with the pistol tore her blouse down from the back of the collar, stripping off the buttons and separating its front. The woman had a good, clean smell and soft skin. He yanked her head back so that he could look at her. Zhan walked by without the least display of interest.

Really, the woman was not bad at all. She looked better with the blood smeared over her face. It gave her character. Mitya tore at her bra. When it wouldn't rip in two, he pulled so hard the woman dropped to her knees.

"Please don't kill me."

He understood her. It made him smile.

Nolan slammed down the receiver of the wonderful state-of-the-art cellular communications unit that never failed to operate perfectly.

"Son of a bitch." Nolan reserved obscenity for special occasions. "Can you believe this piece of shit?"

"Should've got MCI," Lopez said.

"Son of a bitch."

"Saves me lots of money on calls home to Puerto Rico."

"Son of a bitch."

"Want to try a pay phone?"

Nolan shook his head. He picked up the receiver one more time, but the machine was just as dead. "No time. Something's going down."

"We going in?"

Nolan looked at him in the rich darkness.

Compromising a surveillance operation was bad enough. But you never went in without reporting your action. It was a fundamental rule.

"We're going in," Nolan said.

"Please don't kill me," Charlee begged. It was so strange. She had made no conscious decision to say such a thing. But then, there were no decisions left. Every time she tried to think, her tormentor hurt her with a power that disordered everything inside her. Now it was as if her body had taken over from her brain, determined to survive. "Please don't kill me," her body said.

At first, she had been too surprised to do or say anything. This sort of thing happened to other, distant women, to the victims she had pledged her life to protect. It was not supposed to happen to her. At home in America.

When she realized fully what was happening to her, she tried to fight back. But the man was so much larger and stronger. He seemed like a giant. He struck her on the side of the head and it felt as though he had shot his pistol into her ear.

She saw him in flashes as he herded her from room to room, tearing at her clothing. His face rushed toward her again, scarred and unshaven, with boils down his cheeks. He stank.

He kissed her, laughing and covering her mouth with wetness. His breath made her think of the fumes off a corpse. He smeared his face over her cheeks, then drew back.

He was bloody.

Then she realized the blood was her own.

He tugged at her bra, then jerked her down to her knees.

"Please don't kill me." Her voice was very clear now.

The crotch of his trousers brushed against her, and the smell made her irresistibly sick. She began to vomit over the floor. Some of it caught the man's shoe.

He kicked her away, shouting at her in a language she could not understand.

It's him, she realized. *It's him.* He was every sweaty, back-country, self-appointed colonel with his gut hanging over his gunbelt. Every nationalist partisan who had been nothing but a common criminal before the civil war began and who would go back to being a common criminal after the fighting ended. If he wasn't running the government.

This is how it is, Charlee thought in wonder, *this is how it is.*

The man lifted her and hurled her into a room with a bed. She knew the room, its fixtures. But everything was much more vivid now.

The man spoke to her in a softer voice. Then he laughed again.

Charlee fell backward onto the bed.

Maybe if I let him do it, she thought. Maybe if I don't fight . . .

He pushed her legs apart, then frustrated by her panty hose, he shoved her skirt higher with sandpaper hands, seeking the waistband.

Oh, God, no, she thought. *Please, God, no.* Even a moment before, it had not been this real. She felt the fabric stretch away from her skin.

"No," she screamed, grabbing for his hands.

He slapped her so hard her neck seemed to pull away from her body. But that same body had made another decision. She kicked at him, struggling to get a knee up to where she could hurt him.

But he was too quick. She kicked air. He landed another blow that sent her into the beginning of a daze.

He cursed her. She did not know the words from his language. But she understood that they were horribly obscene. And she realized that sex was only a part of what was happening to her.

He pulled out a knife. She believed he was going to kill her. But he only cut away the last cloth keeping him from her. Then he tossed the knife onto the floor, a thousand miles out of her reach.

His face, perched above her, had nothing human left in it. With a shudder, she felt something thrust into her and she thought it had already begun. Then she realized it was only his hand, fingers rough as wood.

She closed her eyes and began to pray. With words remembered from childhood. All of the recent, gender-neutral liturgy had fallen away, and the old, powerful words came to her aid. They were all she had left.

Wetness spattered off the man's face as he lifted away from her. For an instant she believed her prayers were being answered. Then she heard the familiar sound of a man opening his trousers.

She shut her eyes and sank back into her prayers, thinking at the same time that she might be able to pretend this was all happening with someone else, with someone she wanted.

Why should it matter? It was nothing really. Statistically, it made no difference.

Oh, God, she thought. Dear God, help me.

It made all the difference in the world.

Please, God, help me.

He split her legs apart and she understood that this wasn't about sex at all, only about hurting her in a special way.

She realized she was crying. Praying and crying. She felt his skin fall against her, and a fraction of a second later, his entire weight bore down. His mouth covered hers.

Someone knocked very loudly at the door in the front room.

"They're not going to open up," Lopez whispered. His statement was really a question: What do we do now?

Nolan did not have time to respond. The door opened suddenly and the enormous sound of gunfire filled the hallway.

Lopez watched stunned as his partner staggered backward. As though a ghost were punching Nolan in the stomach and chest. Blow after blow. Nolan looked at him with an expression of immeasurable surprise and collapsed.

Lopez threw himself down on the floor, clutching his pistol with both hands. A huge man filled the doorframe. He had a gun.

Lopez fired. The big man twisted away. Lopez fired again.

Lucky shot. The big man's skull exploded, red blood erupting from blond hair.

Lopez tried to roll out of the light. But his body would not respond. Then other details of the past few seconds caught up with him, and he realized that he had been shot.

In the last second of his life, Lopez saw another man in the apartment. This one was smaller, with impossibly white hair and the red eyes of a demon. He had a gun in his hand and it was pointed at Lopez's head.

Zhan listened to the building and the world beyond: no one else. Only the dead.

And the woman.

Zhan went calmly into the bedroom. The woman sat curled in a corner beside a stack of magazines. She did not look up.

"You," Zhan said, testing his English. "We will go."

The woman did not move.

He walked over to her. Considering her disordered hair and the rags of clothing she had tried to draw over herself.

"We go now. Or die now."

He wanted her to respond. He did not want to kill her yet. She was the only link he had left. And the situation had worsened markedly. It was obvious that someone had known he and Mitya existed. He could feel the press of time and sense the solemnity of dying.

He longed for his own world. Where he understood the city streets and the mountain passes. For the first time, he doubted Rakhman's wisdom. It had been folly to send him here.

But a man's fate was a man's fate.

He hardened himself. Breathing the gunshot air.

He was going to get the photographs.

Grasping the woman by an arm, he drew her to her feet. Half of her clothing fell from her body. Zhan looked away.

"Cover yourself." He walked into the other room. A woman's nakedness always had the power to embarrass him and offend his moral sensibility.

Shaking, Charlee hunted through the chest of drawers. Seeking a sweater or anything else that might cover her nakedness. She had so little control over her body that she pulled one drawer out too far and it escaped her grasp, falling noisily and tumbling its contents onto the floor.

Automatically, she stooped to right her wrong. And she saw the knife.

It had fallen between the chest and a cardboard box, a bright, criminal tool. She traced it in her memory, saw it rise again in a monster's paw, then watched it fly through the air as he discarded it to dedicate himself to her. The blade shone between little tumbleweeds of dust.

Instinctively, she reached for it. But her hand stopped short. She did not know if fear restrained her, or some deep judgment. But her hand would go no farther, and after a last pulse of doubt, she retreated, hand still empty.

A moment later the other thug reappeared in the doorway. He looked pathetic and mad. But that might have been the effect of his abnormality. He reminded Charlee of the bunnies her mother had occasionally produced at Easter. Except that this white-furred, red-eyed animal was a murderer.

He held a gun in his right hand, her raincoat and purse in his left. With a face as impassive as cement, he extended her property to her.

"We are going now," he said. Then he, too, saw the knife.

He smiled at her irredeemable folly.

THIRTEEN

"She's got the photos," Bates told Ritter. "It all fits to-gether perfectly. She's got the photos and she's going to pitch you. Just wait. She'll call and tell you the Russian mafia or somebody wants money for the photos or they're going to kill her. And all you have to do is agree to whatever she wants."

Bates grinned, a happy child. He was wonderfully pleased with his analysis, which he had shared at length with Ritter. The details had included the complete history of Nadya Morozova.

Ritter was not smiling.

He knew he should praise the older man, who had done a masterly job of putting together some very jagged pieces. But Ritter could not bring himself to speak yet. He had not expected much of the woman. But he had expected better than this. Out-side, in the world beyond his apartment, cars on late errands hissed along wet boulevards. A police siren rose and fell.

Belatedly, the older man got it. "Well, I guess you're a little disappointed."

Ritter met the colonel's eyes with a quartz stare. "I didn't think she was Bernadette of Lourdes. But her own father . . ."

"She did it. I couldn't prove it in a court of law. Not yet. But she did it. And you know it, too."

"Yes."

"As a professional, you have to believe it."

"Yes."

Bates sighed and idly scratched at the black uniform sweater spanning his stomach. An irregular bulge betrayed a pager fastened to his belt. "There are some things you never get used to."

Ritter began to speak, then stopped. It occurred to him that, if nothing else, the women in his life had always been interesting.

"Have a drink, if you want to," Bates said.

"I'm not that kind of guy."

Bates nodded. As if he had known all along that Ritter was not that kind of guy. "She impresses the hell out of me, though. I've got to give her that much. That woman has the survival instincts of a virus."

Ritter looked through a bookcase into the immediate past. "She has," he said slowly, "strength of will. She's a woman with a sense of purpose." He smiled slightly, rupturing the glacier his face had become. "She told me about her life in Russia. Brilliant tactic. She told me about the shitty things she did to get out of there. She didn't tell me everything, but she told me enough to show me my own weakness. In comparison to her. Because there are lines I would never cross, things I just would not do." His smile broadened grimly. "I cherish all the stuff that lets us tell ourselves we're decent and honorable. I am . . . romantically involved with the niceties of civilization. With morals and manners and handshake deals." His smile dissolved into bleak earnestness. "I believe in the fundamental importance of honesty. Even when I'm lying. But all of that's a luxury she can't afford. You and I are privileged. We can indulge in stylized codes of behavior. But she's fighting tooth and nail to survive." Ritter smiled again, almost wistfully. "I suppose, from her perspective, we're frivolous."

Bates leaned forward, balancing his elbows on his knees. "But *you* don't believe that. I mean, you still don't believe that values are frivolous."

"No. But maybe only because I'm too much of a coward. I'm afraid that, if I believed as she believes, my world would fall apart. I'm not strong enough to live without rules."

Bates shrugged. "Well, that's the point, isn't it? Of 'Yes, sir' and 'No, sir' and of all the little customs that work like glue to hold a defeated army together or to keep a society functioning?" He ran a hand back over his thinning hair and glanced at the picture of Ritter's wife that had taken up permanent residence on the coffee table. "You know, I've always felt that anybody who doesn't believe in an all-powerful God should be clinging to the values, to the earthly components of belief, for dear life. Even if those values are utterly arbitrary in a cosmic sense. Even if mankind just worked them out through trial and error. In a godless world, values, morals—even table manners—become barricades against the darkness. I am what I believe. In the absence of belief, I am my habits." Bates smiled, looking up at Ritter. "But that's neither here nor there."

"Do *you* want a drink?"

"I'm not a drinker, either."

"Bad luck."

Bates brightened. "We're lucky in other ways, you and I. We get a glimpse of what's on the other side of the hill. Even if it's only a swamp." The older man softened. "You really were starting to feel an attachment to her. Weren't you?"

Ritter let himself sink back into his chair. "Nothing serious. She just fucked my brains out."

"And now you hate her for it?"

Ritter perked up, surprised. Reminded that he and Jeb Bates were two different human beings after all.

"No. I'm grateful for it."

Bates moved the discussion back to business. "So you really have no idea where she and her boyfriend—or whatever you want to call him—might be?"

"None. I really thought it was a kidnapping. Silly me." Ritter remembered falling pathetically to the sidewalk as he tried to follow the woman and her abductor. He recalled the faces staring down at him as they hurried past. And he did not think he would ever forget the multileveled pain. A street person, a young man in a ragged red, black, and green knit beret, had been the only passerby unafraid to help him.

Bates pushed out his lips as if preparing for an unusual kiss.

"Well, it would've helped. But I suppose it doesn't matter. She'll call. I'd bet my eagles on it. She'll call you."

"What about the guy you said you had watching my building?" Ritter asked, voice slightly caustic. He still could not quite master his irritation at being kept in the dark so long, at not being fully trusted.

Bates extended open palms, offering to let Ritter drive in the nails. "The kid was too young. And I didn't have a partner for him. Christ, we're short of everything these days—and they're cutting the budget again. Anyway, it's my fault. I had to make some tough choices, and I figured there wouldn't be any real danger in your sector. So I ran the op on you with one agent per shift." Bates raised one hand in a plea for understanding. "I mean, let's face it. You're kind of slow on your feet these days. I figured one guy could keep up. How's the leg doing, anyway?"

"Shitty."

"Anyway, my boy sees you and the woman heading for the taxi stand over by the Ritz Carlton. So he decides to tail you, after I've beat him up for past sins of omission. Except that, once you're over in Georgetown, you can't keep up with her, and my guy makes the wrong call—he stays with you."

"She knew I could never keep up with her. That was part of the plan."

"She's a clever woman. Would've made a great tax attorney. Anyway, I think my agent felt sorry for you. He said you fell down."

"Yes. I fell down."

"And nobody would help you up."

"Times are hard."

"And he had to help you."

"That was your agent? The derelict?"

Bates smiled proudly. "Got a better cover for somebody hanging out on the streets of Washington, D.C.?"

"Well, tell him thanks."

"I'll tell him. He's feeling pretty bad right about now. I had to spank him."

"So who else are you covering? Or am I still an outsider?"

"No. You're in it now, my friend." Bates shifted his weight, grown too big a bear for last year's uniform. The sweater's black ribbing swelled. "You know that I've got limited resources. I have a spot on Charlee Whyte's place up on the Hill. We weren't tailing her, though. Too manpower intensive. And that was your job. My best team's on Miss Morozova's apartment. I figure that for the likeliest action scene." Bates considered for a moment. "Quiet so far, though. And I've got to admit I totally missed her boyfriend. She was better than all of us put together."

"You look thirsty. Want a Coke?"

"Diet?" Bates asked, automatically stroking his paunch.

"Sure." Ritter tried to rise. But the effort went badly and his face told how his knee felt.

"Sit down. I'll get it." Bates jumped up and headed off around the breakfast bar, an old fighter with a couple more good rounds left in him.

Ritter spent a moment worrying about his leg and his future as an Army officer. Then he said:

"All right. So what's your theory about Charlee? Where's the payoff for her in this? She's risking everything."

Bates looked at him curiously and did not answer immediately. Ritter caught the inflection. He wondered if Bates was holding something back even now.

Bates gave a time-delay shrug. "Maybe not." He bent to the refrigerator, raising his voice to be heard. "I mean, who knows? Cromwell's the one who wants the photos. Charlee Whyte's just his girl Friday in this."

"Charlee owes Cromwell. Big-time."

Bates laughed with uncharacteristic meanness. "Without the good senator, she'd be out on her rich-girl ass. He's calling in the chits." Bates held up two cans of diet Coke. "But who knows? Maybe the Honorable Miss Whyte's got some personal angle on this, after all. Ever talk to her about it?"

It was Ritter's turn to shrug. "Yeah. She's evasive."

Bates opened his mouth, then closed it again. Ritter felt irritated, certain now that Bates knew more about Charlee's motivation than he was willing to share. But Ritter was a good soldier and he kept marching where the old colonel wanted him to go.

"So why," Ritter asked, "does Cromwell want the photos? Did you ever turn up anything on that name I gave you, by the way? Charles Turner?"

"No. Where do you keep your glasses?"

"Above the sink. So what's Cromwell's angle?"

"I wish I knew." Bates let a cupboard slap shut, parking two glasses on the countertop. He opened the freezer in search of ice. "He's taking one hell of a risk."

"Which means that there must be one hell of a reward."

Bates poured the colas and brought the glasses into the living room. "Looks crazy to me. Everybody who touches this baby's going to get dirty. I mean, I always figured Cromwell had it all. Power broker on the Hill. And elsewhere. Money. Reputation. And he's never had the least interest in POW/MIA affairs—so why jeopardize his career by getting mixed up in this mess?"

Ritter took a drink. "Sounds to me like it may not have anything to do with POW/MIA affairs."

Bates held his glass suspended halfway to his mouth.

Ritter leaned in over the coffee table, massaging his knee. "Maybe I'm too skeptical. But it strikes me that, if a guy like Cromwell has no interest in the POW/MIA morass and suddenly shows up ass-deep in it, somebody or something just might have pushed him in. Or lured him in."

"Give me something concrete." Bates sounded anxious, enthused by the line of reasoning.

Ritter shook his head. "Can't. I'm a stranger in these parts. Listen, can't you get a wiretap order on Cromwell's phone? I thought you spooks had connections. Can't you just tell the judge he's talking to the Russians?"

Bates put on a look of resignation and took a slug of cola as though it were whiskey. "Chris, getting a wiretap on anybody is next to impossible these days. And this peckerhead's a United States senator. I mean, the judges are all gun-shy as it is—I just got the order on Charlee Whyte's phone today, and it took a bomb and half a dozen dead Indians. Plus something else that turned up in what's left of her office."

"What's that?"

"The remains of a whole lot of cash. Looks like hundreds of thousands of dollars. Maybe more."

"To pay for the photos. It was a million, by the way. Charlee told me about it."

Bates looked at him. "Only poor old Morozov brought something else instead."

"Okay. If you can't get a tap on Cromwell's phone, how about at least putting a tail on him?"

"The FBI would have to do it. And, I can tell you, they won't."

Ritter tried to think, yearning to discover other options. Swimming through mental tar. "So what else has your Russian source told you, sir? Does he have any feel for who's calling the shots on the Russian end? Do they just want to get the photos back to avoid national embarrassment? Or has somebody got a personal stake in it?"

The doorbell rang.

Bates leapt to his feet.

Ritter managed to stand up as well. "Let me get it," he whispered.

He limped to the door. His leg had gone stiff as if it were in a cast. But he felt markedly less pain. He wondered if that might not be a bad sign. He motioned for the colonel to step out of the line of sight, but Bates was already moving. The old man was surprisingly deft.

The doorbell rang again.

Ritter was not at all certain he was ready to face Nadya. The whore with the heart of iron. Yet he hoped to find her standing in his doorway.

Despite everything.

He opened the door.

The couple standing in the hallway made him think of discount department stores and steak-house chains where you stood in line with an orange plastic tray. The woman was not particularly old, but she looked impatient for age to come. Her hair possessed an artificial perfection recalling the days before beauticians were born again as hairstylists, and her suit was a hard chemical blue. The man wore his belt down under his belly. He shifted his neck inside his collar and tie, holding an umbrella with a taped plastic handle and carrying both their raincoats on his arm.

The woman smiled as though hustling a line of cheap cosmetics. "Are you in favor of the murder of children?" she asked.

Ritter stared at her for a moment, not understanding. Her hair looked as though it would crunch if he touched it.

"Do you support the slaughter of innocent babies?" she asked again.

Ritter took her meaning now. Such matters had been far from his mind this evening.

"Madam," he said quietly, "I think your time would be better spent elsewhere."

The man and woman exchanged a knowing glance: a hard case. Features sharpened for battle, the woman edged closer to the door, as though ready to sacrifice a limb to prevent its closing.

"This is about the right of little children to have a full, rich life in Jesus," she said. "We don't ask for money. We're just asking all Americans who are against the cold-blooded murder of the innocent unborn to stand on the Lord's side tomorrow. Satan's handmaidens are bringing their coven to our nation's capital. There will be tens of thousands of them, for their name is legion. But the Lord's servants are going to be there, too. Have you heard about the Call to the Mall?"

Ritter opened his mouth. He did not wish to be rude or insulting. But he did not want to hear any more.

The woman prevented him from speaking. Inching closer to his threshold. "It doesn't matter what walk of life you're from. The Lord needs you to help stop the genocide going on in this country and—"

"Madam," Ritter said icily, "you don't know the first thing about genocide. And this building has a no-soliciting code."

"Jesus loves you," the woman's companion said quickly. The woman just looked mean.

"Good night," Ritter said, shutting the door. A muffled male voice called, "God bless you, sir."

For a long moment, Ritter and Bates looked at each other across the apartment. Quietly sharing their understanding of how unfashionable they had become, with their dedication to the ideals of service, to a reasonable level of tolerance, and to something as outmoded and foolish as a belief in the rule of law. Finally, Bates shrugged and spoke:

"It's the revenge of the creeps. *Those* creeps to the right of you, and the politically correct storm troopers on the left." He smirked. "Where's a Truman Democrat or an Eisenhower Republican to go?"

Ritter lifted a corner of his mouth as though a fishhook had snared him.

Bates sat back down and gestured to Ritter to join him: rest that leg. "Speaking of creeps," the colonel said, "you asked me about the Russians Cromwell's dealing with. I'm not a Russian linguist, so I might butcher the names, but there are two heavy hitters who keep coming up. There's a security-services general named Birov or Pirov. Something like that. Ring any bells?"

"Virov. Who's the other guy?" Ritter tensed. Anticipating the answer.

"Some big wheel out in Central Asia. Sounds like 'Rockman.' "

"Rakhman."

"You know him? Jesus, what's the matter with you?"

"I know him." Ritter did not want this. He had been struggling against it.

"He bite you on the ass or something?"

Ritter felt an unaccustomed liveliness under his skin. As if his body had been invaded by parasites. "He ... touched my life. What can I say? He's a modern-day khan. He prospered under the Soviet system as a KGB general and thug of the highest order, and he's prospering now as a warlord. He calls the shots in a wanna-be country with enormous natural-gas deposits and maybe the world's third- or fourth-largest oil reserves." Ritter smiled at fate. "One of his star pupils fixed my knee. And killed Ben Williams."

Ritter sensed that Bates was no longer listening to him. The colonel had sailed off onto his own mental sea. And he was not yet ready to invite Ritter on board.

Ritter let it go. He sat quietly, with plenty to mull over. Rakhman. And the Johnny Winter look-alike who had done the job on Ben. Was *albino* permissible terminology? Maybe you were supposed to say *person of no color?*

Bates stood up and walked over to the sliding door that led to the balcony and the great world. He stared out into the night.

"Chris," the older man said finally, without turning back to face his conversational partner, "who does Cromwell represent? What is the number-one business in his part of the country?"

That was the first easy question of the night:

"Oil. Gas. Fossil fuels and—"

And there it was. As clear as day in the desert.

"That *bas*tard," Ritter said. "Cromwell's cutting a deal with Rakhman and his crowd. I should have seen it coming. I had the evidence in my *hands.* In black and white."

"And the photos could screw it up," Bates said, completing the thought and turning around at last. His face had taken on an impassioned look. "Congress just might be a little bit hesitant to bless a deal with folks who murdered American POWs."

The colonel sat back down. But he couldn't keep still. He looked even more pleased with himself than he had been an hour before, when he had gutted Ritter's universe with his revelations about Nadya.

Ritter was not as pleased. The thought of Rakhman and company did not make him smile.

"We have to get those photos," Bates said earnestly, happily. "It's not just a history lesson anymore."

The colonel's stomach began to beep.

Bates reached under his sweater and fiddled with his pager. Then he looked at Ritter. "Something's up. Mind if I use your phone?"

"Be my guest."

Bates hurried back into the kitchenette, picked the receiver from the wall, and poked in a number. The other end answered immediately, and Bates identified himself.

Ritter could just see the lower half of the colonel's face behind the line of suspended cabinets. The mouth closed. Then the lips tightened. And tightened again.

"When?" the mouth demanded. *"How long ago?"* The lips fastened shut again. The older man's jaw seemed to grow weary, declining toward his chest. Yet the lips remained tense, a thin brown-pink line.

"I'll be right there," Bates said, and he hung up.

He came back around the breakfast bar and showed Ritter his full face. He looked as though he had heard terrible news about his family.

"What's the matter?"

Bates just shook his head. Then he said, "The dumb sons of bitches."

"What's wrong, sir?"

"I've got two dead agents. And one dead hostile in Russian clothes, with foreign dental work and tattoos. At the Morozov apartment. It looks like we've got some new players in the game."

"Rakhman's people. Or maybe Virov's." The parasites had come back to life under Ritter's skin. Fate, fate, fate.

"I've got to go."

"I'll go with you."

The colonel extended an invisible hand. Halt. "No. You stay here. Our little Russian sweetheart's going to call you, I'd bet my next LES on it. And I need you to be here when she's in the mood to talk." He looked at Ritter solemnly. "Agree to anything she wants. And I'll see that she gets more than she bargained for." Bates reached into the hall closet, retrieving his raincoat with its little silver eagles. He was about to let himself out of the apartment when his face turned into a human question mark:

"By the way, do you have any idea where Charlee Whyte could be? My people have lost track of her."

"You can't talk to me like that," Cromwell told the telephone voice.

"Ollie, get real. You've got promises to keep. And folks out here don't care if you're a goddamned senator or the king of Jebip. You need to get this situation under control. Damned fast."

"I thought we were all friends."

"We *are* friends, Ollie. But you're the friend who made promises. And a lot of your friends have laid out a downright dangerous amount of money based on their friendship with you."

"Are you threatening me?"

The voice laughed. "Ollie, we're *friends.* You said it yourself.

Why, I knew you back when you were nothing but an over-educated, social-climbing young huckster with sand in your ears and shit on your shoes. I'm just trying to put things in perspective for you. Not all of your constituents feel you have been duly attentive to their needs."

"Everything's under control. I've told you that. It just takes time."

"Ollie, have you seen the news within the last hour or so?"

"No."

"I didn't think so. Maybe you'd better turn on CNN. There's been a leak about that Pentagon-bombing business with Larry Whyte's little tart of a stepdaughter. News folks say the investigators found bits and pieces of a whole lot of cash. Now that sounds to me like it just might be the beginning of a problem for a friend of mine in Washington. What do you think?"

"I—"

"Ollie, get off your butt. Do the right thing. For everybody's sake. I mean, you're a patriot, aren't you? You want the Brits or the Dutch or maybe the goddamned Italians to move in on that oil? Instead of your fellow Americans? Instead of your friends, who covered some very impressive gambling debts for you *and* considered your future needs?"

"I have the situation under control."

"Well, I'm glad to hear that. I truly am. And when do you expect to have those items of interest for the friends of your friends?"

"Soon. It takes time." Cromwell thought bitterly of the Russian thugs who were out there somewhere, undoubtedly making things worse. But he did not want to raise that additional issue with his old friend.

"When, Ollie? Tell me exactly."

"Tomorrow." But Cromwell was sorry as soon as he had spoken the word. He had spent the evening drinking heavily and trying to contact Charlee, who had apparently been spirited away by a UFO. Everything seemed to be coming apart.

"That's good, Ollie. I like that. Decisiveness. Confidence. The spirit of America." The voice paused long enough to let Cromwell hate the man who had once been his golfing and whoring partner. Then his old friend resumed:

"And let me give you a tip, Ollie. Between friends. Stay away from Atlantic City. It's not a suitable environment for a U.S. senator. You're mixing with real trash up there. Stick to your own kind."

"Is that all?"

"Just a little friendly advice. You get a good night's sleep now. I'll tell the boys you said howdy."

After hanging up the phone, Cromwell wandered over to the floor-to-ceiling windows that looked toward the Capitol. The glass was wet and lustrous, but he did not sense rain at the moment. He opened the central door and stepped out onto the balcony.

The night air was cold and sodden, and he realized that he was a very long way from home. Clouds the color of oil flowed across the sky. The low-lying city shone. He wondered where on earth Charlee had gone off to, then he wondered how on earth he had gotten to the place where he found himself.

Ritter lay on his sofa, leg propped up, waiting for the telephone to ring. He had put on a McCoy Tyner disc, but abruptly changed his mind and shut off the stereo. Music didn't work now. Nothing did.

He felt beaten down, worn at least halfway to giving up, and his thoughts drifted. He remembered, with sadness but remarkably little anger, the Russian woman's body and her lies. And he thought bitterly of Rakhman, of the white-faced, white-haired murderer in the desert night, and of Ben Williams. Drowsing, he resolved to call Ben's wife, Karin, when all of this was over, to see if her rage toward all men in uniform had softened and if she needed any help. Then he thought of Charlee, wondering why he had not heard from her.

He remembered the day he met her. He had sauntered blue-jeaned and late into a political science seminar, expecting to find a professor notorious for his disinterestedness. Instead, he had encountered the incensed glare of a graduate assistant, a regal young woman in a black silk blouse, shimmering with blond hair and ideas. The other males found Charlee so physically attractive they could not speak in complete sentences. But he had been enchanted by her intensity, her resolution, and by the out-of-control fire of her intelligence. He wondered in retrospect if he had been the only male in the history of the human race who had slept with a woman because he believed she was too smart to pass up.

He dozed. Unclear dreams slithered over his soul. But none of the images had sufficient power to draw him all the way down into sleep. Then he imagined that the phone was ringing and he sat up, wild-eyed.

There was only silence in the well-lit room. He relaxed and settled back onto the sofa pillow, then, mindful of his leg, shifted onto his side.

Confronted by the photograph of his wife, helpless with sudden waking, he found himself replaying the night she had died, the last time he had seen her alive.

They had argued over some trivial thing, a matter so small he was never able to recollect it. But Lena had been temperamental with sickness, and he had grown short-nerved in his exhaustion and terror of losing her. Within moments, they were shouting at each other, a thing they had never done before. The combat escalated until it reached the point where men and women say things they do not mean, could not mean, and will always regret having said.

"If you had the least shred of fucking decency," he told her, "you'd just fucking die and get it over with."

He left their home then, slamming the door behind him, and he drove. His anger soon dissipated—there had been no real basis even for annoyance, let alone such a rage. There had been only a need for two frightened humans to let off the tension that had come near to breaking them. He saw the situation clearly before he had spent a gallon of gas. Yet he could not bring himself to return home immediately. He was too ashamed of the words that had escaped his mouth.

When he finally got up the nerve to go back and face the woman he loved, he found her corpse.

FOURTEEN

CHARLEE NEEDED SOMETHING TO DRINK. IT WAS A HORRIBLE FEELING—
she did not know how much longer she could control her kid-
neys, yet her mouth and throat were parched with a chemical
bitterness. She wanted to shriek, to summon help, to prove that
she was still alive. But her vocal cords refused to obey her.

Her entire body was unmanageable. Cramps spiked her muscles and it was impossible to move her limbs to relieve the
stress. Spasms of white pain made her feel that she was on the
edge of a breakdown.

Whenever she had read about someone kidnapped and shut
in the trunk of a car, she had imagined that person sunk in
darkness. But it was not so. The taillights leaked inward and
her separate world shone as if lit by Chinese lanterns. Only
there was nothing to see.

She feared that the fumes would kill her. She could smell
the exhaust. It smelled of death.

But she did not die. She only became sicker to her stomach.
From the fumes. And the fear.

She was terribly afraid. Not with the shocked, incapable fear
she had experienced when the other thug assaulted her, but
with a cold, horrid, intelligent fear. She lay hunched in a car
trunk, waiting to die. Waiting to be killed. By the foreign murderer behind the wheel.

They drove endlessly. But she sensed that they were still in the city. The car started, then braked, stopped . . . resumed its progress. Thumping over the ill-kept D.C. roads.

She felt nauseous, tasting all of the body's sourness at the back of her mouth. Yet she found herself laughing. Then she began to cry.

She stopped that, finding a reserve of strength, determined to be brave now. It was such a joke. After all of the murderous places through which she had passed unscathed, after becoming a connoisseur of the sufferings of others, she was going to die in her own town, where she knew the connections and the restaurants, the shortcuts and the places not to go.

She could not think of one reason why she should not die. So many others died daily, cutting short far less satisfactory lives. She had, after all, possessed so much.

There was her work. She needed to live in order to carry on her work.

Yet even her work seemed small now, a catalog of failures.

No. No, she was not going to give up. Not even now. If she had to die, she would die believing.

What was left to believe in? No matter what you did, they kept on killing, raping, torturing, starving their brothers and sisters. How could you ever make them stop?

She recalled that she had a haircut appointment the next afternoon, and before she regained control of herself, the thought threw her into a panic.

The car smashed through a pothole and Charlee's head struck metal.

She wanted to drink. To urinate. To smell fresh air. To stretch out her limbs. She tried, again, to kick and pummel her way out of the enclosed space. But her movements were so restrained that she managed only to bruise herself and bring back the cramps.

"No," she screamed. *"No, no, no, no, no."*

The car jounced along. She wondered if the bizarre-looking killer in the driver's seat could hear her.

In Sudan, the women were too weak to call out. If they raised a hand to beg, the terrible effort just brought them closer to death. The phenomenal lack of muscle between their skin and the long bones left you in awe of how much a human being could endure.

In the ruins of Yugoslavia, there were special, if ill-equipped, clinics for the expectant mothers who had been gang-raped over and over, then interned until they were too pregnant to abort. In Armenia, the addled grandchildren of the century's first genocide dyed their uniforms black and wore homemade swastikas.

In the Kurdistan that did not exist, the women risked death from land mines, from border guards and exposure, to smuggle sugar for the men's tea, and in Tajikistan neither side took prisoners. Across the border in Afghanistan, the freedom fighters so recently adored by Westerners stoned women to death for suspected adultery and tortured teachers before murdering them.

In country after country, on continent after continent, the rebels butchered the loyalists and the government troops burned the villages suspected of aiding rebels. In Tibet and Iran, disallowed religions were being erased. And no one cared except a few stray academics and Hollywood stars so astonishingly stupid they couldn't order lunch without a script. The world was coming to an end. It came to a new end every day.

Only the misery was endless. And Chris did not believe you could do anything about it. Why was he so unwilling? She had lost him so soon. Why had he, of all the men, infected her soul?

She wondered if God were punishing her. For helping Ollie. Perhaps there was justice on the earth, however irregular and intermittent. She knew she was doing wrong. She had always been in the vanguard of those fighting the cover-ups and falsifications. Now she was a part of one.

And people had died. For Ollie and his friends and their greed. She had tried to convince herself that there were always trade-offs. And the POWs were dead. Her father was dead. And there were so many others still alive who needed her help.

She had hated the memory of her natural father so deeply for so long. The man-boy who had chosen to fly his airplane instead of remaining with his family. The father who had held her in so little regard that he had not even waited to see her born. She had believed him dead, her mother believed him dead, the government said he was dead. And now the stupidest of fates had driven a wedge of doubt into her snugly carpentered world. What if her own father had been one of those prisoners?

The prisoners, she knew, were dead. That was the whole point. Yet, it somehow changed things to think that her father might have been alive for years after the war, that he might have been alive on some other part of the planet when she was going to school and enduring her first loves. She could not understand why it should change things, but it did. And she found that she wanted to know the truth.

Perhaps her father had suffered even more than she had wanted him to suffer. For deserting her. Perhaps her longing for his suffering had somehow made it all worse.

He was dead, in any case. Nothing could be done. Yet she sensed that a thousand things remained unfinished.

She threw up. She almost choked and had to struggle in the cramped space to clean out her mouth with her hand.

She hated the smell of herself. She had always hated the smell of herself.

She began to cry again, but this time she could not stop it. It was no good trying to be brave. She wanted her mother. And her father.

She did not want to die. Not now. Not like this. She realized that, if she could make a bargain, she would trade all she had done or might do for the common good just to live.

No. She refused to be such a coward. She had seen cowardice enough, and she had always despised it.

If the photographs had been in her possession, she would have given them to Ollie. So that she could carry on her work with the living. The dead were dead. And any notions she had about finding her father in the photographs were born of pathetic sentimentality. And sentiment was the enemy of clear thinking, of achievement.

You had to do everything yourself. What had she expected of Chris? A white knight who could ride to her rescue? She laughed, or imagined herself laughing. In real life, the cavalry arrived to find smoldering ruins, corpses, and fat crows.

She cried, with vomit clinging to her hair. No one had ever been strong for her.

She was glad now that she had never had children. She had always known that she would be a bad mother. And it was a blessed thing that she had aborted the child Chris had started in her. So long ago. He had been so naive. He had not even known. And she had resisted telling him, convinced that he would insist on doing something stupid for the wrong reasons. She had wanted him. But not like that.

Not one of the other men who had filled her body had come so close to filling her heart.

"I'm dying," she said, "I'm dying."

But Charlee was not dying. The exhaust fumes were not strong enough to kill her. And at least one man still needed her

Zhan hated the powerlessness of his situation. Through ruthlessness and strength of will, he had mastered his own world, defying the trick God had played on him at birth. He had become a feared man in the desert cities and mountain valleys into which fate had cast him. But he felt lost in this flashing foreign place. Washington in America. He drove past its monuments and through streets lined with a more vulgar form of pageantry. He did not know what to do.

He supposed he would have to kill the woman eventually. But he disliked the thought. He did not mind killing men—it could be entertaining. But he did not like killing women. Usually, he let others do it. In principle, he stayed apart from all women, uneasy with them, suspicious. Neither did he have male friends. But that was different. He could handle himself around other men, a genius at recognizing their weak points. He had picked up that knack early on, in the orphanage in Dushanbe.

He had no idea who his parents had been, whether they had been swept away by the avenging broom of the state or had simply abandoned him in disgust at the oddity their lust had created. The orphanage, which was supposed to make children love Father Lenin and the succoring Party, had been nothing but a school for criminality. Above all, the experience had taught him that no man or institution could resist an opponent who knew how to keep his mouth shut while displaying remorseless cruelty.

Later, he had exchanged a juvenile detention camp for an adult prison long before reaching the legal age for such incarceration. The local authorities had made an exception in his case, given the special climax of his string of offenses. He had waited, quietly, until an older, stronger rival passed out from drunkenness. Then Zhan had bound him to his bunk, soaked his blanket in gasoline, and burned him to death.

Prison had been an improvement. You worked, but the food was better. And the camp outside Karaganda furnished him with connections that enabled him to embark upon a career after his release.

He had been astonished to find how simple it was, in the twilight of Soviet power, to transition from being one of the jailed to being one of the jailers. In prison, he had learned scraps of German and English, and ingenious ways to kill. In the orphanage and detention center, he had spoken Russian and Tajik, along with Uzbek swear words, and he had learned to survive. The experiences were fulfilling and complementary, and when General Rakhman took an interest in him, he was ready to serve. Rakhman, still wearing a KGB uniform in those days, had simply ordered his early release from prison. As a congratulatory gift, Rakhman also gave him his first legal weapon. Rakhman had always been a man of vision.

Zhan's own vision grew dark. This bright, inconstant world of America, of the American capital, was like quicksand. He had needed Mitya, after all, if only for his slightly greater knowledge of the customs and the language. Alone, all Zhan could do was to drive on, waiting for inspiration and quickening each time he heard a siren or saw a police car. He had begun to pulse with terror. At the thought of failing Rakhman. Whose vengeance would pursue a man beyond the grave.

He did not want to telephone his contact. That would mean admitting failure. And it offended his pride, as well as worrying him that word of his ineptitude would fly back to Rakhman prematurely. But, after driving the streets for two hours, he forced himself to accept that there was no alternative.

He drove on until he saw a telephone on the edge of a deserted parking lot. This was a part of the city where no one walked in the darkness. Zhan pulled the large, difficult car over to the curb, striking the cement with its tires.

He bolted out of the door and hurried to the trunk as though under fire. When he opened the compartment, the woman looked up at him in wonder.

She was filthy. She had soiled herself. She stared up at him but did not move.

He grabbed her by the shoulder, fixing his hand to her raincoat at a spot that looked unstained. He lifted her, pulled her.

"You come out," he commanded. "You come out now."

The woman attempted to comply, but her limbs failed as though she were drunk. She stank like the waste from a camp infirmary.

"Faster." Zhan felt an urge to slap her, to make her move. But he did not want to soil himself with her filth.

"You have money?"

She looked at him, standing in the street.

"You have my purse. There's money in it. I don't know how much."

He believed he understood. He shoved her toward the front of the car, prodding her with his pistol so that he would not have any more physical contact with her than necessary. He gestured for her to open the door and take her purse.

"I want small money. For the telephone."

She looked at him, then at the phone stand, then back into his eyes.

"You'll be lucky if that one works," she said, and he believed he heard an unreasonable note of sarcasm in her voice. But she quickly produced a handful of coins.

"Come with me. For noise, I kill you. You go away, I kill you. Come."

She walked beside him to the telephone.

"You are my friend. Everyone must see that."

The woman did not answer.

Masking the pistol, he primed the telephone as Mitya had taught him. But a strange, official woman's voice came on the line, then it quit.

He tried again. With the same result.

In great, helpless embarrassment, he gestured to the woman to come closer. With her unclean smell.

"The telephone does not work. You must help me."

She stared at him for a moment. Then said:

"What number are you trying to call? Show me the number."

He drew back. Afraid of a trick. Then he realized that it did not matter if she saw the number, since she was going to die. He showed her the scrap of paper.

"That's here in Washington. You don't have to dial the area code."

He did not understand her. After a few seconds of frustration, he stuck the pistol barrel in her ribs.

"Make the telephone work."

She took the receiver from him, eyes bright with fresh fear. Her hand shook as she placed the instrument against her ear, against her stained hair. She almost dropped the coins he returned to her.

"It's ringing," she said, handing it back to him.

The smell she left on the phone revolted him. But he had no choice but to bring it against his ear and mouth. He decided that he truly hated America.

"This is forbidden," the voice said. "You're only supposed to call me in an emergency."

"This is an emergency."

There was a pause. Then the voice returned: crisp, bureaucratic Russian. It was the voice of an educated man, and educated men were always weak.

"Explain the situation to me. Don't embellish."

"The Americans surprised us. Mitya's dead. He was your man."

"My God. My God, you shouldn't have called me."

"If you don't help me, Rakhman will kill you." It was a bluff. But Zhan was certain the other man was too weak to resist it. "Rakhman will kill you. And he will kill your family. And the family of your family."

"Where are you?"

It was an embarrassing question. Zhan did not know where

he was. Somewhere in Washington. He covered the receiver with his hand.

"What is this place?" he asked the woman in English.

She looked around, then shrugged. "Not my neighborhood. Looks like Anacostia."

"What is the name of this place?" he demanded.

"Anacostia."

He spoke into the phone. "I am in Anna-Kostya."

"What in the world are you doing *there?*"

This, too, was an embarrassing question. Zhan decided to take control. "You listen to *me.* We went to the apartment of the Morozovs. As you said. But the girl wasn't there. Only an American woman. Then the Americans came and we had to shoot. I had to leave Mitya there. I took his identification, but he has tattoos. From the camps."

"God in heaven." Then silence. And suddenly, "What about the woman? You said there was an American woman."

"I have her with me."

"God in heaven. Who is she? Do you have any idea?"

"She's blond. Looks like a big shot's wife. Forty."

"That doesn't tell me anything. You said she's with you now?"

"She's standing beside me."

"Do you speak English?"

"Enough."

"Well, ask her who she is. Find out."

Zhan covered the receiver again. He looked at the woman. Her face was pale. Almost as pale as his own. He reached for the English words he needed. But he had come to the end of his vocabulary. It sent him into a rage.

He shot out a hand and grabbed all the blond hair his fist could encompass. Jerking her toward him, toward the phone stand, he smashed the receiver into the side of her face, against her mouth.

"Say who you are," he commanded.

She gasped. As though she could not breathe. Then she whispered:

"Charlene Whyte." She fought to replenish her lungs. And suddenly she found her voice. "This is Charlene Whyte speaking," she said imperiously, "Assistant Secretary of Defense for Humanitarian Affairs."

Zhan let go of the woman's hair and brought the phone back to his own mouth and ear. The other end of the line was so silent that he thought his contact had hung up on him.

"Are you still there? Should I kill her?"

The silence continued. Zhan almost hung up. Then a small, frightened voice told him:

"Don't even talk like that. God in heaven. She's on *our* side."

Nadya sat on the motel bed, watching television to help her think. A late-night talk-show host interviewed a singer who warbled out of a tiny little mouth under an arrangement of blond hair so exaggerated that it reminded Nadya of portraits of Catherine the Great. Nadya realized that such a hairstyle was unacceptable for anyone who was not a performer. She was a quick study, and in any case, mastering the surface effects of a culture was not difficult. The hard part lay in getting the nuances right, in digesting the fine contradictions. Details were important to her, because she was determined to Americanize herself in the best possible way.

The remaining stumbling block was her lack of money. She wanted money to buy the things that determined an American's identity. The American class system was remarkably complex, fluid on the surface but brutally rigid underneath. She saw the issue of class in America essentially as a matter of negatives— knowing what *not* to wear, understanding what kind of car *not* to drive. When she first arrived in America, she had been disarmed by the apparent freedom of choice. But she had quickly realized that freedom of choice existed only within carefully defined parameters. And even money was not enough to guarantee your social position—you had to grasp the proper application of that money. She had learned, slowly, never to buy a single thing she liked.

Money. The drab, droning teachers from her school years had been absolutely right about its fundamental importance in America. But they had utterly missed the complexity of money's role in American society. Without money, you were nobody. But you could be nobody with money, too.

Nadya was determined to be *some*body.

She sipped cold coffee, cradling the paper cup with the fast-food logo as though she might warm its contents with her longings. Almost randomly, she reached across her sleeping lover and took up the remote control. Volodya moaned with a quiet, drowsing sound and turned slightly. Nadya wandered through a world of channels, looking for inspiration. Television had been wonderfully helpful to her in her campaign to refashion herself as an American woman. During the day, the soap operas furnished excellent texts on dress and casual manners, although she found their gritless view of sex naive. Talk shows taught her how Americans responded to conversational stimuli, what they did and did not discuss, where social boundaries lay, and what Americans truly believed to be important—as opposed to what books and newspapers imagined worthy of consideration.

Her favorite shows, however, were police dramas. She took a deep interest in how the American legal system worked, and no library she had visited had offered half so much insight as television. Between commercials—also powerful in their educational value—the television criminals came up with all sorts of clever devices no heavy-handed Russian thug would have imagined. Of course, the police usually solved the crime and arrested the wrongdoer. But Nadya did not take that part so seriously. The endings were the stuff of fairy tales. In any case, her informal statistical analysis told her that American criminals failed for three fundamental reasons. First, they grew overconfident, sloppy. Second, they repeated crimes. Finally, and most telling, they lacked the strength of will to triumph over their enemies.

Nadya did not intend to make any of those mistakes.

Yet now, in her hour of need, television was letting her down. No inspiration flared out at her, and there were no crime shows. Only talk, movies whose gutless romances could have been taken from the films she had left behind in Russia, and music videos with hideous, cartoonish young black men who looked authentically criminal.

Her position was nearly unbearable to her. She had come so close. She had the photographs in her bag beside the bed.

Riches, security, were a brief exchange away. Yet she could not envision how to make that exchange, photos for dollars, without becoming vulnerable to the police or some other hostile force.

The woman, Charlee, could not be trusted. She was a snake. And she was too strong. The only possibility remaining to Nadya was the American officer. Chris. So terribly befuddled. It was always the physically capable men who overestimated the power of sex. Such men, not women, were the true romantics. Only men threw away safe, established lives for love. Men of a certain age. The Moscow hotels had taught her that. Women were survivors.

Nadya knew that she had to work through the officer. But it was vital to maintain control at every step. Too many people had become involved, there was too much knowledge available, and she feared that any deal, if not perfect in conception, would end in disaster. With others waiting in ambush. To ruin her dreams.

She needed a mechanism to make the exchange work. But she still did not know Washington or the United States well enough to see how it could be done. Where could you go to trade a parcel of photographs for a million dollars without feeling a policeman's hand on your shoulder a moment later? In Moscow, she would have known a hundred ways to do it. Here, she was lost. And the clock ticked against her.

She rose, feeling the coffee needling through her system, and went into the bathroom. When she finished, she looked in the mirror for a long time, appalled at the darkness under her eyes, the loss of elasticity in the skin of her neck. In the late hour, she sensed that she was beginning to pay the debt of hard years.

But she was still young enough. In the morning, after a bit of sleep, everything would be fine again.

She did not leave the mirror. She turned, tilting her head in the harsh light, and marveled at a human being she had never quite seen. For all that she had experienced, Nadya had never possessed a sense of her own mortality. She was the sort of person who could walk through plague-haunted alleys thinking about lunch. But tonight, in the dream world of economy-priced motels and rootless America, death grinned over her shoulder as she examined herself in the bathroom mirror.

There was no poetic taint to her character, so she stood before the mirror untroubled by any need to express what she felt so suddenly and so deeply. Cold waves of time reached for her feet and ankles, and emotions so profound that mankind has overexpressed them and reduced them to clichés pierced her like darts. She realized that, although money could, indeed, buy love and more of it than any single human being could explore, it could not buy time. Time, the great spoilsport, was the single incorruptible ruler of the living. Even God could be bribed. But the clock was Robespierre.

She snapped back to her accustomed sense of worth and hurried back to the bed and the sleeping presence of the one man she had found worth loving.

The television meandered into a late news update. Nadya had little interest in the news. It mattered so little. Still, she watched for a bit out of inertia, comforting her hip against the warmth of her lover's flank.

The screen displayed grisly film clips from the Balkans that neither moved nor surprised her. U.S. senators offered their identically self-important views on a trade agreement. Then a female reporter with a voice like a knife striking a chopping block announced that hundreds of thousands of pro-choice advocates would rally on the Mall in the morning, with a number of distinguished American women scheduled to speak from the steps of the Lincoln Memorial. The event would last the entire day, and tens of thousands of antiabortion activists were expected to mount a counterdemonstration. A commentator noted that the police would have their hands full preserving order between the opposing groups.

Nadya smirked. Americans were unfathomable. Such a big fuss about abortion. She had gone through five, and where was the harm? She laughed silently in the near-darkness. If they ever banned abortions in Russia, there would be more Russians than Chinese in five years. Such nonsense. The Americans could be so childish. They were so spoiled.

Abortion was just a thing you did so you could get on with your life. Nadya had never understood the women who became emotional about it. And here, in America, the men wanted to stick their noses in, too. As if they hadn't already stuck in enough parts of their anatomy. Russian men knew when to mind their own business.

The problem with Americans, Nadya decided, was that they just didn't have anything serious to worry about.

She was pointing the remote control to switch off the television when her hand stopped in midair. She realized that she had just been given a gift. And she had almost thrown it away.

She rolled onto her side, dropping the remote and reaching for the telephone. Then she caught herself.

It was important to be careful. To not become sloppy or over-confident, the way the television criminals inevitably did.

She swung her legs over the side of the bed and reached down for the jeans she had dropped on the floor. In moments, she was sufficiently dressed to leave the motel room, keys to the rental car in her hand. The sky was clearing and the air smelled fresh and lush.

She drove until she judged that she had covered a safe distance from the motel, then pulled up to a pay phone in front of a darkened shopping center. She had a good memory for numbers and did not even need to check her notebook before calling the American officer.

He answered, sleepy voiced. She spoke to him in Russian, so that she could control the nuances of the conversation. It took a moment's babble for him to come to himself, and she watched impatiently as a police car nosed along the storefronts.

"Chris? Please. Listen to me. Please. They're going to kill me. Please, you mustn't go to the police. It would only make it worse. These people are Russians. I know what they'd do."

"Nadya . . . for God's sake, where are you?" The officer's voice sounded both weary and alarmed as he struggled with pronunciation and syntax.

"I cannot tell you that. I cannot tell you anything else. One of them is listening to me. He makes me speak Russian. The man who took me. He says he will kill me if I cannot exchange the photographs for money for him." She paused to let the officer absorb the information. He did not respond, and she pictured him shocked, worn, unable to think words into speech.

"They have the photographs," she continued. "They showed them to me. I cannot tell you how horrible these photographs are. You can see everything. There are prison pictures of Americans. With names. And then there are the pictures of the executions. They are so terrible. The man who took me and his friends say you must bring one million dollars tomorrow, and then they will give you the photographs. After they count the money, I will be freed."

"Where?" the officer asked quickly. "Where do they want the money delivered?"

Nadya smiled. At the boundless folly of the male. "There will be a demonstration tomorrow, a very big one. By the Memorial of Lincoln. They say you must come there. You, but no one else. Or they will not turn over the pictures. And they will kill me."

"Nadya . . . how will I know them? Will they recognize me? What—"

"I will be there. You will see me. And I will see you. By the Memorial of Lincoln. I will carry the photographs and they will watch me. You must bring the money from your government or from the woman, it doesn't matter."

"It takes time to raise that kind of money."

"It must be tomorrow. I mean today. At noon. There will be no other chance. And they will kill me. And I will never see you again, my love." She sighed so he would hear her. "Please, my Chris. You must help me. Only you can help me. Don't let the police come. Or anyone else. It will only ruin things. And we will never be together."

"Nadya, the crowd's going to be huge."

"I will find you. By the Memorial of Lincoln. Don't worry, my darling. I will always find you. I would find you at the end of the world."

"I'll do my best. I promise. I'll be there, Nadya."

"It will be easy for you. I have faith in you. You will save me."

"I'll do my best."

"Yes. I love you, my Chris. They say I must go now."

She hung up and closed her eyes. Breathless, she felt as though she had just run a hard race. But she had him. She was convinced of it.

It would all work out. Because it had to work out. And life would be wonderful.

But, standing alone in an empty American parking lot in an hour when prostitutes yearn for their last customer to tire, Nadya realized that she had never been so afraid. She reached down into her purse and touched the gun the way she might have sought out a strong, reassuring hand. She had no intention of using the weapon, and no active vision was associated with the feel of the metal. Only a sense of commitment, of irrevocability, and of determination.

Volodya awoke and found himself alone. For a moment, the sweat of panic began to wet his undershirt. He switched on the light, bumbling, and called his lover's name. Then he saw her green plastic travel bag off to the side of the bed.

She had not deserted him. God only knew where she had gone. But she would return.

Then, in his solitude, with Nadya's smell warm off the bedclothes, he saw her absence as fate. He was being given a sign, and an opportunity. To save them both.

He had been thinking about the act for days. But he had not found the courage, the strength. Now he realized that God had decided to help him.

He rose from the bed and felt the rug cool under his feet. He picked up Nadya's bag. And he stepped into the bathroom.

He took out the envelope with the photographs—the photographs that had robbed her of her soul, that were bound to destroy them both. He could not understand how, given her cleverness, she could fail to see that. The photographs were not going to make them rich. They were deluded children, and they had done evil. The photographs belonged to the devil.

He had failed at everything in his life. But he had come to believe in redemption. Even if, in the end, God was absent, redemption had to be possible. If a man acted in time, if he sacrificed, if he did one great, true thing out of love . . . then salvation had to be possible. In any case, he hoped to keep Nadya from prison or worse.

He took out the photographs, refusing to look at them. Squatting in front of the commode, he began to tear them into pieces. He almost put the scraps into the toilet, but stopped himself, afraid they would not flush away. Instead, he tore them directly into the plastic bag lining the wastebasket.

There were a great many photographs, and Volodya still possessed the methodical nature of a scientist when important matters were involved. He ripped the snapshots and file photos into very small bits. It took a long time, and he began to worry that Nadya would return and find him. He even paused to go into the other room and hook the safety chain across the door. He did not want her to interrupt him. He knew she would be furious, and that he would not be able to resist her.

When he bent back to his work, a centered photograph caught his eye. He read the English slowly:

Captain Luther Schwartz. United States Air Force. #4193769.

The man looked up at him with wide-open, accusatory eyes. Volodya looked away, feeling the heft of the photo and the others clipped to it. He knew that the bottom photograph would show the man's death. Holding the photos was almost like holding a shriveled corpse, like holding death in the hand.

Volodya began again. He tore the photos once, twice, with his strong fingers. Then he had to separate the shreds to reduce them further.

Despite his fears, he was able to finish destroying all of the photographs before Nadya returned. He took the nearly full plastic bag out of its container, tied its top ends into a series of knots, then hid it in the cabinet under the sink.

Afraid of Nadya's wrath, unready to tell her what he had done, he took a book from his slight luggage, wrapped it in a hand towel, and put it in the envelope that had held the photographs. He put the envelope back in her bag and placed the bag near the bed as exactly as he could remember.

He got into bed, nervous, fearful, yet confident that he had done a good thing. His heart pounded. Then he remembered the door chain and rushed from the bed to unhook it, unwilling to give Nadya a clue as to what he had done.

He knew in his soul that he had saved them both. He just did not know how he was going to explain that to her.

"We've got her." Bates's voice sounded positively joyous over the phone line. "Between my people and the FBI, we'll have so many agents in that crowd she'll never slip through. All you have to do is stand there and pretend you're a flag waving in the breeze."

Ritter lay on his bed. He wished he could remain like that until the entire business was done. "And then what?"

"Then we've got the Russians, too. If everything tracks, we'll have POWs by name, date of death, the works. The Russians won't be able to stonewall us anymore. The families will know what happened. And we'll be able to bring the bodies back— God willing and the creek don't rise." Bates briefly ran out of exuberance. When he began again, his voice had a Sunday-morning sobriety. "If it's the last thing I do in my career, I want to stand on the apron up at Dover and salute when they off-load those caskets."

"Yeah. But what happens to the woman? To Nadya Morozova?" Ritter spoke the name as though it hurt his tongue to shape the sounds.

"Nothing she'll like very much," Bates said matter-of-factly. Ritter imagined the colonel shrugging at the other end of the line. "I haven't thought it through, I'm more concerned about the photos. But I guess it depends on whether they'll try her in Virginia because that's where the bombing took place, or in D.C. Virginia's got the death penalty, although I don't know if they push it when it comes to female offenders. In D.C., it's a life sentence. Unless somebody decides it's all too much trouble and they just deport her." Bates thought for a moment. "I don't know the Russians the way you do, but I don't imagine that's a very attractive alternative for her, either."

"No."

Bates roused himself again. "Snap out of it, Chris. She's a murdering snake, for God's sake. Let it go. You know better."

"It just seems . . . a terrible waste. I can't explain it. But I really do see her side, in a way."

"Well, you can be a character witness for the defense." Then

Bates caught himself. Ritter could read the other man's psychology by the weight of his pauses. "Sorry, Chris. That was uncalled for."

"No. You're right."

"Okay. Let's move on. Because now I've got another mission for you."

Ritter cringed.

"I want you to call Charlee Whyte. She's home now. Surveillance picked her up going in with some white-haired geezer. They couldn't get a good look at him, but he had hair as white as Methuselah's. Probably one of Cromwell's poker buddies. Anyway, you call her and tell her what the deal is. Don't tell her you're talking to me, of course. Just that the Russian woman called you and wants a mil—"

"Wait a minute," Ritter interrupted. "Why does Charlee have to be involved in this? You'll get the photos. Why can't we just leave her out of it?"

"Because . . . damn it, Chris, because two of my agents—two of *our* fellow soldiers—are dead. And I don't know who the hell's responsible. Because there's a Pentagon office full of corpses and Charlee Whyte's in this thick as mud soup." Ritter had never heard Bates so angry. "And," the colonel went on in an iron voice, "because she's the channel to Cromwell. And I don't want to see that son of a bitch just walk away from this all fresh and clean and rosy. Do you?"

"No."

"Then call Charlee Whyte."

"Sir, I can't—I don't—believe that Charlee's motives are bad. We may not like what she does, but she's a straight shooter, and—"

"Chris," Bates said, voice calmer but utterly uncompromising, "listen to me. You're an extremely talented officer. A dutiful officer, and a very good man. But you're the worst judge of women I've ever come up against. Now call Charlee Whyte and tell her about Miss Morozova's proposition."

Given the tone of the colonel's voice, Ritter expected the conversation to end abruptly. But Bates was not to be underestimated, and he picked up again in a changed, almost fatherly manner:

"Chris, if you're right about Charlee, she'll do the right thing. Play the hand you've been dealt, and let her play hers. We'll see what happens."

It was Ritter's turn to reach for words. He felt as though he had failed in all things, and he just did not want to do any more damage to any human being who had ever cared for him.

"Sir," he said finally, "I don't want to hurt her."

"I know," Bates answered in a quiet voice. "Just do what's right."

Sen. Oliver Cromwell stood on his balcony, staring down. He tried to imagine what it would feel like to fall through space, then strike the concrete. Would a man feel much at all? Would there be an instant of terrible pain as the neck and back snapped? He told himself that the building was high enough to guarantee death. That was important. He didn't want to end up as a cripple and a laughingstock.

That was the trouble with suicide, of course. You would still be humiliated. Cromwell could not bear the thought of public embarrassment, even after death. He was proud—he believed he had reason to be proud—and he wanted to leave a proud legacy. Suicide was, ultimately, too undignified. Not the way it had been with the Romans, running onto their swords and all that. Now the newspapers raised embarrassing questions, and if you were genuinely unlucky, there were shameless photos.

He had known all along that suicide was not really an option. But it gave him an oddly luxurious pleasure to contemplate it, drink in hand. He had put down a great deal of whiskey, almost an unprecedented amount, given that there was no party and there were no women. Unlike suicide, whiskey was a genuine comfort.

He despised men who could not or would not drink. He hated the self-righteous little assholes who spent their lunch hours jogging down on the Mall, bodies as thin as their personalities. *His* generation had been the last generation of real men. Men who drank bourbon or Scotch and knew how to handle women. He snorted, then grinned like a skull for no one to see. These days the women on Capitol Hill were twice the men any of the skimpy little males would ever be. The age of the lions was almost over, and he was one of the last. Who else was left? Teddy, of course. Now there was one man with whom you could still empty a bottle. But he was certainly no genius. Not half the man either of his brothers had been. No, Cromwell told himself, there weren't many left. He was among the last of a dying breed. He drained his glass and regarded its emptiness fondly. It took twenty-five years to make a good Scotch, and twice that long to make a good man. And anyone who didn't believe that could go to hell.

The phone rang. Cromwell stumbled back inside, grateful to leave the cold air and his colder thoughts behind him.

It was Charlee. She sounded positively unnerved. Well, to hell with her, too, Cromwell thought. Letting him down like that.

"Ollie, listen to me. Are you awake? Are you sober?"

"Of course I'm sober."

"She called, Ollie. The Russian woman called the officer I've been working with. She has the photos. She wants a million dollars."

Cromwell rubbed his eyes. "I already *gave* you a million dollars."

"Please, Ollie." Charlee's voice sounded downright terrorized. Women, Cromwell told himself. They just can't tough it out in the end. "Ollie, this is your last chance. The million's gone, remember? The bomb? You remember that?"

Cromwell mumbled something as spiteful as it was inarticulate.

"*Please,* Ollie. I *beg* you." Then she tried a different approach. "Fix yourself a drink. Make yourself a fresh drink and we'll talk."

"I don't need a damned drink. Who do you think you are?"

"Try to remember. The photographs. The Russian woman has them. She'll hand them over to the officer I've been working with. At noon. In front of the Lincoln Memorial. You can watch. But you've got to come up with the money."

Cromwell laughed. "And where am I supposed to get this money from? I don't have a million dollars in my wallet. Do you have a million dollars in your wallet?" But the thought of money, of a lot of money, lifted him partway out of the haze. He began to feel his toughness rising, the spiritual muscle that always pulled him through. "You're a fool, Charlee. Just a damned little blond fool. You know as well as me that a body can't come up with that kind of cash that fast. Didn't you learn a damned thing from your stepfather?"

"Ollie, I'm *des*perate."

Cromwell laughed. "We're all desperate. And ain't this a hell of a mess, though. Ain't it just one hell of a mess." He chuckled, infinitely amused at man's fate. "Don't worry. We'll figure something out." Then he remembered his squandered evening. "Charlee, girl, where in the name of Jesus are you, anyway? I've been trying to call you since dinnertime."

There was a dark little silence on the other end of the line. Then Charlee said:

"I'm just sitting at home with a murderer, Ollie."

FIFTEEN

THE DAY WAS AS BEAUTIFUL AS ANY GOD ALLOWED. THE LATE-autumn sky was so blue and filled with grace that it made the worst loneliness easier to bear, even as it challenged new lovers with an echo of their frailty. The sun fell on human shoulders like a steady gift, and the countless demonstrators whose expectations had been conditioned by their wet, morose arrivals found themselves rolling up parkas and peeling off the sweatshirts whose inscriptions spoke of each individual's selected being. The air drank up the last puddles and the grass dried, welcoming jeans and picnic lunches. The solemnity, the certainty of causes, remained, but softened, and even the most committed, listening as the loudspeakers poured passion, took long moments to close their eyes and raise unplanned smiles to heaven.

Ritter carried his leather jacket over his left arm, and the sleeves of his old chamois shirt were half-rolled. The cane he had taken reluctantly to hand helped him both with the act of walking and in making his way through the crowd. Perhaps, he thought, it made him appear suitably earnest. Or punished. In any case, the women, the astonishing variety of women who had come to tell the world that their bodies were their own business, made way for him with unexpected goodwill. He worked his way forward under the bare trees beside the Reflecting Pool, heading for the day's epicenter, for Lincoln.

The organizers had chosen to speak from the steps of the Lincoln Memorial for its symbolic value. But it meant that the bulk of the huge crowd was held at a remove, centered on the hillock from which the Washington Monument thrust skyward, a fitting symbol for the Father of His Country, but perhaps less appropriate to the day. Despite his preoccupations, Ritter did not miss the difference in mood between the subdivisions. The girls and women gathered around the obelisk clanned in friendship, satisfied with the day, while their puritan sisters at the base of the Reflecting Pool waited for revelation.

An abrupt squeal from the loudspeaker system stung Ritter's ears. The latest speaker had come too close to the bank of microphones. Even from a hundred yards away, she was recognizable by her trademark hat. As Ritter closed on the makeshift stage, she spoke of the need for legislative protection, of the danger of rights being chipped away until there were none left. From the side of the Mall over by the National Academy of Sciences, a voodoo chant rose and fell, unintelligible, yet clearly hostile to the women and ornamental men gathered at the speaker's feet. Earlier, Ritter had maneuvered through the fringes of the right-to-life crowd, repelled by their general rage and misspelled signs, and two things had struck him. First, a surprising proportion of men reinforced the contingent opposed to abortion rights, and second, he had never before realized the degree to which the abortion issue involved class warfare.

By their bearing, their clothing, their speech and uneasy facial expressions, the right-to-lifers appeared either lower-middle class or what had once been termed working class. Only their firm-faced leadership could claim secure middle-class status—and that had more to do with that leadership's economic situation than with its view of the world. In the postmodern age, these were the downwardly mobile.

As soon as Ritter limped through the police lines, passing the bored reserves in riot gear and the park police on horseback, he found himself among the upper half of American society, among women whose studied carelessness announced that they had been to college and would not be bound by any tyrannical, unexamined views other than their own.

He saw, too, that no matter what his personal views on abortion might be, he was obliged to stand on the side of the women gathered before the Memorial. Although they would assuredly have tested less "patriotic" in a traditional opinion poll, they were the truer Americans. These women had come to Washington in the spirit in which their ancestors had crossed oceans and prairies—to insist on their worth as individuals and on their right to determine their own fates. Their forbidding opponents, whose slogans appropriated American values, stood on the side of the bullying mass against the individual. Even the gift of sunshine and sky could not reconcile these opposites, and Ritter felt a genuine sorrow at the divisions in the land he was pledged to defend, and he resented feeling the need to choose sides against any of his fellow countrymen.

He made his way down to Lincoln, past a raggedy encampment of alleged Vietnam vets shilling POW/MIA knickknacks. A "veteran" in a faded field jacket wore a Screaming Eagle patch on his right sleeve—but he wore the old Women's Army Corps brass on his black beret, a fair indication to Ritter that he had no more served in the Army than Ritter had served in the Three Stooges. Anyway, the women had not come to commiserate with him and buy his trinkets, and the bearded impostor looked forlorn behind his sunglasses.

Ritter left the softness of the grass and inched his way over concrete and macadam, finally positioning himself before the lowest terrace of the Memorial. Up on the makeshift stage, a row of familiar symbols sat applauding at appropriate moments and now and then exchanging bits of chat. Other than the woman in the hat, closing her speech to gunfire applause, Ritter recognized the woman in the aviator frames and the transplanted Englishwoman with the wild mane of graying hair. A black woman wore her trademark neo-African costume, and the fabric cascaded poetically. A female novelist lent her remarkable paleness to the day, and the woman seated next to her wore the same expression of self-righteousness she had worn when testifying during televised Senate hearings. These women, too, were distinctly American in the way they had been packaged—recognizable more as personalities than as purveyors of ideas. Well, Ritter told himself, ideas had not found much of a welcome on his continent since the disappearance of the men who had risked their lives by meeting in Philadelphia.

With the blessed exception of Lincoln. Waiting for the day to unfold, waiting for Nadya and Charlee and fate to find him, resting his leg on an old man's cane, Ritter looked up past the thicket of microphones and the black woman reading her poem, to the shadowed face of America's greatest son.

Lincoln.

The sculptor had done a brilliant job in capturing the soul of Father Abraham. The marble man sat frozen between thoughtful repose and a readiness to stand up and speak words of fire. Lincoln's eyes looked as though they had seen more than a mortal man could bear, yet he bore it, and his hands lay ready on the arms of his chair, one fretful at the thought of his impulsive children, the other prepared to leverage him into action. He looked tired. Yet he sat without anger or malice, Christlike in his capacity for forgiveness, though possessed by an Old Testament determination to put things right. Only the humor, the plain man's love of a pointed tale or a sassy joke, was missing. But it would have been unfair to blame the artist for that. He had done rich and remarkable work in chiseling out the least marble of America's presidents.

Ritter suspected that Lincoln's vision of his country, despite the man's homespun practicality, had lofted into the realm of dreams—into a beautiful, robust dream of a land where each human being might stand unfettered by false birthrights. Lincoln, champion of the individual, had cherished unity with a suppleness of vision that transcended surface contradictions. It struck Ritter as a bit sacrilegious that such a day of division should play out under Lincoln's marble eyes. He could not say what a contemporary Lincoln would have made of the abortion issue, but he knew that the divisiveness, the venom that poisoned the dream, would have broken his heart.

An actress took the podium and tormented the English language in an effort to pass on her notions of sisterly solidarity. Ritter smiled at the little irony that Lincoln had fallen victim to an actor's vanity again.

He felt a light touch on his forearm and turned to find Charlee at his side.

She had a black eye and her lower lip was swollen. But her hair streamed as golden as the day, flirting with the breeze.

"My God. What happened to you?"

She smiled and showed intact teeth. It was a smile he found inexplicably generous. "Occupational hazard. It's good to see you, Chris. It's good to see you just once on a sunny day."

He tried to smile, but it did not quite come off. "You have the money?" He looked down as he asked the question and saw a large, worn briefcase in her hand.

"No. I couldn't get it so quickly." She followed his gaze. "It's full of the week's newspapers."

She moved closer to him. A woman recognized her, started to greet her, then dropped her jaw as she got a closer look at Charlee's face. The fan turned away with a look of confusion.

"Chris? Are you there for me?"

"Yes," he lied.

"I need you to be there for me. Because I'm afraid."

"We can pull it off without the money. We'll get the photos. If she shows up."

"I know. She's a fool. A mean fool, that's all." Charlee looked at him. "You see that now?"

"Yes."

A folk singer, famous almost as long as Ritter had been alive, adjusted the microphones and offered an anthem of freedoms already attained. Some of the older women in the crowd sang along, but the younger ones, unacquainted with the lyrics, just let it go by.

"I lied to you, Chris. Listen to me. Cromwell's a bastard. He wants the photos so he can destroy them. So there won't be any record. It's all about an oil-and-gas deal. No matter what happens, you can't let him get his hands on the photographs."

"I won't. I promise."

They stood in a private silence for a moment, superficially listening to the old song they both knew. It had been featured on an album they had once shared. When Ritter looked at Charlee, the sun seemed to cover her, as though she had been chosen for God's special kindness.

She met his eyes, but did not speak. So much between them.

"I've done wrong," she said at last. "I didn't mean to. But I did it."

"I know you didn't mean it."

"Chris, I've never hurt anyone on purpose."

"I know that, too. Who hurt you?"

She looked at him with an intensity that seemed determined to frustrate time's advance. To hold the two of them in that breeze-swept moment, under that pure sky.

"Don't look around," she said calmly in a clear voice. "There's a man watching me. You won't have any trouble identifying him. He's an albino and—"

The singer finished to indulgent, committed applause. But it did not register on Ritter.

Charlee was quick. She had always been the quickest of Ritter's lovers. Even quicker than Lena. And, perhaps, kinder, in the end.

"You *know* him. Don't you?"

"Yes."

"He's a Russian or something. I don't know. One of *them.*"

"Yes," Ritter said. "I know him." Without looking back. Because it had to be the same one. Because the feeling of fate was as crisp and clear as the air.

"He's a murderer," Charlee said steadily.

"I know that, too."

"He's on Cromwell's side. Cromwell's in it with the Russians or whoever they are. It's their gas and oil. It all has to do with export licenses and transshipment rights and government-to-government agreements."

"I know."

"They all want those photographs. And this man—he's dangerous, Chris."

"It's going to be all right, Charlee," Ritter said slowly, as though impressing the message upon himself, as well. "Everything's going to be all right."

Zhan passed through the crowd and the bright day with the caution another man would have brought to the exploration of a snake-ridden cave. It was indescribably painful to him to realize he had grown afraid of the blond woman. As soon as she realized that he would not—dare not—hurt her, she had taken charge of him with humiliating force, dictating not only the terms of their relationship but his actions, as well. He defied her only when she tried to insist he remain at her home while she fetched the photographs. That was too much. So he had pointed his pistol at her head, casually, saying:

"I think we go together."

He hated the blond woman. And he hated America. It was too much to digest, too utterly confusing. He had so many questions, but he could not ask the blond woman. He had too few English words and too much pride.

This great demonstration, for instance. It shocked him. At first, he had been baffled as to why so many women should stage a protest. Only slowly had he been able to piece the story together. The key, he decided, lay in the banners and shirts with the slogan PRO-CHOICE. He understood the word *choice. Pro* he found confusing—until he realized that Americans did the same thing to English as Russians did to Russian. They truncated words, slamming the first sound of one word up against the following word. The only English word of which he could think beginning with *pro* was *professional.*

That made it all clear.

The women, young, old, and almost uniformly devoid of pride in their appearance, were demonstrating for the right to choose their own professions.

So much of what he had learned about the United States had been wrong. He had believed that American women were not only as consistently elegant as the women of Hollywood films, but that they were, in all senses, possessed of more freedoms than the women of any other nation. But here was proof that American women were not only slovenly, they were far more restricted in their lives than the women of the former Soviet Union. Even in Central Asia, many women became doctors or judges or professors with much knowledge. But here the women had been so oppressed that it had come to this: a nation on the verge of revolution. It amazed Zhan that no one in his homeland knew of this, and he decided that he would caution

Rakhman about dealing with representatives of a nation that was so obviously unstable.

The blond woman had explained to him that she had to work through an American man and that it was necessary for Zhan to remain apart from them. He complied. But he made it clear to the blond woman that he would not allow her to stray very far.

They pushed to the front of the crowd together before she insisted they separate. He watched her go forward, moving in on the terrace where a platform had been erected for speakers in front of a monumental tomb with a statue of a seated man. Zhan decided the mausoleum probably honored some great capitalist who had made fortunes by exploiting women and downtrodden countries. The women had chosen this site for their protest because the tomb was a symbol of contrary might, of power, exactly like the tombs of great men back home. Zhan glanced up at the statue. Lurking back in the shadows, in conspiratorial darkness. Like an evil king. Sitting in judgment. Then he shifted his eyes back to the blond woman's head, afraid to lose track of her.

As he focused in on the woman, he suddenly stopped. As though a massive foot had punched down on brakes deep inside him. She had taken a position beside a man Zhan recognized. One of the many valuable things prison had taught him was to see and remember, and he remembered this man's profile, even glimpsed from a bad angle. Zhan maneuvered to a vantage point behind a group of young women who had seated themselves on the ground, tight as a flock of sheep in winter.

It was unquestionably the same man. The American officer. If any proof were needed, the cane on which the American leaned supplied it.

"I should have killed him," Zhan muttered to himself, punished with regret. "I should have killed that one, too."

Zhan realized that he had been betrayed, and his fist closed around the pistol in the pocket of his jacket.

Col. Jeb Bates watched the albino from the middle of a group of startlingly aggressive, unfeminine women. The largest and most vocal member of the group wore a T-shirt stretched over her chest and biceps, its logo proclaiming that she counted herself among the LESBIAN MOMS FOR LIBERTY. She reminded Bates of an old sergeant major he had known in Vietnam. Even the officers had been terrified of him.

The albino, on the other hand, reminded Bates that things could still get out of hand, despite the dozens of FBI and Army agents positioned to intervene. The albino kept one hand in the pocket of his jacket in a manner that made it obvious to Bates that he was armed. Worsening the situation, the man looked nervous. And Bates did not like nervous murderers with loaded weapons.

He was glad the FBI had come in. They were amazingly good at some things, and they had domestic resources forbidden to the military by law. Within an hour, the FBI had traced the vehicle in which Charlee Whyte and the albino had arrived at her town house on the Hill just after midnight. It was a rental vehicle, licensed in New York State, and under contract to a customer who did not exist except as a false identity for a Russian member of the United Nations staff. They had also surprised Bates by identifying the dead Russian who had been found inside the Morozov apartment.

Dmitri "Mitya" Karpovich had been a particularly unpleasant slimeball affiliated with the Russian Foreign Intelligence Service and suspected in the rape-murder of a Russian émigré in San Francisco the year before. He had been identifiable thanks to his web of jailbird tattoos.

The FBI could not get a fix on the albino, though. Because of his white hair, the agents on stakeout had assumed he was an older man—until they got a look at him in the morning light as he and Charlee Whyte emerged from her front door.

Charlee Whyte. Up to her plucked eyebrows in shit. Bates did not feel the satisfaction he might have expected. He simply felt disgusted. That the people who made things go inside the Beltway were such utter swine.

He was disappointed that there was still no sign of the great Sen. Oliver Cromwell. It was clear to him now that nailing Charlee Whyte alone would be the booby prize. Cromwell was pulling all of the strings, but he had been careful as a Mafia don to insulate himself from the hands-on side of things. The senator had used Charlee Whyte with the careless disregard a businessman felt for a rental car.

Bates had hoped Cromwell would show up to put in an immediate claim on the photographs. But it looked like the old bugger was too smart for that.

What had begun as a search for the grail had turned into a cesspool-cleaning operation. Bates knew he should be hot about the prospect of getting his hands on the photos, proof positive that the Russians had taken those men and murdered them. But any excitement he had felt had given way to weariness and a bitter sense of duty. He just wanted to bring the filthy business to a close.

He also wanted this mission to end for a very personal reason. His wife had suffered through a bad night, most of it spent alone. She was scheduled for another operation in ten days, but Bates suspected that the date would have to be moved up. They were going to cut open her abdomen again. But he knew that the doctors were looking in the wrong place. The real sickness lay in her heart.

America had never caught fire in her soul. Grateful for sanctuary, unquestionably in love with him in the best possible way, and dedicated to her family, she still longed for home. Vietnam. Where things made sense, even in the middle of a war. So unlike America, where even children who turned out well appalled her with their independence and reduced her to tears with their lack of respect for tradition. His wife was dying. For love of her lost homeland. And it broke his heart.

Perhaps that was why the day and all its strident causes depressed him so. Here, on the grass, the forces of selfishness had marshaled themselves, determined to "control" their bodies and lives, but allergic to any self-control. While over on the right—and coming closer, despite the police lines—the spiteful and jealous took their stand, attempting to imbue their empty lives with meaning by shackling others with their values. America was sick with selfish causes. Everyone had a cause that excused them from personal responsibility for their actions and failures. Everyone had become a willing victim.

Bates looked past the foreign killer with his tense shoulders to Ritter and Charlee Whyte. They made a startlingly good couple—not in their physical beings so much as in their plain bad luck. Born under a bad sign, Bates told himself. He wondered what his wife's astrologer would have made of their fates.

Waiting, as he had waited in Vietnam, in Lebanon and El Sal, in Germany, Panama, and Kuwait, Bates looked past Ritter and Charlee Whyte, up past the dreary speaker of the moment, to the monumental double row of columns screening the statue of the Great Emancipator. If it had lain within his power, Bates would have torn the Memorial down.

He had nothing against Abraham Lincoln, who had been a very good man in very bad times. Bates just hated history. Not the way a high-school student might—casually, fitfully, and stupidly—but with resolve.

He had seen firsthand what too much history did to men and women. History was the best excuse to hate your fellow man, even better than religion or race. Historical crimes were tangible—and usually so gruesome they did not require much embellishment. In dying empires and hardscrabble new states, history became an excuse for atrocity and greed. History had never made one man love another. History did not promote understanding. History was the most powerful growth hormone for hatred that nature had ever produced. And Bates wanted none of it. If anything had enabled the United States to achieve greatness, it was the *lack* of history.

There was so much hatred in the world. The hatred that exiled his wife to a far, cold land. The hatred metastasizing here, under God's golden sun, on a day when he would otherwise have been able to sit out in the garden with his wife, by the fountain he had built for her with his own hands.

The talons of professionalism plucked Bates from his reverie. Brushing past a burly man in a plaid shirt—who looked distinctly out of place amid the pro-choice set—Nadya Morozova hurried toward Ritter and Charlee Whyte. Clutching a small travel bag against her side, she looked as though she could barely hold back her rage.

One of the Russian woman's hands hid inside the travel bag: another participant had come armed. And she had not come alone. A slender, eyes-elsewhere man in a shapeless suit followed her like a dog.

Instinctively, the colonel's eyes shifted back to the big man in the plaid shirt. He wore a camouflage-patterned baseball cap and cradled an odd-shaped satchel under his arm. Bates had a visceral sense that something about the man was not right.

But this was a city full of weirdos, and rallies like this attracted outside oddballs, as well. Anyway, there was no time to worry about anything but the matter immediately at hand.

As he attempted to regain sight of Nadya and her wilted-looking escort, sudden motion fixed the colonel's attention. The albino was moving, swiftly, with animal assurance. Aiming for the Russian woman.

Nadya trembled. Little things were going wrong. Volodya, in one of his blubbering fits, had begged her not to go through with the exchange. He had been so stubborn she had briefly suspected him of knowing something she did not. But that was impossible. Finally, she told him she would go alone, if he were too much of a coward. That worked.

It had been impossible to park the car. She had not been sleeping enough and had not thought things through as thoroughly as usual. There were no parking spaces anywhere near the Mall. Exasperated, she had driven all the way to the National Cathedral, returning by taxi, nervous that her last bit of cash might not cover the fare. Volodya, deprived of alcohol, was no help at all. But she needed a man's muscle by her side. Someone who could knock down the American officer, if necessary. Someone who could hurt him.

They had to shove their way through hordes of women, all clamoring for something, all spoiled, none of them sympathetic. American women were intolerably coddled. How on earth could anyone respect American men?

Finding the American officer proved harder than she had anticipated. The crowd was thick—although that was good in other respects—and she had put too much trust in her instincts. Mockingly, she recalled her words to the American to the effect that she would always be able to find him, and she grew angry at herself for her ineffectuality, angry at the world.

At last, she spotted him. And grew angrier still. He had not come alone, despite her warnings. The bastard. Standing there like some holy martyr with that unbearable woman by his side. Nadya thrust her hand into her travel bag, clutching the pistol.

It was too late to turn back, too late to try another approach. She did not have enough money left to buy lunch for herself and the man she loved.

Suddenly, she felt panic flush down through her body like cold, cold water. What if it were all coming apart? What if *she* had been the fool?

Enraged, she pushed her way around a big Siberian bear of a man. Enormous, he mothered a parcel against a plaid shirt that smelled of sweat and tobacco. He mumbled something, and the sound of his voice made her think of an Orthodox priest. Something about him chilled her, and she hurried past him.

She did not even look back to see if Volodya was keeping up now. Her life's focus was on Ritter and his blond slut of a partner. The two of them had probably been manipulating her all along, playing with her. Determined to cheat her.

Her grip on the gun tightened.

Then she saw that the blond woman held a briefcase in her hand. It was large enough to hold a great deal of money.

For the last time in her life, Nadya felt hope.

The next moments of Ritter's life stitched themselves to his soul.

He saw Nadya. Hurrying toward him with a terrible expression on her face. She looked furious and worn. Yet indelibly beautiful. A gaunt, ravaged man in a cheap suit pressed up behind her.

Centuries too late, he noticed a third figure, a plaid-shirted lumberjack, his face covered in tears under a baseball cap. The big man drew an automatic weapon from a satchel.

The weapon, one of the various brands of boutique machine guns popular with special-operations forces and terrorists, looked small to the point of fragility in the man's hands. It flared with tiny blips of light. An amplified sewing-machine sound followed after an instant's delay.

The rate of fire was very fast. The lumberjack emptied the first clip into the crowd of women before Ritter could pull

Charlee to the ground. Blessedly, the fan of bullets closed just to the right of where they stood.

Nadya was still on her feet. But the man following her stumbled, then collapsed at her side, reaching out an arm to touch her as she turned to stop his fall.

Ritter discarded his cane and rushed for the gunman, struggling to reach him before he could reload.

The big man moved quickly, though. He knew weapons and his oversize hands went nimbly through the drill of ejecting the first clip and slipping in another.

As he closed the distance between them, Ritter saw mad, jeweled eyes.

The lumberjack raised his weapon again, aiming randomly into the throng—at women screaming or just stunned, running, scrambling, or utterly unaware of what was happening.

"Thou shalt not kill," the lumberjack shouted. *"Daughters of Satan, thou shalt not kill . . ."*

Ritter could not reach the gunman in time. His leg refused to cooperate. Desperate, he cast his body across the line of fire.

Then, just as the gunman depressed the trigger, Ritter saw a wonderful thing. A woman, equal in size to the big man, flew through the air. Her hair had been trimmed for combat and she wore a purple T-shirt that said LESBIANS MOMS FOR LIBERTY. She hit the lumberjack at waist level with the impact of an NFL tackle. The big man fumbled the weapon and struck the ground with a thud audible over the shrieking and screaming.

The weapon fell close to Ritter. He plunged toward it. But another hand got there first.

Jeb Bates.

Relieved, Ritter switched his attention back toward Nadya and Charlee. He expected to find them locked in a struggle over Nadya's travel bag. But he discovered a different scene entirely. Nadya sat on the ground, cradling the head of her companion in the bad suit on her lap. The man's eyes were open and still, and blood trickled from his ear.

Charlee stood above her, a disinterested commuter waiting for a bus, briefcase in hand.

A young woman crept past Charlee's shoes, gasping blood

and pressing her denim jacket into her stomach. Charlee did not even notice.

A mounted policewoman struggled to control her horse. Sirens rose. Up on the stage, the interrupted speaker asked the crowd, "What happened? What happened?"

Men and women with official faces closed in, weapons drawn.

Nadya began to rock back and forth, clutching the dead man's head ever more tightly and weeping with an intensity Ritter had never witnessed.

She screamed. Once. So that even the deafest, most distant God would have to hear her. And she held a pistol up in the sunlight.

"No," Ritter shouted. "Charlee, get—"

But Nadya had no interest in Charlee now. Or in anyone else. She fit the barrel of the pistol to her temple, just in front of her ear, at a spot Ritter remembered touching with his lips. And she pulled the trigger.

Blood spattered over Charlee's legs. She winced briefly, but showed no further reaction as Nadya slumped at her feet.

Ritter thought it was all over. Until he saw the albino.

He was fast. Faster than Bates. Faster than Ritter would have been even without an injured leg. He was faster than every one of the gun-wielding agents and police officers.

With a motion smooth as dance, the albino dipped his arm under the strap of Nadya's travel bag. Rising again, he grasped Charlee and turned her so that he could hold her back against his chest and steer her, with a pistol fixed to the underside of her jaw.

Charlee dropped her briefcase. But there was no one left to care about that. She was free to scream or speak, but made no sound. Her eyes stared vacantly.

The albino began to draw her back toward the steps of the Memorial, jerking his shoulder to keep the strap of Nadya's bag in place. Every few seconds, he glanced backward, and as he did, he screwed the pistol deeper into Charlee's jaw, forcing her head to the side. She blinked in pain. But it was an animal, unintelligent reaction.

The panic in the crowd manifested itself in doomsday noise and motion. Near Ritter, more controlled voices shouted orders and directions back and forth. The sirens multiplied.

The albino tugged Charlee awkwardly up the first quick series of steps. Ritter looked into the face of the man who had killed Ritter's best friend and crippled him. And he saw something unexpected:

Fear.

The albino looked terrified.

He's lost, Ritter realized with a shock. *He doesn't know what he's doing, what to do next.*

For whatever reason, the Memorial drew the foreign murderer. Stray demonstrators, sound-crew members, and organizers with walkie-talkies scurried out of his path, and a close-in quiet began to develop against the backdrop of human tumult and sirens.

The armed agents swarmed around the albino's flanks, angling for a clean shot.

But they would not shoot, Ritter realized. Not as long as the pistol burrowed up into the soft cleft of Charlee's jaw, reaching for the roots of her tongue.

She was coming back to herself. Ritter could see it as he limped along in her wake, forgetful enough of his own pain that he could just keep pace with a man walking backward and pulling a hostage behind him.

Bates came abreast, weapon ready. It made Ritter aware, again, that his own hands were empty. He had no real power to affect the outcome. But he could not stop his pursuit. If nothing else, he wanted Charlee to know that he was with her now.

"Will he shoot her?" Bates asked. The armed pack moved slowly toward the steep main steps.

"Yes," Ritter said with certainty.

Zhan had been afraid before. In the orphanage. Sometimes in prison. But that fear had been a transient, little, manageable thing. Now, for the first time in his life, he felt Fear.

The fear made sweat. Down his back and sides. Sliming the pistol's grip. When he breathed, it sounded like a roar to his ears. The smell off the woman, her alien softness, sickened him. He did not know what to do.

He cursed the place, this damned country. Where he had no grip. Where everything was so unexpected.

A dozen men and women with sidearms maneuvered like wolves just beyond his reach. He wanted to send out a few bullets, to drop one or two of them to warn them off, to regain space. But he knew that the moment he moved the barrel of the pistol away from the woman's head, he would be shot.

No place to go.

No solution.

In the past, there had always been a solution.

He watched the American officer limp along behind him. The ass. As empty-handed now as he had been that night on the pass. A man who would always be defenseless.

The woman moaned slightly. He tightened his grip, pressing the pistol into the pouch of flesh at the top of her throat.

"No noise," he commanded, as though he were sneaking her down a darkened corridor. He could think of no further English words.

They reached the first of the two upper banks of steps. His intelligence knew that he was doing a foolish thing, that the mausoleum or whatever it was offered no safety. But his muscles were making decisions for themselves, his body acted more quickly than his intellect, and he felt a unique powerlessness. In convict's Russian, he ordered the woman to be careful not to trip them both.

His pursuers had nearly completed a circle around him.

"Get back," he screamed suddenly in Russian. "Get back or I'll kill this bitch of yours."

He felt for each next step with his heel, terrified as a beast about to be gnawed to death. He did not know how much longer he would be able to control his bodily functions. His hands had begun to tremble the way he had seen old alcoholics quake in prison.

"Get back," he shouted again, entirely forgetful that his hunters would not understand his language.

He jerked the woman up another step. As they climbed, a panorama of thousands of Americans, tens of thousands of them, spread out before him. All watching him. Red and blue flashing lights inched through the crowd.

He judged that, at the last moment, he would be able to kill the woman and at least one—possibly two—of his pursuers before they brought him down.

"Give him some room," Ritter yelled. "Goddamnit, he just wants some space."

None of the agents backed off. Nor did Ritter. But they stopped closing the distance. The hunted, hostage, and hunters moved up the Memorial's steps like a template.

"He's crazy," Bates said quietly. "Why on earth is he taking her up there? There's no way out, for Christ's sake."

Ritter used both hands to swing his leg up another step. He wished he had not thrown away the cane. He wished none of this had ever happened. He saw the brief flame bite Nadya's temple again, erasing his last kiss. The sight came to him again and again: her head snapping with the force, then recoiling as the skull exploded behind the opposite ear. When she fell, he saw a large black powder burn on white skin and tawny hair. She had died with her teeth bared like a rabid dog.

"He doesn't know what he's doing," Ritter said. "He's fucking lost."

Not her, too, God. Don't let her die, too. He felt no love, no desire, for the woman in the albino's arms. But he felt a bond that cannot be reached with language, that would settle cheaply for the word *friendship*. And he did not want her to die. Not here. Not on this day.

Not at this man's hands.

They staggered up through perfect air, with the blue of the sky bringing the white stone to life. It was a day to celebrate the act of breathing. Not to die.

His eyes met Charlee's. He saw that she was fully conscious and awfully afraid. Her lips shaped a word, and he thought it was his name.

The albino reached the top step. He moved more quickly on the level, drawing Charlee back into the shadows, fixing her with the pistol as he looked madly from side to side, hunting salvation.

His attention settled on Ritter, canceling any power Charlee's stare possessed. He flooded the space between them with hatred, drenching the air with it.

Ritter sensed that he was on the receiving end of every shred of viciousness the other man had ever felt and stored away. The albino wanted to kill him, whether or not the act made sense. In that instant, Ritter understood him better than any other living thing had ever done. Better even than Rakhman understood his own disciple.

In that instant of cognition, Ritter realized the other man was about to pull the trigger.

It did not happen. A new figure emerged from the shadows at Lincoln's side, an old man in a park janitor's uniform. Holding a push broom as if it were a baseball bat, he shuffled up behind Charlee's captor.

Ritter opened his mouth to shout a no, afraid the pistol would go off. But the old man was quicker than anyone else in Washington, D.C., on that particular day.

With the finesse of a master polo player, he brought the broom around like a mallet, smashing one end of the crosspiece into the side of his target's head.

The pistol skittered across the marble floor. The albino took a fall from an overachieving comedy routine, losing Nadya's bag as he toppled sideward. He settled facedown and still.

Freed, Charlee stood apart in her astonishment.

Everyone was astonished.

Except for the old janitor, who just shook his head in disgust, fixing the albino's body to the floor with his broom.

"You can't come around here behaving like that," the old man said.

In a movie, Charlee and Chris would have embraced to satisfy their audience. Instead, they remained apart, unable to look at each other for more than a few seconds at a time. The shadow of a relationship that lay between them now had nothing to do with the future or even "quality time" shared between old friends. Neither of them could have endured the other's touch for more than a few seconds. The bond between them—a tiny, wrinkled thing gasping for air—simply had to do with the avoidance of further loss. And Chris's leg hurt. Charlee, for her part, wanted to hide from the whole world.

Others were livelier. Now that the violence was over, the number of brave men and women increased dramatically. A man in a fine Shetland sweater ordered his agents to keep the crowd back. A helicopter thundered overhead, then moved on along the Mall.

Jeb Bates reached for Nadya's travel bag.

Another hand grasped the bag's strap while the colonel's hand was still a few inches away.

"I'll take that," Senator Cromwell said. "This bag contains evidence in a senatorial investigation."

"Fuck you," Bates replied, locking two big hands onto the cheap plastic, quickening at the feel of its weight.

Cromwell yanked at the bag.

Bates, much stronger, pulled it against his belly.

But Cromwell refused to surrender. *"You,"* he barked, catching the eye of the agent in the country-weekend sweater. "This man's breaking the law. He's interfering with a Senate investigation."

The sweatered man stepped closer, walkie-talkie crackling like a cabdriver's receiver. "Senator, no one's going to interfere with this investigation."

Cromwell stiffened. "Well, if you know who I am, then you know that I speak with the authority of the United States Senate." He gave the travel bag a quick, sneaky jerk. But Bates held steady. "The contents of this bag bear on the national security of the United States."

Suddenly, Jeb Bates smiled. He eyed Cromwell, who looked as though he had not slept well. Then he exchanged a glance with the FBI agent, with whom he was on an insider-story basis.

"I guess the only way we're going to settle this is to open it up right here. Let's just see what's inside."

Cromwell's right hand strayed off as if reaching for a drink.

"Okay with you, Bruce?" Bates asked the agent.

Soft wool shoulders shrugged.

Cromwell grabbed the bag with both hands again, pulling

with all of his strength. The effort surprised Bates, who almost let go.

"*Damn* you," Cromwell said, "you are *not* going to expose the contents of this bag to all these . . . these *people*. This is a matter of national security. It's not for the public's eyes."

"He's full of shit," a woman's voice said. It was Charlee. Returned from the dead, moving in on the struggle. She looked at Bates, then at the FBI agent. "Don't let him have it, guys. He's a lying bastard."

Cromwell, still clawing at the bag shut against the colonel's belly, turned his face toward her. He looked sunburned.

"You're history, bitch."

On the ground, the albino twitched. The old custodian bore down harder with his broom. "You folks want to look after this fella?"

With a mammoth effort, with all of his old soldier's reserves of strength, Bates wrenched the bag cleanly from the senator's hands. As Cromwell lost contact with the vinyl, it was as though he had been separated from his source of energy. He sagged.

Bates squatted down, tugging at the cheap zipper. The bag opened in stages.

The colonel dumped the contents onto the marble floor. A golden lipstick tube rolled toward Lincoln's throne, and a compact snapped open with a puff of dust. Falling heavily amid the junk rain, a worn manila envelope landed flat.

For a moment, everyone stared at it.

Slowly, reverently, Bates picked it up and undid the end.

He reached inside.

The first veil of concern passed over his face as he felt the contents. With a hurried gesture, he pulled out a folded white hand towel.

Fumbling, the colonel unraveled the cloth. Inside, there was a book.

The huge grumbling of the helicopter returned, passing low overhead, then scooting down over the Potomac. A slight wind, winter's first kiss, swept through the stone hall.

"What the hell?" Bates asked.

Nobody answered.

The colonel turned the book over in his hands. He opened it, fanning the pages, looking for anything at all. He reached back into the bag, testing, then upended it again. He peered into the empty envelope.

Belatedly, the public address system admonished the crowd to remain calm.

Bates looked up, turning from one face to another. His eyes reached Ritter.

"Chris. Here. Look at this." The colonel held out the book. "It's in Russian. Does it tell us anything?"

Ritter stepped forward. His leg was too stiff to allow him to squat beside Bates, so he just reached down and took the book from the colonel's hand.

Even without seeing the foreign alphabet, Ritter would have recognized the book as Russian, given its distinctively cheap, no-nonsense binding. He read the title, then turned to the back where the Russians hid tables of contents. His eyebrows tightened toward the bridge of his nose as he strained to read the faint print. As usual, the Russians had gone sparingly with the ink.

"What is it?" Charlee asked, coming closer. "Does it mean anything?"

All of the faces waited on Ritter, wearing their expectations and fears openly.

Ritter was bewildered at first. His Russian was very good, but the language of the text was densely technical and strewn with opaque equations. He took a long time, laboring through the pages.

Suddenly, he got it. And he smiled the smallest smile of his life, as he looked at the waiting faces. Each of them had been deceived, as surely as he himself had been.

"It's nothing," he said matter-of-factly. "A puzzle book for scientists. Problems with unexpected outcomes."

ECHOES

IN AN ECONOMY MOTEL ON THE VIRGINIA SIDE OF THE RIVER, A CLEANing woman found a bag under a sink. Whenever Adelaide discovered such a thing, she opened it. Although the contents usually ranged from the useless and bland to the revolting, people occasionally threw away or forgot useful items. This time she was disappointed. The little plastic trash sack contained nothing but shredded photographs.

She did not try to piece them together. She was a churchgoing woman and had her suspicions as to the subject matter. Once, while making her morning rounds, she had entered a room in which several people were making a film that would not be shown in any theater to which she would have taken her granddaughter. A body learned a great deal about God's children working in a motel.

After sifting the torn bits one last time to make sure nothing of value was mixed in, she put the little bag into a bigger trash bag meant for the Dumpster. Then she looked at her watch, sighed, and knelt to clean the toilet.

The president frequently calls on Senator Cromwell for advice on trade and technology matters involving the states crawling out from under the wreckage of the Soviet Union. Given his remarkable success as midwife to the largest international gas-and-oil deal in history, Senator Cromwell is also much in demand by the United States business community. He gives farsighted and entertaining speeches on the pitfalls and potential of joint ventures, on the need for patience with young countries learning rough-and-tumble democracy, and on patriotism. His editorials on foreign policy and trade have brought him near-staff status at the *Washington Post,* yet he maintains remarkably healthy ties to conservative, even fundamentalist, groups. Senator Cromwell is emerging as something of a renaissance man among politicians—or, better put, as the youngest, handsomest, and most able of our "elder statesmen."

Senator Cromwell is guaranteed reelection, at least partly thanks to the income his international endeavors have generated for influential citizens in his home state, but rumors on the Hill have him moving on to bigger things. He has been mentioned for a cabinet post, and his regional clout could balance a presidential ticket nicely. Thus it came as a shock when he recently told Barbara Walters he is giving serious consideration to leaving the political arena for an executive position with Argent Oil. "After all," he explained to the television audience, "good business—a healthy and growing economy—is our nation's first line of defense."

Viewers were also privileged to catch a startled look on the face of the usually well-prepared Ms. Walters as Senator Cromwell took advantage of the occasion to announce his engagement to a young woman from Palm Springs whom he described as "seriously concerned with the environment and things like that."

Col. Jeb Bates was exiled to an obscure command in deepest, darkest Maryland. Senator Cromwell had begun calling in chips to have Bates forced from active duty—until a staffer pointed out that, as long as Bates remained in uniform, the colonel would not be free to air his views with the public.

The entrenched POW/MIA bureaucrats at the Office of the Secretary of Defense and at the Defense Intelligence Agency also wanted to see Bates hung and left to twist in the breeze. Charlee Whyte had sent some Army major a photograph she claimed showed a U.S. Korean War–era POW who had been taken to the Soviet Union and shot. Bates had pressed the issue to embarrassing extremes, even though it was obvious to the experts at OSD and the DIA offices at Clarendon that the photo was a forgery, if a good one. After all, OSD and DIA had spent more than twenty years proving that no U.S. POWs had ever been left behind anywhere. Bates and his organization were loose cannons on deck, endangering careers and reputations. Bates was nothing but a spoiler, and he had to go.

So Bates went. But he did not go terribly far. The Army protected him. The Army leadership knew the colonel's worth, and a number of general officers had become convinced that they had been lied to for years about the fate of their comrades-in-arms. The Army could not save the POW/MIA research team Bates had put together, given the opposition by government agencies interested in keeping the waters smooth between the United States and Russia. But the colonel's disciples took his message with them as they dispersed back to the various military organizations and agencies from which they had been borrowed. Someday, one of them might even talk to the press.

The colonel's new assignment may turn out for the best, since it provides a potential springboard to the general-officer ranks. But, whether or not Jeb Bates receives a promotion he never expected, the job has one immediate and welcome advantage: it's a much shorter commute. Although his hours are long, he manages to spend more time at home with his wife, who is responding well to treatment with an experimental drug. When the weather is good, they sit outside in the garden, by the fountain the colonel built to please her, and they reminisce in her language about those clear, wonderful days during the war when they fell in love.

Maj. Christopher Ritter volunteered for any position that might open up in Yugoslavia. He volunteered for a U.N. position in Africa. After careful consideration and an off-the-record phone call from Jeb Bates, the assignments manager in the Hoffman Building cut orders on Ritter sending him to Fort Hood, Texas, where a Military Intelligence battalion over on the West Fort needed an executive officer. Ritter complained bitterly that his skills—so appropriate to the times—were being misused. Then he went to Texas.

His leg may never be completely normal, but he has already recovered to the point where he runs in the battalion's morning physical-training formations. Otherwise, he spends a great deal of time in the unit motor pool and in the countless briefings that reassure higher-level commanders and their staffs that the Army's cutting edge is prepared for war. Ritter reads the newspapers, watches CNN, and eats books on the rash of fires between Zagreb and Dushanbe. He works hard to maintain his language proficiency. Although he understands that he was sent down to the XO's position to guarantee him promotion to lieutenant colonel and to set him up for his own battalion command, he wishes he were elsewhere.

He rents a house in Harker Heights where he can play his stereo as loud as he wants. He also has a weekend sort of relationship with a female captain who is recovering from a disastrous affair with a helicopter pilot. They drive down to Austin, eat Mex, and listen to good raw blues at Antone's. She's bright and fit and would not mind marrying him, but they both know it isn't a permanent relationship.

Charlee Whyte resigned from her position in the Department of Defense and, after a few months far from the public eye, took a low-level job with Enough For All, a nongovernment organization dedicated to providing food and hope in countries where both are in short supply. Based in Nairobi, Charlee spent most of her time down-country in Mozambique or Rwanda, in Somalia or Sudan. She took risks no soldier would dare and saw things—good and bad—of which the Department of State, with its exclusive affinity for capital cities, had no inkling. Her work soothed her.

In a half-massacred village on the Upper Nile, she met a woman of similar age named Gail. Gail had studied her way out of small-town Pennsylvania only to fall in love with Africa, and Charlee encountered her at a time when Gail had, perhaps, loved Africa too long and too well. The chance meeting led to the first real friendship of Charlee's adult life, and one morning in Maputo, when nothing in the hotel worked and her cassette recorder had gone missing, Charlee just sat down on the veranda and thanked God for the good fortune of her life.

During one of the paperwork sieges back in Nairobi, Charlee's mother came to visit. Charlee packed her off on a luxury ooh-there's-a-lion safari, but the deprivations told on the older woman. Upon her mother's return to the city, Charlee fetched her in one of the agency's Land Rovers, determined to ask about her real father. The conversation did not go well. Charlee's mother declared that she saw no point whatsoever in dredging up the past, which was always a bore, while Charlee drove in a dense near-daze, haunted by the thought that her father might have lived for decades in a prison camp in the Soviet Union. Neither woman could bring to speech that which wanted to be said. Instead, they argued. Rounding a corner, Charlee shrieked an insult at her mother, meaning to hurt, just as a truck smashed into the vehicle on the driver's side.

Charlee's mother got a nasty bruise on her calf that limited her wardrobe choices for weeks on end. Charlee nearly bled to death. At the hospital, she was well-attended and repeatedly transfused. The blood saved her life, but infected her with the AIDS virus.

She chose to remain in Africa, keeping her job. For now, she remains exemplary in her health, with tremendous reserves of energy. Not everyone in her organization likes her, since her accomplishments tend to reflect badly upon other relief officers who do not fully share her dedication, having grown fond of their neocolonialist lifestyles. The males resent her terribly. But no one really wants to see her fired. She gets things done.

About the Author

Ralph Peters is a novelist and Army officer who specializes in the graveyard of the Soviet empire. From August 1992 to October 1993, he served with Task Force Russia (TFR), an organization formed in the wake of President Yeltsin's statement that U.S. POWs might have been taken to the former Soviet Union. TFR sought to investigate the POW/MIA issue honestly and thoroughly, in Russia, the United States, and elsewhere. TFR broke with tradition by dealing openly with POW/MIA family members and the American public. And TFR quickly found itself at odds with the government's POW/MIA establishment, since its analytical conclusions contradicted more than twenty years of denial that any U.S. POWs might have been left behind anywhere. By the end of 1993, TFR was dismantled.

Acknowledgments

For better or worse, this book
would not exist were it not
for the rare skills of my agent,
Mr. Robert Gottlieb, who would
have made a fine combat commander,
had his life taken a different course,
and "Colonel" Paul McCarthy, my editor,
who is remarkable and wise.